LET'S BE FRANK

(THE NURSE NATE SERIES, BOOK 1)

BREA BROWN

WAYZGOOSE PRESS

CONTENTS

NURSE NATE

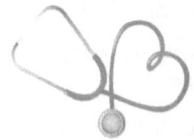

YOUNG HARRISON WEBSTER'S TONSILS ARE DISGUSTING. Not only are they extremely swollen, but a white discharge coats them, like yogurt. As a pediatric nurse, I see stuff like this all the time, so it doesn't gross me out as much as it would the average person. It's still nasty, though. I'm glad I'm wearing these latex gloves.

After a thorough look around in the ten-year-old's mouth, I pull back and turn off the otoscope.

"I feel real bad, Nate," Harry laments, holding his hand against his neck.

"I bet!" I say with more cheer than I feel as I pocket the otoscope, peel off my gloves, and toss them in the trash. During a thorough hand-wash, I say over my shoulder, "Looks like you have a very angry throat, bud."

I dry my hands and toss the paper towel into the trash as well. Then I prop one butt cheek on the edge of the paper-covered examination table and shoot a sympathetic wince at the boy's mom. "We'll have to do a test to be sure, but it looks like strep. This is the sixth time this year," I tell her what she already knows, unless she's lost count.

She nods and blushes, like she has something to be ashamed of. It's not her fault kids share gum and always have their hands in their noses and mouths, sometimes in quick succession.

"Yeah, so what do we do?" she asks me.

Flipping open Harry's chart and making a note in it, I say, "The next step is up to you. I'll have to consult with Dr. Reitman, obviously, but she'll probably recommend that you have Harry's tonsils removed."

"Oh, man," Mrs. Webster mutters.

I look up sharply at her dismayed tone. "Is that going to be a problem? It'll be better in the long run, you know."

She waves her hand at me as if to dismiss her own outburst. "No. That's fine. It's just, you know, surgery." She whispers the last word, but the previously spaced-out kid in the room jumps on it.

"What? Isn't surgery where they cut you open with a knife and stuff?"

Before I can answer, his mom soothes, "Nobody has to cut you open for this. Right, Nate?"

The near-pleading in their matching green eyes prompts me to immediately reply with a reassuring smile, "No. No cutting *open*."

My too-honest qualifier isn't lost on Harry. "Is it gonna hurt?"

I take a deep breath. "Not at the time. You'll be asleep. Afterwards, you'll have a sore throat for a few days. But they'll give you medicine to make it hurt less."

Spying the time on the clock over the door, I hop from the table and cross to the computer monitor and keyboard mounted to the wall, where I type some information into Harry's electronic chart and say, "Hey, I had my tonsils removed when I was about your age. Not a big deal. I got to stay home from school and play video games and eat ice cream and Jell-O. It was awesome."

Harry eyes me suspiciously. "They had video games when you were a kid?"

His mom and I laugh at the dig, and I shake my head. "Uh, just how old do you think I am?"

Following a head-to-toe inspection, during which I flex my muscles and show him the "best side" of my face, he guesses, "Like, twenty-five?" with a wrinkled nose that clearly expresses his opinion of that ancient figure.

I relax my posture, shrug, and go back to the computer. "Yeah. Close enough." If he thinks twenty-five is old, there's no way I'm going to reveal my real age. "And yes, we had video games back then. They weren't as fancy as they are now, but we didn't know any better, and they kept me busy while I was recuperating."

After I log off the computer, I say to his mother on my way to the door, "I'll be right back to do the strep test and give you Dr. Reitman's official recommendation about that tonsillectomy."

In the hallway, as I'm pulling the door closed behind me, I hear Mrs. Webster say, "Harry! It's rude to call people 'old!'" with more bemusement in her voice than embarrassment.

"I didn't!" he objects.

I grin and turn to head in the direction of the doctor's office, bumping into the woman herself on her way past, with her eyes down on a handful of charts. "Oops. Sorry about that," I say while she blinks comically, holding onto my forearm for balance.

"Whoa," she laughs, and shakes her blonde bangs from her eyes. "What's the rush?"

Apologizing again for the collision, I explain, "I'm running behind on appointments, and I need to get out of here on time tonight."

"Hot date?" she teases, then sobers when I'm unable to hide my chagrin. "Oh. Sorry. None of my business. Anyway, I'll stop holding you up." She lets go of my arm, leaving cool spots where her fingers had been. "Literally. Sorry about that." The files in her other hand reclaim her attention as she continues toward her office.

"Actually," I stop her by raising my voice. "I was coming to talk to you anyway." Her eyebrows lift. "About a patient," I finish.

Her brow smooths, then she bobs her head toward her office. "Come on in."

I follow her and close the door behind me, since we'll be discussing confidential information. She rounds her desk and sits in her high-backed leather chair, closing her eyes and rolling her head. Standing with the desk between us, I clutch Harry's chart in the crook of my arm and give her a lowdown of the situation.

In order to see as many patients as possible at the clinic, nurses and nurse practitioners see the patients Dr. Reitman can't fit into her finite schedule. The family nurse practitioners (FNPs) are a bit more autonomous and don't have to consult the doctor on straightforward cases, like Harry's. I'm still just a master nurse, so Dr. Reitman does have to sign off on my recommendations. Eventually, I'd like to become an FNP; I simply haven't gotten around to it yet.

Okay, to be more honest, I'm not very enthusiastic about the course. It'll only take me a year, but academics have never been my strong suit. Although the FNP certification course is clinical and doesn't take place in a traditional classroom, I'm still not relishing the idea of another year of schooling in any form. After all, I just finished my Master of Nursing (I love how that sounds: Nate Bingham, Master of Nursing!) less than six months ago. It seems like I've been in school my whole life. Then again, I know I'm prolonging the agony by putting it off.

Now there's another obstacle, though. I need Dr. Reitman's referral for my enrollment paperwork. Right now, I'm not comfortable enough around her to ask.

After I give her the spiel about Harry Webster, the doctor comes to the exact conclusion I predicted she would, then says abruptly, "Hey. Are things going to be awkward now? Between us?" She flaps her hand over the desk, like the piece of furniture is the issue.

Sweat breaks out under my arms. I shift Harry's file from one arm to the other, then tug on my earlobe. The folder slips and almost falls, but I catch it at the last second, and stutter, "Why would they be?"

She smiles at my obtuseness and rapidly clicks her pen, leaning back and rocking in her chair. "You know, because of..."

I clear my throat. "Oh. No. I mean, it was nothing personal, you know?"

"Exactly! *I* know that."

"It's just that it's a pretty big commitment, and it didn't feel right."

"You were absolutely right to go with your gut."

My shoulders relax. "Really? So you weren't upset?"

She laughs. "No! Good grief! I received an offer from someone else later that same night. Don't worry about it." Sitting up and resting her elbows on the glass-topped surface in front of her, she adds, "The buyer and I negotiated back and forth a few times, but eventually came to an agreement. We close in a couple of weeks."

The neat resolution to our recent failed real estate transaction fills me with relief. "Whew! I'm so glad everything worked out. It's an awesome house; just not exactly what I was looking for."

That's putting it mildly. Her house was *all* wrong for me. From the wall-to-wall carpeting to the in-ground pool in the backyard, everything was too perfect. Perfect for teenagers' parties and swanky soirées with crudités-crunching doctors, that is. But it held no potential for me to put my own stamp on it. It was already exactly the way it should be, fit for two middle-aged professionals with the perfect—or so it seemed— family with a busy lifestyle.

Plus, it was huge. Four bedrooms, four bathrooms, and a cabana? No way. It was priced to sell quickly, so I could have afforded it, but just because I could didn't mean I wanted to.

"I hear you found a place, too?" she queries pleasantly.

"Yeah. I moved in last weekend."

She smiles warmly. "See? No worries."

Conscious of the time passing and worried I'm keeping the Websters waiting, I nevertheless expound, "It's, uh, in my brother's neighborhood, but I decided to overlook that major flaw."

The medical community here in Green Bay is a relatively small one, so she knows my older brother: thoracic surgeon Dr. Nicholas Bingham. I can tell she's trying to keep a straight face when she remarks, "Oooh! That's a pretty fancy neighborhood."

I roll my eyes to let her know I know it's trendy as hell and don't necessarily approve; but at the same time, the house I ultimately purchased is perfect for me. Fairly new, all modern amenities, hardwood floors (that I've covered with area rugs, since hardwood is nice to look at but notoriously hard on one's joints), and plenty of possibilities for customizing to my own specs. I spend a lot of weekends staining and painting, but I have nothing else to do, so DIY is a good way to pass the time.

"I just have a cottage on the outskirts," I add. "A lot smaller than his house... or yours. You know, your house was too big for one person," I say, then immediately regret it.

She shuffles papers around on her desk. "Yep. That's why I sold it."

Way to step in it, Nate. Why don't you spout some interesting statistics about the negative health effects of divorce on the average fifty-something-year-old professional woman? Just in case this isn't awkward enough.

"Anyway," she segues smoothly, "I wanted to make sure you knew I wasn't upset. You've seemed tense since the showing, and it only occurred to me the other day—when you stopped talking about your new house to Lynette after I walked into the room—what the problem might be."

Now I realize how ridiculous I must have seemed to her. Dr. Reitman has never been anything but professional and friendly and fair to me in my six years working here—even that time I accidentally shot blood across the room when I forgot to release the tourniquet before removing the needle during a blood draw. She took the situation in stride and stepped over the kid's passed-out mom to help me restore order to the room. (Hey, I was new!)

"It was dumb for me to even view your place."

"I thought I made it clear that you weren't under any obligation—"

"You did!" I hasten to interject. "But it occurred to me that a house with so much history would take on a life and person-ality of its own and become more than a structure. When I realized it wasn't for me, I worried you thought I was rejecting everything that was important to you." When that soliloquy meets silence, I open my eyes.

She blinks at me and tilts her head.

I laugh nervously at her shocked, almost alarmed expression. "My parents are psychiatrists. Sometimes stuff like that kind of"—I make a hand gesture to simulate something we see often around here—"spews out."

Looking away, she says quietly, "Well, that observation was very astute, and sensitive. But you presumed a bit much."

"I'm sorry!" I quickly respond to what feels like a rebuke.

With a chuckle, she shakes her head at me. "Forget it. Uh, Nate..." She seems to think better of finishing whatever she was going to say and merely smiles after a deep breath through her nose. "I'm glad we cleared this up. Now, we have a full patient load this afternoon. Let's get back to that."

I nod and edge toward the door, reaching behind me for the doorknob. My fingers brush against the smooth metal, and a welcome cool draft rushes in when I pull open the door. "Right. Thanks."

Her attention officially away from me and on her computer monitor, she murmurs, "Mmm-hmm."

With that overt dismissal, I slip into the hallway, feeling oddly lighter and heavier at the same time. So she's not offended I didn't buy her house; but I questioned her professionalism by worrying she might have been offended. Geez. If I had time to obsess about this right now, I'd be in trouble.

As it is, I don't have time. I rush to the supply room and gather the materials I'll need to perform Harry's promised strep test. Back in the exam room, I glove up, apologize for keeping Harry and his mom waiting, and swab the boy's throat. After sealing the swabs in a plastic tube and tossing my gloves in the trash, I give Mrs. Webster the name of the ear, nose, and throat clinic she can expect to hear from in the next few days.

To Harry, I direct while tapping the sealed swab tube against my palm, "Stop licking doorknobs, all right, bud? Didn't we talk about this last time?"

He manages to giggle while holding onto his neck and rasps, "I didn't lick any doorknobs."

"Riiiiight. Well, after you get your tonsils out, the doorknobs will shock your tongue. Don't say I didn't warn you." When he seems to take me seriously, I wink and he relaxes, making me wonder if he really *does* have a habit of licking door hardware.

Again, with no time to contemplate the odd proclivities of young boys, I let it drop and simply wish them a good afternoon. After they've departed for the reception area, I do a five-count and jog in the same direction toward the front office, where I hold out Harry's handwritten referral to Lynette, one of the receptionists.

She stares at it but doesn't take it from me. "What's the diagnosis?"

"Haven't done the culture yet, but I'm sure it's strep." I subtly shake the piece of paper, the international sign for *Take it already*. "Can you input this, please? I'm so behind."

"Yeah, I know," she acknowledges, finally pinching the slip between her fingers and squinting at my bad handwriting. "The patients are piled up out there, and parents are getting antsy."

"Well, I'm not thrilled about it, either. I have that thing tonight."

Again I receive a blank stare from her. Then she blinks and shakes her head. "Oh! That *thing*. What thing?"

Smiling tightly, I back away from her and snatch the next patient folder from the tray by the waiting room door. "You know, my blind date."

"Right. What's her name again?"

Fully aware I'm giving her information she already knows—or at least that she's already been told—I nevertheless answer, "Frankie. Frankie Lipton."

She giggles, crushing her hand against her mouth. "So many jokes. Can I just make *one* about tea-bagging?"

"No!" I look around us, paranoid someone impressionable may hear her. "No, you may not! Shhh!"

With an exaggerated sigh, she lowers her hand. "Fine. Hmmm. Now you're sure this is a *woman* you're being set up with?"

I narrow my eyes at her but don't dignify her question with a response, partly because I've triple-checked the same thing with my friend, whose friend-of-a-friend works with my mystery date at Quimby-Rex, a pharmaceutical supplier headquartered here in town.

My reaction only elicits a louder laugh from her. Then she seems to take pity on me and says, "It'll be fine, and if it's not, you'll have a great story to tell us on Monday. Now, get movin'." She turns away and peers at the form I've handed her, tutting. "Sheesh. Are you *sure* you weren't supposed to be a doctor, like your brother?"

I also don't dignify that question with a response but open the waiting room door to call the next patient.

"Yo, Niles! Ooh, that looks like a nasty boo-boo." As he and his dad walk past me, I lean down and say, "Just so you know, your neck is not a pencil holder. Let's get that taken care of, bud."

2

BLIND DATE

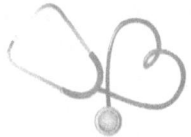

CRASHING AND CURSING THROUGH MY FRONT DOOR NEARLY three hours later, I kick off my shoes and peel off my Buzz Lightyear scrubs as I hurry down the hallway to my bedroom. The afternoon patient load was relentless, so not only am I home late, resulting in very little time to prepare for my date with Frankie, but my bladder's about to explode. This is how people get bladder infections and kidney stones, you know? Well, maybe *you* don't know, but *I* do.

In the bathroom, I run the water in the shower while I stand in front of the toilet, moaning as if experiencing a completely different kind of release. "Better than sex," I try to convince myself, shaking off the last drops and flushing without thinking. Damn. Now I'll have to wait for the water to return to below skin-searing temperatures.

Rushing naked into my bedroom, I stand in front of my closet and fret over my pathetic wardrobe. Not many people can say they wear glorified pajamas to work, but something tells me my first date in a long time warrants wearing pants with a zipper and button. Possibly even a belt. Although drawstrings do lend a bit of whimsy to any outfit.

Outfit? Whimsy?

Maybe I should lay off the chick lit for a while. Next I'll be calling my clothes *ensembles*, with the proper French pronunciation.

If memory serves (and I have to think way further back than I'd like to admit), the semi-casual first date—which I've been assured this is—calls for khakis, an Oxford shirt, and nice shoes—not tennis shoes. And no tie.

When *was* my last date? It must have been sometime fairly soon after... Oh. Right. Well, I won't be thinking about *that* tonight. No siree. Tonight is about the present, not the past. Anyway, that was a depressingly long time ago.

I throw the only date-worthy clothes from my closet onto the foot of my bed and sink down next to them. My shoulders slumped, I let my hands dangle between my knees like Cro-Magnon man and stare into space, wondering if tonight will be just another bad date or the beginning of something I've almost stopped daring to hope will happen.

This house is proof my *Leave it to Beaver* fantasy is dying faster than a skin cell in winter. When the dream was alive and well, only a few short years ago, I determined I'd do things in the right order: wife, house, kids. Well, I'm a grownup (most days) and grew tired of renting, so I've put the house before the wife. As happy as I am with my new place, it's still just a house, and it sucks that age is requiring me to manage my expectations.

Not that thirty-two is old, by any stretch, no matter what Harry Webster thinks. Sure, my parents were married, well-established in their private psychiatry practice, and had both Nick and me by the time they were my age, but times are different now. Nowadays, we're not in as much of a hurry. We take time to figure out who we are and what we want out of life before we settle down.

So, at this rate, I'll be about eighty by the time I'm ready.

I was ready once, though.

Snapping from my indulgent reverie, I whisper "Shit!" when I realize how much water I'm wasting and that I have a blind date in less than an hour. And a lot of grooming to do between now and then.

My cell phone rings in my carrier bag as I walk past it. "Fuck," I continue my stream of obscenities, digging through the bag for the device. With any luck, it's Frankie calling to cancel. *Her* luck, anyway. Let's face it; she's not going to be missing out on any charming conversation, based on my vocabulary tonight.

When I see my brother's name flashing on the screen, I carry the phone into the bathroom with me, set it on the edge of the sink, and activate the speaker phone, despite his immediate protests.

"Speaker, bro? Really?"

"I'm jumping in the shower, so it's either speaker or nothing."

He sighs. "Fine. Whatever. You can't delay your de-boogering for five minutes to talk to me? I get it."

I step into the stall and pull the door closed behind me. "No, I can't. I just got home, and I'm supposed to be meeting a date in less than an hour."

"Oh, yeah. That's tonight. Where you taking her? Please, don't say Chuck E. Cheese. It's *not* the best way to show you're a fun-lovin' guy. It doesn't say, 'I love kids;' it says, 'I'm a pedophile.'"

"Did you have a purpose for this call?" I prompt, squeezing shampoo into my palm and rubbing it vigorously into my hair.

He's quiet for a few seconds, so I think the call's been dropped. "Hello?" I check.

He clears his throat. "Uh, yeah. I actually do have a reason for calling. It's funny, um..."

While he dithers, I place my head under the stream to rinse and wait for him to get on with it. It's unusual for my self-confident big brother to have such a hard time expressing himself, so I figure this must be about someone of the fairer sex.

Sure enough, he finally says, "I'm calling to invite you to something. Something important."

"Yeah?" I massage conditioner into my head. "Well, I already told you I'm never going to one of your girlfriends' interpretive dance recitals ever again, so if that's what this is about, I'm busy. Whenever."

I expect him to laugh, so when he doesn't, I hold my hands still against my head and stare at the tiled ceiling. "Aw, man! No. Tell me you're not back together with that nutjob. What's her name? Zanzibar?"

"Zaskia. And no, I'm not going out with Zaskia."

"Zaskia! That's right." I continue conditioning. "Thank God. She was crazy! Remember how proud she was of being from Transylvania? She always said she was here to meet and marry a rich American, because that was what she always dreamed about, growing up. That recital—that wasn't dancing, by the way. That was—"

"Nate!"

I freeze, then pinch water away from my eyes. "What?"

"Bro—shut up. Here's the deal. I'm inviting you to my engagement party on Sunday."

"Hardy har har. Good one." I tilt my head back under the water. "Seriously, if you don't have something real to talk about, I need to let you go. I haven't even thought about what I'm going to say to this woman tonight that doesn't have to do with puking kids or our weirdo parents." I turn to face the stream and grab the bar of soap from its shelf on the wall.

"I'm serious. I'm getting married, and the engagement party is on Sunday."

None of this computes. None of it.

Well, I take that back. Maybe some of it does. Now that Nick's finished with med school and is part of an elite surgical team at the area's biggest hospital, it makes sense he's settling down in his personal life, too. Everything goes according to plan with Nick, after all.

"Where's this party going down?" I inquire, still waiting for him to say, "Just kidding!"

"At the Plotzlers' house."

I don't want to think about my former fiancée or her family tonight, of all nights, so his mention of them is extremely unwelcome. That being said, I can't ignore it or pretend it's completely normal for that name to come up in our everyday conversation. Gripping the soap as if my life depended on it, I stare at the rushing water in front of me while I try to make what Nick's said make sense.

"You there, bro?" his voice cuts through the steam.

"Um. Yeah. But wait a second. Why are the Plotzlers hosting your engagement party? To a person I've never even heard about, much less met?"

The growing cramp in my intestines tells me I'm sure I know why, and I don't want it confirmed right now, so I quickly say before he can answer, "Listen, I bet it's a funny story, but you'll have to tell me later."

Unfortunately, I can't reach my phone from here, so there'll be no hanging up on my brother before he says with a shaky voice, "I'm marrying Heidi."

I say, equally shaky, "You're not marrying Heidi."

As if staying in motion will mean none of what he's saying

is true, I scrub the now-mangled bar of soap against my chest to work up a lather.

His tone is firmer, more like him, when he says, "Yes, I am. I'm sorry to tell you on the phone, but it's not an easy conversation, you know? I've been trying to think of how to tell you for a long time."

The soap slips from my grip and lands squarely on the top of my foot. I barely register the pain. It's just as well I've dropped it; I need both hands to brace my weight against the wall as he explains about running into Heidi at The Cheesehead "a while back" and how they didn't mean for anything to come of it, and he hoped it wouldn't be weird, because "the last thing we want is to hurt you, bro."

A part of my brain comes alive and helps me say, albeit in a more robotic manner than an acting coach would have preferred, "Of course. It's fine. I'm happy for you two. Obviously."

"Really?"

Injecting a skosh more enthusiasm into my tone, I claim, "Yeah. I mean, it's been three years, right? It's not like I still... Anyway! This is great news!" I'm on a roll now. "Of course, I'll be at your engagement party on Sunday. Wow, you weren't kidding about waiting to tell me." I reanimate, retrieving the soap from the stall floor and getting back to the task at hand.

"And you'll be my best man, right?"

I pause, my hand hovering protectively over my foamy private parts. I close my eyes and count to three, silently begging my voice to stay steady when I answer, "Sure. Absolutely. If that's what you want."

"I do," he solemnly states, then chuckles. "Oh, good practice, huh? '*I do.*' But really, I'd really like that, for you to be my best man."

His repeated use of the word "really" tells me something

else, but I don't push it. I can't possibly continue this conversation another minute.

"Great. It's settled then. I'll see you Sunday?"

"Yeah! And, hey, good luck on your date tonight. Lief Heineman says he knows this Frankie chick, and she's hot."

Normally, I'd ask how the heck Lief "I-still-live-in-my-parents'-basement-and-think-hockey-mullets-are-the-height-of-style" Heineman knows anyone "hot," but I simply say, "Good to know. Thanks." I'm glad when Nick gets the hint and hangs up without any more lingering goodbyes.

Fortunately, this is yet another thing I don't have time to obsess about right now. I can't get too carried away, imagining what everyone in our families is thinking and saying about all this. I can't worry about the pitying looks I'll be receiving at the wedding, at the reception—*at Sunday's engagement party.*

I groan as I rinse the suds from my body, turn off the water, and fumble for the towel hanging over the shower door. I can't think about how many times people—namely, my mom—are going to ask me if I'm okay. I can't think about how "Heidi Bingham," a name I'd relegated to my list of "could have beens," now actually *will* be. Just not because of me.

I can't.

I lurch from the shower, drying off while I walk into my bedroom, where my uninspired clothes still await, looking blander than ever. Whatever scant hope I had for tonight (a one-night stand would have been cheap and sleazy, but at least it would have been a result) fizzles. After all, what's this "hot Frankie chick" going to see in me? My clothes are the generic dust jacket on a textbook about abnormal psychology.

Historical events prove I'm incapable of normal interaction with the opposite sex. I'm going to babble about the bread sticks or confess I don't like football or admit my addiction to chick lit or blurt my desire to get married and have kids as soon as possible. Or any number of other things that have had past dates nervously eyeing the door and muttering excuses about "early mornings." Early mornings that have nothing to do with waking up next to me.

I'm suddenly about a million times more insecure than I was before I talked to Nick. This date holds so much more— yet so much less—significance somehow. Part of me wants to call her and cancel; nothing's going to come of tonight, anyway, except more opportunities for me to humiliate myself in front of a stranger. But another part of me taunts that this could be my last chance at that life I desperately want.

I have three choices: I can stay home and sulk, go on the date and do my usual sabotage job, or show up and prove everyone wrong.

I dress with the urgency of someone escaping a burning building, my fingers shaking as they work feverishly on my shirt buttons.

Screw sulking.

3

FRANKIE

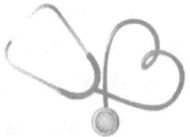

GOOD NEWS: I HAVEN'T MADE ANY OF MY USUAL FIRST-DATE verbal gaffes so far.

Bad news: That's because I haven't been able to get a word in edgewise.

Worse news: I don't care.

Worst news: Sulking at home alone would have made for a more interesting, enjoyable evening.

I nod and make encouraging noises from my side of the table while Frankie yammers on and on about her job as a traveling corporate trainer for Green Bay's only pharmaceutical drug supplier. I swallow the food I don't taste, and I pray for time to speed toward a socially acceptable date-ending hour.

It's not that she's awful; she's quite attractive, or "hot," as less evolved members of my sex would say. I suspect her verbosity has more to do with nerves than her natural personality. But my heart's not in this. My heart is at home, under the covers, wallowing.

My brain's pretty pissed off, too. After all, I'm botching what I know is my best chance at getting laid in... well, I'm not going to do the math, because that's crude. Suffice it to say, it's been a long time. I wasn't expecting it to happen tonight (hoping, maybe), but it'll never happen if I don't get past the first date with anyone.

Nick claims I'm impossible to please, nobody will ever be good enough, and I'll die alone. (Okay, I added that last part.) I'm *not* impossible to please. Do I have standards? Doesn't everyone? The women I've dated had standards, too. They seemed to spend a lot of time trying to mold me to fit them. (*Ahem*, Heidi!) So I don't think it's asking a person too much to cover her cough if we're going to have a chance at forever.

Anyway, let's say I *did* get past the first date, and even the second and third dates. Even if I'm willing to invest the time and energy it takes to form a bond strong enough to lead to physical intimacy, and then further, to a long-term relationship, who's to say that person won't tell me it's still not good enough, after months of my trying to be everything she wants me to be? Frankly, it's not worth it. That's what I read in a self-help book about commitment-phobia and self-sabotage.

Fine, it was an article in *Cosmo*, and it was written with a female audience in mind, but that doesn't mean it doesn't apply.

Tonight, the scene outside the restaurant window—a usually bland view of the strip mall parking lot—repeatedly pulls my attention from my date's face. Mini mountains of plowed snow lend an otherworldly, unfamiliar feel. Everything's already decked out for Christmas, although we're still a week away from Thanksgiving. With all the snow on the ground, though, we feel more justified hastening the arrival of the holidays than cities in more temperate climates. Winter is more than a season here; it's a way of life.

Looking at the white scene makes me cold. I'm not sure I'm ready for the next six months of snow chains and snow plows and snow shovels and snow and snow... and snow. As if on cue, the flurries ramp up their intensity into a full-out shower, coating the cars in a matter of seconds. I sigh.

That's when I notice how loud it was, because for the first time all night, the other side of the table is quiet.

As if in a trance, I slowly turn my head to look at my dinner companion.

Her jaw juts to the side and then resets so she can suck her lips into her mouth, clamping her teeth down on them. Not a good look, even on someone as pretty as she is.

After an awkward pause that I'm too apathetic to fill, she opens her mouth and says primly, "I'm sorry. Am I boring you?"

"No!" I lie.

She starts to get up, but I place my hand over hers, which has landed on top of the table between us, and is now gripping her clutch purse.

"No, please. Don't leave," I implore.

What are you doing, fool? Let her go! Then you can end this nightmare date and do what you really want to do: throw yourself a giant pity party at home. Alone.

Lowering her chin, she looks at me through her eyelashes. "And why should I stay? I might as well be talking to myself in my own apartment."

I blush and sweat as my normal personality finally struggles to take control of this runaway jerk train. "I know. I'm sorry. I just... I got some really bad news right before coming here, and —well, it wasn't *bad* news, I guess. More like weird news. My brother's getting married. Not that my brother is weird or it's weird that he's getting married. Actually, he's kind of a catch— a real doctor, not 'just a nurse,' like me—but his choice of bride is... unnerving. Not because I still have feelings for my former fiancée."

"Your brother's marrying your ex-fiancée?" I feel her

muscles slacken slightly under my hand as she decides to keep her seat, for now.

The sick knot in my stomach tightens. "Yes. It was years ago, but still..."

She wrinkles her nose. "Still," she agrees. "You and she... I mean, I'm assuming."

I shake my head and close my eyes, hoping she'll stop. When she mercifully does, I say, "Right. Exactly. We have memories of each other."

Now I feel her hand slide out from under mine and cover it. "I'm sorry. I can see why you're distracted."

With a weak smile, I open my eyes and lift my left shoulder in a half-shrug. "Yeah, well, it's no excuse for being rude. I'm sorry. I just can't help feeling like she traded me in for my more masculine, more successful older brother."

"Do you think they were... *you know*... while you and she were still together?" Her eyes widen at a possibility I hadn't even gotten around to contemplating. (I'm sure it would have hit me eventually—maybe at 2 a.m.)

Immediately, though, I dismiss the theory. "No! I mean..." I try to think about it more objectively, remembering their rare interactions with each other back then. "No," I answer more surely. "Nick had just graduated from med school. He was working insane hours, and we never saw him."

"*You* never saw him," she points out, smirking and leaning forward in her chair.

If I didn't know better—which I don't—I'd say she was starting to enjoy this.

I shake my head. "No way. Anyway, that was three years ago. Even if they had been doing something behind my back— which neither of them would ever do—it wouldn't have taken them this long to go public. That's extra-sneaky. Like, diabolical. Nick's not smart enough to be diabolical."

Still looking skeptical, she says, "I thought you said he was a doctor. You have to be smart to be a doctor."

"He's a surgeon, and yes, he's book-smart, but he's straightforward. And not very imaginative. He doesn't have it in him to be deceitful. Or to keep a relationship with someone like Heidi a secret for three years."

She finally seems to believe me, and that's when her interest in the topic wanes. "Well, then. What can you do? I know all about selfish family members, trust me."

"Nick's not selfish," I feel I need to state. "He's a good guy, mostly. You can't help who you fall in love with, but... Yeah, I wish they would have widened their dating pool a little to try to fall in love with other, newer people."

Her laugh is tinged with sympathy. "Again, I'm sorry."

I rub my hand over my face. "No, *I'm* sorry. I really have heard everything you've said. You're an only child, born and raised here in Green Bay, but your parents have lived out in Arizona for several years now. You work at Quimby-Rex, traveling during the week to educate sales reps about new product lines. Why is it that all prescription drug names sound like stripper names? Or is that just me? You're a University of Wisconsin alum—Go Badgers! You love the Packers. What else?" I tap my lips, frantically searching my memory.

"Okay, okay. Please!" She laughs. "You've proven you can listen while moping."

Fingering the edge of my frayed cloth napkin, I mumble, "Ouch. I guess I deserved that."

"Maybe I'll give you a pass, since your situation is unique. You seem like a nice guy otherwise; maybe I just caught you on a bad night."

I look away. "Oh, I probably would have done or said something even more repulsive if I'd been focused on this date. You're... Well, you're gorgeous. And smart. It's a combination that usually results in my making a complete ass of myself." I chance a peek at her reaction to my confession. I can't tell if she's skeptical or scared.

"Are you always this honest?" she asks, making it sound like it's not necessarily a good thing.

"What's the point in lying about myself?"

"Usually on first dates, guys try to put their best foot forward."

I wince. "This *is* my best foot."

She nudges my real foot under the table with hers. "So far, I'm intrigued. You're not like other guys."

God, if she only knew.

* * *

TWO HOURS LATER, our server is giving us dirty looks. I guess now that I've paid the tab, she's annoyed we're still breathing her air. Too bad. I'm amazed at my recovery. I thought this date was going to rank in the Top 5 Worst, up there with the one during which I talked about resuscitating a newborn who had stopped breathing in the office, and I started crying. In my defense, it had just happened earlier that week, and I was still shaken up from it.

And she didn't have to laugh at me. After all, I didn't make *her* feel bad about her thinning hair, did I? No, I didn't. I didn't even mention it or recommend some simple changes in her diet to try before taking a more drastic approach, like investing in hair plugs. I stared at her three-inch part and nearly bit through my tongue, but I didn't say anything. Why? Because I have feelings and also care about other people's feelings.

Anyway, the point is, this date is going much better than that one did. Frankie seems fascinated by my unmanly (or what I like to call "non-traditional") quirks. Her intense interest encourages me to keep finding more ways to surprise and delight her, too.

"Oh! I just thought of something else! I love chick lit!" I boom, as if that's the most brag-worthy trait of them all.

This revelation garners more disdainful glares from our server and rapid blinks from Frankie over the edge of her water glass.

Sure I've finally said too much, I laugh nervously. "I know... one more strike against my man card."

She sets down her glass and narrows her eyes at me. Rubbing her chin in an exaggerated fashion, she studies my face. "Chick lit, huh? You know, *you* could sell a million books with that face."

"No! I'm definitely *not* a writer. But every time I read something from another genre—what some may say is a more gender-appropriate genre—I find myself wishing I were reading something a little funnier, a little more romantic, and a little more hopeful and happy."

"How did you find this out about yourself, though? I mean, most guys wouldn't even pick up a pastel-colored book to read the first paragraph, much less read the whole thing to see if they enjoyed it."

"I was in college; it was a confusing time," I joke. Then I say, more seriously, "It *was* during college, though. Freshman year. I was taking a gender studies course as part of my general education requirements. One of the assignments was to read a mass market work of fiction geared toward the opposite sex. I picked up *Good in Bed,* by Jennifer Weiner, thinking I would at least get to read some steamy sex scenes."

"No steamy sex scenes," she says, acknowledging what my initially disappointed nineteen-year-old self discovered.

"Nope. But an addiction was born." My face burns. I'm

committed to owning this peculiarity, though. "I mean, in what other genre do nice guys more consistently get the girl?"

She laughs and shakes her head. "The good guys always win in those action books. You know, the ones with the complex military maps inside their front covers?"

I dismissively wave my hand in front of myself. "I didn't say *good* guys. I said *nice* guys."

She squints an eye at me.

"It's not the same thing!" I insist. "James Bond is a 'good guy,' but I wouldn't call him a 'nice guy.' As a matter of fact, he's sort of a d-bag.'"

She nods. "Yeah, well, most love interests in chick lit start out that way, too, right? The guy's a jerk, usually some bossy cop or ranch foreman or some other macho profession; he and the protagonist don't get along, they're like fire and ice, blah, blah, blah—"

I wrinkle my nose. We may have a problem here. If she lumps all women's fiction—including those Harlequin Romance things—under the heading "chick lit," that could be a deal-breaker.

That's one of the hundreds of reasons it never would have worked out between Heidi and me. She thought the epitome of a romantic lead was a stalker-esque, sparkly vampire with control issues. She and Nick, who probably hasn't read a book for pleasure—ever—will make a great couple.

"You're describing a romance novel," I point out. "Chick lit is *not* strictly about romance. You don't read it?"

She smiles and looks at me through her eyelashes. "Of course I do. I just wanted to make sure *you* really do, that you're not feeding me a line."

My relief makes me laugh louder than I probably should. "Not a line. Haven't I given you enough first-date confessions to reassure you that I'm not gonna hand you any lines?"

The way she pushes her lips together and looks askance at me makes me think she still doesn't believe me, but then her face relaxes into a broad smile. "Hmm. True."

"So why don't you return the favor, then?" I say.

Her mouth drops open. "What do you mean? I spent the first forty-five minutes of this date telling you everything about me."

I fake a yawn. "I don't mean your eHarmony profile." When her eyes widen, and her tongue peeks at me from between her teeth, I laugh to let her know my teasing is in good fun. "I mean, tell me something you don't tell just anyone."

Her smile completely gone now, she stares me down, and to keep from squirming, I analyze the precise shade of her irises. (Nutmeg? Milk chocolate?) Finally, though, I give up on classifying her eye color and getting more information from her. "Never mind."

"No," she quickly capitulates. "I'm thinking, that's all. Trying to decide if I want to tell you this. It's something I've only told one other person, my best friend I've known since second grade."

I swallow loudly, suddenly afraid of the intensity radiating from her. "It doesn't have to be something *that* secret. I was thinking more along the lines of, 'I get chills when I hold babies,' or 'I pee in the shower.'"

"*Eww.*"

"I know, right? It was just an example. I don't do that." I rub my neck and continue to wait as she taps the toe of her shoe against the table leg. Here it comes. The deal-breaker to end all deal-breakers. *"I'm married,"* springs horrifyingly to mind, along with, *"I used to be a man;" "I am a man;" "I came on this date on a dare;" "I don't shave my underarms;"* and *"I'm a chip double-*

dipper." (Because that's just nasty.) Or worse, *"I love Nascar romance novels."*

Oblivious to my building panic—or getting off on it—she takes a deep breath and her sweet time before saying, "I don't just read chick lit; I write it."

"Okay..." Still bracing for the bombshell, I ask, "So, why's this such a big secret?"

With a toss of her hair, she answers, "I don't know. I could wallpaper Buckingham Palace with my rejection letters."

"Idiots, all of them. I'm sure you're a great writer."

I'm not sure at all, but that's what you say, right? I mean, for all I know, she's terrible. It seems everyone—except me—fancies themselves a writer nowadays. There's a ton of shit out there. I've read half a ton of it.

She folds her hands on the table in front of her. "Oh, I'm an excellent writer."

Something tells me not to say, "Oh-ho!" or anything equally deprecating, and I'm glad I don't when she continues, and it becomes obvious she's being completely earnest in her self-assessment.

"My writing's not the problem; my image is the problem. I'm another thirty-something woman writing about women finding their way in their late twenties and early thirties, you know? I'm a staticky television in a sea of white noise. Not enough of a standout."

"A staticky television in a sea of white noise"? Yikes. I know it's not fair to judge everything that comes out of her mouth based on the new knowledge that she's a writer, but she invited it with her *"I'm an excellent writer"* boast. Bragging is such a turn-off.

Still, I feel obliged to ask, "Can I read something you've written?"

"No, I hardly know you. Plus, what if you didn't like it? I

mean, it would be totally subjective, and I know it wouldn't be a reflection of my talent, but you'd be put in the position of lying to spare my feelings."

"Oh, I wouldn't lie. I'm picky about my chick lit."

"Then definitely no."

I laugh, suddenly understanding how "great" her writing must be. It's not nice to pick on someone's weaknesses, so I steer the conversation back to the facts.

"Your best friend is the only person who's read your books?" I ask.

"Betty's the only one who *knows* about my writing, period. Or did. I guess you know now. Not even my parents know."

"For real?"

I can't relate to that *at all*. It was only until recently that my parents didn't know *everything* about me, unfortunately. I think I'll keep that information to myself.

In response to my shock, Frankie asks, "Do your parents know about *your* hobbies?"

"My parents are psychiatrists. They helped me choose my hobbies when I was a kid, based on complex profiling and personality algorithms." I punctuate that with a laugh and turn it back around on her before she has a chance to think about how messed-up it is. "Man, I feel bad that I know something about you that your parents don't even know."

"Well, don't. Why would they even need to know? I'm not sure they'd be interested, anyway." The way she says it brings the conversation to an abrupt halt. She smiles tightly. "That's not a first-date conversation, anyway. Let's save something to talk about on our second date."

Hmmm... Do I want a second date? Ah, what the hell else do I have to do?

I grin across the table at her. "Deal."

4

RULES OF ENGAGEMENT

Pastel-colored balloons tied to the mailbox sway in the cold November wind. Wedding-themed paraphernalia dots the snow-dusted front lawn and lines the cleared and salted concrete walkway. Even if I'd forgotten in the past three years where my former future in-laws lived, there would be no mistaking which house on the block is hosting the engagement party of the year.

Heidi's parents, Walter and Mary Jo, know how to do this, having married off two other daughters already. Not to mention, this isn't Heidi's first engagement party. Let's not forget that. Yeah. This may be a tad more awkward than I even imagined, and I imagined "awkward" on the scale of chirping crickets, fake laughter, sweaty armpits, and the kind of drinking that usually ends badly.

As my Prius glides to a stop and I jam it into park next to the curb, a voice as real as the one on the radio says to me, "*It's not too late to drive away. Nobody's seen you yet. Pull a U-turn, and—*"

"Nate!"

My brother bursts through the front door and tiptoes through the yard ornaments and muddy snow to get to the salt-stained sidewalk. A goofy grin on his face, he peers through the passenger window and shouts, "C'mon! What're you doing out here? We're waiting for you!"

I alight from my car. "Hey," I say, failing to achieve the level of I'm-cool-with-this enthusiasm I was aiming for, but he has enough energy for both of us.

"I'm so glad you came, man. I was starting to think you weren't going to." He meets me at the front of the car and grabs my arm, as if making sure I'm not going to bolt.

I run my hand through my hair. "Uh, yeah. I, uh, overslept."

I *was* in bed, with the covers over my head, until less than an hour ago, so it's almost the truth. Close enough for today.

He pretends to believe me. "Well, come on in. The party's in full swing. Plus, the game's about to start. We need to get all the crappy speeches out of the way so we can turn on the TV."

My brain almost doesn't know which part of his statement to hate the most. *"The party's in full swing"* means several of our relatives are already loudly drunk; *"the game's about to start"* refers to the Packers game I'm going to have to get drunk to pretend to care about; and *"all the crappy speeches"* may refer to something I'm supposed to take part in, but I don't have anything prepared, and there's no way I can wing something gracious and coherent.

I decide to focus on the most alarming thing: "Speeches? Am I expected to say something?"

While dragging me into the house, he laughs, but he doesn't turn around, so he can't see the growing terror on my face. "Good one, best man! No, this is *my* gig. You already had your chance with Heidi."

I laugh nervously and try to stay conscious as I remember with relief that the bride- and groom-to-be are the ones who talk at the engagement party. "Yep. Blew it," I mutter, barely getting the words out before he comes to a stop, pulls me forward to stand next to him, and puts his arm around my shoulders in a jovial squeeze.

"Hey, guys! Look who finally decided to show up!" he practically yells into the crowded open-plan living/dining/kitchen area of the Plotzler home.

The room falls quiet.

"My brother and best man!" Nick announces, squeezing me harder.

Mom tilts her head, squints, smiles, and mouths an, *"Oh!"* as in, *"Look at my darling boys, such good friends!"* when I know she's really thinking, *"Oh, poor Nate. As soon as things settle down, I need to corner him and interrogate him about his mental state."*

My other head-shrink parent is strangely absent, I note, searching the room for Dad. Before I can get too far into my survey, though, Heidi almost tackles me with a hug.

"Hey, Nate! Thanks so much for coming and for agreeing to be Nicky's best man!"

Please, make it stop. The public Nate sandwich is unbearable. It's going on forever.

Finally, I wiggle loose and give what I hope is a bemused chuckle. "You may not be thanking me after you hear what I have in mind for the bachelor party."

Heidi's megawatt smile freezes, and her eyes deaden. Uh-oh. I know that look all too well.

"Just kidding," I say unconvincingly, pulling her back toward me and giving her a fierce noogie.

She ducks from my reach, trying to smooth her long, blonde, shiny locks. "Nate!"

Nick shoots me a dirty look and lets go of my arm, raising his voice to be heard over the guests who have returned to their conversation and plates of food during our threesome. "Now that everyone's here..."

He launches into a long, sappy speech, including the entire story of his and Heidi's relationship to date, starting at The Cheesehead over a year ago (What the fuh?) and ending at Lake Wenskaug, where he proposed to her during a romantic picnic. The women are lapping it up, complete with goo-goo eyes and oohs and aahs. Heidi looks like she could probably have an orgasm in the middle of her parents' living room.

The men, on the other hand, are looking longingly towards the den, where they'll be watching the football game after Nick shuts up. Or they focus on the food on their plates, or employ their best poker faces to hide their *"Can-you-effing-believe-this-guy?"* reactions to Nick's smooth delivery. I hope my poker face is working better than Uncle Mort's. I also hope it's better than the face I used when I lost all that money to Uncle Mort in an actual poker match at my parents' Fourth of July barbecue.

Finally, Nick stops talking, and he and Heidi kiss like they're alone in the room. After about ten seconds, my psychological discomfort manifests itself into physical fidgeting. I avert my eyes and scratch my ear, willing the two lovebirds to stop making out. Much longer, and I'm not going to be able to silence the annoying voice in my head that wants me to acknowledge that I know *exactly* what it's like to kiss those lips (Heidi's, not Nick's). And other things.

"Oh, shit, I need a beer," I hiss, wishing I hadn't said it out loud but figuring the resultant end to the makeout session is worth it.

While I'm cracking open a beer and chugging it with my back turned to the rest of the guests (as if that means they can't see me), Heidi begins her speech. I'm congratulating myself on how well I'm *not* listening to what she has to say when some of her words filter through.

"...and I thought I'd never find a man who would measure up to

the example of husband and father my dad has always been, until Nicky."

My fist tightens around the empty beer can, creating a loud, metallic crunch. I don't have to turn around to know everyone's staring at me.

Heidi giggles. "Oops. No offense, Nate."

Everyone else nervously titters, too.

I take a deep breath through my nostrils and face the audience. "Hey, none taken. I think it sort of went without saying, but... Please. Go on."

To everyone's chagrin, she does go on. And on. And on. And on. Finally, after several choke-ups and restarts, she wraps it up, and we endure a slightly shorter, more chaste kiss to underscore her love for my brother.

"All right, then. Go, Pack, Go!" Uncle Mort says, making a beeline for the den. Several people, including Heidi's siblings, Hans, Greta, and Sonya, follow.

I dig in the ice-filled sink for another beer.

Mom sidles up to me. "I'm proud of you," she says in greeting.

"You have such low standards." After three long gulps from my drink, I rest, stifling a carbonated burp behind my fist.

She rubs my upper arm. "I know this isn't easy—"

"It's not about 'easy' or 'hard.' It's uncomfortable. That's all. Everyone's staring at me, expecting me to... I don't know. Break down sobbing? Punch Nick in the throat? Beg Heidi to take me back? What are they expecting?"

"I think they want you to give them a sign that you're okay, that you're happy."

I snort. "I'd be a lot happier if I weren't under the microscope. Oh, and if people wouldn't tiptoe around me. Or treat me like the second-place finisher in an arm wrestling competition. It's been three years. I'm okay. Really."

I feel her staring at my profile, so I force myself to turn my head and look down into her eyes, eyes that are so much like mine, it's almost creepy. Holding her gaze, I say firmly, as if saying it to both of us, "I'm okay. It's fresh, all right? He just told me Friday night. I've hardly had time to process the news, you know?"

"I do know."

"Yeah. Everyone knows. Everyone's known for a while, obviously. This is not an impromptu party." I wave my hand at the bedecked room.

I shut up and stop gesturing when two of Heidi's siblings come closer to graze at the buffet. We smile painfully at each other and make stupid small talk.

"Still a nurse, Nate?"

"Yep. Still nosy and self-righteous, Greta?"

OK, I don't really say that, but I want to. I actually say, "Yep. Nothing's changed for me. For the most part."

Heidi's big brother, Hans, pops a cheese cube in his mouth and says while chewing, "I see you still don't watch football."

"And I see you're still thirty pounds overweight, carrying that 'sympathy weight' from your wife's last pregnancy four years ago."

Yeah, I don't say that either.

Admitting to not liking football in this town—especially if you also possess male genitalia—is tantamount to treason and blasphemy combined. It's another favorite pastime of the other 99.5% of people in this town to give people like me shit for not liking football. As if it's the worst thing possible, ranking right up there with pedophilia and being a Vikings fan. I'm surprised I haven't been strung up or at least evicted from the city.

"Right-o. Still not my thing. I do enjoy *fútbol*, though."

This prompts a disgusted snort from Hans. "Soccer. A bunch of pansies, compared to American football players."

I'd like to see him sprint up and down a soccer pitch for nearly ninety minutes straight and see if he still thinks soccer players are pansies, but I merely concede, "If you say so," since it's not worth my breath to argue with him.

"Good seeing you again," Greta and Hans say at nearly the same time, making us all chuckle woodenly before they head back to the den.

As soon as they leave, I return to my conversation with Mom. "Don't worry about me, all right? I'm fine. Do I wish you hadn't made Nick ask me to be his best man?" She opens her mouth to protest, but I cut her off, laughing. "Trust me, I know that was your doing. I'm sure he has six or seven golfing buddies he'd rather have asked."

"He only has one brother."

"And I bet he's thankful for that most days."

"You joke, but he loves you. This has been stressful for him. You know, he almost broke up with Heidi before it got too serious because he was so worried about you. I convinced him you'd be fine, that you only wanted him—and Heidi—to be happy." She hugs my arm. "Don't prove me wrong."

Pulling my third beer from the ice, I say, "I *am* fine," punctuating my statement with the hiss and pop of the can's pull tab. "I'd be better if they'd refrain from playing tonsil hockey in front of everyone, but I guess you can't have everything."

She laughs. "Gosh, that went on forever! I almost reminded them their parents were in the room, but I didn't want to sound like a fuddy-duddy."

"Speaking of parents, plural, where's Dad?" I ask, hoping to permanently change the subject.

"Oh, he's around somewhere. Watching the game, most likely."

I'm not all that concerned or interested in his where-abouts, although I'm curious, as it relates to me. I'd prefer not to be cornered for a man-to-man today. I know he's trying to help, but sometimes his heavy-handed pep talks do just the opposite, and they depress the crap out of me.

With a parting pat on my bicep, Mom says, "Slow down on those beers, huh? Load up a plate and go watch the game." She moves off, flagging down Heidi's mother to compliment her on the food and the decorations.

I look down into the nearly empty can in my grip and sigh. She's right; nothing good will come from getting drunk. At the very least, I'll have to get someone to drive me home. But I'll need to keep drinking to watch the game. It's a conundrum.

Not hungry—at all—I decide to seek out some different company, some people with whom I'm more comfortable. Since I'll be forever relegated to the kids' table at these joint family things, I might as well get chummy with my peers.

* * *

WHEN I ROUND the bottom of the basement stairs, I see ten kids, aged nine and younger, clustered around a board game on the floor. It physically hurts to look at Heidi's sister Sonya's three blond boys, because they look like the mental image I had of the kids in my fantasy life with Heidi.

Most of her nieces and nephews were babies when she and I broke up, so they don't remember me, but the older ones do. I stitched Kingsley's eyebrow when he split it open on the corner of a coffee table one Christmas. He's the first one to acknowledge me.

"Hey, Uncle Nate!" The nine-year-old, unaware the title he's given me no longer fits, scrambles to his feet and points to the board on the floor. "We're gonna talk to dead people with the Ouija board."

His announcement shakes loose my irrational and self-indulgent melancholy, and I have to stifle a laugh. "Cool. Mind if I play?"

Seven-year-old Remus scoots so I can squeeze between him and his four-year-old brother, Percy. I place my hand on the pointer, or planchette, and wiggle my eyebrows across the board at Hermione. The eight-year-old giggles.

"We're gonna ask to talk to our Grandma June. She died," Hermione informs me.

"I heard about that," I say seriously, "and it made me sad. I liked Grandma June."

June, who's been dead for a couple of years now, was Heidi's grandmother and the kids' great-grandmother. She and I kept in touch after the break-up, and she once confided in me that she thought I was probably better off without Heidi.

Oh, Grandma June, I wish you were here today.

In addition to Greta's gang, Hans's three daughters—Amber (eight), Ruby (six), and Violet (four)—and Sonya's three —Jude (six), Justin (five), and Jeremiah (three)—surround the old Parker Brothers game board. Since Kingsley's the oldest, he takes charge of asking the questions of dearly departed Grandma. Hermione has a pencil and a pad of paper, which she says she'll use to write down the letters for the longer answers.

"Grandma June, are you in Heaven?" Kingsley intones earnestly.

Nothing happens. Bless their hearts, none of them has figured out that someone has to move the planchette. I gladly take up that responsibility and move it to *Yes.*

The kids squeal, and I struggle to keep a straight face.

"Do you like it in Heaven?"

I slowly and smoothly nudge the pointer around the board, resting briefly on each of the letters: F-O-O-D-I-S-G-O-O-D.

When Hermione reads the words in their entirety, she glances at me, as if to verify that's what Grandma June meant.

I shrug and pull the corners of my mouth down in a contemplative frown. "I hear the food's excellent in Heaven, so that makes sense," I state.

She nods earnestly.

Next question: "Are you here in this room with us?"

Yes.

More squeals.

"What do you want us to know?"

The felt pads on the legs of the pointer squeak against the laminated game board. E-A-T Y-O-U-R V-E-G-E-T-A-B-L-E-S.

"Eat your vegetables?" Remus questions, his freckled nose scrunched up. "Grandma June's upsessed with eating."

I hang my head and cough to hide my laughter.

Amber pipes up, "Let *me* ask the questions. You ask dumb ones, Kingsley."

Seemingly unoffended, Kingsley yields to his peer.

"Grandma June. Who do you think is more handsomer, Nick or Nate?" she asks, all business-like. I can tell by the giggles from the girls that this is not a new topic.

"Now, guys," I say. "Grandma June doesn't—"

I jerk the planchette into motion, making a beeline for the "N" on the board. Widening my eyes at the kids, I say, "The next letter will give us our answer," pretending to anxiously wonder. Our hands take the quick jump from the lower row of letters to the "A" directly above the "N."

I gasp. "Grandma June!" I fan my face with my free hand. "Thanks, but we all know Nick is the handsome one."

"Yeah!" Amber agrees, too quickly.

"Nuh-uh!" say Hermione and Ruby in unison.

The boys all make gagging noises.

"Who cares?" yells Jeremiah.

"You were pushing the thingy!" Amber accuses her Team Nate cousins.

"Was not!" Hermione insists, shoving the planchette for real. "If I was pushing it, it would move like that. Grandma June was moving it!"

"Ladies, ladies," I coax. "Settle down. It's just a game. For fun."

"But Uncle Nate, they're cheating!" Amber cries.

"Are not!" Hermione insists. "And stop calling him 'Uncle Nate.'"

"What else are we s'posed to call him?" Kingsley asks.

All eyes lock on me, and while I try to figure out what, exactly, I am to them now (nothing, I finally come to the depressing conclusion), Hermione butts back in with, "I don't know, but I heard Mom say to Dad that we have to walk on our tippy-toes around you. Why? Do you like to pretend you're a ballerina? I like to pretend that sometimes."

"Me, too!" Ruby pipes up.

"Nobody has to tiptoe around me," I assure them all.

"*My* daddy said Nick was the better choice, and my daddy's always right," Amber boasts.

"Tell that to his cholesterol levels," I mutter, before smiling brightly and sing-songing, "Let's talk about something happier, like super-viruses."

"Wait!" Kingsley shouts. "What do we call you? I always call you Uncle Nate, but now I'm not allowed?"

I sigh and make eye contact with each of them in turn. "Listen. It's complicated. So you guys can call me whatever you want, all right?"

"Poop Head?" Remus suggests with a giggle.

"Penis Butt?" Percy chimes in with a four-year-old's version of extreme profanity.

Laughing at their silly potty mouths (hey, they're not my kids, so I don't have to be a mature role model), I say, "No! C'mon! At least make it something cool. How about *Captain Poop Head*?"

They shriek and squeal at my joke, getting louder and louder as they throw out more outrageous "illicit" names. Suddenly, from the top of the stairs, Hans's voice booms at us, "What's going on down there?"

I cover my mouth and widen my eyes, shaking my head at the rest of them.

After a suitable pause, Hans barks, "Cut it out, will ya? We're trying to watch the game."

When I'm sure the coast is clear, I stage whisper, "Who wants to talk to Grandma June again?"

Ten voices chirp, "Me!" as I set up the board once more.

5

BETTY

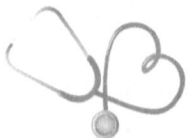

THIS IS A TEST. I KNOW IT IS. I GET IT. "CHICKS BEFORE dicks," and all that business. Or, as guys like to say, "Bros before hos."

Whichever offensive, profane way you like to express it, the sentiment is the same: friends will be around *after* the inevitable breakup, so loyal friendship trumps romantic partnership every time. Or it should, I suppose—until you're married. Then you're supposed to reverse position on that and forsake all others. Is it any wonder we don't have a clue as a society what we're doing when it comes to all this shit? I mean, it's confusing as hell.

I will say one thing for men, though: at least we don't parade potential mates in front of our friends for premarital inspection.

I might understand that if I don't pass muster with Frankie's best friend, Betty, it's game over, but that doesn't mean I don't resent it. Why does this Betty person get the final say? And what if I don't even *want* to move on to the next level with Frankie? It's sort of presumptuous of her to assume that's the case.

As a matter of fact, after a few dates, I'm starting to think she's not worth the trouble. I'm not only talking about sex. Give me *some* credit. I'm not one of those guys who thinks a woman owes it to me after a few dinners and drinks and my sitting through some godawful comic book movie (during which she moaned and drooled over every silicone-coated man in tights that flew, zoomed, and leapt across the screen). I don't feel even close to the way I need to feel about a woman to go *there* with her.

But—at the risk of sounding like a misogynist asshole— she's said more than one or two things about her past relationships that make me think she doesn't have the same standards for sleeping with people that I do. There. I said it without using any ugly, judgmental words. I'm not judging her; I'm merely observing and comparing.

But I'm starting to wonder what about me doesn't meet her seemingly low standards for sexual candidacy. It's messing with my head a little, and leading me to do uncharacteristic things, like obsessively checking my breath and chewing gum, even though it aggravates my temporo-mandibular joint dysfunction (TMJ, or jaw pain, for those of you laypeople out there); dressing more preppy, and then less preppy; experimenting with body sprays and colognes and deodorants, etc. It's costing me a fortune, all for something purely academic, since I don't think I'd say "yes" even if she did suggest we have sex.

And now *I'm* being evaluated by the best friend? It chafes, that's all. Honestly, if I weren't feeling so vulnerable right now, like I'm running out of chances, like maybe I've bailed too early too many times in the past, I would have already lied several times about being too busy to hang out with her, hoping she'd give up on *me* before I had to have that awkward "It's not you... well, yeah it is" conversation.

"So, is she always late?" I ask Frankie as we nurse our second drinks and wait for Betty to arrive.

She rolls her eyes. "Yep. I have a feeling she likes to make an entrance."

This insight makes me laugh. "Just a feeling? You've never called her on it?"

With a tiny shake of her head, she replies, "Nope. But when she gets here, you'll see. In the meantime, I need to use the bathroom."

Before I can object to her leaving me alone as her best friend is about to arrive, she practically climbs over me in the booth with a "Be right back!"

"But—" I sigh and watch her trot toward the bathrooms. "Great," I mutter. I face forward and train my eye on the front door.

Not too much time elapses before the door opens. A black-haired woman in a black cashmere coat, red scarf, and matching red leather gloves blows in with the cold, snow-scented air. She pauses on this side of the threshold, stretches even higher in her three-inch heels, and scans the room, ostensibly to find Frankie and me. Since I'm in the first booth directly in her eye line *and* I'm only one of a half-dozen patrons in the place this early on a Friday, she sees me right away, but she takes her time acknowledging me with a regal nod and slow smile.

We have a live one.

She sashays toward me in slow motion. Drawing even with the table, she pulls her gloves from her fingers, one-by-one, and waves one of the gloves in the direction of the bar. "Cab Sav, Russell!" she calls to the server, who's kept his eyes on her every move from his vantage point, leaning against the bar.

Turning her full attention to me, she stands expectantly next to the table.

"You must be Betty," I say, for lack of any better way to kick off the introductions, since our mutual acquaintance has apparently fallen into the toilet. There's no chair for me to pull out for her, but I slide from the booth and stand, offering her my hand to shake.

In a whimsical role reversal, she pulls my knuckles toward her face and brushes them against her blood red lips. "*Enchantée*, Nathaniel," she murmurs, studying me through her thick eyelashes. She drops my hand so she can glide into the booth across the table from me.

As she unwinds her red cashmere scarf from around her neck, I retake my seat, covertly rubbing her lipstick from my knuckles onto my jeans. "Actually, it's Nathan, not Nathaniel," I casually correct her original greeting. "But everyone calls me Nate."

"Nurse Nate," she croons, touching her top lip with the tip of her tongue.

Russell arrives, setting a cocktail napkin on the table directly in front of Betty, then placing a large, round wineglass on top of the napkin.

She beams at him. "Thanks. You're a doll." The smile dies in her eyes but stays on her lips. "Now, scram."

How did she...? Before I can marvel at the shift in demeanor and the speed with which Russell complies with her command, her laser beam eyes return to me. "I think I like Nathaniel better," she declares.

Frankie returns to the table, and I stand once again to let her in. "So, you guys have met?" she inquires, taking her seat and fishing the chocolate kiss from the bottom of her martini glass.

I watch her fingers, feeling a strange mixture of mesmerized and repulsed. Knowing what's lurking on the average person's hands—even someone with good hygiene—makes me shiver at her dipping her fingers in her drink, especially since she just came from the bathroom. I only hope she washed those hands thoroughly.

That being said, she has long, graceful fingers, and neat, short nails, painted a deep red that's almost black, a color probably named something dramatic, like "Black Currant." It immediately makes me think, "Deoxygenated Blood." That's not helping the queasy feeling her behavior's prompting. Oh, and it's probably a good thing cosmetics companies don't consult me on names for nail polish.

Betty pulls my attention back to her by answering Frankie, "Yes. I was about to explain to Nathaniel how I like to come up with special names for people." She pokes her thumb in our server's direction. "His name's Rusty, but I never call him anything but Russell, which I think is more dignified." The smile has returned to her blue eyes, which sparkle playfully.

Frankie rolls her unsparkly brown eyes. "She calls me Francesca, which I hate with a passion. Anyway, this is all just an act. She watches too many black-and-white movies." Directly to her friend, she demands in a stern tone, "Stop it, Barracuda. You're making Nate sweat."

"No!" I quickly deny. "I'm fine. I mean, alcohol always does this to me. It's warm in here. I shouldn't have worn a shirt under this sweater, but it's itchy, so I don't like to wear it without something under it."

Betty arches her right eyebrow in a feat of facial flexibility I don't think I could ever mimic, even though I suddenly have the urge to try. She says to Frankie, "You don't normally go for the awkward ones, but this one is cute."

I'd resent the "awkward" assessment if it weren't true. I prefer to focus on the fact that she thinks I'm cute.

Beaming at her, as if she's given me the biggest compliment in the world, I say, "Thanks!"

"Oooh, and eager-to-please, too," she croons.

"That's enough." Frankie says mildly, wiping her fingertips on her cocktail napkin. She slides her hand under my arm, giving my bicep a squeeze.

I flex it so it's not a squishy tube of toothpaste against her hand, but immediately feel like an idiot for doing something so transparent.

She either doesn't notice or does a good job pretending not to. "Leave him alone. Gosh! You come in here, looking like Katy Perry and acting like Lauren Bacall—"

"I was named after her, you know. Lauren Bacall. Betty was her real name." She sips her wine.

"Yes, you've mentioned it a few *thousand* times," Frankie says.

"I was telling Nathaniel. Sorry!" For the first time since arriving, she seems like a real person, not a caricature in her fit of pique.

Frankie sighs but raises her hand to flag down Rusty. She motions for him to bring us another round, then lets go of my arm. I relax it.

"You got any hot friends, or brothers?" Betty asks. "And when I say, 'hot,' I mean a tad edgier than you." She punctuates this with a wink.

I clear my throat, running through a mental lineup of my friends to see if any of them fit the bill. Thing is, most of my friends are either married or about to be married. I'm one of the last single ones left. (And yes, I know what that says about me.)

She waits, gulping her wine while I think, and then says, "If you have to think that long, the answer's no."

"My brother's engaged to be married," I explain, then want to punch myself in the crotch, since the last thing I need is to get on the topic of Nick's upcoming nuptials. I quickly add, "I only have the one brother. Plus he's not edgy. He's like me, only"—*where the hell am I going with this?*—"richer," I finish flatly.

She looks at me like she's found out my IQ (or some other measurement), and I've come up woefully short. "Richer?"

"He's a doctor. A surgeon, actually."

"Doctors don't do it for me," she claims. "They seem to have a God complex."

Rusty returns, sliding a new martini in front of Frankie and replacing my empty pint glass with a filled-to-the-brim glass of dark amber liquid.

"Big boy beer," Betty approves with another wink.

"Am I going to have to hurt you?" Frankie asks. But she doesn't sound all that upset by Betty's shameless flirting or my response to it. Not that I want her to be jealous. Or do I? I don't know. Maybe a *slight* response would be nice, to show she cares.

"So, you're a murse, huh?" Betty continues her questioning, trailing her index finger along the rim of her wineglass.

Her hybrid of "male nurse" makes me laugh. "Uh, yeah."

"Sexy. Do you sport any tats under your scrubs?"

"No tats here," I inform her unapologetically.

"Uh-oh. What are you, afraid of needles?"

"That would be a bit inconvenient, don't you think?"

"But it would make you more interesting," she muses.

"Oh, I'm plenty interesting in other ways," I retort, which instantly erases any examples from my mind. Fortunately, she doesn't make me back up my claim.

"Never mind. 'Interesting' isn't one of Francesca's requirements."

"Well, I'll keep my eyes open for fellow murses who like body art, and I'll send them your way," I offer.

"I'm not into ink," she says with a moue and an impatient flick of her wrist. "I was just making conversation."

"Can we talk about something that involves *my* participation?" Frankie demands in that baby-talk sulky voice that drives me up a wall almost as much as the duck-lips face that goes with it.

I clench my teeth but manage to turn it into a smile before facing her. "Yeah. You're quiet tonight."

"Didn't want to interrupt." Her tone and the way she's now moved as far away from me as the wall will allow suggest otherwise.

There's no point in being a jerk, so I cover her hand with mine and squeeze it. "Hey, I'm sorry." She pushes my hand away but doesn't say anything.

Rejected, I bury my nose in my beer glass and drain the rest of it.

Betty observes us for a few seconds. "This one's really not your usual type, sweetie. Good for you for broadening your horizons and stepping away from Doucheville for a while." She leans back in her side of the booth, cradling her wine glass against her face and scrutinizing me like someone would an abstract painting.

"You're one to talk," Frankie snaps. "Do you really want to get on the topic of past relationships?"

Betty's face pales. "Fair enough," she mutters.

Willing to do anything to dispel the sudden cloud that's descended on our table, I set down my glass, finger the coaster under it, and blurt, "Yeah, the guy whose former fiancée is marrying his brother in less than six months would appreciate steering clear of that conversation."

Betty's smile has an appreciative edge to it. She chuckles. "Gosh, I heard about that! Interesting family dynamic you have there."

"Lots of material for a writer like Frankie," I concur. To the writer, I say, "Make sure you change the names to protect the innocent. That would be me, FYI."

"I'm not sure anyone would believe a book about you." What would normally sound like a compliment seems less than one when paired with the smirk on her face.

"I *am* too good to be true."

I meant it sarcastically, but Betty hoots, "Smooth!" Before I can defend myself, she continues, "And speaking of smooth, what are your thoughts about body waxing? Francesca usually likes guys with less..." She pinches at the skin at the base of her throat, as if she's fluffing an imaginary tuft of hair.

I instinctively finger the fuzz to which she's referring. "I, uh..."

"Your body hair is fine," Frankie assures me through clenched teeth while shooting her friend a wide-eyed warning glare across the table.

I can't help but wonder, though. Is *that* the problem? Am I too hairy? You'd think a guy into chick lit would be all about manscaping, but except for the obligatory nose-hair taming and neck shaving, I'm an "If-it-grows-there-it-goes-there," sort of guy. Part of it's laziness. Another part of it is I've never considered it an issue. That was one of the few things Heidi never tried to change about me.

Anyway, it's not like I'm sporting a hair sweater or anything. But if Frankie really does like a guy who waxes his eyebrows, chest, back, and dangly bits (I hear it makes guys look bigger down there), then maybe it hasn't been my breath or my clothes or my deodorant that's been holding her back.

I stare into space while gauging the thickness of my eyebrows with my fingertips and trying to recall the last time I examined them in a mirror. Too thick? Untamed? Not well-shaped?

Betty cuts through my mental measurements (my brows are bushy and huge, by the way, and I'm trimming them as soon as I get home tonight, since I'm sure it'll be an early night, and I'll be alone, as usual) by setting down her wine glass with a clink and saying, "So, you know about Frankie's writing, yeah?"

Blinking, I try to remember what we were talking about before any mention of my body hair. "Uh, yeah. I think it's great."

Hypothetically, of course. I still haven't read a single word of it, although I don't admit that to Betty. Something tells me she already knows, anyway. I signal for another round, despite starting to worry I'm not going to be able to drive myself home. This brand of beer is good, but it's kicking my butt tonight. Lunch was a long time ago.

Betty nods her approval of my support but stares down at the table and mutters, "Her books *are* great."

Frankie smiles tightly. "Thanks. I think I'm ready to publish, but the thought of strangers reading my books.... It's like they'd be looking into my soul."

"Your books are autobiographical?" I inquire.

That might explain why she's so opposed to me reading them. A glance in my peripheral vision reveals a squirmy Betty, who's finding her final drops of wine to be quite interesting as she makes them chase each other around the bottom of her glass.

Frankie shakes her head and blushes. "No. I mean, maybe a little. Not all the time. But readers will assume they are."

I make a face. "Who cares? And anyway, I don't think that's true. Do you think Samuel Pembroke has lived or thought all the things he's put his characters through?"

"Uh-oh," Betty mutters across the table. "You had to say *that* name."

Frankie's face hardens. I look from her to Betty and back. "What'd I do? What'd I say? Samuel Pembroke? The guy who writes all those CIA epic thingies? Why's that bad?"

"I get so tired of everyone thinking he's the end-all and be-all of fiction writers."

Betty signals for another round. "Here we go."

"Okay," I reply warily. "He's a genius. Nobody can argue that."

"Samuel Pembroke," Frankie says with a sneer. "Samuel Fucking Pembroke. I'm not saying he's not a great writer. If you like those sorts of books."

"Even if you don't. I mean, *I* certainly don't, but he's a legend," I say.

"Whatever! The point is, he wrote a few dozen bestsellers and a how-to on writing, so now it's impossible to have a discussion about writing without his effing name coming up. 'Samuel Pembroke says…' 'According to Samuel Pembroke…' You know, I think if Samuel Pembroke wasn't Samuel Pembroke, he'd tell Samuel Pembroke to go fuck himself."

Speechless, I stare at her.

Betty drums her fingers on the table.

Frankie holds my eye, jutting out her chin for good measure. "I'm sorry," she finally mumbles, looking away and shredding her cocktail napkin. "I just get so annoyed with the Samuel Pembroke references."

"I see that. His name was the first one to pop into my head, and it illustrated my point, that's all," I explain. "I don't even like his books. They bore the crap out of me."

She puts her hands on either side of my face and plants a playful peck on my lips. "I'm sorry," she repeats. "That rant was so random."

"Kind of," I admit, feeling like I'm riding the Bi-Polar Express, with Frankie as the conductor.

She lets go of my face but grabs my hand. I squeeze it, more to appease her than to show affection. It's all I can do not to snatch my hand away and put it in a safer place. I'm not sure she doesn't bite.

Instead, I use soothing tones when I suggest, "Sounds like you'd be the perfect candidate for a pen name."

I look to Betty for affirmation. She merely nods, like this is all something she's said before to her friend.

"I'll take it under advisement," Frankie replies. "It'd be different if I could hide behind a different name *and* a different face."

Another full beer appears in front of me, and I dive into the milky, smooth dark ale.

Betty and Frankie exchange a glance that definitely means something, but I can't quite interpret it in my fuzzy-headed state. Holding Betty's gaze, Frankie says, "Women love it when a guy writes chick lit."

"Heck, *I* love it," I agree, trying to control the slur creeping into my words. "It usually sounds just like all the other books, but it's the perception it's different that makes it great. 'A *dude* wrote this? He must be so in touch with his feminine side.'"

"Grrrowl," Frankie says with a giggle.

I laugh. "Exactly! Makes me wonder, how many of those guys are the actual writers of the books? Maybe their wives or girlfriends—or ghostwriters—are doing all the writing while the men are posing for headshots and making appearances in front of screaming ladies."

Frankie squeezes my hand to the point of pain, that is, if I could feel pain, but I don't seem able right now. I feel warm and happy. Mmm, beer. I love beer.

"That's just it," she says with a pout. "I need a face. A man's face." Her hand lands on the inside of my thigh. High.

"I can be your face," I toss out carelessly.

"Yes!" she cries. "Yes, yes, yes!"

My eyelids are so heavy that it takes a while for me to focus and remember what I said that could be eliciting such orgasmic agreement. The concentric circles she's tracing so close to my Happy Zone aren't aiding concentration.

I give her a goofy smile. "What she said."

"No, what *you* said!" The hypnotic thigh-rubbing ceases. She taps me on the tip of my nose. My blinks feel about ten seconds long as I try to follow her finger, and the conversation.

"What did I say?"

Betty snorts. "I think it's time you took Nurse Lightengale home before we have to carry him."

Frankie shoots her friend a dirty look. "No. He's fine. I want to explore this topic a little more."

"He's getting sauced!"

"No, I'm not," I claim, not wanting either of them to think I can't hold my liquor any better than a skinny sorority girl. "I'm fine. I'll be fine in a minute. I just gotta use the bathroom."

I make my way to the bathroom, managing to walk in a straight line (I think) and not bump into anything or anyone in the now-crowded bar, nodding and smiling at the people I pass, who either ignore me or bestow on me looks that convey everything from pity to disgust to— Hey, that woman was totally checking me out. Glancing over my shoulder at her while I pass almost destroys my precarious equilibrium, so I whip my head back around and focus on getting to the door with the correct silhouette on it.

Inside the bathroom, I take care of business at the urinal, glad I'm alone (I have a shy bladder). When I look at myself in the mirror while washing my hands and silently singing the alphabet to make sure I'm washing them long enough, I note with surprise that I don't look as drunk as I feel. I pull two paper towels from the dispenser by the mirror, using one to dry my hands and one to protect them from the door handle as I pull on it. I must not be too far gone, since I'm still worried about touching the handle that some jackleg touched after handling himself—and whatever—and not washing his hands.

When I get back to the table, a huge glass of water sits in place of my empty beer glass. I slide into the booth and chuckle. "Geez. Your concern is touching, but I'm really okay. That last one hit me hard, but now that I've walked around, the buzz is fading. Why don't we order something to eat?"

When my speech receives no response, I look from one woman to the other. Frankie's lips are absent, sucked into her mouth as if she's already eaten—a lemon. Betty laconically signs the credit card slip in front of her with a flourish, and slaps the pen on top of the tiny plastic clipboard.

"Are we leaving? What did I miss?"

I seem to recall everyone was happy before I left, but something obviously happened in my absence.

"Nothing," Frankie replies. "Drink your water."

Like a chastened child, I start to do as I'm told, but a few gulps in, I stop and say to the silent table, "Seriously. What's up?"

As if I haven't said a thing, Betty pushes the receipt holder toward the edge of the table and tucks her wallet into her purse. "Well, kids, I'm out of here. There's a big shoe sale tomorrow at Younkers, and the doors open early."

"Yeah, fine, bye," Frankie says.

I tense, hating even the hint of confrontation, much less the uncomfortable aftershock of it, when I don't know what actually went down. My body's response to the psychological upset I'm feeling sobers me better than a head-dip in a cold barrel of water.

I stand with Betty and say, "It was nice meeting you."

"Likewise," she says, sounding sincere for the first time all evening. Her bright blue eyes soften around the edges. "Have a nice night."

"We will," comes the firm assurance from behind me in the booth.

Betty rolls her eyes and turns on her heel, waving at Rusty on her way out the door. "Left you a big tip, Russell. You're welcome."

I watch her go, wrapping her scarf around her neck and sliding her hands into her gloves before she pushes on the pub's door to reenter the cold, now-dark world.

When I turn to sit back down, I bump into Frankie, who's exited the booth and is standing right behind me.

"You okay to drive?" she asks. She sounds uninterested in the answer.

"I will be in a few. Are you?"

Instead of answering my question, she merely gives me a cold kiss on the cheek and says, "I'm traveling all next week, so do you want to do something this weekend?"

Still thrown by the rapid change in the evening's tone, I merely grunt an unsure, "Sure," before recalling, "Oh, I told Mom and Dad I'd bring you with me to their place for lunch on Sunday, remember? But if you'd rather not do it this weekend, I'd totally understand."

Unfortunately, she brightens at the reminder. "I'm looking forward to meeting them. It just slipped my mind. Unless *you'd* rather not."

I've been putting it off for a couple of weeks now. If anyone's waiting for me to *want* to do it, it's never going to happen.

I smile bravely. "I think my mom's about to take matters into her own hands, and that's always a dicey proposition, so it's probably best if I take you to her. And Dad, of course. But he's echoing whatever Mom wants, because—" I stop myself before mentioning anything about getting laid this century, since it comes too close to kicking the elephant in the room right between the legs. "He's a nice guy," I finish lamely.

"Apple must not have fallen far from the tree," she purrs, pressing herself against my chest and leaning into my lips.

Alcohol and biology conspire against the civilized, enlightened guy who usually controls things in my brain. "I can take a vacation to Doucheville, if you like it there."

Before her mouth makes contact with mine, she retreats, her face closing off.

"Or not," I mutter.

She shrugs on her coat and pats my shoulder on her way past me. "Don't forget to pay the tab," she instructs. "I'll see you Sunday."

Apparently, my trip to Doucheville will be via Wanktown.

6

PSYCHOANALYSIS

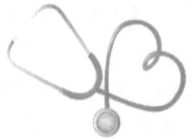

"Okay, so here's the thing. My parents…"

"Yeah, I know. They're psychologists."

"Psychiatrists."

"Whatever."

I sigh. This is going to be a long afternoon.

She looks around the big brick porch, where we're shivering as I deliver my final disclaimers before she meets Mom and Dad. "Nice house," she declares. "'Crazy' pays well."

"They do okay," I admit, trying to refocus her attention on me. Finally, I grip her upper arms and bend my knees so our eyes are level. "Hey. Just listen for a second, all right? I don't want you to be blindsided by anything in there." I bob my head over my shoulder toward the front door. "They don't really believe in boundaries."

"You've already told me they're quirky. Trust me, when you meet my parents you'll understand why quirky doesn't faze me."

She tries to kiss me, but I pull my head back. I'm not in the mood for making out on my parents' front porch.

"Yeah, okay. Everyone says that. Then they meet *my*

parents, who say and ask some pretty intrusive, personal things, and they get pissed off because I wasn't more specific, so—"

She laughs. "What? Are they going to ask us about our sex life?"

My steady eye contact is all the confirmation she needs.

It makes her laugh harder and louder. "Seriously?"

I nod.

"Well, that's an easy one. I'm saving myself for marriage."

I gulp, not sure whether to feel relieved or devastated. "You are?"

She shrugs like it's no big deal nowadays. "Yeah."

"But you're not..."

Waving away her long-lost virginity like a pesky fly that's managed to survive weeks of freezing weather, she says, "I *have* had sex before, yes. But..." Now she cuddles up to me, pushing me against the front door. "I think you're special. I think, I mean, maybe it would ruin everything if we had sex."

"I'm not so sure about that."

"I am. Why do you think I haven't already tried to jump your bones?" She twines her arms around my neck and breathes against my jaw. Her hot breath leaves a moist patch there.

Lizard brain kicks in. "Uh, well, I hadn't thought much about it," I lie. "I just thought, you know, we were taking things slow."

"We are. Really slow." Her voice is little more than a growl. "It's hard. I think about it all the time. But I think the wait will be worth it."

She kisses me, soft and slowly at first, then hard and hungry. I moan, and she smiles against my lips, obviously aware of what she's doing to me and enjoying it.

Suddenly, the door behind me swings open, almost causing me to fall backwards into my parents' foyer.

"Oh, sorry!" Mom chirps. "I heard something out here and thought it was the Sunday paper delivery."

"At 1:00?" I ask, trying to my balance by hanging onto the door jamb. I also have a handy counterbalance now sticking from the front of me, but I hope nobody notices, or at least pretend not to notice.

Frankie tucks her hair behind her ear and extends her hand. "Hi. I'm Frankie."

Mom shakes the proffered hand with a sheepish smile. "I'm Yvonne. I didn't really think you guys were the Sunday paper."

While I regain my footing, Frankie nods and bites her bottom lip. "Well, I see Nate comes by his honesty naturally."

I sigh, chagrined we couldn't even get through the introductions before things got weird.

"Oh, don't start sighing already," Mom implores on her way past me into the house. "Please, come in. Lunch is ready."

Frankie kisses my cheek as she follows Mom. "Relax," she whispers in a husky voice that has the exact opposite effect on me.

Thirty minutes later, over post-lunch coffees, Frankie listens raptly to Mom and Dad pontificate about birth order and how it relates to Nick and me.

"We tried to avoid all that middle-child rot by only having two," Dad pipes in when Mom takes a breath. "But Nate's thwarted those efforts, exhibiting many tendencies of middle children. He's a blend-into-the-background guy, and he's also the peacemaker."

Yes, I'd like to remind everyone here that I'm nearly thirty-three years old, and my parents still talk about me to people like I'm a child in a psychological study they're conducting, like I'm not even in the same room. I prefer this, though, to the way they used to act when I was younger and would introduce them to girls I was dating. At least they haven't asked Frankie to take a Myers-Briggs test or any other psychological profile quizzes "just for fun."

Frankie squeezes my hand. "Well, I'm excited about having kids someday with someone special." My heart lifts and races at this information, something she's never shared with me before. Coyly looking away from me and back to my parents, she continues, "But I'm an only child, so the dynamic between siblings is fascinating to me. Psychology in general is really interesting."

"It's a pseudo-science," I mumble, earning a glare from Dad.

"Being an only child comes with its own set of issues," Mom says cheerfully, as if it's such a wonderful thing there are enough psychoses to go around.

I quickly intervene. "We don't have to get into them today, though, right? We should save that for a special occasion, like Easter."

Mom rolls her eyes. "Oh, Nate."

"I mean it. Why can't we talk about the weather, like normal people?"

"I think Nate's worried we're going to tell you something embarrassing, like about his bedwetting, which is actually common and not anything to be ashamed of."

"When I was a kid!" I hasten to clarify. "Not now."

"I think that went without saying," Dad says, as if I'm the one being inappropriate.

Frankie laughs behind her hand, then says to me, "It's okay. I knew what she meant."

"What would you prefer we talk about, your brother marrying the woman *you* were going to marry a few years ago?" Mom asks, as if she's been doing me a favor by talking about my need for plastic sheets well into elementary school. (I was a deep sleeper, all right? Like she said, and I know from my work in medicine, a *real* science, bedwetting is a widespread issue, especially with young boys.)

"Oh, I already know all about Nick and Heidi," Frankie casually assures my parents.

Mom laughs. "I should hope so. You'll be Nate's date to the wedding in May, right?"

There are so many awkward assumptions in that question that I don't even know where my pique should begin.

Fortunately, nobody requires my participation in this conversation.

Frankie winces. "My dad's sixtieth birthday is that weekend, and I already have plane tickets to Arizona to visit them."

"What crappy timing!" Mom laments.

Dad begins clearing the dessert dishes. "It's probably for the best."

I'd love to ask him what he means by that. *How* could it be for the best that I go alone to the wedding of my brother to my former fiancée? How? I'm dreading it. I can't think of any way that it could be for the best. But I'd love more for this conversation to end, so I decide to table that discussion for another time, when he and I are alone. Now, I merely stare at his back as he walks away from the table into the kitchen to set the dirty dishes by the sink.

Frankie sips her coffee, then says, "I know it's going to be a hard day for Nate—"

"Only because everyone's going to be staring at me, waiting for me to make a scene," I try to explain to a room of people apparently not interested in a single word I have to say on the topic.

"I wish I could be in two places at once. It would take a lot of the pressure off you if you had a date," she says.

"It's a long time from now." I try to make it sound authoritative, like the last word. "We could all be dead by then."

"Nice," Dad grumbles upon his return to the table.

I laugh. "Sorry. I didn't mean to sound that hopeful. I just meant that it's not worth worrying about right now. It'll be fine."

Frankie gasps and grasps my hand. "Oh, my gosh! I have the best idea! You can take Betty."

At first, I think she's kidding, but as soon as I study her eyes, the laughter dies in my throat. "You can't be serious."

"Who's Betty?" Mom wonders, a grin spreading across her face. I can already tell she likes this harebrained idea, and that means I'm in trouble.

"My best friend," Frankie explains.

"I thought you guys were, you know, arguing." I still haven't been able to get out of Frankie what transpired between them at the pub while I was in the bathroom, but I know I wasn't imagining the tension when I returned.

Ignoring my observation, she pushes, "Betty's a ton of fun at family gatherings."

I'm not sure if our definitions of "fun" sync up yet. Does she mean "fun," as in, "gets rip-roaring drunk and silly within five minutes of having access to the open bar," or "fun," as in, "does a mean Conga," or...?

Frankie interrupts my musings with a leg-jolting brush of her fingers against my upper thigh under the table while she says to Mom and Dad, "You guys will love Betty. And she's a workhorse. If you need help with last-minute stuff on the day of the wedding, she'll pitch right in."

I wonder if Betty's aware of all this work for which Frankie's volunteering her. Then again, it's hard for me to concentrate as Frankie's fingers creep closer and closer to my lap.

To me, she urges, "C'mon! It would be perfect. You'd have a date, but I wouldn't have to worry—"

"You don't have to worry, because it's not gonna happen."

Mom smiles warmly at the two of us. "I think it's a sweet, thoughtful idea."

"Yeah, don't dismiss the idea out-of-hand," Dad agrees.

I *am* dismissing it out-of-hand. "I don't need a date for the sake of having one. Now, let's talk about something else. Did I mention that Frankie's a writer?" I blurt, hoping Frankie doesn't kill me for telling my parents.

To my relief, she grins when they look suitably impressed with this piece of information.

When Mom takes the bait and asks, "What genre?" I breathe a full breath for the first time in several minutes (it helps when Frankie returns her hand to her own lap).

"Women's fiction. Chick lit, more specifically," Frankie answers.

"Are you published?" Dad inquires.

Frankie's lips pinch over her teeth.

"She's kind of shy about sharing her work right now," I jump in, before anyone thinks of abandoning this conversation in favor of one of the more hideous ones we've already explored. "She's still considering her options and... and... thinking about pen names. Right?" I consult her, realizing I'm doing that annoying thing where I talk about someone in the third person, even though they're sitting right there.

I know I've made the right decision to rescue her, though, when I see the gratitude—something I've rarely seen from her —in her eyes. She grips my hand on top of the table and says to my parents, "Actually, I was thinking about keeping my last name and shortening my first name to Frank."

"Giving yourself a literary sex change, huh?" Dad jokes. "Interesting."

Frankie nods enthusiastically. "It was Nate's idea."

I nearly choke on my coffee. "It was?"

"Yeah, remember? You suggested it at the pub. It's great, because you're right; even though a lot of guys write chick lit, they're still a minority and somewhat of a novelty, so they sell a ton of books."

Mom and Dad exchange a look. I might not know Betty and Frankie well enough to accurately interpret their nonverbal communication, but I've had decades of experience reading my parents'. The look they just shared was similar to the one they gave each other when I announced I'd decided to become a pediatric nurse with my biochemistry major and was no longer pre-med.

Nick was already only a semester away from graduating —and certain to be accepted to med school, of course— and everyone assumed I'd follow smoothly in his wake. Looking back, I'm not sure why they made that assumption. I'd never done things exactly as Nick did. He played football and hockey; I ran track and played soccer. He dated cheerleaders; I didn't. He was the life of every party; I was the guy everyone asked for copies of class notes the day before a test. He got As without studying; I had to spend hours studying to get that same A. It's not that we were opposites, exactly, and everyone knew we were brothers, but nobody could accuse our parents of cloning.

When Nick and I both decided to pursue medical careers, it felt right. At first, I thought it was cool we would be doctors together someday. We even talked about starting a private general practice. But Nick decided he wanted to specialize ("That's where the money is, bro"), and I didn't want to spend half my life in school, racking up all that debt before ever entering the workforce. When I did a nursing internship in pediatrics and fell in love with helping kids, our different fates were sealed.

Now Mom muses, "In this day and age, it's hard to keep something like that a secret. Aren't you afraid it'll backfire?"

"Writers do it all the time," I intervene. "Even J.K. Rowling had a male pen name, for about two seconds. When her true identity was discovered, it helped her sell more books, so it's not like it was a huge scandal that hurt her career."

"Hmm," Mom utters noncommittally before saying, "I was thinking more about what it does to the psyche to live less-than-honestly, but I see what you mean. I'd love to read your books, Frankie, no matter what name you decide to put on them."

Like that, the tension dissolves at the table, and Dad sweetens the situation by suggesting we go into the living room to watch the football game.

I volunteer to clean up the kitchen. Watching football is bad enough. Watching it with Frankie is a whole new form of torture, which my parents are about to get an education in. I'd just prefer not to witness it.

7

GUY TIME AND SELF-CARE

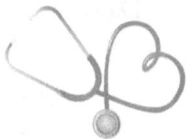

My fifth consecutive swing and miss prompts Nick to say, "What's your problem tonight, bro?" He is standing behind the chain link fence.

I shrug off his question and whiff at the next ball that flies at me from the pitching machine. I'd be embarrassed if we weren't alone here on this freezing weekday evening in the indoor, unheated batting cages.

I let the next pitch go past without swinging. It clanks against the fence and joins its friends, amassing at my feet. I kick the baseballs away, so I won't trip on any of them, and get back into my stance. The next ball whizzes at me, and I manage to get a piece of it, but it soars straight up. I duck and hold my plastic helmet more tightly against my head, anticipating the hardball's fall. It misses me and thunks at my feet.

"Get out of there before you get hurt," Nick demands.

My heart's not in it, and I'm almost out of the pitches I've paid for, anyway, so I don't bother arguing. The point of this exercise was to work off some frustration, but it's only causing more.

As soon as I round the fencing, I remove my batting

helmet and toss it and my bat toward my equipment bag under the pine bench. I sink to the bench, prop my elbows on my knees, and watch Nick prepare for his turn. He feeds money into the machine, stands next to home plate, and crouches into his stance. The first pitch comes flying toward him, and he hits it hard, almost immediately preparing for the next ball.

"Mom tells me she and Dad met Frankie a couple of weeks ago," he says, hitting another line drive.

I stare at his elbow a few seconds, contemplating what I'm going to say before replying dully, "Yeah."

He straightens his legs, letting his bat hang impotently at his side, and turns to me between pitches. "Why are you so glum?"

"Watch the balls, all right?" I implore, before answering, "I don't know."

"You don't know? How can you not know?"

I sigh. "It's complicated." I tuck my hands into the front pouch of my hoodie and hunker lower into it.

He snorts. "All right. What is it with this one? Did she use your toothbrush or something?"

"What do you mean?" I ask, hoping if I play dumb, he'll drop it.

"There's always something. With that one chick, it was her breath."

"It was bad! When I ended it with her, I recommended she see a doctor about it."

"I'm sure that softened the blow and really endeared you to her," he says with a laugh.

I snarl at the back of his head. "Hey, I was worried about her! What do you think I should have done? Kept dating her, even though kissing her made my eyes water? In a bad way?"

He shrugs. "Okay, I'll give you that one. That's pretty insurmountable. But what about the chick in college?"

"You'll have to be more specific," I say with plenty of smarm. It's fun to pretend I was a real ladies' man at some point in my life.

"The one who farted when she sneezed."

"I didn't break up with her because she snarted. She picked at her feet, which is gross and unhygienic." I wrinkle my nose and suppress my gag reflex at the memory.

"Okay, what about the one who swallowed her gum all the time?"

"Same person. She also didn't know that Jerry Lee Lewis and Jerry Lewis were two different people; she paid people to write her term papers; and—oh, yeah—she screwed my roommate—on my bed—every Wednesday for an entire semester while I attended my biology practicum. I stand by my decision to break up with that one, thank you."

Recovering from his first strike, he says, "Okay, fine. But my point is, you always find something."

We both know there's at least one exception to the rule: if Heidi hadn't broken up with me, I'd be married to her right now, resigned to the many things about her that annoy me. Being her husband and the father of her children was worth whatever irritants came with the job. That's what I thought at the time, anyway.

I was devastated when she broke up with me, when she gave voice to what I was too scared to face: something was missing between us that would be essential to our long-term success as a couple.

So I've gone back to being the pickiest bachelor in Green Bay. It's better to reject than be rejected.

Out of balls, the machine winds down with a whir and shuts off. Nick removes his helmet and joins me on the bench.

"You never answered my question," he remarks, sliding his

arms into his coat and zipping it up to his chin. "Fuck, it's cold in here!"

I agree with him, but the coldness I'm feeling can't be helped by putting on my coat, so I don't bother. I straddle the pine bench then recline, lying flat on my back, crossing my arms.

Shivering to generate warmth, he prods, "Go on, then; give me Frankie's fault list."

Immediately, I reply toward the high metal rafters above, "She's a slob."

"Here we go."

"No, you don't understand. She's not messy in an 'Oh-you-haven't-loaded-the-fully-functioning-yet-unused-dishwasher-in-a-day-or-two' kind of way. I'm talking, I nearly went into anaphylactic shock thanks to the mold growing on the dishes in her sink the last time I was at her place. I don't even have a mold allergy. It was nasty."

"So don't go into her kitchen."

"If the kitchen sink was the only problem area, that would be a fine strategy. But there's stuff *everywhere* in her apartment. Outdated magazines, expired coupons, written-on window envelopes. Every surface has paper trash piled on it." I squint at the stadium lights that are supposed to lend the cages a big-league ambiance. "It's like she hasn't thrown away a piece of junk mail since Obama's first term. Probably before then. It makes me twitchy."

"But that's *your* problem, not hers."

I think about that for a second. "Okay, yeah. But I have to decide if I want that to be my problem *forever*."

"Why? You gettin' married?" He pokes my knee with his forefinger. "C'mon, bro. Don't take everything so seriously."

I sit up but keep the bench between my legs. "I do take things seriously, though. If I'm not considering marrying her, then what's the point in dating her?" When he shoots me an incredulous look, I defend myself, "I'm not just looking for a piece of ass anymore, all right? I'm looking for a wife."

"You could—I don't know—train her to be tidier," he suggests.

"She's not a dog! You should never go into a relationship thinking you're going to change someone."

Nick shrugs. "I guess."

I can feel us edging too close to one of the major recurring issues in my relationship with Heidi, so I refocus the discussion on Frankie before Nick remembers all the times I complained to him about being Heidi's "project."

"Then there's her obsession with football."

"That's sexy, man. I don't understand how that one goes on your crap list. I'd be in heaven if Heidi watched more games with me, with her face in my lap."

"Hey, hey! Do you mind?" I push his shoulder hard.

He falls sideways, giggling like a twelve-year-old. "Sorry. Just sayin'."

"No. Don't 'just say' anything like that to me ever again. Inappropriate."

He sniffs while righting himself. "Jealous."

"Anyway!" I shake my head to rid it of the mental image of Heidi blowing my brother during halftime and say, "I know I'm in the minority around here with my apathy for the sport, but Frankie takes fandom to a whole new level. Like, she makes most of the guys we know look like fair-weather *poseurs*. She can recite the entire starting roster and each player's position."

"Anyone can do that," he scoffs, quickly adding, "except dorks like you."

"I wish it ended there. She also knows the names and specialties of the guys who ride the bench week-to-week. She can name the backup to the backup quarterback. She calls them all by their first names, like she's best buddies with all of them." When he still seems unimpressed, I claim, "That's weird!"

He closes one eye as if considering it. "Maybe a little, but big deal. It's no weirder than you knowing all the character names on your nerdy shows."

Determined to make him understand the depth of her obsession, I continue, "She can—and does—recite word-for-word every single commercial that features a Packers player."

"Whatever!" He laughs. "That's every other local commercial that airs during any given game!"

"I'm not exaggerating. You have to see it—and hear it—to believe it. Ask Mom and Dad. She did it at their house. I think Dad's going to nominate her for a stupid human trick on Letterman."

"Sweet."

"Not sweet. Obnoxious. Just like it's obnoxious that she shops at a grocery store across town from her place, because she heard some of the players and their wives shop there."

"A bit stalker-y..."

"Right?" I take a deep breath, considering whether to reveal the detail about her using the same shampoo as one of the long-haired players. I'd like to pretend it's not true, for one thing. For another, I'm starting to feel bad griping about all this stuff. It's not very loyal. It's definitely not what a good boyfriend would do. I mean, if it bothers me so much, I should break up with her, instead of badmouthing her behind her back.

On the other hand, he needs to know. He needs to get the full picture. He needs to see *I'm* not the freak. He needs to take my side.

While I'm trying to decide to tell him about the shampoo,

he raises an eyebrow and says, "What? You look like you're about to tell me she likes it all freaky-deaky in the bedroom. Like she makes you wear an Aaron Rodgers mask during the nasty."

I laugh, relieved it's not *that* bad, before deciding to just drop the whole thing.

Nick studies my face, then shakes his head when it's obvious I'm not going to continue. "Anyway... She's hot, right?"

"Yeah, but—"

"And the sex is good?"

I bend over and make a big show of untying and retying my left shoe.

"No way." Nick breathes when I move to the right shoe, still not giving him an answer. "You two haven't had sex yet?"

I blush, even though it's hardly something to be ashamed about. It's not like we've been dating for years or like we're married and still haven't consummated our relationship. Still, I know Nick thinks it's just as bad.

"The right time hasn't presented itself," I say.

"What do you mean? Any time is the right time!"

I straighten and face him like a man. "Not really. She doesn't seem to be in any hurry, and I don't want to pressure her to do something I'm not all that excited to do."

"You might want to get that checked out. Low testosterone is nothing to screw around with."

"My testosterone level is fine."

"Not if you're okay with this current situation, it's not."

"Quit joking around."

"I'm not joking. I'm saying this to you as a medical professional."

"Screw you."

"I'm not having any problems in that department."

Blocking more disturbing mental images, I blurt, "Frankie wants to wait until she's married."

It's not often my brother is speechless, but that does it, temporarily. Eventually, he clears his throat and says, "Oh. Uh, I didn't... I mean, why didn't you say so?"

Because I don't believe it myself?

I simply shrug.

We sit in stifling silence until Nick regroups and says, "Well, Mom and Dad seemed to like her okay."

"They did? When did they say that?"

"A few days ago, when I saw them. They said you guys had a nice afternoon." He turns his head and looks at me from the corner of his eye. "Why? Did something happen?"

He knows something always happens when our parents meet our friends or girlfriends or co-workers or bosses or neighbors or... anyone we know, so his question translates more into, "*What* happened?" Only this time, for once, I can't tell him anything specific.

I make a face. "Nothing, really. I just got a vibe from them that they didn't like her all that much."

"So what? Aren't you past needing Mommy and Daddy's approval?"

I know it will make me sound as lame as I am if I answer truthfully, so I merely say, "I don't want things to be awkward in the future, that's all."

"They won't be."

"How do you know?"

He starts packing his bats and helmet and batting glove into his duffel bag. "'Awkward' is the time Mom took Karin Fowler aside at the church Easter egg hunt and assured her that she'd told you and me all about how to please a woman, because she felt she had a moral obligation to raise men who were considerate lovers."

GUY TIME AND SELF-CARE | 75

I laugh at the eighteen-year-old memory.

"It wasn't funny! Karin thought Mom was confessing to something illegal. It took me forever to convince her we'd never been molested and Mom was simply relaying to her—however inappropriately—that she'd contributed to the torturous 'birds-and-bees' talk Dad gave us."

"Gosh. I still can't even read the word 'clitoris' without hearing it in Mom's voice," I reveal with a wince.

Nick shudders and zips his bag. "I went months without so much as a wet dream after that talk. I was terrified Mom would show up in my sex dreams. That well-intentioned stunt delayed the loss of my virginity by nearly a year. Karin dumped me, and she told a bunch of her friends what Mom had said."

"Sounds like free PR to me." I shove my baseball equipment willy-nilly into the main compartment of my duffel, promising myself I'll reorganize it later, before I put it back in storage.

"My point is..." He stands and loops his bag's strap over his shoulder. "It sounds like it was a normal first meeting, for our parents. If they didn't like Frankie, they would have told me for sure, right?"

"Unless they think she's the best I can do." I zip my bag and stand, pushing my arms into my coat and buttoning it.

Nick watches me, letting his mouth hang slack while he looks me up and down. He fingers my wool collar. "What the hell is this?"

"It's a peacoat," I say while hoisting my bag.

He claps a hand on my shoulder. "This coat—which looks like something mom would have made us wear with sailor hats for a portrait when we were pre-schoolers—is about to prove my point."

"This should be good."

"Maybe you don't have the luxury of being all that picky

anymore." When I snort, he talks louder. "Hear me out, bro." I put my hand on my hip but quickly let it fall to my side when he gestures derisively at my posture. "You're not getting any cooler. Or younger. Maybe if you had a better sense of style or made more money or drove a flashier car, but that would be a negative on all fronts, so..."

"I need to aim lower, is that what you're saying?"

"From what I've heard, Frankie is hardly 'aiming low.' Still haven't seen for myself, since you can't seem to make up your mind about her enough to introduce us, but that's a whole other discussion."

He turns and leads the way from the building to the parking lot. I follow, lengthening my strides to catch up, feeling like I always did when we were younger, and I tagged after him. I think I was perpetually out-of-breath until we hit high school.

Halfway across the lot, he pushes a button on his key fob to pop open the trunk on his gleaming black Audi, which is already idling in the snow that's accumulated since we've been inside the batting cages. White clouds billow from the car's dual exhaust pipes. Who knows how long it's been running out here, sending pollution into the ozone for the sake of my brother's ultimate comfort.

When I mutter something to that effect under my breath, he says, "I make a living saving lives. I think it evens out," as he tosses his duffel into the yawning trunk and closes it just firmly enough for it to latch. A hydraulic mechanism hums, finishing the job and bringing the trunk flush with the rest of the car. Using the end of his scarf, he wipes his hand's oils from the surface. "Now, are you ready to hear what I think you need to do?"

"Are you going to tell me, no matter what?"

"Yes. Because you filled my entire evening whining to me

about your love life, when I could have been with my fiancée—"

"Don't say it."

"—doing a lot less talking."

I sigh.

"So now I'm going to do the talking, and you're going to listen."

I close the hatch of my car and lean against the cold, dark taillights. Shoving my hands as far down into my woolen coat's pockets as they'll go, I grumble, "Fine."

His arms crossed over his chest, his legs spread wide, he takes a deep breath, as if about to debrief a group of surgical residents. "Here's how I see it. You want some kind of lifetime guarantee on a life partner, but guess what? That's not gonna happen, bro. You're gonna have to give someone a chance to prove to you that moldy dishes and a cluttered coffee table aren't deal-breakers."

"But—"

"And are you gonna make it easy for her to stick to her cute abstinence pledge?"

"Yes, because that's what decent guys do. They respect the wishes of the women they're dating, especially in regards to sex. What's wrong with you?"

"If that was really her wish, I'd completely agree. But it's like when Heidi says she doesn't want..."

"Careful..."

"...*dessert* when we go out to eat. She wants dessert; she just doesn't want to be the one to order it. She wants me to know what she wants and order it for her."

"Gosh, I used to hate that."

"Yeah, well... she makes up for it in other ways."

I throw up my hands. "I don't know how we're even brothers. You're such a pig."

"I know women, that's all."

If I didn't suspect he was right, I'd continue to argue, but—as uncomfortable as the comparison makes me—something tells me Frankie's using her sexuality like I use Saf-T-Pops with the kids at work, as motivation to coax me into giving her what she wants. I'm always straightforward about the agreement with the kids, though ("Hold still for this shot;" "Let me look into your hot, painful ear;" "Try not to flinch while I press on your boo-boo to check for broken bones"); I haven't figured out what Frankie's aim is. I don't understand her motives for keeping me in the dark. She's not usually averse to asking—or demanding—anything.

Barely short of whining, I ask Nick, "Why can't I meet someone who's funny and smart and good-hearted? Someone who doesn't play games. Someone who's relatively normal. And tidy."

"Because that person doesn't exist."

"I can't believe that. I *won't* believe it."

"You're free to believe whatever the hell you want to believe. Doesn't mean it's true. All I'm saying is, maybe you shouldn't be so quick to quit on Frankie. Instead of focusing so much on the negative, focus on what life can be like if you stop holding back because you're afraid to be vulnerable."

I laugh. "Whoa. Heidi's been reading Cosmo out loud in bed, hasn't she?" His sheepish smile confirms my hypothesis. "I knew it!"

"It's still good advice. Plus, I'm assuming Frankie's seen your scrubs organized by color, and she's seen you in that coat, but she's still hanging around, so... she sounds pretty tolerant to me. She has a good sense of humor, if nothing else." He blows into his hands and squints through the flurries at me. "I'm freezing my nuts off. You wanna go grab a beer and continue this conversation, or what?"

I shake my head and push away from my bumper. "Nah. I'm gonna head home and... defrost."

"You're going to take a hot bubble bath, aren't you?"

"Maybe," I grudgingly admit, swiping the fine layer of snow from my car's back window with the sleeve of my coat.

With a shake of his head, he unlocks his fully defrosted car with a chirp and slides in. "Seriously. Examine what you really want. What's scarier, coming to grips now with the reality that there's no such thing as a perfect woman and dealing with it, or being in stubborn denial about it and ending up alone for the rest of your life?"

Frankly, neither of those options appeals to me.

* * *

I DO my best soul-searching in the bathtub. Don't judge, guys. Like I tell Nick, it works. Check out Mr. Darcy (the Colin Firth one). He was a smart guy, ruminating in the tub. Try it sometime. Get the water as hot as you can possibly get it, so hot it makes you sweat. Yeah, it'll feel counterproductive, but you're not in the bath to get clean. You can—and should— shower later. After all, you're soaking in your own sloughed-off skin cells, hair, and body soil. But don't think about that! Add some bubbles to make it at least smell good.

I find that a nice scent—tonight, I've chosen a manly sandalwood, because I like irony—also softens the blow of some of the less pleasant things I realize about myself and my life while participating in this cleansing exercise.

Scary realization #1: At the very least, I'm becoming *that* guy. You know, *that* guy. The guy who ends up alone for the rest of his life, because he's impossible to please. I'll be the guy who shuts himself up in his immaculate house, barking at kids to stay off his lawn. Who wants to be *that* guy? Not this guy.

I want to be the guy who not only waves to his neighbors as they drive by his house while he's working on the yard or washing his car in the driveway but knows them by name and takes time to actually talk to them once in a while. I want to chuckle good-naturedly with male neighbors about the "Honey-Do" list. I want to share baby due dates and deliver hot dishes to neighbors who've brought home *their* new babies. I want to exchange recipes. I want to commiserate about sick kids and humble-brag about Little League victories and track meet wins.

Entry into that club, however, requires a wife and kids. I'll never have them if I don't stop being so... selective.

Scary realization #2: I'm no better than Heidi used to be when she'd nit-pick me to the point of change... from the way I shaved to the brands of food I purchased.

Heidi had definite ideas about what she wanted and expected in a spouse, and she made it her mission the two years we were together to shape me into that guy before we walked down the aisle. I didn't mind, for the most part. Despite her Type-A personality, Heidi was (*is*, I suppose) a sweet, generous person... as long as the people in her life conform to her ideals.

I considered myself lucky to be worthy of her efforts and was excited to be part of her charmed future. I didn't give a shit what I'd be wearing in that life (nothing from last season... ever), as long as I had that life. It wasn't until she snatched the dream away from me that I realized I didn't even recognize myself anymore.

In an effort to rediscover myself, I stripped my bachelor pad of anything there only because Heidi had made it so. That left me with a closet full of brightly colored and cartoon-character-patterned scrubs, a few mementos from high school, college, and nursing school (including a beer bong), my laptop, and my entertainment system.

I also pulled down a box of chick flicks that had been hiding and gathering dust in my closet, and I loaded up my Kindle with as many funny, quirky girlie books as it could hold by authors like Jennifer Weiner, Jane Green (old school, not her newer, darker stuff), Marian Keyes, Sophie Kinsella, Hester Browne, and anyone else Amazon recommended to me based on those selections. I went on a rom com bender on the naked mattress in the middle of my Beirut-chic bedroom and reacquainted myself with a guy I'd forgotten existed.

When I emerged from my isolation at the end of that weekend, I felt shaky, like someone who's come up on a horrendous accident scene, realizing if he'd not had to backtrack to the house to retrieve his jacket or stop for gas along the way, he might have been one of the people in those body bags.

Unlike medical shock, though, this emotional shock was beneficial, healing. It reminded me that I was, indeed, alive, and I had escaped with my personality intact. Mostly. What I could remember of it, anyway. Some things I'd lost weren't as obvious.

At the time of our breakup, Heidi and I were looking for a house to buy together. None of the ones we viewed had fewer than five bedrooms, five bathrooms, and three living areas, and they all had master suites that looked like they came straight from the pages of Heidi's favorite magazines about celebrities. The properties were sodded and landscaped to the hilt and would require hours and hours of upkeep on the weekends... or a gardener, which I knew we wouldn't be able to afford, on top of the massive mortgage we'd be taking on.

A few weeks after Heidi called off the wedding, I threw away all the real estate listing books, dripping tears and snot as

I stood staring at them in the paper recycling bin. Was I mourning the idea of the crippling debt and all the yard work I knew I would have hated and grown to resent? No. I was mourning the death of the guy who had been willing to take that on in the name of love. I know, it was pathetic.

Once the pain lessened to a dull ache following Heidi's departure from my life (well, when I thought she was departing, anyway), and friends and family truly believed me that I didn't need to be on glorified suicide watch, I'll admit I overcorrected on my personality in an effort to relearn who I was. I promised myself I'd never let anyone—not even a woman I love—make me lose myself so fully again. It's a perfectly good promise, but I may have taken it too far. Now it's time to stabilize.

Scary realization #3: I'm about to blow it with the smartest, most interesting, most beautiful woman to be interested in me since... well... you know.

And why? Because of her brand of shampoo? Because she steals every single pickle from my plate when we go out to eat? (I love pickles, but still.) Because she drinks coffee at 10 p.m., then can't sleep, then calls me at 1 a.m. to ponder why that's the case and asks me to keep her company until she's sleepy? Because she never turns off a light when she leaves a room? Because she mutters to herself and laughs out loud while reading, then refuses to share what's so funny? Because I feel like I need to wear a Tyvek suit every time I enter her apartment? Most of those things don't speak to her character, and if they do, they don't necessarily point to a *bad* character. Just a different character than mine.

Isn't that a good thing? If we were too much alike, we'd drive each other crazy, right? Opposites attract. It's science.

Why is the fine line between compromise and settling such a hard one for me to walk? Why must the two be so synonymous in my mind? And why do I view anything short of my ideal as such a negative? Is all my pickiness a way to convince myself I'm on the road to male spinsterhood by choice, when the reality may be that I'm too odd to find someone who fits, someone willing to put up with *my* quirks?

Because I have plenty of them. I'm not blind to that. Hell, I'm sitting in a bathtub right now. This behavior is... unusual for guys in the twenty-first century. I get that.

It's painful to admit this, but... maybe Nick's right. I'm not getting any younger. My career may be on the right track, but my personal life feels hollow and empty. I want to lead a *full* life, not a half-life. I'm ready to get on with the life I *want*, not the one I currently have. I think Frankie could bring my life a good balance, if I'd only relax.

Like Nick said, maybe I should spend more time recognizing how nice it is that Frankie hasn't tried to change a single thing about me, rather than fret about all the admittedly petty things I'd like to change about her.

It's time to stop being so guarded, so critical, so pessimistic. It's time to be accepting, loving, and open to the idea that "different" isn't wrong. I've been trying to convince people of that my whole life. Shouldn't I give Frankie the same consideration?

In a paraphrase of a line from one of my favorite movies, I'm ready to get the shit kicked out of me by love.

VALENTINE'S DAY

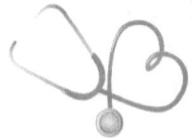

IT'S BEEN A MONTH SINCE MY BATHTUB SOUL-SEARCHING AND my conversation with Nick at the batting cages. During that time, I've been like someone who's resolved to go to the gym "every single day," at the start of the new year. In other words, I'm failing miserably.

Fortunately, I didn't tell anyone about my resolution to be more accepting, and I only see my girlfriend on the weekends, when I can usually fake it pretty well, so I'm the only one who knows what a failure I am. As far as everyone else knows, things are progressing well with Frankie and me. Frankie doesn't even suspect anything. And that's good, because I just need more time.

I tell myself it's taking me a while to come to grips with everything because I so seldom see her that it takes half of the weekend for me to reacquaint myself with all the things I'm supposed to be more accepting about. By the time I have the hang of ignoring the things that niggle at me so much, it's Sunday night, and she's pushing me out the door so she can pack for her next week on the road.

I'm seeing *some* improvement, though. Like the new runner

who finds his endurance increasing with each session on the treadmill or lap around the block, I'm noticing the weekends are feeling shorter and shorter. I actually missed her this week while we've been apart, and I'm looking forward to seeing her this evening.

That anticipation is tempered by the fact I've barely heard from her all week. I know, technology works both ways; I could have called or texted or even emailed her, and I have. Once or twice. But she never answered me.

I'm sure it's nothing, though. Sometimes she just has busy weeks, in and out of airports and conference rooms, and she barely has energy to eat dinner before passing out in her hotel room. That's probably been the case this week. When I see her tonight, I guarantee that's what she'll tell me.

First, I have to make it through the last day of one of the longest weeks of my life. There's been an outbreak of stomach virus, which everyone keeps calling "the flu" (*major* pet peeve of mine), so I've been up to my eyeballs in puking kids all week.

I'm sighing over the latest file for a ralphing patient when Lynette breezes by. "TGIF, Nate! Got any special Valentine's plans with Frankie this weekend?"

Oh, yeah, I forgot to mention that, didn't I? It's Valentine's Day. Well, it *was* Valentine's Day yesterday, but even a "holiday" as contrived as this one gets its own weekend nowadays. (What's up with that, anyway?)

I ignore Lynette's banal chit-chat and ask with as much patience as possible, "Does Riley Poehler already have a barf bucket with her in the waiting room?"

Lynette blinks at me, obviously stung by my curt rejection.

I soften. "Sorry. I'm busy, and sick of vomit. I'm also paranoid I'm going to come down with this crud, since it's so contagious."

Her smile widens as she accepts my apology. "I get it. To answer *your* question, yes. Everyone, including Riley, is receiving a barf bucket upon check in. It's this week's must-have fashion accessory."

"Great."

"Now, what do you have planned with Frankie this weekend? Indulge a lonely single girl, huh?"

Thinking about it makes my stomach lurch in a way I hope has nothing to do with germs. "Not much. I'm going to surprise her at the airport tonight."

"Oooh! How romantic!"

"You think so?" Truth is, I've been going back and forth on the idea all day. A few times, I've been a button-push away from sending her a text to tell her I'll see her in the morning.

But Lynette gushes, "Totally! We love when you guys make the effort to be spontaneous and fun."

"Well, that's me. Spontaneous and fun," I mutter with a tight smile as I retrieve Riley's file folder and push open the waiting room door.

The sounds of retching and splashing greet me. It doesn't take me long to locate the source of the noises, and when I do, I'm dismayed to see a bucket sitting in the chair next to Riley, while she throws up on the floor in front of her. Her dad watches helplessly.

I rush over, skirt the puddle of muck, and position the pail under her face.

"I—I don't know why she did that," her dad, looking pale and shaky, tells me.

Maybe because she's sick and five and needs a grownup—that would be you, Dad—to show her how it's done?

I set Riley's chart aside so I have a free hand to rub her back while she continues to expel the contents of her stomach. "It's okay," I reassure both of them as calmly as possible, focusing on the child so my irritation at her father doesn't show.

The other patients and parents avert or close their eyes to the disgusting sight. Lynette's voice tinkles over the pager, calling a custodian to the waiting room with all the cheer of someone announcing a lottery winner.

When it seems Riley's current biohazard event is over, I thrust the puke pail at her dad, letting go of it the second I'm sure he has a grip on it. Grasping Riley under her arms, I lift her over the mess on the floor and rest her on my hip while I squat to retrieve her file and carry her through to the back rooms. Her hot forehead presses against my neck.

Hmm, feels like she's sittin' at about 102 degrees. That's hardly dangerous for someone her age, so her case isn't urgent, but based on my experience with other patients this week, I have about ten minutes, tops, before she spews again. That's my motivation for rushing.

At the scale, I set her down just long enough to get a digital readout before hoisting her again and carrying her into one of the empty exam rooms.

She whimpers, which I know is a sure sign that bad things are about to happen. I whirl to grab the bucket from her dad, but he's nowhere in sight.

"Really?" I mutter, setting her on the examination table and sliding the room's trashcan between her feet, stomping on the pedal and flipping it open just in time for it to receive the kind of material its red bag promises.

"Get it all out of there, sweetheart," I murmur while holding her wispy hair away from her face.

Between stomach spasms, she cries for her dad.

"He'll be here in a sec," I promise, not sure if he will, because I have no idea where he could possibly be. Just as I'm about to pick up the room's phone and alert a search party to his disappearance, he catches up to us, sans bucket.

"Oh, there you are," he declares.

"Yes. Where's the pail?"

He takes in the room's activities. "I gave it to one of the front desk girls."

The last frayed nerve I was counting on to keep me out of prison today snaps. "Dude. Just..." *One... two... three... I love my job... I love my job...* I get to ten before I'm sure I can address him professionally and sympathetically and wave him over. "Come here and help her stay on target. Please. I'll be back in a second."

I stride out to reception, checking to make sure the Plexiglass sliding windows to the waiting area are closed before asking, "Okay, which one of you 'front desk girls' was the lucky recipient of Riley Poehler's stomach contents?"

Lynette turns from her insurance data entry and says, "Oh, that was Pam. Do you need the bucket?"

"Uh, yeah!"

"Well, it's not here anymore. Did you think we'd set it under the counter and go on with our day?"

She's got me there. I guess it was dumb to come looking for it in here. I'm not going to admit that, though. Instead, I spin and exit the area, heading for the supply closet, where I can find a new receptacle. And Bio-Mat bags.

When I return to Riley's exam room, she's sacked out on the table, her sweaty, blonde hair stuck to her forehead. Once I determine she's only sleeping, not unconscious, I set aside my supplies and rub the back of my neck.

"Her mom usually handles all this, but she's sick, too," her dad sheepishly explains. "Should I have tried to keep her awake? She didn't get any sleep last night."

"Well, sticking a tongue depressor down her throat would

probably only lead to more problems, anyway," I say, regaining my diplomatic equilibrium while I wash my hands. "So, tell me what's been going on."

He describes what countless other parents have described to me this week. Then I explain for what feels like the thousandth time the difference between a viral and bacterial infection and tell him there's nothing I can do to hasten the running of this particular virus's course. Ten minutes later, he leaves with his daughter and my reassurances she's going to be okay, plus some suggestions for keeping her hydrated and minimizing her discomfort.

I look at the clock, dismayed both at how quickly and slowly time is passing.

* * *

LEG JIGGLING, foot tapping, and fingers drumming, I wait in the arrivals greeting area at the airport a few hours later, clutching the bouquet of red roses I picked up on the way as part apology, part welcome home gesture, part Valentine's gift, and trying not to feel like a loser, biologically incapable of playing it cool.

Flowers? Really? How unoriginal! I wouldn't blame her if she pretended not to know me.

Hold up, Eeyore. Just take a deep breath and get a grip.

I obey myself, closing my eyes to focus my attention on hyperventilation prevention.

Surprising Frankie this evening is a lovely, romantic gesture. Like Lynette said, she'll be impressed I put forth the effort after a ten-hour day of pretending to be positive and upbeat and all, "Oh, you threw up on my shoes? No problem. It's not like they were my favorite. Plus, only an idiot in my income bracket spends $150 on a pair of athletic shoes to wear around sick kids."

The goal is to woo her, to say, with both actions and words, "I want to be un-alone with you for the rest of my life. Maybe. If that's what you want."

Shit. I should have practiced what I was going to say. Maybe it's best if I say nothing and let these lame flowers speak for themselves. Sometimes—especially in my case—silence truly is golden.

Sure, *her* silence this week has been unnerving, but it's not unprecedented. The only reason it feels more sinister is that everyone's been obsessed with Valentine's Day, while she and I have largely ignored its arrival and passing. That's not normal, in my experience, between two people in a relatively new relationship, but maybe it's a sign that what we have transcends all that shallow nonsense. Sounds good, anyway.

My eyes have been pinned to the arrivals board for nearly thirty solid minutes now, so I flinch when the status of her flight changes from "In Air" to "Arriving at Gate B4." A few seconds later, a bored voice reiterates the information on the loud speaker.

Oh, gosh. She's here.

Okay. Um. Breath check. Good. This gum is making my jaw ache, but I'm minty. Totally worth it. I stand and pace but quickly stop when I notice a nearby woman watching me with a private smile. I smile back uncertainly before realizing she's eyeing the flowers. I wonder if it would be bizarre if I gave these to her instead of Frankie. Could I pass it off as a random act of kindness, or would it be obvious I was losing my nerve, too insecure to pull off the big gesture?

Stop.

No wussing out. I've thought about this all week, during

lucid moments, when my mind was fresh and able to make decent decisions. These are Frankie's roses. I can do this.

I edge toward the furthest place non-passengers are allowed to go to wait for travelers. I won't be able to see her coming from far off, due to the layout of the airport, but as soon as she rounds that corner, we'll only be about a hundred feet apart, as opposed to the hundreds of miles that have separated us all week.

I hear her laugh before I see her.

Oh, gosh. Where is she? Is she laughing at me? It's the bouquet, isn't it? Damn it! I should have thrown it in the trash.

However, when I finally see her, I'm relieved to see she's not laughing at me at all. That relief lasts about 0.6 seconds, since the next thing I notice is that she doesn't see me, because she's focused on whatever the six-foot-four god of a man she's walking with is saying to her.

I feel like an even bigger idiot, standing here with these roses, my frozen, anticipatory smile fading from my face, as I wait for her to turn her attention from the Adonis in the suit to little ol' me in my faded long-sleeved t-shirt, jeans, and Vans. Oh, yeah, and my peacoat.

Jet-Set Ken tears his eyes away from Frankie and catches me sizing him up. He nods in my direction and says something to Frankie, who turns her head and sees me for the first time.

For a sick second, I'm not sure she's going to acknowledge me. But her hesitancy must have been my imagination, or it was taking her a second to register what she was seeing, because just as my heart stutters out of rhythm, she smiles vaguely and gives me a tentative wave.

I wave back but stay where I am, worried it will seem territorial for me to walk toward her while she's still talking to whoever that guy is. She turns away from me, so I can't see her face, and all he says is, "Okay," giving me no clues regarding her side of the conversation. I have a vivid imagination, though.

"Oh, my gosh. This guy sends me a Hoops and Yo-Yo ecard on Valentine's Day, then thinks he can show up here with flowers, and it's all good? Don't leave me alone with him."

Or...

"How pathetic is that? Red roses? When I dump his ass for you, don't ever do anything that lame."

Or...

Fortunately, she gives her mile-high man a final arm pat and a parting "See ya!" over her shoulder as she walks toward me, so I don't have time to think of any further devastating dialogue.

He smiles at me over her shoulder in a way that a more jealous man than I am could construe as smarmy or cocky. I grant him an acknowledging nod before focusing all of my attention on Frankie, who's broken into a trot, her small wheeled suitcase wobbling behind her, her laptop bag bouncing against her butt.

She shortens her strides to try to slow down in her slick shoes before she runs into me. "Hey! What the heck are you doing here?"

I'm relieved she sounds pleased and not like she's about to signal for security at any second.

I give her a tentative hug, which she firmly returns. "I wanted to welcome you home," I explain, letting her go and holding the roses out to her. "I wanted to say sorry. For a lot of things."

Her wrinkled brow tells me she's thought nothing of our radio near-silence all week. "Okay? Anything in particular you're apologizing for? Do I need to be worried?"

"No!" I suck my gum down my throat and cough as it slides down and lands with a plunk into my stomach. "I mean, no." I chuckle. "I just feel bad that I didn't talk to you all week or do anything special for Valentine's Day."

"I was too busy to talk, anyway," she says dismissively, relieving me of the flowers in a loud crinkle of cellophane.

I wait a beat while she attempts to smell the hothouse blooms, but she merely grins expectantly at me after giving up on an olfactory experience.

The suddenly awkward silence makes me blurt, "So, who was that guy?" since it's the only thing I can think about right now.

She blinks at me. "What guy?"

He's no longer there, but I nod in the direction of where I saw her talking to the mystery man and answer, "The suit. You know, the one you were walking with."

Her mouth remains fixed in the shape of a smile, but it's as if a curtain has drawn to a close behind her chocolate irises, blocking any light from my view. "You mean, Kyle?"

"I guess. Is that his name?"

"Yeah."

"How do you know him?"

She laughs nervously. "He's just a guy who rides that shuttle from Chicago nearly every week, like me. He's the CEO of a software company or something down there. But he's from here and stays here most weekends."

"Oh. With his wife and kids?"

"No, he's single. Why?"

I shrug, trying to rearrange my features into something less pouty. "No reason. Just... you two seem friendly."

"I know you're not jealous."

"Don't be ridiculous."

"Exactly. That would be insane."

I'd like to know exactly why she thinks it would be crazy, but since I'm supposedly not jealous, it's not worth pursuing.

Before I can recover, she goes in for a kiss. "This week was nuts," she says against my lips.

Primal parts of my body react to the contact. "Uh, yeah. It was."

After a soft, glancing smooch, she grasps hold of her luggage handle and walks ahead of me. "Thanks for the roses. They're gorgeous."

I take over driving her suitcase for her. "You're welcome. I... I hope it's not too cliché. I just wanted to show you I missed you. Happy Valentine's Day, belatedly."

"Well done."

"Really?" The muscles in my shoulders relax for the first time in hours.

"Yeah. I love flowers. Did Betty tell you that? She's such a sneak and didn't let on at all that you were planning this."

Mentally smacking myself in the forehead for not thinking about consulting Betty, I merely admit, "It didn't occur to me to ask her."

It's true, but in addition, I'm wary about being in touch with Betty when Frankie's out of town. Don't get me wrong; I like Betty. The more I get to know her, the more I like her. She's fun to be around, and I count her as one of my friends. But she's a couple-friend friend, you know? I mean, I hang out with her when Frankie's around, but if Betty and I were to hang out alone, that would be odd. Not awkward or uncomfortable, but not natural-feeling, either, so I don't seek out her company. It's my way of ensuring I don't talk to my girlfriend's friend more than I talk to my girlfriend.

"Well, next time, you should consult her. She knows everything about me, including my underwear size."

I slam into a guy on his way into the airport as I process the last part of her sentence, and my brain (yeah, we'll pretend that's the body part at play here) nearly short-circuits.

"Hey!" the stranger barks.

"Sorry," I mutter, too busy following Frankie's swaying hips to stop and give the guy a more sincere apology. Catching up, I say, "Duly noted."

She smiles then winces and rubs her head.

"Are you okay?"

She nods wanly. "Yeah. I didn't sleep well last night, so I have a bad headache."

"Oh." I push down my disappointment. "Let's get you home, then. You probably need to eat something, too. We can pick up something on the way. Or I can drop you off and go to the grocery store to grab something for you." I stop, then say, "This way," leading her to the row in the short-term parking lot where my car is.

She's quiet for the rest of the walk, but as I stow her laptop bag and rolling suitcase into the trunk, she says over her roses, "I ate during my layover. I just need to sleep."

"Of course." I hurry around to the passenger side of the car and open the door for her. She rewards my chivalry with a kiss on my cheek on her way down to her seat.

When I take the wheel, she waits for me to start the car, then places her hand over mine on the gear shift. "You went to so much trouble. I feel bad putting a damper on your plans."

I shoot her a brave smile and lie, "This is the extent of any 'plan' I had. I wanted to meet you here so you didn't have to take a cab home. I'll help you get settled, and I'll leave you alone to get some rest. We can do something tomorrow."

She nods, setting her bouquet by her feet. "Okay. I have a mountain of laundry to do, but..."

"I'll take it home with me tonight."

"You will?"

I back from the parking space. "Might as well. That way, we can do something fun tomorrow and not worry about it."

She draws her knees to her chest, rests her forehead against her knees, and mumbles, "You're too good to me."

A statement that should make me proud fills me with irrational dread, but the feeling is fleeting, replaced by tenderness as I glance over at her, spying a sliver of milky, white neck peeking through her hair. I make a mental note to kiss that spot tomorrow, when she's feeling better.

9

GROCERY RUN

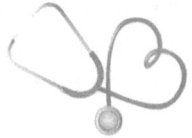

BEFORE I COULD TAKE HOME FRANKIE'S MOUNTAIN OF laundry (she wasn't exaggerating about that, by the way), I spent an hour de-funking her refrigerator and kitchen, since it smelled like something died in there while she was away last week. Turns out, a carton of already-expired milk doesn't improve with age and neglect. Leftovers in Styrofoam takeout containers also don't stand the test of time.

She bravely stood by for a few minutes, insisting she'd take care of it, but the deepening green around the edges of her eyes and mouth as we unearthed more and more rotten food told a different story, and she eventually wandered off to take some aspirin and a shower.

By the time I dumped the bleach water, disposed of a huge black trash bag of "food" in the dumpster out back, and returned to her apartment, she was fast asleep on her bed, her wet hair splayed on her pillow. I resisted the urge to watch her while she slept, telling myself I was too busy for such melodramatics, but I indulged in a kiss to the top of her head. Then I took three trips to my car with basket after basket of her dirty clothes.

Nothing says "I love you" like housekeeping, right? It's a decent start on the huge undertaking I now know is before me, after seeing her with that guy in the airport.

Frankie and I have been dating exclusively for three months. That might not sound like a long time, but it's a veritable eternity compared to every other relationship I've had in the past three years. I'll admit, though, that I've been coasting. I'm hardly putting forth any effort at all, as if just because she's not around during the week, that means I'm off the boyfriend hook.

And on the weekends, when we are together, I've become complacent and lazy. A typical Friday or Saturday night consists of us going out to eat and seeing a movie. I swear, we've seen every new release, including the animated ones, since we met in November, but I couldn't tell you the last time we had a deep, meaningful conversation.

Even today's surprise was something planned more out of obligation than because I wanted to do it: "It's that time of year; we were apart for Valentine's Day; I guess I should make some kind of romantic gesture, because that's what decent boyfriends do. Sigh."

But seeing her face all lit up when she was talking to Kyle at the airport, before she realized I was there, stirred a jealousy in me that I didn't even know was possible. I didn't think I cared enough to be jealous. Well, I do. That's a huge relief, but she didn't seem to appreciate my brief display of territoriality. If I don't get a grip and start showing her I care in ways that don't make her want to punch me, she won't stick around much longer.

And how do you show a woman you care? You cook for her. At least, I do. Tomorrow, she'll experience a home-cooked meal from my kitchen. She doesn't have to understand the significance; I know it's big. With one load of Frankie's laundry tumbling in the dryer and another spinning in the washer, I tug a purple fleece-lined sweatshirt over my other layers and head for the grocery store, everyone's favorite place to be on a Friday night.

At the store, I grab one of those mini-carts for the lonely— I mean, single—and zoom through the aisles, tossing in the ingredients for chicken tortellini, salad, marinated eggplant, and my homemade tiramisu.

I'm double-checking my list, making sure I didn't forget anything, when a sultry voice behind me says, "Not many men can pull off purple like that."

I whirl to see Betty behind her own sportscart. I give her a nervous smile. "Oh. Hey. You're here."

She does that acrobatic eyebrow thing while patting herself. "Why, yes. Yes, I am. I'm not a mirage."

I blush at my stupidity. "I meant... I've never seen you at this store before."

"I always shop here on my way home from the gym, so I've been here..." She closes one eye and looks up toward her bangs. "Three other times."

"New gym membership?"

"Nope. I just never go. It's such a meat market."

My eyes gravitate toward her cart. I can't help it. I have a thing about analyzing the contents of other shoppers' carts, and I have to say, I'm particularly fascinated to see what Betty's basket says about her. Anything to give me some clues as to what makes her tick.

I still haven't quite figured her out. Frankie likes to tease me and say I'm afraid of her, but that's definitely not it. I've seen for myself what Frankie told me the first time I met Betty: her toughness is a big front most of the time.

It's the other part of the time I'm not so sure about, though. One minute, she's confident and sassy; then, a simple, seemingly innocuous word from Frankie renders her quiet and contemplative. Usually, she excuses herself at that point and leaves. It's odd.

As for her reactions to me, I never know if she's going to laugh along with something I've said or eviscerate me with a scathing comment about my bushy eyebrows. (Okay, she hasn't mentioned them since that first meeting, but now I have a complex.) Other times, she'll take me completely by surprise by complimenting me, and I'll feel like we've made a break-through and have finally started to feel comfortable around each other. The bottom line is, she's unpredictable. Unpredictable makes me nervous.

Tonight, as I'm silently approving of the Listerine and dental floss in her cart, it moves, and she clears her throat dramatically. "Excuse me, but none of your business!"

I raise my eyes to her face and say, "Sorry. But there's no expectation of privacy in a shopping cart."

"It's an unspoken social norm. It's like when guys stand next to each other at the urinals. You don't sneak a peek then, do you?"

Horrified, I reply, "No! But that's different. Anyway, there's nothing shameful in your cart. Oral hygiene is closely linked to heart health, and red wine is full of antioxidants." I pause, then mutter, "That's a lot of antioxidants you have there, but..."

"Thank you for your concern," she replies drolly, pulling even with me and poking her fingers through my basket. "Now, your turn." When she can't find anything to criticize, she accuses me of being boring, then says, "You hit the junk food and personal hygiene aisles last, don't you, so you don't have to wander around the store with a bunch of embarrassing stuff in your basket. Smart."

I laugh. "You got me."

"I know your type. Mr. All-American, with your whole

foods in clear containers on your kitchen counter for everyone to see, but your locked pantry is full of high fructose corn syrup."

"Like, in bottles? For chugging?"

"In all forms. I bet you love fruit snacks."

I smile guiltily. "I've been known to partake."

"Oh, my gosh! I was kidding."

I shrug. "I wasn't. They're better for you than most candies."

"How about nature's candy, Nathaniel?" She gestures to the bananas, grapes, and strawberries in her basket."

"It's the middle of winter. Fruit sucks right now."

She nods. "I know. I end up throwing half of it away." Suddenly, she pounces on something in her cart. "Oh, here's something you *must* approve of!" she says, hoisting it at eye level.

I pull my head back to avoid being smacked in the nose with the half-gallon pump bottle of antibacterial hand gel. "Good for you. Actually, I'm not a fan, but whatever."

"Not a fan?"

"Nope. Why not just wash your hands?"

"Sometimes I don't have access to water."

"You carry that around in your purse? It's huge!"

She laughs. "Okay, no. I refill my travel-sized bottles with bigger bottles like this. It's cheaper to buy in bulk, you know?" She sets the gel in her cart, carefully avoiding a half-dozen egg flat, and wipes her hands against her yoga pants, as if she's handled the bottle after someone dirty.

"Well that stuff's not good for the environment," I inform her, trying not to sound too preachy as I state the facts. "And it's responsible for antibiotic resistance and, in some extreme cases, UV sensitivity and hormone reactions."

"You're making that shit up."

"I'm not! Google it!"

"I have better things to do, like clean behind my refrigerator."

I give a conceding nod and wince. "Yeah. I'm way overdue for that."

She shoots me a look that tells me she's not sure if I'm being serious. Good. See how she likes it.

Before she can zing me I say, "Well, my skim milk's sweating. I'd better get moving."

"Sounds like something you might want to get checked out, Nathaniel."

I chuckle. "No comment."

We both head for the checkout. Casually, she remarks, "I heard you're not joining us up at the cabin weekend after next."

I freeze. "Oh. Yeah. That." Quickly, I make the impulsive decision to say, "Actually, I'm in."

"Really? The last I'd heard from Frankie, you had to work."

Okay, hard truth time: I lied and said I had to work at Urgent Care that weekend, to avoid coming right out and saying, "I'd rather spend my Saturday cleaning behind my fridge than freezing my soaking-wet ass off on snowmobiles at Betty's parents' cabin with you and a bunch of people you've known since elementary school." It was a white lie to spare Frankie's feelings—and to make me seem like less of a dick than I am.

Contrary to what Frankie thinks, I'm not pathologically honest. "Working at Urgent Care on the weekend" has been one of my go-to excuses for years. That's not going to change now. There have also been a few times I've told her those jeans didn't make her butt look big (back pocket size matters). Since I'm laying it all out there, I do prefer having sex to not having sex. It's not my fault if she's naïve enough to believe my statements of indifference.

Now, I swallow and half-smile at Betty when I say, "I switched with someone, so I'm all set."

She pauses, studying my face, before saying, "Hm. That's... unexpectedly convenient."

I ignore her implication and make a big show of finding an open self-checkout station. "I haven't had a chance to tell Frankie yet." I loop my canvas bags over the holders in the bagging area. "She fell asleep almost as soon as I got her home from the airport."

Betty situates herself at the station next to mine and begins scanning her items, flashing her driver's license to the attendant when her jugs—of wine—set off an ID alert.

After the attendant goes back to her podium, I ask, "So this is something a group of you does every year, snowmobiling?"

"Well, *they* do. I supply the cabin in the woods by the lake. I'm not a big fan of riding around on deadly machines in the cold," she says while scanning and bagging. "I read by the fire while everyone else is out freezing off their fingers and toes. Sometimes I cook for everyone, if I'm in the mood. I make a mean meatless lasagna."

"Comfort food."

"Yeah. I use portabello mushrooms in place of the meat. It's amazing."

My stomach growls at the thought of it. I love meat, but portabello mushrooms are one of my weaknesses. I grill them like steaks in the summertime.

"Sounds great."

"Yeah, I guess I'll do it this time, too."

"Looking forward to it." I swipe my debit card, key in my

pin, take my receipt, and lift my canvas bags from the bagging area. "Well, have a good night."

Concentrating on weighing and keying in her fruit, she nods in response, her tongue poking from the corner of her mouth. "You, too. See you next Saturday."

"That you will."

10

COLD WEEKEND

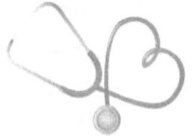

IT'S PROBABLY UNBELIEVABLE THAT I'VE LIVED IN WISCONSIN my whole life and I've never been on a snowmobile before today. I've never worn those snowshoes that look like tennis racquets, either, so stop stereotyping. But maybe it's not all that surprising. I'm sure by now it's clear I'm not the rugged outdoorsy type.

I've always been apprehensive of snowmobiles and four-wheelers and jet skis and all those other adventure machines my brother and most of our friends spent the majority of their teens and twenties riding, depending on the season. If I'm not going to drive a car to get somewhere, I'd rather my own muscles provide the power. I like walking, running, and cycling. On smooth pavement. I'm not a fan of abrasions, cuts, fractures... or death. Not that my brother or my friends are, either, but while it seemed like a fairly big warning to me that at least one person we knew died every year on the back of a recreational vehicle, Nick saw it differently. "Survival of the fittest. The dumb die."

Somehow, I don't think the valedictorian of our high school was too dumb to ride a three-wheeler. Nevertheless, he's six feet under in the cemetery I drive by every day on my way to work.

My point is, I'm smart enough to quit while I'm ahead. By "ahead," I mean "still alive after being dumped three times by a laughing Frankie." When everyone else is bundling up for Round Two after thawing out by the fire for a couple of hours in the custom-built log cabin Betty's mom and step-dad call home when they feel like "roughing it" (a.k.a., "living without wi-fi"), I cheerfully announce, "I'll stay here and help Betty with dinner."

Frankie frowns. "Are you mad at me?" she asks in front of everyone.

They all wait expectantly for my answer. I look around at the four faces I've known for about five hours, most of that time fearing for my life or envisioning catastrophic, life-changing injuries, and chuckle nervously. "Uh... no..."

"I won't dump you this time. It was just a joke."

"It's fine."

"She was only hazing you, dude. The new guy always gets dumped," Dan (Ben? Manuel?) says, pulling on his gloves with his teeth.

"I'm not mad," I insist again, this time with less of a smile. "I'm still cold, though. You know, it's not my thing, that's all. But you go ahead."

"And ride alone?" Frankie asks with a pout. "Great. That'll be a blast."

"I'll ride with you, Frankie," Tina (I think) volunteers. She turns to Dan/Ben/Manuel. "You don't mind, right, Babe? Then you can go as fast as you want without me getting scared and yelling in your ear."

He smirks. "I like when you scream in my ear."

"It would be easier if you'd come with us," Frankie points out. "We're not staying out as long this time."

Betty pokes her head through the doorway from the living room to the entryway, where we're grouped, discussing what a party pooper I am.

"What's going on? It's getting dark."

"Nate doesn't want to go with us," Warren (or some other old-guy name he probably hates his parents for giving him) tattles.

"So? Last time I checked, even numbers weren't a requirement for idiocy." She shoos everyone out with two hands. "Now, go!"

With a final doleful look over her shoulder that I assume is supposed to make me cave, Frankie leaves with her friends.

I shoot her an apologetic smile and call, "Have fun!" before Betty closes the door in my face.

"Bunch of immature assholes," she mutters, striding back to the kitchen, where she sticks her head in the fridge and pulls out ingredients.

I follow and stand on the other side of the breakfast bar as she places the food in a precise line on the counter, arranging and rearranging each item in an order that obviously matters.

"Can I help with anything?" I ask. "I might as well make myself useful."

"You can help me by staying out of the way," she answers shortly, splashing more wine into a large, nearly empty glass. "I have a system."

I purse my lips. "Okay, then."

She looks up from her ingredient shuffling. "Sorry. I don't mean to be a bitch. I'm just used to doing things alone."

I raise my hands in front of my chest. "I get it. No need to apologize."

She spins toward the refrigerator, opens it, and comes out with a bottle of beer, which she thrusts at me after twisting off the cap. "Here. You can sit over there by the fire with this and relax. I'm sure you've earned it."

"What do you mean? I'm having a good time so far."

Tilting her chin down, she looks at me through her lashes while I take the beer from her. "Right." She returns to her cooking. "Even if you weren't lying through your teeth, you run your ass off all week at work with sick kids, so you deserve a quiet, relaxing weekend."

I open my mouth to object to her canonization of me, but she cuts me off. "Really. Sit. You're throwing off my routine." She tosses back the majority of her glass of wine and pours herself another.

I back away. "Fine. I'll read. Or something."

After retrieving my e-reader from my bag in the bedroom I'm sharing with Frankie, I choose a cushy leather chair big enough for two people and settle into it. Setting my beer on a coaster on the end table next to the chair, I open the device and tap it to life. As it pulls up the titles stored on it, I call toward the kitchen, "If you change your mind, let me know. I can dice an onion like nobody's business."

She laughs. "So I've heard. Frankie told me you made quite the romantic belated Valentine's Day dinner for her."

"She told you about that, huh?"

"Bragged, more like it."

I grin. "Oh. Well. I like to cook. I had to make it up to her somehow for being such a lame boyfriend lately."

After some busy clanging with pots and glass casserole dishes, Betty asks, "What are you talking about? All she does is rave about you. Haven't heard her this excited about a guy in a long time."

"You probably shouldn't be telling me all this."

The clip-clop of a rocking knife on a chopping board keeps time as she replies sardonically, "Yeah. It'll give you a big ego."

That's not what I meant, but I drop it. The more I think about it, the less I want to talk about that night, anyway. It's not that it went badly; on the contrary, it was apparently a major success... according to Frankie. I just walked away from it more confused than ever.

I wanted it to be special; I wanted to delight Frankie. Mission accomplished. Too well, maybe. During dessert, between seductive sucks on her spoon, she stared into space and laid out our entire life together. Yeah. It was weird, and a little scary. I pushed away my plate and listened, hoping she was too enthralled with her own fantasy to pay much attention to my facial contortions as I tried to maintain a neutral expression.

"I'll stay home and take care of the kids. That will give me a chance to write. When they're babies, I'll work during nap times and in the evening, when you're home. When they're in school, I'll have all day to write, but I'll also be available to volunteer at school and car pool and do all the things my mom certainly never bothered doing."

I "uh-huh"-ed and "yeah"-ed and "okay"-ed in the right places while reassuring myself, *This is way in the future, all hypothetical. This isn't a contract negotiation. This is Frankie's fantasy. She's dreaming out loud. Isn't it cute that she feels comfortable enough to do that in front of me? Yeah. It is. She's gorgeous. And we'll have beautiful children. That's what I want, anyway, right?*

I even saw those children while she continued to lay out how many books a year she'd write and publish and where we'd go on family vacations with her royalties. I saw myself holding those babies for the first time. I saw them toddling across my living room. I saw them wading in the surf during one of those royalty-funded vacations. I saw them hunched over homework at the very dining table where I was sitting. I ignored the fact that I didn't see Frankie with me in any of those visions.

My heartbeat slowed, a genuine smile returned to my face, and I reached around the dishes and across the table to clasp her hand in mine. "Plenty of time for all that," I told both her and myself.

She squeezed my fingers, laughed, and blushed. "Yeah. Of course. Sorry. I get carried away sometimes."

"Me, too," I admitted. I'm sure it will be more and more true as time passes, too. Surely.

"So, whatcha readin'?" Betty interrupts my discomfiting memory.

I blink down at my e-reader. "Uh, nothing. I just finished the latest Jennifer Weiner book, and—"

"Oooh! I love her. How was it?"

"Amazing." I jump from my chair, snagging my beer and carrying it with me to the breakfast bar, where I set down my Kindle and my bottle. Perching on a stool, I lean on my elbows on the counter and add, "It's going to be hard to find something to follow it. Any ideas?"

She tosses a few names out, but they're all authors whose entire catalogues I've already devoured. "I'm ready for something new. Something *new* new."

"That shouldn't be hard. Start browsing. The biggest challenge will be narrowing it down. There's so much out there now."

I tap around for a while before murmuring distractedly, "I want to read something written by a man."

"Sexist!"

I laugh at the irony of her accusing a man of being a sexist after he's waxed rhapsodic about a Jennifer Weiner book. "What I mean is, I want to discover the next Patrick Fox, Matt Dunn, or Nicholas Sparks."

She wrinkles her nose.

"Yeah, you're right. Not Sparks. That dude always makes me cry. I'm not in the mood to cry. I want to laugh."

"Check out the 'people who bought' sections on those guys' pages. That'll give you a good place to start."

Fifteen minutes later, she's sliding a heavy glass pan layered with mouth-watering ingredients into the oven, but I'm no closer to deciding on a book. "Too many choices!" I groan. "I need another beer."

She complies with my demand and tosses my empty bottle into a tidy stacking recycling bin. Returning to the counter, she mirrors my pose, so we're nearly forehead-to-forehead. I turn the Kindle sideways so she can see, too.

Thumbing through the book sales lists, I swig from the beer bottle, then set it aside so I have better control of the e-reader. I drill down into the lists, narrowing, narrowing, narrowing.

"I'm looking for writers like Nick Hornby—ooh, there's a good one! Lad lit!—but *not* English," I explain.

In a horrible Cockney accent, she demands, "What's wrong wiff British blokes, eh? Top o' the mornin' to you, laddie."

I nearly drop my beloved e-reader as I wheeze, "You went from Michael Caine to Lucky Charms in about two-point-six seconds."

She punches my shoulder. "Shut up. My question stands. Why no British guys? They're hot."

"They may well be, but a) that's not one of my requirements or concerns and b) Fox and Dunn and Hornby sometimes use expressions that would probably be a lot funnier if I knew what they meant."

"It's not their fault you're not multicultural, Nathaniel." She pulls the device away from me and taps at the screen, eliminating parameters to widen my search. "Broaden your horizons."

I grab my property back from her. "My horizons are plenty wide, thank you. It's not that I *never* read that stuff, but this time, I want someone American. It has nothing to do with xenophobia and everything to do with laziness."

The list of candidates dissolves from more than a half-million to less than ten thousand in a matter of taps. I reclaim my beer.

As we scroll down the page, Betty calls out the names we see, in case I can't read, I guess. I dismiss them for various reasons.

"Nick Alexander?"

"No Nicks."

"Evan Llewellyn?"

"Too many 'l's."

When she shoots me a disbelieving look, I keep my eyes pinned to the screen and state, "I don't have to have good reasons. This is all about gut instinct."

She snorts but stops staring at my profile and goes back to reading from the screen. I fill my mouth with more beer and continue scrolling.

The next name on the list, however, makes her gasp, and it turns my insides to ice.

Frank Lipton.

Clinging to the pathetic hope that someone who's *not* my girlfriend has already published ten books with sweet, illustrated pastel covers and under the name Frankie's been planning to use for her pen name (bummer for her!), I tap to the "About the Author" page to see what this Frank Lipton dude looks like.

Oh... My...

Beer sprays from my mouth and onto my face... on my e-reader. I mean, my face is on my e-reader. In it. On it. Whatever. It's *there*!

"Motherfucker!" I hiss, losing my grip on my beer bottle while jumping down from the stool. Golden liquid spreads across the granite as the bottle rolls. Betty straightens to avoid having her arms drenched, and the bottle drops between the counter and her body, landing with a sick crash at her feet.

"It's okay!" she immediately says, but I'm not sure to what she's referring. If she's talking about my picture out there on the Web, associated with a bunch of books I didn't write, then she's way off-base.

I wipe the e-reader against my butt, effectively making me kiss my own ass. "Oh, shit!" I hiss when I make that connection. Holding the device in front of me again, I demand to a suddenly empty kitchen, "Do you know about this?"

Her head pops up to counter level again, followed shortly by the rest of her body. In her hand is a kitchen towel and several brown pieces of glass.

When I look at the screen, I half-expect the picture to have changed, and it has, because I've activated a link with my all my butt-rubbing, so I'm faced with a list of "Frank Lipton's" book titles. I read them out loud, watching Betty's face become paler with each title.

"Oh, my gosh," I whisper. "You *do* know."

She tosses everything in her hands into the nearby sink, rounds the counter, and stands in front of me. Grasping the drawstrings of my hoodie, she pulls them, bunching the hood against the back of my neck and pulling my face closer to hers, little puffs of alcohol-and-grape-scented air making me blink with each syllable when she says, "I had no idea. You have to believe me."

I nod sickly but pull away from her, afraid my one-and-a-half beers are about to make an encore appearance. At the risk of hastening that occurrence, I reread the titles. None of them sound remotely familiar, but one—*Hippocratic Oaf*—practically bitch slaps me. I navigate to the previous page, my fingers tacky against the dried beer residue.

Yep, there I am again. I hold the device out to Betty so she can see. "When the eff was I ever wearing those black glasses? Never!"

She examines the picture. "Looks like a Photoshop job. A good one, but still. Where'd she get the original picture?"

I edge closer to her so I can look at the photo over her shoulder. At first, I draw a blank, but then I recognize the background as my parents' living room. And that shirt... that was the one I wore the day we went to their house for lunch, the day I introduced her to them, and it all comes flooding back.

"C'mon, just a little picture. I don't have any of you!" It was half-time of the game the three of them were eventually successful in forcing me to watch.

"Why now?" I asked, trying to evade the tiny circle on the back of her phone.

"Nathan! Let the girl get a picture of you," Mom interfered from the other sofa, where she sat next to Dad.

I sighed but rearranged my features into something that felt unnatural but possibly acceptable. As soon as Frankie took the shot, I held out my hand. "Let me see."

She clutched the phone to her chest. "No."

"Yes! I want to make sure I don't look like a moron."

"You don't look like a moron," she promised. "You look like you. I like it."

It was the first time anyone other than my mother had said something so accepting, and it took me aback. "Oh. Okay. But don't put it all over Facebook," I muttered.

"I won't," she reassured me, pocketing her phone without showing me the snapshot and cuddling against me to watch the rest of the game.

I rub my face at the memory. "She took that at my parents' house," I answer Betty.

Sounding shell-shocked, she says robotically, "It's a good one. You're photogenic."

"I look like a smug hipster!"

A handsome, smart, smug hipster, but that is beside the point!

I scan "Frank's" author bio. "Oh, shit the bed," I grumble.

A sigh comes from Betty. "Green Bay? She didn't even change the hometown to something bigger? How about New York City? Isn't that where all writers live and blend in and get lost? Not here, where skimming the Sports section counts as 'extensive daily reading.'"

My heart thunders. Sweat pops out along my hairline and on my upper lip. I manage to land a butt cheek on the nearby couch in time to ride out my lightheadedness.

Betty follows me and relinquishes the sticky e-reader. "This sucks," she understates.

When I feel relatively composed, I go back to the page for *Hippocratic Oaf* and, dry-mouthed, silently read the blurb.

Pediatrician Bing Nathanson...

A squeak escapes my throat.

...never dreamed being in touch with his feminine side would be such an impediment to finding true love with a woman. But crying at weddings, singing to babies in the NICU, knitting baby booties in his spare time, and avidly reading women's fiction has only resulted in one thing: ridicule from his family and utter loneliness.

Fed up with being labeled "too sensitive," he gives himself a personality makeover, adopting the opposite of each of his natural personality traits to present a new and "improved" Dr. Nathanson to an online dating site.

There, he finds Kris, the perfect woman for him. Only she's perfect for the old him, the real him. She can't stand the macho Dr.

Nathanson. His quest to convince Kris of his true nature lands him in some outlandish situations as he works harder and harder to win her over. But a cynic like Kris isn't an easy sell...

Swallowing repeatedly, I stare at the simple-yet-eye-catching cover art for *Hippocratic Oaf*. After a few seconds, I wordlessly hand the device to Betty. I can tell by her ever-widening eyes that she's reading the blurb, and it's new to her.

After a couple of minutes, she lifts her eyes warily and winces at me. "You don't look so great," she observes, perching on the arm of the couch and pushing down on my back. "Here. Uh, put your head between your legs or something."

Her advice is appropriate, so I obey. Staring down my boys, I muffle, "What am I going to do?"

"I guess you can start with telling her what you found."

I laugh mirthlessly. "Oh, yeah. Sure. Here? With an audience?"

"I'll keep everyone occupied out here, and you guys can have some time alone in your room."

"I want to go home."

She pauses, then says, "I don't blame you. I don't think you should be alone tonight, though. Do you think you could stay with your brother?"

I gulp. "I'm fine. It's not the end of the world. I'm just... stunned and upset she did all this behind my back."

"Don't leave," Betty urges.

"I don't want to ruin everyone's weekend. They'll hate me. Even more than they already do."

"Nobody hates you."

We both laugh at her unconvincing tone, and I marvel at my ability to laugh at anything right now.

Her cheeks flush, and her eyes flash. "Anyway, if they do hate you just because you don't like zooming around on stupid snowmobiles, they're morons. Forget them."

I wish I could. But their presence is a huge factor in my decision. If it were just Frankie, Betty, and me here, I'd stick it out. Betty made the discovery with me, so it wouldn't be a big deal if she heard Frankie and me talking about it. "I don't want a bunch of strangers hearing Frankie and me argue."

She bites her lower lip. "They won't. There's a bar in the closest town. We sometimes hang out there, so it won't seem weird if I suggest we do that tonight. You guys'll have time to talk, and if you want to leave after talking, you can, without a bunch of people watching you load up and drive away."

The smells wafting from the kitchen remind me, "Your dinner. What about that?"

"You think you can pretend everything's okay through dinner?"

I shake my head. "Probably not. I'm sorry. There's no pretending *this* isn't happening." I flick the back of the e-reader in her hand.

She nods. "Okay. You're right."

We both jump to our feet when we hear the others' voices as they stamp the snow from their boots on the front porch.

Thrusting the electronic device at me, she hisses, "Go to your room. I'll tell everyone you... you have diarrhea."

"What?"

She pushes on my shoulder, prodding me toward the hallway leading to the bedrooms. "Go! I'll think of something to keep everyone away from you. Then I'll suggest Frankie stays here with you when we go out later."

I stumble down the hall with her pushing on my lower back. "Okay, but don't say I have diarrhea. A headache will work just fine. Say I'm sleeping. Or something."

"Whatever!"

She shoves me into the bedroom and slams the door.

I back up to the foot of the bed to sit and wait.

In the meantime, I know what I'll be reading. I stab at the button that will send *Hippocratic Oaf* to my sticky e-reader and wait while it downloads.

* * *

I'M A FAST READER, so by the time I hear the cleanup efforts underway in the kitchen, I'm about halfway through *Hippocratic Oaf*.

First of all, can we discuss the title for a second? If I weren't the obvious inspiration for the oafish protagonist, I'd get a kick out of it, so I guess I have to give Frankie props for being clever. But it seems obvious, based on what I've read so far—heck, based on the protagonist's name and some of the details in the blurb!—that I *am* the inspiration. Therefore, I'm offended to have inspired such a spaz of a character.

Propped against the headboard, I close my eyes and set the book aside on the bedspread, concentrating on breathing without hyperventilating. I need to detach if I'm going to continue reading without having a panic attack. Because if this is really how she sees me, why are we still together? I thought *I* thought some unflattering things about *her!* My petty complaints are nothing compared to how she's portrayed this Dr. Bing Nathanson character.

Which brings me to the writing. I was hoping it would be amateurish and flat, but no... Frankie's smugness when she talks about her writing is absolutely justified. That doesn't make her attitude attractive, but it's warranted. She's good. Damn it. If she can market this well enough, she'll be a big deal. Or *Frank* Lipton will be, anyway.

And the story. I'm hooked. Not just because I can't turn away, either. No, she's figured out that thing that good writers do to keep you saying, "One more chapter," after every single chapter. She's going to keep a lot of people up way past their bedtimes if all of her books are like this one.

The bedroom door creaks, and my eyes fly open.

Frankie tiptoes toward the bed. "Hey," she whispers, taking in the scene. "How are you feeling?"

"Pretty sick," I answer honestly and shortly, trying to contain my rage.

The corners of her mouth turn down in a huge frownie face reminiscent of an emoticon, and it's all I can do not to scream at her sickening insincerity.

"Is everyone else gone?" I check, realizing it sounds to me like I'm making sure there are no witnesses... to her murder.

I must not sound as menacing to her, because she nods and perches next to me on the bed. She reaches out to brush my hair from my forehead. "Yeah. I wanted to stay here with you, though."

I jerk my head away from her fingers. "I'm sure."

Her face hardens. "What does that mean? Are you still mad about earlier? Is that what this is all about? Are you in here, pouting?"

When I snort a denial, she says, "Well, that's what it seems like."

I toss my e-reader into her lap. It's been idle for so long while I've taken a break from looking into its horrific hall of mirrors that it's gone into sleep mode, so I wake it up with a push of the power button and a swipe across the screen. Chapter Seventeen pops up, but it takes a few seconds of Frankie reading the words for her to recognize them as her own.

Her jaw slackens. "Uh," she grunts as she expels her held breath.

"Don't bother trying to figure out how to spin this. I've

already met Dr. Nathanson and Frank Lipton, both of whom seem very familiar."

"Which one are you more upset about?" she asks.

"Does it matter?"

"Of course."

"I'd say I'm equally pissed off about both. For different reasons."

She gulps. "Okay. Well, which one do you want to yell at me about first?"

I swing my legs over the side of the bed and stand, so I'm no longer close enough to smell the cold, smoky outdoors still lingering on her hair and clothes. I show her my back to avoid seeing her infuriating victim's eyes.

"I don't even know where to start," I tell her.

"Dr. Nathanson isn't you," she chooses for me.

"Fuck me," I say with my hand over my burning eyes. "If we're going to have this discussion, you're at least going to respect me enough not to lie."

"It's true!" She comes up behind me and rests her face against my back.

I shrug her off and move away, but the room's not big enough for me to get as far as I want to be from her. I'm afraid the state's not big enough. But the rest of the house will have to do.

I rush from the bedroom and lead her on a speed-walking chase to the living room, where she's smart enough to keep her distance. She sits on the brick hearth in front of the fire. I pace behind the couch.

"So, what did you do? Start writing that book the minute you got home from our first date?"

"When I met you, I got the idea for this character," she admits. When I huff like a sullen teenager, she rushes on, "But you were only the start! Most of his traits are made up.

Anyway, the guy's not *all* bad. He loves kids, he's a registered voter, he donates to worthy causes..."

My stomach knots. "He's also a passive-aggressive, whiny asshole who reads chick lit and constantly wonders why he can't find his other half. You know why he can't? Because he's a passive-aggressive, whiny asshole."

"But—"

"I'm not done. I'm assuming at some point in the book, this Dr. Nathanson's personality does a complete one-eighty, and he becomes the type of guy worthy of being a chick lit leading man, not an *oaf*."

"It's an affectionate label!"

"My ass."

She sighs. "I can't believe this! He's not you!"

I stop pacing and stare her down. "You're right; he's not. You gave him plenty of upgrades. He's a doctor, for one. I guess nursing isn't glamorous enough for your hero, huh?"

"Oh, come on!"

"And he's hung like a horse. Not that you'd have a clue about my dick size, since you're not interested in seeing it."

She shoots to her feet. On her way out of the room, she yells, "You're *being* a dick!"

I figure I've earned the right, so I'm not going to apologize for it. This time, I'm the one following. I arrive at the door to our room in time to see her throw her bag on the bed and stomp into the bathroom. She comes back with her toothbrush and other toiletries and throws them slapdash into the open bag.

"Where are you going?" I demand.

"Away from you!"

"I don't think so. You still haven't explained yourself about using my picture for your literary identity."

Without a glance at me, she zips her bag. "You said you'd be Frank Lipton."

"In what parallel universe?"

"At the pub, way back in December."

When I continue to look blankly at her, fearing she's had a complete break with reality, she adds, "When you first met Betty. We were talking about pen names and ghostwriters. You said you'd be my 'face.'"

I laugh bitterly when I finally remember the conversation. "I was kidding!"

"No, you weren't. At least, I didn't think you were. I took you at your word."

"My 'word'? It was a joke!"

"How was I supposed to know that? You don't have the best sense of humor."

"Hey! My sense of humor is—" I stop, refusing to allow her to distract me with something unimportant. "Never mind. The fact that I was half-drunk that night may have been a clue."

"You're the one who kept insisting you were fine!" She crosses her arms over her chest. "So, now what? You're going back on your offer?"

I release a frustrated moan. "My offer was never a serious one!"

"Well, I took it seriously. I take my writing seriously. I'm sorry it's such a joke to you. I'd think you, of all people, would understand how hurtful it is when people don't place any value on what you love to do."

Her statement brings me up short. I open my mouth to say something, then close it again. Suddenly, I'm too tired for this conversation. Too tired for this scenario. Too tired for life.

She slumps next to her bag and stares at her hands in her lap. "I'm sorry. I thought you were sincere and wanted to help me with my writing."

"Then why didn't you tell me what you were going to do, before you did it?"

"I thought it was already understood and agreed upon!" she says irritably. "I didn't think you wanted a play-by-play. Sometimes when I talk about my writing, your eyes glaze over. I figured you weren't interested in the details."

"What?" I breathe the word more than say it. "Where did you—"

"And anyway, it was an experiment. I didn't expect it to work. I thought I'd put the books out there as Frank Lipton, and nothing would happen, so I'd go back to Plan A, submitting to agents and publishers, trying to get published the traditional way."

"Still using my face?"

She shrugs. "I don't know. I didn't have to think that far. The thing is..." She stands and slinks toward me, part hesitant, part eager. "It *has* worked. I mean, the books have only been out there for about a month, but... they're selling. A lot. Based on the emails Frank gets, most of it has to do with you."

I look down into her wide, brown eyes. Envisioning one of our future children looking up at me with those same eyes, I feel something in me soften. I try to regain my grip on my righteous indignation, but it's running away from me, and I can't grab it in time.

"Frankie."

"Nate, please. Don't be mad at me. The readers love the idea that *you're* the face behind the stories. I can't do this without you." Now the eyes go from glistening to full, and she chokes, "I just want to write, and be with you. Maybe this was my way of combining those two things." She blushes and looks down at her chest. "I don't know. It sounds stupid when I say it out loud."

I chuck her under the chin to entice her to look at me the

way she did before. It's intoxicating, and I want more. "No. It's not stupid. I wish you'd told me yourself sooner, that's all."

She smiles self-consciously. "I realize that now. I'm sorry."

Weakening. Weakening.

"I guess you're forgiven."

"And Nate?"

"Mmmm?"

"I like Bing Nathanson." She pulls me closer to her with a tug of one of the belt loops on my jeans. "A lot. And I've seen —and felt—enough of you, pressed against me, to know his physical traits aren't exaggerated."

My breathing speeds up in direct relation to my heart rate. "I don't know about that."

"I do." She trails a finger lightly along the zipper of my jeans. "All of his best attributes are yours. The others are fiction, to make him less perfect, more believable."

I gulp. She kisses my bobbing Adam's apple. Against my neck, she whispers, "I love you."

Before I can return the sentiment—true or obligatory— she catches my lower lip in her mouth and sucks on it. I wrap my arms around her back and let lust kick aside what little remains of my anger and hurt. After all, lust feels so much better than anger and hurt.

11

BECOMING FRANK

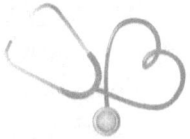

I'VE NEVER UNDERSTOOD THE CONCEPT OF SOCIAL MEDIA, but Frank Lipton loves that shit. And to help Frankie out and allow her to have more real writing time, I've taken over Frank's online presence. It's not that big of a deal. Twice a day, I sign in as him and drop a line or two. I've been instructed to be self-deprecating, yet confident, whatever that means. I usually talk about what "Frank" had for lunch. Isn't that what everyone else does?

However, I've drawn the line at writing Frank's blog, *Quite Frankly*, a collection of "his" rants about everything. Mostly about publishing, some about writing, and a little about being a man in a woman's world. Like I told Frankie when she suggested I pen the posts, I haven't written anything since college, other than a strongly worded email (and I conveniently left out that it was to a TV station that pre-empted *Dancing with the Stars* to air a football game), so she's better off writing *Quite Frankly* herself. Or not blogging at all. (Again, what's the point?)

Frankie doesn't share my opinion about the uselessness of blogging, but she did see the detriment to letting someone like me write more than 140 characters at a time, so I dodged that chore. Unfortunately, that means she dedicates an afternoon every weekend to writing several posts she can schedule to publish throughout the upcoming weeks, at her convenience, and that's one less afternoon she spends with me.

I didn't mean that to come out as petulantly as it did, but I'm going to let it stand. I have a right to be petulant, anyway. Right now, I spend most of my weekends either cleaning Frankie's apartment and doing her grocery shopping and laundry while she writes, or working shifts (for real) at Urgent Care. I figure I might as well be making some extra money if I'm not going to spend time with my girlfriend. And I don't count scrubbing mildew from her shower in a room adjacent to her as spending time with her.

Thankfully, my family's in all-out wedding mode, so they don't miss me. But even if they did, I'd be "working at Urgent Care" every single weekend to avoid them. Mom was leery enough about Frankie's proposed pen name; if she knew what was going on now, she'd come unglued. She'd invoke my middle name and everything. (It's Arthur, if you must know. Nick got Andrew; I got Arthur. It's like he and I were a huge psychological experiment from the get-go.)

And things are about to get even more interesting. Betty's been recruited into this scheme as the marketing guru, so she's been lining up public appearances. You know, signings and readings at book stores, conference panels, and the like. I wanted to say, "No way," but Frankie shot me a look I interpreted as, *"I'll give you a b.j. later,"* and at that point, I would have plotted to kill my own mother for one of those, so I capitulated. I know, I'm weak. I'm not proud of it, but there's no use being less-than-honest here.

As it happens, I'm rusty on my nonverbal cues, so that delightful implied favor never happened. Frankie got wrapped up in her writing; then it was late, and she had to get ready for another week on the road.

I guess I could have gone home and taken care of business by myself (well, in some other way, since I'm not that flexible, and if I were, I'd never leave my house), but for once, I can't be bothered. I'm using every ounce of energy to do whatever I need to do to keep Frankie happy. It's my new purpose in life.

Sometimes I'm more successful at it than at other times. For example, the other day, before I left for work, I got a rare early morning text from her. The thrill I felt at hearing the text chime reserved for her quickly nosedived, though, when I read it.

Don't forget to tweet today

I stared into my cereal bowl, watching the shredded wheat bloat, while I absorbed the disappointment. Then I dutifully logged into Twitter, my hands shaking so much that it took me three tries to key in the password, and I thumbed in,

Frank Lipton is pussy-whipped

I had tweeter's remorse almost immediately and added, *April Fool's!* as a reply to my own tweet. Unfortunately, it was April 3, so that didn't quite work. So I deleted the tweet altogether. But Frankie obviously saw it before I performed my lame damage control. The silent treatment I've received ever since can't be a coincidence.

I guess she's right to be pissed. But seriously? Her texting me to do my "job" as Frank is like me texting her to remind her to drink plenty of water and eat her fiber so she'll stay regular. At least if I sent her a health tip, it would be because I cared about *her* as a person, not because I was treating her like a personal assistant.

So she can give me the silent treatment all she wants, because I don't want to talk to her right now, anyway. I'd rather hear nothing from her than any Frank-related whip-cracking. Maybe it's best if we lie low this week.

Plus, we'll get plenty of together time this weekend when she and I fly out to Arizona with Betty as we combine Frank's first author appearance with an impromptu visit to Frankie's parents' house.

I'm not a fan of "impromptu."

I'm also trying to block out the visions of me hooked up to a lie detector machine in her dad's basement.

"Are you doing this Frank Lipton thing for my daughter just to get laid, Nathan Arthur Bingham?"

"No."

ZZZZAAAAAAAPPP!

Did I mention his polygraph includes a taser connected to my testicles? Yeah, in my nightmares, Frankie's dad makes Robert DeNiro look like a teddy bear.

But I don't have time to indulge in silly daydreams that place me in the role of fellow murse Gaylord Focker; I have a clothes shopping date with Betty.

* * *

"EXPLAIN to me again why I can't wear something from my closet," I say to Betty as she buries me in stacks of clothes amongst the disheveled racks at TJ Maxx.

"Frank's not a khakis-and-Oxfords kind of guy," she states, adding another two layers to the crippling pile in my arms.

"What's wrong with khakis and Oxfords?" I grumble.

"Nothing. For you. But they're not the image we're going for with Frank. Plus you don't have enough clothes. You can't wear the same thing to different appearances."

"Why not? There will be different people at each one."

The look she shoots me clearly conveys her assessment of

my intelligence, but in case I'm not sure, she follows it up with, "Don't be a dumb-ass, Nathaniel. People will take pictures with you and post them on Facebook. At least, we hope they will. We also hope the media will show up at a couple of these readings."

"We do?" I'm not sure if her vision of my future or the mound of clothes I'm buried under is making me sweat more.

"Yes. Exposure is important. I don't expect a lot of buzz at your first few appearances, but as word spreads..." She pushes me in the direction of the dressing rooms. "Okay, that should get you started."

When the dressing room attendant balks at the number of items I'm proposing to take into the stall with me, Betty levels him with a withering glare. "Just go with it," she commands him. "We're about to spend a shit-ton of money here."

He grudgingly allows me to stagger past, with Betty calling after me, "Even if you don't like the way something looks, come show me. I'll be the judge."

"Great," I mutter, throwing the heap of garments onto the floor in the nearest open stall I can find. I guess I should be glad Betty didn't insist on joining me back here.

Sixty sweaty minutes, half a dozen flashbacks of shopping trips with Heidi, and two near-panic attacks later, I have a whole new wardrobe for Frank that includes skinny jeans and pants in nearly every shade of the rainbow, denim and plaid flannel shirts with pearl snaps (I thought only cowboys wore those, but Betty told me to stop thinking and try on more clothes), wing tips, waistcoats, scarves (scarves!) and knit beanies to go with the black-framed glasses Betty already procured to match the Photoshopped ones in Frank's author photo.

As I hand over my credit card to the clerk, it must be obvious how sick I feel to be spending so much money on such ugly clothes, because Betty pats my arm and says, "Frankie will pay you back."

Not in the way I'd like, I can't help but think, but I smile bravely and say, "Whatever."

"No, really. It's part of her marketing budget."

Of course. All business.

I sign the receipt with the staggering total and grab the bags full of mass-market hipster clothes.

"Well, it's been real, Betts," I say in front of the store, stepping off the curb to walk in the direction of my car. "See you next—"

"Wait a second!" she interrupts. "We're not done. I told Frankie we'd work on your image today."

"Done," I state, lifting the shopping bags as evidence.

She laughs. "The clothes are only the beginning."

My heart plummets into my stomach. "Oh. Really? Because... I was hoping to get some stuff done around my house today. You know, since we'll be gone next weekend, and —" I back away from her, but she doggedly pursues.

"You'll have to clean out your gutters some other time. Put those clothes in your trunk and meet me over at that coffee shop." She nods in the direction of the café nestled in the strip mall. "I'll have a drink waiting for you. What's your poison?"

I debate running, but that's not very dignified. Plus, I wouldn't get far with all these bags, and I'm not dropping them, considering how much debt I went into to buy them.

Flatly, I reply, "Salted caramel latte," ignoring her barely contained smile and apparent judgment of my sodium-and-sugar-laden choice. She can bite me.

"Don't strand me with your fattening girlie drink," she dictates to my retreating back.

Confident she can't see it, I roll my eyes and stick out my tongue.

"And don't make faces at me! I'd rather be shoe shopping!" she shouts as she takes her X-ray vision in the opposite direction, heading down the strip mall's sidewalk.

* * *

OUR COFFEES WEREN'T EVEN cold before it was obvious we couldn't continue our conversation in public. For one thing, I felt ridiculous talking about someone imaginary as if he were a real person, much less as if *I* were that person. For another thing, it's one of my biggest fears to have someone approach me and test our ruse, so talking about Frank in the open is too risky.

I have a story (lie) ready, of course; I'm just not in a hurry to use it. We've decided I'll tell people I'm a nurse in real life (which some of them will already know) who wrote and self-published some books under a pen name. It's an elegantly simply cover. The question is, can I pull it off? I'm obviously okay lying to myself and the people closest to me, but when it comes to lying to strangers and mere acquaintances, I seem to always locate my conscience and become a stuttering, fumbling ninny.

When I lament this to Betty at her house (her immaculate house, I note with relief), she dismisses my worries. "You just need to say the lie enough to start believing it."

"Uh... I'm not sure I ever want to get to that point."

"You're going to have to, if this is going to work. When you're in Frank's clothes"—she nods to the bags in the middle of her loft office space—"you'll *be* him." Her eyes sparkle hopefully. And I like that. A little too much.

Whoa, Bingham. Do not *go there.*

With a cough, I insist, "I'm not an actor."

"Have you ever tried?"

I think back to high school when a couple of buddies and I auditioned on a whim for *Fiddler on the Roof*. I couldn't sing, but I somehow didn't think that would be a problem in a musical. And oddly enough, I was okay at the crazy Russian dancing we had to do. The drama teacher gave me a non-speaking/non-singing part (everyone was guaranteed a role) and told me I was part of the "ensemble." "Just dance and lip sync," she said.

Then one of the bit players got leveled on the football field and ended up in traction. He had one line. *Surely, Nate can handle that*, the drama teacher must have thought. Yeah. No. I was eventually able to do it in rehearsals without sounding like I was reading from a cue card, but on all three nights the show ran, I flubbed it.

I sip at the dregs of my coffee and set down the biodegradable paper cup that has started to make the drink taste like biodegradable ass. "Yeah, I have, actually. And I suck. There's something about memorizing lines that makes me freeze up."

She digs through the bags and pulls out a pair of black skinny jeans, a "vintage," bought-an-hour-ago-in-a-chain-store t-shirt, a waistcoat, and a scarf. "You're not going to be memorizing any lines here, so no problem. Go put these on." She nods toward her bedroom through an open archway in the loft.

Rubbing my neck, I sigh, "Really?" but rise from the sofa and take the clothes from her.

Mindful of the doorless room and positioning myself at an angle so she won't be able to see me unless she stands in the doorway, I strip to my skivvies.

From the other room, she raises her voice to be heard when she says, "By the time we're done today—and with some practice on your own during the week—being Frank will be second nature. There'll be no flubbing, because there'll be no thinking. Only instinct."

"No thinking. Perfect," I mutter at my ridiculous reflection while fumbling with the last piece of the outfit, the scarf.

How does this thing work, anyway? Something tells me I'm not supposed to wear it like I would one of my winter scarves. I'm not supposed to wind it around my neck and tuck it down into my vest, right?

Betty suddenly appears in the mirror behind me, making me jump.

"Hey! How did you know I wasn't naked in here?" I squeak, outraged.

"I peeked," she answers matter-of-factly, spinning me around by pulling on my shoulder and taking control of the scarf-winding. "Pay attention," she bosses, doing a series of complicated over-under maneuvers that results in a sloppy, bunched-up, "I-don't-give-a-damn" look. She produces *the* glasses from the neck of her sweater, where they've been hanging out with her girls for who knows how long. When she slides them onto my nose, they're warm and smell like fabric softener.

I turn back to the mirror and want to cry. "I look—"

"Like Frank. That's all that matters. Do you feel different?"

I think about it. "No. I generally feel ridiculous, and these clothes don't change that."

She laughs and pushes on my shoulder, holding on while she talks to my reflection. "Come on. Be serious."

"I am! What's the point in wearing such a pretentious t-shirt if I'm going to cover it up with this?" I finger the fringe (yes, fringe) on the scarf.

"Hipsters wear clothes for themselves, not for show."

"Bullshit."

Again, she laughs, but she releases my shoulder and moves away. "Yeah, I know. But that's the answer they'd give." She disappears into the en suite bathroom I wish I would have noticed earlier, considering it has a door.

"Well, this isn't 'hipster.' This is 'I'm trying hard to *look* like a hipster,' which is even worse!"

"Most people don't know the difference."

"Oh, that makes it okay, then. I feel like so much less of an idiot."

She returns with a hand mirror. Leading the way back to the office area, she tosses back at me, "Enough whining. Now, let's make Frank your bitch."

"For you, anything," I say, following her. Just how much I'm beginning to mean that is yet another pesky part of my current predicament, which I push to the back of my mind.

MEET THE AUTHORS

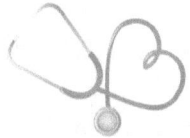

FLYING'S NOT MY FAVORITE THING. IT RANKS UP THERE with snowmobiling. Logically and intellectually, I have faith in the physics that make air travel possible—it's science, after all —but on a more primitive, base level, I don't know how it's possible. How is my body, plus the bodies of so many other people and thousands of pounds of luggage, encased in a 45-ton hunk of metal, suspended 35,000 feet in the air? Not even suspended. Moving. At more than 500 miles per hour. A sane person can't believe that's possible. It makes as much sense as believing in time travel.

I'm holding it together, though. I've been told all the statistics about flying being safer than driving so many times that I can recite them, too. I do, actually. In my head. Unfortunately, they're not all that comforting, and they merely highlight the improbability of my ever living to see age forty, but they manage to distract me from my surroundings.

Plus, I'm downright chill compared to Betty. She's done everything short of breathe into her barf bag during this flight. Frankie wanted the window seat, which was fine by Betty, who wanted the aisle seat so she could "climb the fuck out of here easier if shit starts to get real." That left me with the middle seat. When I'm not repeating death statistics in my head, I'm wondering if Frankie's parents will have alcohol and antibiotic ointment for me to treat the puncture wounds caused by Betty's nails in my right hand.

"Tell me again why we couldn't drive?" I hiss toward Frankie.

She leans around me to look at Betty and rolls her eyes. "You two are ridiculous."

"Us two? Why are you lumping me in with her? I'm perfectly calm."

She nods to my forehead. "It's freezing in here, but you're sweating."

With my free hand, I swab my forehead and wipe the moisture on my khakis. "I have a naturally low body temperature, so I'm hot-natured," I explain.

"Whatever. You're not in control of this thing, and it's freaking you out."

"That's..."

Actually, that's pretty astute. I've never thought of it that way before. But I'm not about to give her any credit for pinpointing part of my discomfort.

"That's silly. I'd be sweating a lot more if I suddenly had to fly this thing."

"What? Why would you have to fly the plane? Is something wrong with the pilot?" Betty screeches. Several people turn to stare. A tense hum builds around us.

For the fourth time, I extract her nails from my hand and set her claws in her own lap. "Nothing's wrong," I say loudly enough for the closest passengers to hear before leaning closer to Betty's ear and murmuring, "Get a grip. On something other than my hand."

"I'm sorry," she replies, uncharacteristically meek. "I'm scared shitless."

"Yeah? I hadn't noticed." No longer as embarrassed by her outburst and the ensuing attention it garnered, I soften and say, "Hey, I'm not thrilled about this, either, but it's going to be okay. Really." I take back her hand and ball it into a fist, which I tuck neatly into my palm. "There. If you had told me how freaked out you are by flying, I would have scored some Valium for you."

"Did you take some?"

I shake my head. "No. I don't like taking stuff like that."

"Why not?"

"Control," Frankie intones by the window.

"Do you have a problem with me?" I snap, my anxiety level too high for me to filter my irritation at her sudden interest in psychoanalysis.

Widening her eyes, she mildly replies, "I'm just stating the obvious. Sheesh."

"Well, now's not the time."

"Knowing is half the battle," she huffs, turning fully toward the window, showing me her narrow back. As if speaking to the clouds, she adds, "It's surprising you even drink, because you like being in control so much."

"I'm complex like that, I guess," I grumble.

"I could use a drink," Betty states. "Where's that cranky flight attendant with her annoying, aisle-blocking cart when you need her?"

The fasten seatbelt light comes on with a ding, and a nearly inaudible man's voice delivers a soliloquy that basically amounts to, *"The rest of this flight will be pure Hell. Hope you like those fingernail marks."*

On cue, the plane bounces, and Betty squeaks.

I look at my watch and sigh.

* * *

THE THREE OF us arrive in Arizona cranky, argumentative, and —in Betty's case—just shy of drunk. The hour-long drive from the airport in the rental vehicle (gas-guzzling tank, more like it) doesn't help. Frankie didn't want to drive, even though she was the only sober one of us who knew how to get to her parents' house, but I suppose she thinks I know the way by osmosis, because she's spaced out on her side of the SUV and won't say a word unless I specifically ask, "Which way now?"

The fourth time I have to backtrack, I explode, "This thing has the turning radius of a rhinoceros, so if we could avoid any more three-point turns, that would be fabulous."

"I assumed you'd be able to follow highway signs, since you know the name of the town we're going to," Frankie snaps back.

"The least you could have done was get a rental car with GPS if you didn't want to navigate."

"Anything else you'd like to bitch about?"

"Yeah! This vehicle is single-handedly killing rain forests in Borneo."

"We needed the space for our luggage!"

"It's a weekend! I still don't understand why you guys needed two full suitcases each. I fit everything I needed in my carry-on. A change of underwear and a toothbrush."

"Whatever. You have your own suitcase, so stop acting like you're such a rugged minimalist."

"Correction: Frank has a suitcase."

A moan comes from the backseat, followed by, "Do I need to come up there and sit between you two?"

Frankie whirls to say into the backseat, "Oh, you're already plenty in the middle."

"What's that supposed to mean?" Betty demands.

"You have an MBA. Figure it out." With that, Frankie folds her arms under her breasts and faces front once more while I try not to react too vehemently to what she's said.

"Maybe we should all just be quiet for a few seconds," I suggest, "before someone says something truly stupid."

"Someone already did," Betty grouses.

When things have cooled considerably (as in, icicles are forming between the three of us), I say to Frankie as innocuously as possible, so as not to start another argument, "Please, summarize the directions for the rest of the trip. Simple stuff. 'Turn left on Highway Blah-Blah, right on Wisteria Lane,' etcetera."

Staring straight through the windshield, she mumbles mulishly, "I don't know the street names or highway numbers. I just know how to get there."

I'd close my eyes, but that would be a conflict of interest with driving, so I breathe in deeply and hold it, along with my tongue. Finally, I trust myself enough to say, "Okay. Then you'll have to direct me."

"Fine. That's all you had to say."

Oh, I see. So, it's my fault now? I guess it is, if you trace this back to the night I drunkenly joked about posing as a male chick lit author. Or we could go even further back and blame me for accepting that blind date with Frankie in November. Hell knows I'm starting to rue that day. More than "starting to."

While I fume about the unfairness of it all, Frankie grumbles monosyllables at me.

"Right."

"Merge."

"Left."

By the time I jump down from Bigfoot in the Liptons' hot driveway, diplomacy isn't high on my social resumé. So when

Her Highness walks toward the front door, leaving Betty and me to sort out the luggage, I yell toward Frankie, "Hey! We left the porter back at the palace!"

I'll be damned if I'm going to be her flunky all weekend. I figure I've done enough already as her chauffeur, with much more to come later as her stinking alter ego.

Still, I can't say I blame her when my sarcasm results in her stomping away without a word.

Betty heaves her own bags from the cargo area and sets them on the blinding driveway. "She can come out later and get her stuff."

"Yeah, right. Like I'm going to go in there, meet her parents, and say, 'Oh, and your bags are waiting in the trunk.'" I extract said heavy, rolling suitcases and set them next to Betty's while I climb into the back to retrieve my duffel bag and smaller case, which have slid all the way against the back seats, out of my reach.

"Then take them in with us," she supplies mildly. When I step onto the driveway again and reach up to close the back hatch, she rests her hand on my arm. "Hey."

I stop, looking into her face to receive what I know is going to be a lecture I probably deserve.

"Listen. I know you don't want to be here."

"That's not—"

"And I don't blame you! You're an amazing guy to do this for her. I ask myself all the time why you agreed to it, and why you continue to do it, but you did. You do. So as long as you're in, let's at least try to have fun."

I stare at the tan and white pebbles that make up Frankie's parents' front "lawn." "Why do *you* do it?" I finally ask her what I've also been wondering for weeks now.

When she doesn't answer right away, I blink to focus my eyes and try to read her expression. It's difficult to translate.

Mostly, she looks perplexed by my question, so I clarify, "I mean, she treats you like an employee, not a friend."

She laughs. "Oh, that. Well, that's how it's always been with us."

"You don't strike me as the type who would put up with that, though. It doesn't gel with your personality."

Her right eyebrow lifts. "And what would that be? Demanding? Bossy?"

"No!" I try to reconcile the Betty I met back in December —and the one who shows up when Frankie's not around—with the one standing in front of me now. "Just strong-willed. I always thought you didn't take any crap from anyone."

"Not just anyone. She's different, though," she says, nodding toward the front door.

I'm about to ask why when Frankie's head pops out the door, as if we've summoned her by talking about her.

"What the heck, you two?"

"Hold your horses!" Betty snaps. "We're trying to figure out how to carry three people's luggage with only four hands."

Chastened, Frankie emerges fully from the house and walks toward us.

"See? I'm not a total pushover," Betty murmurs with a sly smile.

Frankie grabs her suitcases but says, "My parents are waiting inside, and you two are out here, whispering on the driveway."

I slam the hatch. "Nobody's whispering."

"Whatever. I know you're talking about me."

"Self-important much?" Betty mutters.

Before I can answer Frankie's accusation more seriously than Betty has, we arrive inside the house, which I now register to be one of the biggest private homes I've ever set foot in. The sun streams through the uncovered east-facing windows, but it's still cold in here. That's when I realize the air conditioning is on. In April. That's incredible, considering they had to de-ice the plane in Green Bay when we took off this morning.

As I gaze up three stories into a stained-glass skylight, the owners of the house enter the foyer. I turn my attention to them. And do a double-take when I recognize the male half of the couple.

The only picture Frankie has of them on display in her apartment was taken at a Halloween party several years ago. Her mom, Lucy, was wearing a leopard-print mask, a tight, matching bodysuit, drawn-on whiskers, and a tail. Her hair today matches the red hair showing in that picture. Frankie's dad, Sam, was fully kitted out as Batman in what I now realize may have been the actual costume from the Dark Knight movies. Frankie's never offered to show me a more conventional picture or a family portrait.

She's always assured me her parents are "boring" and doesn't talk much about them. The few things she has said have led me to believe they were wrapped up in their careers when she was a kid. This house, their retirement *mansion* in the desert, supports those claims. Still, I imagined them to be like the parents of every other person our age—mid-sixties, be-spectacled, wearing bland clothes from J.C. Penney's retirement line, and sporting blinding white sneakers from sunup until sundown (for arch support) and sun hats for pottering around in the garden.

I took her at her word they were ordinary, uninteresting folks. I guess I'm starting to understand taking Frankie at her word—about anything—isn't a bright thing to do, ever.

While she makes today's stunning introductions, nobody seems to notice me staring at Sam Lipton, the man *I* know better as Samuel Pembroke. Or as Frankie so eloquently called him when I had no idea we were talking about *her father*, "Samuel Fucking Pembroke."

Maybe they don't notice my staring because they've been more focused on Lucy's reaction to *me*. Upon seeing me for the first time, she gasps and covers her nose and mouth with both hands. She then clasps her hands to her chest and seems to be overcome with emotion when she gushes, "Sam, isn't it remarkable how much he looks like Henry?" For my benefit, she explains, "Henry is the love interest in the first book I ever wrote and published," as if it's the most normal thing to say to someone you've just met.

"*I* look like Henry," I try to clarify, while my brain screams at me about the man standing in front of me, one of the best-known pop culture icons of his generation.

Betty tilts her head and studies me. "Hmmm, that's not how I pictured him. Why did I always think Henry was blond?"

"No, no, no! He's tall, dark, and handsome! Nate, you have a bit more of a baby face than Henry, but otherwise it's uncanny!"

Swept up in the insanity of the surreal situation, I supply, "He must look like my older brother, then. Nick's always been described as the manly one."

"I'd like to meet this Nick character," Lucy says with a growl and wink.

"Mom! He's a person, not a character."

Lucy waves away Frankie's irritation. "Yeah, yeah. Fine. It's nice to meet you, Nate."

I stutter something socially acceptable while continuing to sneak glances at Frankie's dad and willing myself not to say or do anything embarrassing.

Lucy motions for us to follow her. "Everyone, drop your bags there. We'll deal with them later. I'm sure you're worn out from traveling. Isn't flying the worst nowadays? When we went to Russia last month for Sam's book research, I swore I'd never get on a plane again. We're going to cruise to destinations from now on. Make travel part of the trip."

In the massive kitchen that looks more like something from a movie set, not a room that anyone actually uses, Betty sits at the table for ten and asks, "So, Sam, what's your latest project?"

Riffling through cupboards, he answers, "It's a spy thriller, set in Cold War Russia. Hence, the research trip. I've immersed myself in the culture. I dream in Russian, and I don't even speak that language!" He opens the refrigerator, the top half of his body disappearing into the appliance's bowels.

Not sure what to do with myself, I lean against a wall, intending to observe while getting my bearings.

Lucy has other plans, though. "Wow. It's remarkable," she says, coming closer to me and touching my face.

I freeze, and she laughs.

"Sorry. It's like I conjured you up from my imagination. But it's been more than thirty years since I wrote that book!"

"Well, that's about when I was born, so maybe you *did*," I say with a nervous, choked chuckle.

"Don't encourage her!" Frankie moans.

Lucy backs away, so I feel able to breathe once more. She shoots a mock-wounded look in her daughter's direction. "I'm just having a little fun," she claims in a pouty voice that's all-too-familiar.

Great. It's hereditary.

I clear my throat. "I had no idea you... That is, Frankie forgot to mention that you and Mr. Lipton are writers, too."

She tilts her head and blinks. "'Too'?"

From near the fridge, Frankie quickly says, "Mom, Dad, I forgot to tell you, Nate's an author. While we're here, he's going to attend his very first public appearance, a book signing in Phoenix."

My eyes nearly bug from my skull at this unexpected development. To my relief, Betty's wearing an expression that looks how mine feels, so I can tell I wasn't the only one who assumed incorrectly that Frankie's parents were in on this whole thing.

Sam, still handing sandwich fixings to Frankie to place on the counter, says from inside the fridge, "You don't say."

"How exciting!" Lucy cries, then taking in my face, sobers. "Oh, my. Are you okay?"

"Uh," I'm not sure how to play my part in this horrific lie.

"He's shy!" Frankie blurts, drawing her mother's attention away from my face. "You know, it's all new to him, and he's worried it's not going to work out, and not many people know about his writing." As soon as Lucy looks to me again for confirmation of this, Frankie shoots me a wide-eyed *"Go with it. Or I'll kill you"* look.

I smile shakily at Lucy and dig deep for some of the Frankisms I've practiced with Betty, who mouths from behind Lucy's back, *"Hobby."* "Uh, yep. Until recently, it was just my silly little hobby. It's weird to know that strangers read what I've written. It would be even crazier if friends and family read it."

"Well, your secret's safe with us," Lucy says with a reassuring pat to my arm.

Sam comes out of the fridge for good and dumps an armload of condiments on the counter. "What genre do you write?" he asks after sniffing a suspect jar of mayonnaise and tossing it in the trash.

Frankie answers for me, again, "Chick lit. Under the pen name Frank Lipton, in honor of me."

At the mention of that detail, I fear Lucy may swoon. "Oh, how romantic!"

"Isn't it?" Frankie asks, blowing me a kiss that I let sail over my shoulder and splat against the wall.

Sam laughs as he peels open three plastic containers of deli meat. "I'm shocked Frankie would be romantically involved with a writer. I thought for sure we'd scared her away from that element for life."

"So, you're Samuel Pembroke," I finally acknowledge out loud.

He grins and nudges Frankie. "You really need to start telling people who we are before you bring them to meet us, Sweet Pea. It's not nice to ambush people."

Sullenly, Frankie replies, "You're my parents. Period. There's nothing else to tell."

"I'm sure Spielberg's kids say the same thing," Betty drawls from the table, where she's rubbing her temples.

"Anyway," Frankie continues, "I wanted to make sure Nate was with me for the right reasons, not because of who you are or what your connections may be."

Looking horrified, Lucy admonishes, "Frankie!" To me she says, "I'm sure there are no worries about that." I have a feeling she's picturing "Henry" when she makes those doe eyes at me and flutters her lashes.

"Huh-huh." I move away before she touches me again. "I'm starving," I lie as I go to work making a sandwich.

Lucy follows me but keeps a respectable distance.

While passing me the mustard, Sam levels a critical look at me that opens the taps on my sweat glands. "I guess I misunderstood something. I thought you were a nurse."

"I am. I—"

"He *is*," Frankie interjects. "Yes. He is. But he writes in his spare time."

"Ah, I see. I remember all too well when writing didn't come even close to paying the bills."

"Whatever, Dad. You don't remember any such thing."

"Yes, I do!"

"We do!" Lucy insists. "We're old, but we're not *that* old."

"You guys have had it so good for so long that any memories you have of the 'bad old days' are as much a figment of your imaginations as the stories you write."

"Are not! I remember eating mac-n-cheese for a month straight. The powdered cheese kind, not that fancy stuff."

"Whatever."

This isn't happening. This isn't happening. I'm not making a sandwich in Samuel Pembroke's kitchen, pretending to be a writer, because my girlfriend has told her bestselling author parent(s) I wrote the books she wrote. Not happening. Not happening.

"Slap together a ham and cheese for me, will ya, Nathaniel?" Betty requests. I glance up at her to acknowledge her request, and the calm in her eyes reduces my heartbeat by a few beats per minute. Her slow blinking conveys, *"It's going to be okay,"* while she tacks on, "Extra mustard and pickles, please."

"Sure," I mumble.

When I deliver her custom-made sandwich on rye, she hisses in a stage whisper, so I can hear her above the three Liptons, still bickering a few feet away, "They're just people. Freak not."

I wish it were that easy.

13
TALL TALES

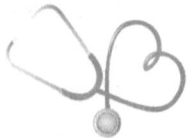

I'VE SPENT MOST OF THE DAY IN THE POOL, ALTERNATELY floating around on a raft and dunking to cool off, so I should be plenty rested, but living a lie is predictably exhausting. Also, soul-searching and sunburn haven't improved my mood.

I escaped to the pool to avoid Lucy's repeated generous offers to use hers or Sam's offices, if I needed some writing time.

The first time she said it, I blinked blankly at her. Then I remembered a "writer" like me would probably be going through withdrawals. It was obvious she thought I was a weirdo when I responded, "Oh, I'm okay. No writing for me this weekend. I didn't even bring my laptop." I might as well have said I left my child at home in a dog crate, with plenty of granola bars and bottles of water.

Lucy must have thought I was simply being strong, because she extended the offer three more times. Finally, Frankie said proudly, "Nate understands the importance of work-life balance. He knows how to engage with real-life people."

I could tell by Sam's sigh and Lucy's eye-roll that the compliment wasn't for my benefit but was, rather, a back-handed criticism of them. I'm not sure what disturbs me most, Frankie's scary acting (lying) abilities, her radiating resentment, or her propensity to turn every statement into a passive-aggressive dig at her parents.

Betty was the one who proposed we hang out at the pool when Sam and Lucy started shooting wistful looks toward their office doors, and I grabbed at her suggestion like a drowning man would one of those foam noodles. Of course, Betty and Frankie didn't want to get in the pool. They preferred lazing under umbrellas on loungers, Frankie in a tiny red bikini, Betty in a surprisingly modest one-piece black number. It was just as well they didn't join me in the water. I liked having the kidney-shaped concrete hole-in-the-ground to myself, so I could better wallow in the current mess I find myself.

Wait. That makes it sound like I think I had no part in getting here, and I'm not claiming that at all. My own culpability may be the most depressing thing about this situation.

Now, Frankie and I are alone in the room we're sharing, another element of the make-believe portion of our relationship. Frankie didn't offer me a separate room, nor did Lucy blink when Frankie told me to follow her to "our" room. Apparently, Frankie's parents don't know about her abstinence pledge, either. It doesn't matter, I guess. What's one more fudged detail?

After she changes into a maxi dress I've never seen before (and which does nothing for her figure, I think uncharitably), Frankie flops onto the bed and turns her back to me, curling up for what appears to be a pre-dinner nap.

That should be my cue to walk my towel-wrapped self into the bathroom with a stack of clothes, get dressed, and go see if Sam and Lucy need help in the kitchen, but I'm worried I don't have all the information I'll need to hold my own in a conversation with them.

"Hey."

She doesn't move, but I know she can't already be asleep, so I continue, "The best con artists know you have to get your story straight with your accomplices before you execute a swindle on a mark. Rookie mistake."

Still, she doesn't react.

"So, if I'm going to be your shill all weekend, maybe you should tell me everything you've told your parents. Or not told them. Or whatever."

"I'm tired. I don't feel like arguing."

"Too bad. I'm tired, too. But if you don't start talking, I'm going to drive my tired ass to the airport and go home."

She rolls onto her back, rests her hands under her breasts, and bestows on me an unimpressed stare. "You know everything now."

"I doubt it, so let's recap. Your parents are authors, one a bestseller of epic proportions. Like, *the* bestseller to end all bestsellers—"

"I knew you'd be like this when you found out."

My chest tightens at the implied criticism. "And I have a right to be! I'm sorry if it annoys you or pisses you off or resurrects childhood demons or makes you jealous—"

"I'm not jealous of either of them."

I snort. "Right. Well, as convincing as that is, my point is, I wouldn't be nearly as starstruck if you'd told me before I was face-to-face with a literary icon."

"You said you didn't even like his books."

"Please, tell me you didn't tell him I said that."

"It's good for him to hear it every once in a while."

I rub my face and groan. "Unbelievable."

She sits up and spins on her butt so she's facing me, her

knees pulled to her chest. "You have no idea what it's like to have parents like that."

"You've got me there; I don't know what it's like to have rich, famous parents. But nobody's parents are perfect. You've met mine."

"Yours are normal."

I laugh bitterly. "On what planet? But at least I gave you a heads up before I introduced you."

"You made them sound like lunatics. But they're human. So are my parents. Flawed, annoying, self-centered humans. I love them, but they're not good parents."

"That's their biggest crime?"

"It's a pretty big one to me, since I'm their daughter."

I lean against the bathroom door frame. "Well, I've had a few hours to adjust to that bombshell, so I'm more pissed off that you lied to them about *me* than I am about your not telling me about *them*. Within seconds of meeting them, I was lying to them left and right about everything! Do you realize how awkward that was for me?"

"So you had to tell a few fibs, big whoop. I've told you before, they don't need to know I write."

"I still don't understand that."

Wrapping her arms around her legs and resting her head against her knees, she whines, "Because that's all we'll ever talk about. It's bad enough already, as it is. It's like they don't know how to talk about anything else. At least when they think I'm just a woman climbing the corporate ladder, they have something else to talk about—usually their disappointment in my not pursuing a more creative career. But still. It adds some variety to our conversations."

I narrow my eyes at her as the true reason finally clicks into place for me. "Ah. You don't want to give them the satisfaction of knowing you inherited their talent."

She lifts her head and rolls her eyes. "Whatever."

"No, no. I'm right." For the first time in weeks (maybe months), that persistent mental heaviness resulting from near-constant confusion lifts somewhat. "You don't *want* them to approve of you. You get off on needling them with what they perceive as your boring career choice. It's your backwards way of rebelling."

"And you fancy yourself inheriting *your* parents' abilities to read and psychoanalyze people."

"Nope. You're just that transparent."

"You know nothing."

As mad as I am at her, the sad way she says that last thing weakens my resolve to punish her for her part in my current predicament.

Now I move to the bed, sitting on the edge, my slumped back to her. "I feel like I *don't* know anything. Even the sleeping arrangements here were a surprise. Your parents think we sleep together?"

She shrugs. "It's none of their business. It's not like this will be the first time we've slept in the same bed."

I run my hand through my damp hair. "I'm flying blind here, being strung along by you, expected to 'just go with it.' Everything. You know me better than that. If I'm going to continue doing this, I need you to keep me in the loop. Better yet, I need you to include me in the decision-making."

"You never would have agreed to lie to my parents about being a writer."

I think about it for a second, then reply, "Maybe not. But that should have been my choice."

The mattress moves, and suddenly she's pressed against my warm-from-the-shower bare back, her chin resting on my shoulder. "I'm sorry. I thought this was the best way. Isn't it easier to stay in character if you're never out of character?"

I bring my hand up to her cheek and press her head against mine. "They're two different characters, though. There's the writer who writes under a pen name and the literary persona of that writer."

She turns her head and kisses my cheek next to my ear, then whispers, "I know who you really are, though. That's all that matters."

My eyes drift closed, and I shiver with pleasure. She rubs her hands across the gooseflesh on my shoulders. My towel twitches and peaks.

"Frankie," I murmur.

"Shhh." She scoots sideways and pulls me backwards until I quit resisting and lie flat on my back, my eyes still closed, my legs dangling off the side of the bed. My lower back cracks, but I barely have time to register the hurts-so-good pop before I feel her tug my towel open and the room's cool air hits my exposed flesh. The contrast of her hot, silky mouth around me makes me gasp. I twine one hand through her hair and hold on.

This *is* happening.

* * *

I LIE on the bed for a while, still out of breath, still seeing stars, still aroused, but feeling cheated, despite what I've just experienced. It was, technically, the most intimate thing Frankie's ever done to me; yet, I'm so alone. I should be basking; I should feel satisfied; I should have perma-grin.

Really, I just feel used.

More than anything, I'd like to be as physically alone as I feel. Fortunately, she refuses my obligatory offer to return the favor, claiming we don't have time. She hops to her feet, straightens her dress, smooths her hair, and says, "I'll see you downstairs," while escaping from the room.

And now I have to go sit through dinner and pretend to be someone I'm not. I guess it's a good thing I'm starting to forget who I really am, anyway.

I throw on some clothes, re-wet and finger-comb my tousled hair, and plod down the stairs to join the others. The house is quiet, so I follow the smell of grilling steaks to the paved outdoor eating area, where I find Frankie and her parents. Lucy transfers dishes from an old-fashioned tea cart to the massive stone and wrought-iron table while Sam layers thick, fresh-from-the-grill steaks on a platter.

"I was glad when Frankie told me you're not a vegetarian," he says to me when I arrive at the table, "because meat's on the menu tonight."

"Nate knows we're all meat eaters," Frankie purrs suggestively.

I gulp and shift from foot to foot, shoving my hands in my pockets, then removing them when they brush against the Judas in my pants.

Lucy glances up from her side dish arranging and laughs. "Oh, my. You've made him blush!"

"I'm sunburnt," I claim too defensively.

The three of them obviously don't buy my excuse but let it go. "Sit," Lucy tells the rest of us. "I have to run back inside and grab the sangria."

We do as we're told as she disappears into the house.

"Where's Betty?" I inquire, in both an effort to change the subject and get information.

Frankie lifts her cell phone from the table and keys a message into it. "She's still upstairs," she says. "Always late, you know."

Actually, that's not true. She's never been late for anything the two of us have been forced to do alone, not even something as casual as our shopping date. I was expecting it, and I *loathe* waiting, so I gave her a meeting time a half hour earlier than I wanted to get started. She surprised me by texting me before I'd even left my house: *Where the eff r u?*

She does tend to keep Frankie waiting, though, I've noticed. When we went snowmobiling at the cabin, Betty showed up nearly an hour after she told the rest of us she'd be there. She had grocery bags in tow, and a large coffee from the tiny donut shop in the closest town, but she offered no apologies for making us wait. Instead, she ordered us to help her carry the food into the house, leading the way to the front door, taking her time unlocking it. The grumbles from the group appeared not to affect her at all.

"Tell her we'll wait for her," Sam says tonight, leaning back in his chair. "She must have been tired, if you two beat her down here."

Before I can decide if his statement contains a double meaning, Lucy returns and fills our glasses with sweet-smelling red liquid that reminds me of Communion wine, only fruitier.

While we wait for Betty, Sam and Lucy fill the time by telling me all about the books they're both currently writing, or their WIPs. I know from the past few months with Frankie that WIP is an acronym for "work in progress," although with Lucy, you never know. She seems like a spunky gal with plenty of real-life stories to back up her fictional characters' peccadilloes.

Oh, man. Did I just get a picture of my girlfriend's parents having kinky sex? Yes. Yes, I did.

I gulp some sangria. It's so sweet it hurts my teeth, but I don't care.

The elder Liptons spout a bunch of other writers' terminology with which I'm unfamiliar, but they think I know all about, considering who they believe me to be. I've gleaned their meanings through context, in most cases, but between ARCs and betas and epubs and mobis and galleys and trads and indies, it's like a whole other language. Frankie's obviously been dumbing it down when she talks to me about her writing, and it hasn't done me any favors. I can't so much as converse intelligently about this stuff at dinner with her parents; how am I going to fake this whole thing at a reading and signing tomorrow?

Eventually, Sam sighs. "I guess we'll start without Betty; the food's getting cold."

"She said she's on her way," Frankie informs us. "Let's eat."

Sounds good to me. Self-loathing is a hungry business. Cole slaw and beans and short cobs of corn beckon to me from their bowls and platters.

Betty shuffles to the table in silk pajamas just as we start to pass around the sides. Rubbing her head and yawning, she says, "This looks delish. I wanted to keep sleeping, but when Frankie texted me what was on the menu, I had to come down."

Sam grins at her. "It's much more fun to cook for a group. Lucy and I become so immersed in writing sometimes that we barely pause to eat, much less to cook. Half the time, we eat standing in the kitchen, just long enough to inhale a sandwich or a bowl of cereal. Then back to the keyboard!"

"I love being in the groove, though!" Lucy simulates typing. "You know, when your fingers can't move fast enough? And the ideas are flowing, and the characters are talking and..."

The clank of the earthenware bowl of barbecued beans accompanies Frankie's loud sigh.

Sam shoots her a look but takes his helping of beans and says to me, "Tell us a little more about your work in pediatrics. That must be interesting."

Relieved to be talking about something I actually know, I reply, "It is. And busy. But entertaining. I love the patients. Kids are funny, even when they're sick."

Lucy shivers. "That's the one part of parenting I never got used to taking care of a sick kid."

"The *one* part?" Frankie mutters.

I chuckle to cover my discomfort and rush ahead before anyone can comment on Frankie's snide remark. "Oh, well, they're not *my* kids, so I guess it's a little different. I feel bad for them that they don't feel well, but there's no worry attached to it. I think that's what makes taking care of a sick kid when you're a parent so much harder."

"No, it was mostly the mess I didn't like," Lucy says with a giggle. "I always knew she'd get over whatever the latest thing was, but it was so tedious and messy and time-consuming. Impossible to concentrate when there's a sick kid around. They're always needing something."

"Pulling you away from your imaginary boyfriends, huh, Mrs. L?" Betty teases with a wink.

"Well, yeah!"

Frankie cuts vigorously on her steak, her knife squeaking against her plate.

Lucy, either oblivious or indifferent to her daughter's obvious anger, says matter-of-factly, "I've never been a nurturer, you know? I could play Barbies for hours or make up fantastic bedtime stories, but the day-to-day nose-wiping and report card-signing and meal-making? Not for me. Sam was always much better at that."

He chortles. "Did I have a choice? One of us had to do it." There's no bitterness in his tone. If anything, he sounds amused and charmed by his wife's self-proclaimed lack of maternal instinct.

Frankie, tossing down her utensils, shows she's neither

amused nor charmed. "I'm so sorry I was such a fucking burden! Raising me had to have been a real chore! Funny thing is, I didn't ask to be born."

I quietly set down my fork and place my hand on her back, between her shoulder blades. "Hey."

"Oh, so you're going to take *their* side now?" she turns on me, jerking away from my touch. "Figures!"

"I'm not taking anyone's side. I'm just... You know, we're trying to eat."

She rolls her eyes. "Well, I'm not hungry, listening to them boast about how unconventional they are, trying to convince you they're the 'cool' parents."

Lucy laughs. "That's not at all what we're saying! If anything, I'm being painfully honest about my shortcomings."

Sam appears not to be concerned by his daughter's outburst, as he continues to cut and eat his steak.

Betty surveys me over the rim of her glass of wine, then immediately goes back to her food, as well.

"I'm sick of it!" Frankie yells. "The minute you two have an audience, you become Samuel Pembroke and Lucinda Rathbone, bestselling author-couple. It makes me want to barf!" She smirks. "Of course, I wouldn't bother you to clean it up, Mother."

"Oh, for goodness' sake."

"You know, Nate's not a reporter with the *New York Times*. He's not here to observe your witty banter or gain insight into your 'process.'"

Quickly, I say, "Although I'm sure it's fascinating."

"Oh, yeah. So exciting," Frankie drawls at me. "Shut away for hours in their pigsty offices, where they stare at their computer screens, scrawl nonsense on note cards, and get lost down the rabbit-hole of the Internet, supposedly researching but not sure what they originally went on there to find. Then inspiration strikes, and it can be *days* without a glimpse of one or both of them, depending on if they're inspired at the same time. When they're not inspired, look out! Miserable, grouchy assholes, both of them." She turns her scorching attention back to Lucy. "Barbies for hours, Mom? Bedtime stories? I think not. I've heard you tell longer, more fascinating tales to a tape recorder than you ever took the time to tell to me, so drop the act. There was a lot more than one thing about parenthood you never grasped. You sucked at the whole thing."

"Tell us how you really feel," Lucy mutters.

That seems to shut Frankie up, but after a few seconds' awkward pause, she looks down at the linen napkin she's twisting between her fingers and says meekly, "I feel abandoned."

The vulnerability in her voice knocks the wind out of me. I take shallow breaths, feeling alarmingly close to weeping, then more-than-close when I see a fat tear, then two, then three, drip from her eyes and soak into the napkin. I cup her shoulder in my hand and draw her closer to my side.

Betty sips her wine and stares at the underwater pool lights.

Sam finally sets down his silverware. "You're a grown woman. And you're here. How have we abandoned you?"

She shakes her head and cries harder but manages to explain, "If I didn't visit you, I'd never see you. And even when I do visit, I spend most of the time by myself, while you guys write, write, write."

"It's how we put this food on the table," he reasons.

Ticking them off on her fingers, Frankie adds, "And the pool in the backyard. And the cars in the garage. And all the other things you have that you don't even bother enjoying, because you're too wrapped up in your fucking imaginary worlds!" She pushes away from the table, the metal legs of her chair scraping against the textured concrete. "Just forget it."

"If you were a writer, you'd understand."

Her mom's words stop Frankie mid-stride on her way to the back door.

"It's not something we can control sometimes," Lucy continues. "It's a compulsion. When I'm not writing, I'm not me."

I try to be as sneaky as possible about wiping the runaway tear from the side of my nose before putting my napkin on the table and rising to stand with Frankie.

When I reach her side, I place my hand on the back of her neck and give her a gentle squeeze. "Come on. Let's go for a walk."

For the second time, she shrugs off my hand. "I don't need to take a walk," she snipes. "Leave me alone."

Stung, I watch her enter the house, leaving me to face humiliation after her public snub.

"Don't worry about her," Sam says, waving me back over. "Come on. Finish your dinner. There's no need for her to ruin everyone's night."

At the risk of being rude, I turn my back to him and stride around the side of the house, where I hope there's a gate. There's not. I return to the pool area, stalking across the patio on my way to the other side.

Betty says, "Yep. That way," but she doesn't try to stop me or say anything else.

Sure enough, I find a gate leading to the front yard. I lift the latch and push on the slatted wood, which scrapes against the gravel path.

Maybe Frankie doesn't need a walk, but I do.

* * *

Two hours later, I'm nursing a blister between my first and second toe, because flip-flops are *not* proper walking shoes, and I'm starting to worry about the wildlife that may be wandering around here that we don't ever have to worry about in Wisconsin. Bears, yes. Scorpions and snakes in April? No.

Plus, the scorching desert temperatures fall off to amazing lows at night. The shorts and t-shirt that were perfectly comfortable during daylight aren't cutting it now that the sun's gone down.

I'm limping and shivering on the shoulder of the road when one of the passing cars slows and pulls behind me, spotlighting my legs. I half-turn but continue walking when I don't recognize the low-slung vehicle. *Please, don't talk to me; don't talk to me; don't talk to me.*

"Yo, Nathaniel!"

I halt, squint at the lights, and backtrack toward them, shielding my eyes with my hand the closer I get. She kills the lights.

Standing next to the passenger seat of the open-topped car, I ask Betty, as if I care, "Where'd you get this thing?"

"It's one of Sam's," she answers. "Get in."

I hesitate. "I don't know."

"Come on. You've been wandering the desert for hours, like some kind of Biblical outcast."

Stroking the shiny turquoise metal and fingering the window slot, I avoid her eyes when I say, "I don't know what the hell I'm doing."

"You're taking everything remarkably in stride. And doing exactly what you've been asked to do."

"Commanded, you mean?"

She tilts her head and tsks. "Now, now. Don't go all self-pitying on me."

I open the door and slide into the leather bucket seat.

After I close the door, the two of us stare through the windshield, but the car remains stationary. I hold my hands out in front of me and soak up the heat blasting through the vents.

"You know, you should be thanking me," Betty begins with excess cheer after a long, gloomy silence.

"Why's that?" I contribute automatically.

"Lucy wanted to come looking for you, but I told her I'd handle it." She cups her hands around her mouth and trills, "'Henry! Henry! Where are you?'"

Despite my melancholy mood, I chuckle at her impersonation.

Encouraged, she continues, placing her hand on my upper arm, "'Oh, Henry! I was so worried about you! You could have gotten lost! Or stung by a double-headed green-dicked scorpion! Come home now, and I'll make you a hot toddy.'" She laughs more than speaks the last sentence, when my own laughter at her monologue proves contagious.

I playfully shrug off her hand.

Giggling, she turns on the headlights and checks over her shoulder for oncoming traffic. As she pulls onto the road in a shower of gravel against the undercarriage (not sure Sam would be thrilled about that), I sober and ask, "Can we drive for a while? I'm sick of walking, but I don't want to go back there yet."

She stops laughing, but the smile stays on her face. "Sure," she replies. "This baby's got GPS, so I'm sure we can find our way back eventually."

I let that be the last word for a while. Propping my elbow against the top edge of the door, I rest my cheek against my hand and watch the desert speed past us. Finally, after a few minutes, I ask, "How'd you find me?"

"Lucy planted a tracking device on you," she immediately

supplies, then laughs and says to my slack jaw and wide eyes, "Just kidding! Gosh. You walked in a straight line."

Relieved the tracking device was a joke, I nevertheless muse, "Yeah, but how did you know that? Or which direction I walked? I could have gone in any number of straight lines."

She sighs but doesn't answer for so long that I think she's not going to answer at all. Then she says, "Fine. I followed you right away."

"You've been following me this whole time? In this car?"

"I was worried about you."

I privately marvel at my lack of awareness of my surroundings that someone could tail me for two hours without my noticing. There go my non-existent CIA or FBI aspirations.

"It's flat around here. I stayed way back and parked a few times, giving you your space but keeping an eye on you."

"Creepy."

"I knew you were upset! And you don't know this place, so I was afraid you'd get lost."

The unsettled feeling I have suddenly has little to do with being creeped out and more to do with the sudden awareness she's still wearing those silky pajamas. That scares me even more.

"Well, thanks, I guess," I mumble.

"You're welcome. You know, we can't lose you. You have an appearance to make at a bookstore tomorrow." She pushes against my shoulder to let me know she's joking. Half-joking, anyway.

Wind noise and the whisper of the tires on the highway are the only sounds for a few more miles. Then I ask, "So, who *is* Lucy, anyway? I didn't recognize her pen name when Frankie said it." And it hardly seemed like the time to delve further into the subject.

Gliding to a stop at a four-way intersection that looks like part of the set of a ghost town in a Western, Betty checks for other cars that aren't there and pulls through. "Lucinda Rathbone? She writes paranormal romances."

I wrinkle my nose. "Like love stories with ghosts?"

"Oh, don't pretend you don't read them. I know you do."

I merely laugh, figuring a stronger denial would only make me look guilty as charged.

"They're not that bad," she continues. "Far-fetched sometimes, but that's kind of the point. She does a good job of poking fun at the genre a little, so her stories don't come off cheesy, like some of the more earnest books in the genre."

"So you've read all of her stuff?"

She snorts. "No way. She's published, like, 70-something books. Two a year since before I was born."

My mouth drops open.

"Yeah. She's amazingly prolific. I read most of her stuff when I was a teenager. I used to skip around and read the sex scenes. They were intense." In the lights from the dash, I think I detect a blush.

Her mention of sex reminds me of what happened between Frankie and me before dinner, and I can't seem to summon the appropriate laughter or teasing tone in response to her admission, so I remain mum.

"I was a teenager," she repeats, a sharper edge of defensiveness in her tone.

"Huh? Oh. Yeah. I mean, that's absolutely age-appropriate," I hasten to reassure her.

"It was!"

"Yeah, I know."

"Then what's up with the judgmental vibe all of a sudden?"

"What? No. I... I... I got distracted, that's all."

"I see. Whatever. As if you haven't read the book."

"What the hell are you talking about?"

She grunts then replies, "You don't have to pretend you don't know about everything."

"I know nothing," I insist.

"As for being preoccupied with sex, I'm not, abnormally. It's just easy for Frankie to think less about it, since she's obviously getting it a lot more regularly than I am."

"Hey!"

"Whatever, Nathaniel. There's no reason to deny it. It's not 1930, and I'm not her mom. Actually, her mom would be more than okay with it, too."

I rub my jaw. "Can we please talk about something else?"

I may be completely flummoxed about whatever else Betty's alluded to during the past five minutes, but one thing's for sure: she's included in the growing list of people not aware of Frankie's abstinence pledge. Hmm. Not sure why Frankie wouldn't tell her best friend something like that, but it's not my place to set Betty straight on it.

Plus, I really do want to talk about something else.

After her outburst, Betty seems embarrassed, and I can't think of anything else to discuss, so the tension builds in the car until, by unspoken agreement, we return to the house. She stops on the driveway, and I get out, even though she doesn't say a word. As soon as I close the door, she zooms toward the back of the house, where the driveway curves and leads to the garage I noticed earlier, behind the pool.

I stare at the after-image of the taillights long after they've disappeared. My shivering has nothing to do with the air temperature.

14

THE BOOK SIGNING

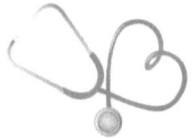

I WOULD HAVE PREFERRED PREPARING FOR THE READING AND signing by myself. Alone. Without other people around. Talking to me. Giving me tips. Trying to encourage me not to be nervous. (That has the opposite effect, people!) Fussing with my scarf.

Okay, actually, I need help with that last thing. The day I don't is when it's time to turn in my man card for good.

Everything else, though? I could do without.

"You're going to wear *those* pants? Can you even sit down in them? What are they, man jeggings?" Frankie fires at me.

I've already tested that I can sit in these, but I'm not going to admit it was one of my chief worries at first, too. Nor am I going to reveal I have to do a bit of shifting of things before-hand to prevent painful pinching of my private parts. Instead, I look down at my legs and choose to address the last in her series of questions.

"Jeggings? No. They're skinny jeans."

"But you're not skinny."

My head snaps up so I can regard her through the bath-room mirror. "What? Well, I'm not *un*-skinny, either."

"No, but..."

Betty fluffs my scarf, then yanks on it to even the fringed ends. I stumble into her before regaining my balance.

"Leave him alone," Betty says. "You're just nit-picking because it wasn't your idea. If I remember correctly, I invited you to go shopping with us, but you were too busy writing."

"Yeah. I'm a writer. I have to do it whenever I have the time."

"Then be content with your choices and stop ragging on the ones you've delegated to us."

"Do these pants make me look fat?" I ask Betty, trying to turn to the side to see my butt in the mirror but unable to do so, since she's still tugging on the scarf.

"No. Hold still. And don't ever ask anyone that again. Frank would *never* ask that. Neither should you. You should be getting into character."

Frankie sighs behind us. "Seriously? Does there have to be a 'character'? Just go out there, read the excerpt you chose, answer a few questions, sign some books. Done."

Finally, my scarf meets Betty's aesthetic approval, so she steps away from me, but she says, "Run your fingers through your hair. It's too perfect."

"Too perfect? It's called 'combed.' It's not like I have it all slicked back." I scratch my neck.

"Don't touch the scarf!"

"It's itchy!"

"You'll get used to it. Don't mess it up. Mess up your hair instead. Tousle it. You know, sex hair. Or 'I've been sitting at a keyboard all day, working hard at a particularly difficult scene.'"

"Hello! Is anyone going to answer me?"

We simultaneously swivel and blink at Frankie. Arms folded across her chest, she does everything short of tapping her foot to display her displeasure at the two of us.

I can't remember her asking a question, but I can tell by the look in her eyes that it would be unwise to admit that, so I gape while desperately searching my memory of the past few minutes for something to answer.

Before I can utter a word, I feel something wet poke my head. I spin to see Betty standing in front of me, her hands glistening.

"What the...?"

"I'm fixing your hair. Crouch down a little, so I can reach."

"What's that crap on your hands?" It looks disturbingly like ultrasound gel. Or personal lubricant. I voice neither observation.

"Hair gel, goofball. Now, let's go! We're going to be late." When I reluctantly comply with her barking commands, she softens and says, "Thank you. And to answer your earlier question, Frankie, yes. There has to be a character. And you've made it necessary, so don't bitch at us about it."

"Excuse me? How have *I* made it necessary?"

"Do your posts on *Quite Frankly* sound anything at all like Nate?"

"No, but—"

"There ya go. We have to be consistent. If he shows up in front of a crowd and acts like himself, your fans will spot right away that he's not the guy who posts those rants." She underscores each point she makes with a jab or pinch at my hair. "There. You have great hair, Nathaniel. Very pliable."

I look in the mirror and groan. "Oh, my gosh. I have a pompadour."

"No, you don't. Your hair's not long enough for that."

"It looks like a pompadour."

"It's perfect."

"Perfectly ridiculous."

"It matches the rest of you."

"Gee, thanks!"

She blushes at her inadvertent insult while sliding the fake black glasses onto my nose. "I mean, it's consistent with Frank's style." With a pointed look over my shoulder at Frankie, she says, "Consistency is key. Now, run through your mannerisms. Facial expressions first. Then hand gestures."

Frankie shoots us her own hand gesture in the mirror and stalks off. "I'm going to eat some breakfast," she grumps on her way from the bedroom, punctuating her announcement with a slam of the door.

"Don't worry about her," Betty says lightly.

"I'm not," I lie.

"You look worried."

"She's not making this easy."

"Well, it was her idea, so she needs to get over herself."

"Maybe she feels left out," I posit.

"Her choice. And we don't have time for her second-guessing what we've decided after having no real direction from her until now. This is it. She should have been bothered earlier, if she wanted input or final say."

Her worried eyes belie her tough talking, and I can tell she's as unsure as I am. In some ways, that's comforting, like I'm not alone in this. But in other ways, it reinforces my doubts. If what we're doing isn't making Frankie happy, what's the point? And what will be the consequence?

Before I can ask that, Betty clears her throat and blinks the uncertainty away. "Now. Someone just asked you if any details in Frank's books are autobiographical. React."

Immediately, I scratch my jawline (careful not to bump the blasted scarf) and allow myself to feel sheepish so the emotion will manifest itself on my face. "I'd be lying if I said no. But anything from my real life is merely a starting point. I embellish from there, and it becomes something much more flamboyant and extreme than anything I've experienced in *my* boring life." Cue the rueful smile and self-deprecating chuckle.

Betty's mouth drops open, and she laughs. "Wow. Excellent!"

I shrug. "Whatever. I've been practicing."

"It's paid off. You're going to be great."

"Yeah?" My heart pounds at her approval, and at the thought of doing this in front of strangers in less than a couple of hours.

"Yeah." She playfully pats my face. "They'll be eating from your hand. And buying out all the store's copies of your books."

"Frankie's books."

She shakes her head as if to clear it and laughs. "Oh, yeah. Frankie's books. See? You even had me forgetting for a minute who the real writer is."

When she exits the bathroom, I look at myself in the mirror one more time and sigh. I think I'm starting to forget a *lot* of real things.

But there's no time to mope about that. The plane ride home will give me plenty of time for introspection. Right now, I need to keep my focus on more immediate problems.

Most immediate is my pissed off girlfriend, who barely glances up from her bowl of cereal when Betty and I join her in the kitchen.

"Nate and I will load up the car while you get dressed," Betty offers with a mollifying pat on her best friend's back.

"You guys have this," Frankie replies curtly around a mouthful of cornflakes.

While I register what she's saying, Betty, seeming a lot less sure than she was upstairs when talking about Frankie's bad attitude, implores, "Come on. Stop pouting."

"I'm not pouting. You guys are right; this is something

I've delegated to you. I do the writing; you do the appearances and marketing. So I'm going to stay here and do my part."

Lucy enters the kitchen and takes in the three of us. "Oh, Nate! Look at you! Very authorial!" I brace myself for her to walk over and caress my face—or something equally inappropriate—but she makes a beeline for the coffeemaker instead.

Betty ignores Lucy's arrival and says to Frankie, "You're supposed to be Frank's agent."

Frankie shoots her friend a warning look, presumably about discussing everyone's roles in front of Lucy. I cooperatively bull up, not sure I can keep straight what I'm allowed to say and not allowed to say.

Lucy, oblivious, asks her daughter while pouring a cup of coffee, "You're not dressed? Don't you guys need to be hitting the road?"

"I'm not feeling well."

"You have to go and support Nate at his first reading!" she insists.

"I don't feel like it."

Twisting her mouth to the side, Lucy regards Frankie with her hands on her hips. "That's not very nice."

Frankie rises from the table and walks to the sink, where she deposits her cereal bowl, still full of soggy flakes and milk. "Apparently, I come by selfishness naturally," she snipes before exiting the room.

Lucy tilts her head sympathetically at me. "I'm sorry."

"It's not a big deal." I shrug. She wouldn't know the truth to spot the lie anyway, so I figure it's one of the most harmless whoppers I've told all weekend.

She shakes her head as she stirs half-and-half into her drink. "I can't help but blame myself. She's right that Sam and I were never the models of selflessness, but..." Instead of finishing her thought out loud, she taps her spoon on the lip of her mug.

I want to tell her she should probably be more ashamed about her daughter's poor housekeeping habits than her childish personality, but there isn't time to have a big debate about nature versus nurture, so I merely turn to Betty and say, "Let's load up and go."

"Good luck!" Lucy seamlessly changes gears. "You look great, and you'll stun 'em. Remember, everyone is there because they love your work, so there's nothing to be nervous about."

I give her a shaky smile and a shakier thanks when I remember none of what she's said actually applies to *me*.

* * *

BACK TO PHOENIX we go in the SUV loaded down with the promotional materials Betty shipped ahead of time. Posters, mugs, t-shirts, bookmarks, business cards, you name it, we have it.

Betty's ranted nearly the entire trip about Frankie's unreasonable behavior and how it's going to look so lame for my "agent" not to be there.

As we approach the outskirts of Phoenix, I say, "It'll be fine. Now, stop obsessing and help me find my way to this place. What's it called again? The Book Nook?"

"The Reading Cupboard," she automatically answers before mumbling under her breath about "not obsessing."

She pulls up a mapping app on her phone to direct us the rest of the way, and I breathe a sigh of relief. With both of us focused solely on arriving at our destination, we make it with no wrong turns—a veritable miracle in this crazy city—with plenty of time to spare before the reading.

Inside the shop, I busy myself setting up our merchandise and stacks of books on a long table reserved for the signing portion of the event, but Betty quickly sidles up to me and hisses near my ear, "Stop it."

She hip-checks me away from the table and smiles tightly at the store employee approaching us.

"What? Why?"

Tucking a strand of hair behind her ear, she averts her face from everyone but me. "Frank wouldn't help with his own setup," she explains quickly before addressing the clerk by the name on her tag and putting her immediately to work arranging mugs featuring *my* mug.

Obediently, I step away, hovering uselessly. I'm starting to hate this Frank guy. He's a Class-A douchemuffin. *Now* what am I going to do? Pace near the podium, in front of several rows of folding chairs that will soon be filled with real readers, and become more and more terrified any time one of the store's employees has to steer people away or direct them to the line that's formed closer to the front of the store, out of my view?

Something tells me Frank wouldn't be afraid, nor would he pace, but I'm making an executive decision to give him a social anxiety disorder. He's brave when he's staring at a screen, interacting with people across the Internet, but he's an intro-vert at heart, so in face-to-face encounters, he's a spaz. Yes. Works for me.

The pacing's working up a sweat, though, so I perch on the bar stool situated next to the squat lectern and open my personal copy of *Hippocratic Oaf* to the bookmarked excerpt I'll be reading.

I chose this book, even though Frankie wanted me to read from her personal favorite, *Girl Noir*. For once, though, I put my foot down. I'm the one who has to read it, and I prefer to read something that strikes a chord with *me,* something I can read with emotion, even if that emotion is mostly shame. Anyway, I don't want to read anything told in a woman's voice, and since *Hippocratic Oaf* is the only book of hers written from a man's point of view, it was a no-brainer. Plus, it's the only book of hers I've read in its entirety, and I plan to keep it that way, even though it makes me decidedly vulnerable when faced with specific questions about her other works.

Must not think about that now.

I'm silently practicing my reading, marking with a pen where I should pause for effect or read more quickly, when, "Mr. Lipton!" startles me from my study.

I close the book and pop to my feet. "Yes! That's me. I'm Frank Lipton."

The man, dressed eerily similar to me, smiles and chuckles, offering his hand for me to shake. "That you are. Bob Meillor. I own this store. Thanks for coming here today." He looks over his shoulder at the people choosing their seats and settling in for the reading. "It's shaping up to be a nice crowd, which is good for both of us. Trust me, I've been at some dead readings. Painful."

I glance toward the grouping of chairs behind him, and, like a patient watching the needle go in during a blood draw, immediately regret it. My mouth dries. I snatch and drain the bottle of water on the podium, imagining the liquid instantly exiting my body through the suddenly overactive pores under my arms.

Bob nods at the empty water bottle. "I'll go grab another one of those for you, just in case, Mr. Lipton."

"Nate," I reflexively correct him.

He tilts his head, his forehead crinkling under his shaggy bangs.

My heart thunders like I was recently given an adrenaline

injection. "I mean, Frank! Frank, of course." I lower my shaky voice and lean closer to Bob. "Nate's my real name; Frank's a pen name. Sometimes, like now, when I'm nervous, I get confused. I don't like public speaking." I chuckle at myself. "You get it, right?" I hope it doesn't sound too much like I'm begging him to buy my story.

He smiles and cups my shoulder with his beefy hand. "Your secret's safe with me, *Frank*," he promises on a wink. "Now, let me go grab that water for you, and we'll get started."

I chance another shy peek at the crowd growing in front of me. An attractive woman in the front row catches my eye and gives me a beguiling finger wave.

Maybe this won't be *too* horrible.

15

DOUBLE DATE

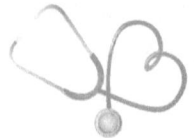

"Eau Claire," Frankie says to me as soon as she opens her apartment door to let me in.

It's an unconventional greeting, to be sure, but maybe we're playing a game—"Name as many obscure Wisconsin towns as you can"—that I'm not aware of, so I reply, "Uh, De Pere?"

We're already running late for our double date with Kyle and Betty, so I'm dismayed when she pads barefoot down the hall to the bathroom, where she's still getting ready.

Abandoning our strange Wisconsin towns shout-out, I ask, "Are you about ready?"

She appears unrushed as she applies another coat of mascara.

Whatever. I don't really care if we're late. Big-shot Kyle made a reservation for us at some swanky French place I didn't even know existed in this town. How does it stay in business? Who goes there? Packers players and coaches, when they're in town? Nobody I know has any desire to eat escargot or anything more French than fries.

Plus, the last person I want to spend an evening playing "Happy Couple" in front of is Kyle, or The Beefcake with the

Briefcase, as I've taken to mentally calling him. But Frankie's suddenly determined to set Betty up with someone—anyone, apparently—and she swears Kyle is Betty's type. I'm not so sure about that. I wouldn't think a big bank account would be a turn-on for Betty. She doesn't strike me as impressed by things like that. I guess that's none of my concern, though.

On the other hand, I have a feeling Eau Claire concerns me, somehow, probably in a way I'm not going to like.

When Frankie doesn't acknowledge my query into her estimated ready time, I lean against the bathroom door frame and submit to the conversation she'd obviously prefer, considering it's the only thing she's said to me so far. "What about Eau Claire?"

She presses her hair between the hot paddles of her flat iron (to straighten her already straight hair?) and drawls, "That's where your next signing is. Three weekends from now. Saturday afternoon."

My stomach drops. "Uh," I say more as an expulsion of air than an expression of an idea or thought. My mind races to provide a valid excuse not to attend another public appearance as Frank.

Not that the one in Phoenix was horrible. It wasn't. As a matter of fact, it went well. So well that Betty and I had to temper our giddy relief when we returned to the Liptons' house, because we didn't want to rub it in Frankie's face how successful it was. I know, that doesn't make any sense, but trust me, if she's not part of the experience, she doesn't want to hear about it. She likes the results (more book sales, increased traffic to her website and blog), but she's not interested in listening to Betty and me bask in the afterglow.

Have I mentioned it's been a tense couple of weeks since our return?

Now, I scramble for a reason—any reason—not to spend

another day in a bookstore in a scratchy scarf. Family? No. Not believable that I'd care enough about a family event to choose it over anything else. Work? Yes! The old standby.

"Well, I can't, because I, uh, have to work at Urgent Care that Saturday."

Her shoulders slump but almost immediately straighten once more. "Oh. So? Switch with someone."

"No can do, because..."

She stares expectantly at me in the mirror. Damn. I was hoping she'd accept my answer without explanation.

Because this is my first interaction with a woman ever?

"I can't, because they're cracking down on schedule swaps!" I nearly yell, then tone it down. "It's been out of control lately, and a few times, nobody's shown up for a shift, because of misunderstandings and stuff."

"Tell them it's important."

"How do I explain that, though? Lie?"

Yeah, because I'm totally averse to that, obviously. I conveniently swat that thought away.

She bites her lower lip, continuing to run her long hair through the straightener. "Hmmm." Her eyes light up. "Oh! I know! Tell them your girlfriend needs you that day for something she booked without consulting you first, and she can't reschedule it." Setting the flat iron on the counter, she slinks up to and rubs against me. "Pretty please? It's all true! Well, Betty booked it, but I do need you." Underscoring that seemingly innocent statement with a brush of her palm against the front of my pants, she smiles wickedly into my eyes.

My heart races. With a tight, painful swallow, I squeak, "That might work." I clear my throat and add more assertively while backing away from her, "But don't get your hopes up. They've been really strict lately. You know, a few asshats spoiling it for the rest of us."

"It's Betty you'd be disappointing," she says in an ultra-casual way, returning to the bathroom counter and avoiding my eyes under the pretense of curling her eyelashes. "And you wouldn't want that."

I refuse to take the bait I've taken so many times since we've been back from Arizona. She's thrust—um, different word, maybe? Thrown?—her best friend and me together to do her bidding wherever and whenever it suits her, and now she's jealous of the time Betty and I spend together? And we're not allowed to have fun or enjoy each other's company while we do her grunt work? I've already told her I don't think it works that way. I'm not going to say it again tonight.

Instead, I ask, "You nearly ready? Your buddy Kyle will think he's been stood up."

Plunking down the eyelash curler, she narrows her eyes at me. "Are you gonna be like that all night?"

"Like what?"

"'Your buddy Kyle,'" she imitates in a deep, dopey voice that sounds nothing like me. "All snide?"

"I'm not being snide. He *is* your buddy, is he not?" I step aside for her to pass, and I wait in the hallway while she roots around in the heap of shoes on her closet floor. By some miracle, she quickly finds a matching pair and emerges with them.

Holding onto my forearm as she slips them on, she answers, "Yes, he's my *friend*. I hope he'll be your friend too." She lets go of me and grabs her tiny purse from the back of the couch.

"Absolutely," I reply, following her out the door.

I only hope Betty puts the kibosh on Frankie's match-making dreams, so I never have to deliver on that empty agreement.

* * *

As I PREDICTED, by the time we get to the restaurant, Kyle's waiting for us in an intimate booth. Even Betty beat us here. They're sitting across from each other and seem to be chatting comfortably, both nursing large glasses of dark red wine.

Oh, great. It's one of *those* places. So, if I order a beer, I'll look like a rube. I'd rather have nothing than drink a mouth-puckering, eighteen-dollar bowl of tannins that gives me insta-headache, so after Frankie asks for a glass of white wine, I say, "Water, thanks," and take the only remaining seat, next to Kyle.

He holds out his hand for a manly shake, but I refuse to participate in one of those grip-strength contests paper-pushers like him are so fond of and keep it firm, yet brief.

"It's good to finally meet you," he says, practically blinding me with his milk-fed smile.

"You, too." For some reason, I glance at Betty when I say that. Her curved right eyebrow lets me know my lame attempts at civility are failing. I can't help it, though; this guy gives me a rash no ointment can cure.

Frankie jumps in. "Sorry we're so late. Bad hair day."

"You must be talking about Nate, because your hair looks perfect," Kyle says smoothly. "No offense," he adds in my direction without taking his eyes off a now-blushing Frankie.

Betty hides her smirk in her wineglass while I try to convert my scowl into something that may be interpreted as a smile in a room full of seeing-impaired people.

"None taken," I mumble, looking over my shoulder for the waiter, wishing he'd return with my tasty, refreshing water.

Frankie tries again to kick-start the conversation. "Kyle owns a computer software company. What's your company's specialty again? Video games?"

He perks up. "Yes! Although, we're not really a software company per se."

"Oops. Sorry!" Frankie giggles.

"No problem." He shoots her a magnanimous smile across the table and lightly taps the back of her hand, which he has to stretch to reach. He doesn't seem to notice me burning a hole in the top of his tan, manicured paw, which lingers on Frankie's fingers. "We specialize in video game development. You a big gamer, Nate?"

Oh, so he *does* know I'm here. For a second, I thought maybe Betty and I were invisible attendees at what feels like a date between Kyle and Frankie.

I shake my head to re-focus my eyes and look away from his audacious mitt. "Me? Oh. No. I mean, some of my friends like to play a bit, so when I'm with them—which is hardly ever anymore, anyway—I play, but I don't own a gaming system, or anything like that."

"Outdoorsy, huh? Hey, I have a boat and a lake house. You and Frankie—and Betty, of course," he swiftly appends, remembering his real date for the evening and smiling at her, "should come up for a weekend and hang out. Lots of trails. You have a mountain bike?"

Starting to feel like the gray crayon in the Big Box, I again shake my head. "Nope. I'm more of a runner."

"Trail running?"

I barely suppress the sigh that wants to jump free from my chest due to this tedious conversation. I also almost lie and agree, if only to end the misery, but instead, I say truthfully, "I usually just have time for quick jogs before or after work, around my neighborhood."

"Right on. I get it. I'm super-busy, too. I hardly ever leave my office to work out. I installed cardio and weight machines in the building a few years ago, so my employees and I can squeeze in some workouts when we're in the middle of a new development."

While the waiter finally delivers our drinks, I say, "Sounds like you have a busy, interesting life."

"I stay occupied," he admits. It would sound more humble without that sarcastic sneer on his smug face.

He turns his attention to the waiter, who seems to be waiting for us to stop talking. Sure enough, given his opening, the server rattles off the chef's specialties for the day and asks if we're ready to order.

None of us has had a chance to look at the menus, but Kyle offers to order for the whole table. I'd rather choose my own food so I know exactly what I'm eating, but then again, I'm sure Monsieur Know-It-All will keep us informed as we go. I nod my consent and struggle not to laugh as he earnestly says the name of each dish in confident French.

When the waiter leaves, Betty clears her throat. "So, Kyle, we know why Frankie's on that shuttle so often, but what has you traveling so much? Business or pleasure?"

Fingering his glass's stem, he replies. "Business. Always business. My company's headquartered in Chicago, but I'm from here, and my family still lives here. I keep an apartment in Chicago—"

"On the Miracle Mile?" Betty inquires in a snooty voice.

Closing one eye in a wink, Kyle laughs. "Yes, as a matter of fact. Are you making fun of me?"

"Maybe," she says. "Actually, I was kidding. I've heard that term a billion times on TV; it's about the only thing I know about Chicago, other than those stinky Bears."

"Hey, I fly my Packers flag high and proud during football season, make no mistake. I'm a major Cheesehead." At this, he turns to me, as if it should matter most to the other guy at the table.

I smile weakly. "I like cheese, too. I mean, go Pack."

"Damn right. Anyway, I have an apartment there, where I

stay during the week. Then, most weekends, unless we're on a massive deadline, I fly here to stay at my house or hang out at the lake and spend time with family. I have three sisters, and I've lost count of how many nieces and nephews I have—I think it's ten now, but my youngest sister has another one on the way." He taps the table. "If you haven't guessed, we're Catholic. Although I'm not practicing."

My gosh. I thought *I* had verbal diarrhea. This guy needs an Imodium martini. I can tell by the look on her face that Betty's waiting for the perfect opportunity to zing him, but Frankie seems captivated, although she must have heard all this before. Clearly, this guy's favorite topic is himself. I've known him for fifteen minutes and could write his damn profile on a dating website. As many times as she's sat next to him on a plane, she must be well-informed enough to write his obituary, which he may need if he doesn't stop looking at my girlfriend like that.

Our soup course arrives. Kyle stops talking about himself long enough to tell us it's a fish soup and adds some pretentious detail about the region in France where it originated and how beautiful it is there.

"You've been?" Frankie asks, holding her spoon near her mouth while she waits for his answer.

Betty rolls her eyes and grabs a piece of crusty bread, which she butters as if trying to punish it.

Kyle shrugs. "Yeah. For business, of course. I tried to get some sightseeing in, though. My girlfriend at the time insisted."

"All work and no play makes Kyle an insufferable dickhead, right?" Betty says sweetly, fluttering her eyelashes over her piece of bread and across the table at him.

He pauses before smiling uncertainly and answering, "Yes, I guess so."

"What's the point in working so hard to make all that money if you're not going to take the time to enjoy it?" Again, her tone is light, but her eyes are hard.

The answer must be hiding in Kyle's soup bowl, because he stares into it for a long time. Finally, he replies, "I enjoy what I do for a living. My source of income is also my favorite hobby. Nothing wrong with that, right?"

"Not at all," Betty chirps. "Only the luckiest of us can claim that."

When Kyle looks up, his eyes are as hard as Betty's. "I *am* one of the lucky ones. I also believe in making my own luck."

I'm not sure what's going on here, but it's simultaneously uncomfortable and fascinating and thrilling. I can't tell if Betty wants to screw him or stab him. Or both.

Before she can deliver what I'm sure would be a delightfully scorching retort, Frankie steps in. "It *is* amazing to be able to turn what you love into a money-making venture. I'm experiencing that for the first time in my life, and it's awesome."

I shoot her a wide-eyed look. Appeasement is no justification for giving away *our* current venture. Her eyes flick away from mine, though, and she grins across the table at Kyle.

"Oh, yeah!" He sets down his spoon and gives her a look reminiscent of a grateful dog being thrown a slice of bacon. "How's that going, anyway?" He claps a hand on my shoulder. I'm too stunned to shrug it off. "Way to take one for the team, Nate. You're a better man than I am. I wouldn't put my face on a bunch of girlie books."

"They're excellent books! And what would you know about it?" I demand.

He stops touching me. "I'm sure they're very well-written, if Frankie wrote them."

"She did."

He laughs. "I know. I didn't mean for it to sound like she may not have."

Frankie reaches across the table but stops short of touching my hand. "I asked Kyle for some advice—you know, on a business and marketing level—and his tips have been helpful."

Betty nearly spits out a mouthful of wine. "Wait a minute. What's wrong with what *I've* been doing so far?"

With a shrug, Frankie says, "Nothing! I wanted some new ideas, that's all."

"Then you should have told me, and I would have brainstormed some for you."

"Ladies, ladies," Kyle interrupts, then pauses as our waiter pays us a visit, exchanging our soup bowls for salad plates and refreshing our beverages. As soon as he's gone, Kyle says, "Nothing I said was earth-shattering. Basic business sense, that's all."

"Oh, so my skills are remedial?" Betty stabs a weed and shoves it into her mouth.

"No!" He chuckles and soothes, "That's not what I meant, either. I was just sharing a few things I've had to learn the hard way, so Frankie wouldn't have to suffer through the same growing pains."

Pointing to him with her fork, Betty orders, "Don't patronize me."

"I'm not!"

Frankie sighs. "Sorry I said anything. I thought it would be something we all had in common and could talk about. Forget it."

"How could you tell him?" I hiss at her. "My parents don't even know!"

"I was excited about it. He's my friend."

"I have friends, too, but I haven't told anyone."

"They're *my* books, though."

"It's *my* face!"

"Big deal. You posed for a picture and play dress-up on the weekends."

"Oh, snap," Betty mutters while I grind my teeth and glare at the person who's supposed to be my girlfriend.

Kyle inserts, "You don't have to worry, man; I'm not going to tell anyone."

Slowly, I swivel my head to look at him. "You know what, *man*? I think you'd be wise to keep your mouth shut, for once."

"Hey!" he and Frankie say in unison.

"Oh, please!" I snap.

Frankie tosses her napkin on the table. "I don't feel well. I'd like to leave."

When I eagerly rise to comply with her wishes, she turns away from me and says to Betty, "Can you drive me home?"

Betty pauses chewing, then resumes and swallows. "But I'm not finished eating."

"I'll take you home," I say to Frankie's steely profile. She continues to ignore me while silently beseeching her best friend.

Kyle slides from the booth and stands next to me. I straighten my spine to make myself as tall as possible without going on tiptoe, so I'll look less like a member of the Lollipop Guild next to him.

"I'll drive you, Frankie," he says quietly but firmly.

"No, you won't!" I immediately protest, drawing looks from the dignified diners around us.

Betty continues to eat, saying behind her hand to hide her full mouth, "Let them go."

Our waiter sidles up to us. "Is there a problem?" he inquires.

"Not at all," Kyle answers for all of us. "My friend isn't

feeling well—nothing to do with the food, I assure you," he quickly adds when his explanation raises panic in the server's eyes. "I'm going to take her home. Can you make sure my two other friends enjoy the rest of the meal?" He digs in his wallet and peels off six one-hundred-dollar bills. "That should cover everything, with some left over for you."

"Of course, Mr. MacDonald. Thank you. Have a good evening."

Kyle cups Frankie's elbow in his hand. "We will, thanks." With a nod to Betty and me, he steers Frankie away.

"Wait a second!" I hiss at their retreating backs, mindful of the stares of the other diners.

I take a step to go after them, but Betty says, "Don't even think about leaving me here like I'm some kind of a loser, Nathaniel. Sit down."

I'm aware that by not following them, *I* look like the loser here, and there will be hell to pay later, but I couldn't possibly deliver an apology right now, and it's clear Frankie's not going to be apologizing anytime soon; or ever. I'm also not the type who would ever challenge another man—especially not a mountain of a man like Kyle—to a Neanderthalish duel over a woman. So what's the point in following?

Does it suck that some other guy is taking my girlfriend home right now? It should probably suck more than I think it does. But at this point, I'm relieved not to have to spend any more time with her tonight.

Plus, I don't want to be the jerk who deserts a woman in a fancy restaurant to finish her meal alone, so I retake my seat and drop my head in my hand.

Betty sets down her fork. After draining the remainder of her wine, she states calmly, "Well. We seem to have fucked that up hardcore."

What else is new?

16

UNEXPECTED VISITOR

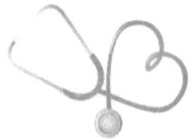

LOUD KNOCKING ON MY FRONT DOOR WAKES ME FROM THE soundest sleep I've had all week. It takes me a few seconds to realize the rhythmic pounding isn't part of the dream I was having about, well, never mind. I collapsed here what feels like seconds ago after working a thirteen-hour day that started before sunrise, and I'm not in the mood for visitors.

When the banging fills the living room after I'm fully aware I'm awake, I groan and sit up on the couch. And nearly poke out my own eye.

I call out groggily, "Who is it?", hoping I don't have to answer the door with a giant erection.

"It's Betty. I need to talk to you."

Dismayed for a number of reasons, I look down at the highly visible one in my lap. "All right. Uh... hang on a boner— I mean, a moment!" I push down on it, but that only seems to be encouraging things. Cursing under my breath, I hobble to the door, my hand cupped over my crotch, and pull open the door the smallest crack I can without looking like Jack Nicholson in *The Shining*.

"Hey!" I say to her, trying to sound normal. "What's up?" *Besides my pecker.*

My silent addition to the innocuous greeting makes me blush.

She looks askance at me. "Aren't you going to invite me in?"

"Do you want to come in?"

One of her eyes narrows while the other widens. "Do you have someone in there?"

"What? No!"

"Why are you acting so shifty? Why don't you invite me in?"

I pull the door wider and, without thinking, remove my hand from in front of myself to make a sweeping, welcoming gesture with my arm. "By all means."

Her glance is drawn immediately south, but she quickly looks away and shields her eyes from the sight. "Good grief, Nathaniel! What the hell are you doing?" She turns completely away from me.

"I'm sorry!" I say, mortified and contrite, covering myself once more and turning my back to her. "I just woke up."

"You're not the only one who's wide awake and perky," she observes.

"You act like you've never seen one before!" I snap, my embarrassment, stress, and exhaustion contributing to some wild mood swings.

"Not yours!"

"Well, you still haven't. I'm fully clothed."

"Those thin scrubs aren't leaving much to the imagination."

We stand back-to-back until finally, my little, er, perfectly average-sized buddy gets the hint and returns to his relaxed (more like humiliated and hiding) state, so I adjust myself and turn to face her, crossing my arms over my chest. "What are you doing here, anyway?" I ask, dreading the answer but figuring it would be best to just get the conversation over with, like ripping off the proverbial Band-Aid from one of my hairy legs.

She bats her thick eyelashes at me over her shoulder and advances into the house, dropping her thirty-pound purse onto the floor by my couch. My heart races, but she simply says, "It's good to see you, too," so it's impossible to tell if she's being coy or truly doesn't remember what happened last weekend. I wish I could say I didn't, that I haven't been thinking about it constantly.

After Frankie and Kyle left the restaurant, I was too mad to eat or even get drunk on Kyle's sixty-thousand dimes, so I sat at the table and pouted while Betty got drunk enough for both of us. Eventually, I started talking. Then it was like I couldn't stop. I whined about everything from never having a day off (thanks to being Frank) to my lack of a sex life (yep) to being treated like an employee by my own girlfriend (oh, yeah). It got ugly.

"What happened to, 'I can't do this without you?'" I wondered aloud over and over.

Thank goodness Betty was too drunk to comprehend half the things I was saying. She kept slurring, "Fuck yeah!" to everything I said.

That was the extent of her engagement for the rest of the evening until she French kissed me when I saw her to her door. But I told myself she was drunk and merely keeping with the French theme of the evening.

I took possession of her keys and unlocked her door, through which I firmly guided her and said a quick goodnight.

Remembering it brings a flush to my cheeks.

"Oh, good grief. Just forget it," she says to me now with a flippant laugh.

I shake my head at her. "What? I mean, I'm trying, but—"

"You had nap wood. Whatever. Moving on." Looking around my living room, she nods her head. "Nice place. Did your mom decorate it for you?" She shoots me a teasing smile and wink.

Trying to keep up with her chaotic conversation, I blurt, "No! I'm an adult."

"Relax! I'm only kidding. This is the first time I've ever been inside your house. It's nice. Probably not as nice as your brother's place around the corner. My gosh, Frankie drove me past there one day when we were bored, and... What type of surgery did you say he does? Plastic?"

I open my mouth to correct her, but she waves away my answer.

"Anyway. Whatever. This place is much cozier, and very tastefully decorated. You know, I've been in some bachelor pads where the owner obviously thought Lego models made for some sweet tchotchkes, the picture frames still held the photos of the model families, and the household's most sophisticated reading material featured women in their underwear... and was located in the bathroom. Don't even get me started on the housekeeping. No, this is nice. You get major points for being a big boy."

Murmuring a sarcastic thanks, I pray she doesn't need to use the bathroom while she's here as I picture that Victoria's Secret catalogue on top of the toilet tank. "So, uh, what can I do for—I mean, what's up?" I inquire, wishing I didn't feel so tired and wrong-footed.

She looks like she's about to answer my question, and it's not going to be something I want to hear, but then she stops short and scrutinizes me. "Seriously. Are you okay? You look... awful."

I rub my eight o'clock shadow. "Thanks. And yes, I'm fine.

Exhausted, that's all. That's what happens when you work an Urgent Care shift the day after your brother's bachelor party."

She winces.

"Yeah. I didn't have any more Saturdays to trade with people, since I've been gone so often lately on the weekends." I look pointedly at her, but she raises her hands in front of her chest as if to say, *Don't blame me.*

I narrow my eyes and snort at her, because it's absolutely her fault. Before I can remind her she's the one who sets the public appearance schedule for Frank, she shakes her head as if trying to puzzle through something.

"Now, explain to me why you had the bachelor party the week before the wedding."

I sigh. "Heidi didn't want Nick to be hung over on *her* wedding day, so she forbade a wedding-eve bachelor party. I couldn't throw my brother's party in the middle of the week, could I?"

"No! Completely lame-o!" She plops on the couch and sits sideways, her head propped against her hand.

"It was still kind of lame, since I couldn't drink, but everyone else seemed to have a good time."

"So do you have pictures from last night, or is that against some Man Code?"

"It's the 'Bro Code,' first of all; and yes, I'll probably be breaking every rule in it *when* I show you the pictures, but... I'm going to, anyway, because they're epic."

If it keeps us from talking about that kiss, I'll gladly bust wide open the precious Bro Code.

She gleefully claps her hands while I come around the back of the couch and sit next to her, pulling my laptop closer to me on the coffee table and opening the files I uploaded from my phone as soon as I got home in the wee hours of the morning. We settle next to each other and cycle through the tame snapshots from the beginning of the evening (Nick and his other groomsmen hamming it up for the camera in the back of the rented limo, everyone taking their turns saluting the camera with their drink of choice, etc.). She giggles as the subjects of the pictures become progressively rowdier, and her jaw drops at a photo of Nick in his underwear on a mechanical bull.

"Oh my gosh! What the...?"

We're still laughing at the picture when my phone rings.

"Speak of the devil. He's probably only been up for a few hours. Bastard," I grumble jealously and tap my phone screen to answer as loudly as possible, "YELLO!"

"Oh, you are such an asshole," he rasps in my ear.

I put the call on speaker so Betty can enjoy the conversation, but I place a finger against my lips. Nick won't say anything interesting if he knows she's listening.

As it is, he immediately asks, "Hey, am I on speakerphone?"

"Yes, but I'm alone," I lie. "I'm... uh... cleaning, so I need both hands."

Since that's consistent with my personality, he doesn't question it but starts moaning about how sick he feels, hypothesizing that someone put something in his drink (singular, as if he only had one).

Betty, pointing to the laptop monitor mouths, *"He's so hairy!"*

I cover my laugh with a cough. "What? No. Nobody put anything in your drinks, bud. C'mon! Would I, your brother and best man, let anything like that happen?"

He mutters, "I guess not."

"I had your back. Maybe you can't hold it like you used to. You're gettin' old."

"Nah, bro. I'm fine," he quickly reverses his earlier claims. "Just a little dehydrated, I guess. I'm glad we did that last night, though. If I was getting married today, I'd be hurtin'."

"That Heidi, she's a smart one," I gush, making a gagging face at Betty, who covers her mouth to contain her laughter.

I motion for her to keep looking through the pictures but move away from the couch, knowing she's about to come across one that I won't be able to see without losing it. I turn my back to her and the laptop and walk to the kitchen, where I open the fridge to grab two bottles of green tea.

"Listen, bro," Nick says now. "You didn't happen to, uh, take any pictures last night, did you?"

Smoothly, I answer, "Just a couple, before things got fun. I sort of forgot to keep taking them. Sorry."

"No, no. That's okay. Don't worry about it. It's probably for the best. I mean—"

Suddenly, Betty's throaty laugh echoes in the high-ceilinged living room, and I know she's reached my favorite pic. It's Nick, drinking from a bottle of beer with one of those novelty penis straws, popular at bachelorette parties. His eyes rolled back in his head, he looks like he's giving a blow job to a Keebler elf.

"What's that?" Nick demands.

Merely imagining the photo makes me giggle. "Nothing," I say, deep breathing to keep it together. "I have *Pretty Woman* playing in the background while I clean. You were saying?"

He pauses. "Shit. I can't remember. Never mind. I'm glad you didn't take many pictures. Although it would be nice to fill in the blanks. I can't remember getting home, or anything. That freaks me out."

"Well, you were perfectly safe. I wasn't even buzzed."

"Thanks, man. I owe you one."

I wonder if he'll still feel that way after I post his bachelor party photos on Facebook, tagging both him and Heidi in every one of them. I figure I'll wait until a couple of weeks after their honeymoon. I want him to be both humiliated *and* firmly wed to the woman who sleeps in full headgear and spends the equivalent of a small country's annual gross domestic product bleaching every hair on her body, and her anus.

It's taken more than two decades, but the time has come to get back at him for blaming me for the slingshot murder of Mom's beloved parakeet, Snacks. This is going to be some sweet, sweet revenge.

Since Betty's now no longer making any effort to be quiet, and she's taken to slapping her hand against the couch, I tell Nick I'm getting ready to vacuum and say a quick goodbye after imploring him to drink plenty of water.

I return to the living room with our beverages and stand over a stretched-out Betty. "Are you going to be okay?"

"No," she gasps. "I'm not. Those... are... incredible."

I grin proudly. "Yeah. I know. By the end of the night, they were all so wasted, they were doing everything I told them to do, no questions asked. I felt like a hypnotist. 'Cluck like a chicken.' 'Eat that peanut off the floor, but pick it up with your mouth.' 'Drink from that bottle with this phallic straw.'"

"You're evil."

"Maybe." I give her a hand up, and she takes the tea from me as she swings her legs in front of her and makes room for me to sit.

"Thanks."

"I'd offer you something more adult, but I don't have any wine in the house, and I know you don't drink beer," I say, trying to sound casual. It's true I don't have any wine, but I'd rather not go into why I'm glad I don't.

"This is perfect," she says over the crack and subsequent pop of the seal breaking on the glass bottle's metal cap as she twists it off.

"So, what's up?" I ask for the third time, leaning back into the couch cushions. "Lonely this weekend, since Frankie's stuck in Chicago?" I stare at the wooden beams over our heads and wait for an answer that never comes. The tense silence holds until I find the courage to glance her way.

She swipes at the lipstick on her bottle. "Um, about that..."

Suddenly terrified about what she may have come here to say, I babble, "I, for one, am kind of relieved. Does that make me a bad boyfriend?"

A tiny head shake is all the response I get, so I continue before she gets the wrong idea, "I knew I'd be busy with Nick's party and work and I'd love to have some alone time, especially since the wedding is next weekend, and we have a book signing in Eau Claire the weekend after that, but my parents have claimed at least part of the day tomorrow. Dad's dusting the snow off the grill, or something. I guess I can't blame them; they haven't seen me in weeks. I wish they'd just wait until the wedding."

Betty suddenly stands. "Well, as long as you're okay with it."

Oh, gosh! She *does* remember the kiss. She's here to hash it out with me. *Am* I okay with it? Is it okay for me to be okay with it? Probably not. I should probably say something responsible here, like, *"You know, Betty, that was wrong. I know you were drunk, but it still wasn't right. And that can never happen again."* But all I can do is squeak a stalling, "Okay with it?" and wait for her to say the next thing.

"Frankie staying in Chicago," she answers with a tiny shrug, heading for the door.

Oh. That. Am I okay with that? I'm much more okay with it than talking about that kiss on Betty's front stoop.

My hair scratches against the upholstery as I crane my neck to follow her retreat, but I don't move any other part of my wasted body. "What's not to be okay about it? She missed the last flight to Green Bay last night. It made no sense to get a flight today, only to turn around and fly back out Monday morning."

"Right, but... Never mind. You're right. I'm being weird."

I laugh. "Kind of. What's going on?"

She attempts her own laugh, but it comes out more like a croak. "Nothing. Probably. I'm sure." With a determined head shake, she holds up the bottle of tea, backtracks to get her purse from the floor, and says, "Thanks for the drink. I guess I'd better go. I don't even have a dress yet for the wedding. I have the perfect shoes, of course, but the dress, well, almost anything will do with the shoes I have. Nobody's going to be looking at the dress. And I don't want to show up the bride. That's bad form."

I thought for sure with Frankie's newfound jealousy, she'd rethink her brilliant plan to have Betty go as my date to Nick and Heidi's wedding, but it seems Frankie's envy is situational, which is convenient for her. Not so much for me.

Plus, maybe this is Frankie's way of punishing me. She apologized for telling Kyle about Frank and for leaving the restaurant with him last weekend, and she's been sweet as can be this week, sacrificing her evening writing time to talk to me every night on the phone, but that only makes me feel guilty and puts me on alert, waiting to see how she's going to make me pay. I have a feeling she thinks taking Betty to Nick's wedding as my date is my penance. I'm just not sure how. That makes me even more nervous, of course.

Considering how much time Betty and I have been spending together lately, it doesn't seem as big of a deal as it was when Frankie first proposed the date at my parents' house four months ago. (Has it only been four months? Seems like a lifetime!) Then again, considering what happened last week after the double date. But Frankie has no idea about that, of course. I hope.

Oh, gosh. Wait. Does she? I frantically recollect every conversation I've had with her since that kiss, trying to determine if she *does* know. Could that explain why she's being so sweet to me? She feels threatened and has decided she should be nicer to me? Or she's trying to draw me off my guard so she can sucker punch me with the information later and guilt me into doing something truly terrible? Like, taking her to a Packers game? Or worse, a *pre-season* game?

Betty interrupts my panicked pondering. "You don't happen to have your tux already, do you? I could take the bow tie with me to make sure I don't get anything that clashes."

At her mention of the hot pink tie and cummerbund I'll be sporting in front of hundreds of people next weekend, I groan. "Don't remind me. And no, my final fitting isn't until Wednesday."

"I'll steer clear of reds and oranges, then."

"Sounds like a great plan," I mumble distractedly.

"I'll leave you alone."

I jump from the couch but keep the piece of furniture between us. "Betty, did you... uh.... I mean..."

She widens her eyes and laughs. "Well, spit it out, Nathaniel!"

Rubbing the back of my neck, I say, "Never mind."

"You sure?"

I release a self-deprecating chuckle. "Yeah. I'm tired, that's all. Sorry. See you next weekend."

She repeats my farewell in a wary tone and pulls open the front door.

As soon as she's gone, I collapse on the sofa again, my mind too weary to fight the rampant daydreams of her lips on mine.

17

MISPERCEPTIONS

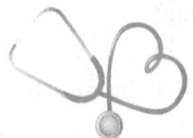

WEDDINGS ARE SUCH A PAIN IN THE ASS, BUT THEY'RE TEN times worse when you're part of the wedding party—and about fifty times worse when you're the best man.

Fortunately (or unfortunately, depending on how you look at it), I'm a pro at this gig, having done it four times prior to today. In this latest case, I've reached the home stretch. The bachelor party has been organized, held, and overseen. The final tux fittings have been suffered through. I've picked up the rings, kept my brother's feet nice and toasty (so glad that's figurative) leading up to that walk down the aisle, and written and delivered a decent speech for the reception. I've even overseen the defacing of the getaway car. Now it's time for me to kick back and avoid everyone's pitying stares and whispers —"Who's that bombshell with Nate?" "Some chick named Betty. His beard, probably." "I thought he was dating someone. Freddie? Frankie?" "Sounds about right. The dude should just come out of the closet already." "No, really. I think it's a woman." "Tranny?" "No, a real woman!" "Whatever. I have some historical artifacts in my garage to sell you, when you're done buying that story."—for the rest of the reception.

I'm also trying not to think of the colossal argument Frankie and I had on the phone last night.

A fight wasn't the objective of my call. The point of the call was to wish her dad a happy birthday, but after Sam returned the phone to his daughter, she was curt and dismissive, so I steeled myself and asked the question I didn't care to know the answer to: "What's wrong?"

She hedged for a while, but when I was about to let it go and hang up so I could sit by myself in my empty house and fully dread the next day's "festivities," she blurted, "Kyle thinks you need to be tweeting and posting more on Facebook as Frank."

"Does he want to take over the job?" I offered through gritted teeth.

"See? I knew I shouldn't say anything."

"Yet you still did."

"You asked me what was wrong!"

Pinching the bridge of my nose, I advised, "Next time, if the answer involves that guy, lie and tell me you have cramps. I'll be a lot more sympathetic."

Her sneer was audible. "Your jealousy toward him is pathetic. And a major turn-off, by the way."

"How would I know the difference?"

"Excuse me?"

"Might as well be honest about how I feel about him, since holding back isn't going to get me anywhere anyway."

"Well, I owe him a lot, and not just for the advice he's given me about marketing my writing. I would have been stuck in some crappy airport hotel last weekend if he hadn't put me up."

Then it was definitely my turn to say, "Excuse me?"

"I stayed at Kyle's last weekend when I was stuck in Chicago. I told you that."

"You most certainly did not!"

"Yes, I did! You weren't listening, as usual."

"My ears would have perked up on that nugget. What the hell, Frankie?"

"Nothing happened!"

That she felt the need to say it spoke volumes.

My breath whistled forcefully through my nostrils while I processed her denial, then remembered Betty's unannounced visit, strange questions, and hasty retreat last Saturday evening.

"Oh, hell," I breathed.

"What? It wasn't a big deal. Once again, you're being a jealous dickhead. And at least he did something to help me."

The implied criticism hit hard enough to distract me from the thoughts I didn't want to be thinking, anyway. "What was I supposed to do? Fly you home on my private jet?"

"You could have driven here."

"To Chicago." Those two words came out about as flat as the head of an infant who spends too much time on his back.

"Yes! We could have spent the weekend up here together. But no."

"I had to work!"

"You always have to work."

"Yeah, usually on your shit!"

"Oh, so being Frank is shit now?"

It always has been, I wanted to say but somehow managed to withhold at the last second. My silence said it all, anyway.

The pout strong in her voice, she said, "Fine. I see. What-ever. I guess you've been doing all this to get laid."

"What? No!"

"Save it. You may have everyone else fooled with your sweet, evolved, in-touch-with-your-feminine-side sensitivity bullshit, but you're just like every other man I've ever been with."

"Have you really *been* with me? Is that an accurate description?"

"Screw you!"

"Got any candidates?"

She hung up on me before I got out that last question, though. It's a shame, too. It was an excellent comeback. I almost called her back right away to say it and then hang up on *her*. Then again, maybe it's a good thing I didn't. Now that I think about it, I would have been proving her point.

Instead, I lay on my bed, drinking, staring at the ceiling, and fuming.

Probably would have been better off hosting a bachelor party last night. I wouldn't have been as hungover, that's for damn sure. And I would have gotten a lot more sleep.

"Holy crap, Cowboy. You look like someone shot your horse and turned it into dog food."

I impart a baleful look over the whiskey and Coke Betty dangles by the rim, her manicured fingertips inches from my nose.

"If you're not careful, people are going to interpret that look as 'heartbroken and scorned,'" she adds.

"They can think whatever they want," I snap, accepting and draining the drink, which is mostly whiskey, I realize too late. I cough against the back of my hand before sliding the plastic, ice-filled cup onto the table next to us.

Now that the toasts and formal aspects to the reception are over (and I'm the proud owner of the garter that was shortly ago intimate with my ex-fiancée's upper thigh, thanks to my mother's insistence that I not allow any of my pimply teenaged relatives to catch it), I've shucked my jacket and moved from the head table to a less conspicuous one near the restrooms. If anyone was sitting here, they've found better seats or are dancing or mingling. Whatever the reason for the empty table, I was enjoying my first chance all day to be alone and sulk.

"Seriously, though. What's your deal? Francesca promised me a good time at this wedding, but—"

"Frankie says a lot of things to get her way."

Cocking an eyebrow toward her elaborate updo, Betty tugs at the top of her downward-creeping strapless dress, then sits and says, "Oh. Now I see. Another fight?"

"You could say that."

She sighs as she slumps in the chair and stretches her legs, crossing them at the ankles. "Well, I should probably stay out of it."

Her word choice strikes a nerve. "Why did you come over to my house last weekend?" I ask, staring down at the ice in my cup. She doesn't answer, so assuming she didn't hear me over the booming music, I raise my voice and begin to repeat the question.

She interrupts me after a few words, "I wanted to consult with you about what to wear to the wedding. How'd I do?" Gesturing to the gown that hugs her in all the right places, she suggestively twitches her eyebrows at me. "Figured silver was a nice, safe, complementary color—"

"You didn't come over to collaborate on wedding attire." My eyes pin hers. "That dress matches those shoes perfectly, which means you bought them at the same time, which means you already had the dress when you came to see me, because you said you already had the shoes and that 'anything would go with them,' which is clearly not the case with those things."

I glance at them and quickly back up at her face, because, frankly, those are the sexiest shoes I've ever seen, and they make me think very wrong thoughts. This isn't about *my* being wrong.

After a guilty swallow, she attempts blithely, "Wow. You've given this a lot of thought, Sherlock."

"Can you just answer my question? Please?"

Lifting her chin, she takes a deep breath and says, "Okay, fine. I didn't need to talk to you about what to wear tonight."

I roll my hand to encourage her to tell me something I don't already know.

Unfortunately, Nick and Heidi pick that moment to wend our way.

Betty sits up more fully in her chair and tucks her knees under the table. Nodding toward my brother and new sister-in-law, she beams up at them when they amble up to us. "Hey, guys! Congratulations!"

The happy couple, clearly high on a mixture of relief and love and unadulterated joy, answer in unison, "Thanks!"

Betty kicks me under the table, so I straighten and mutter, "Congrats." I already gave my semi-sincere best man's speech. How many times am I going to have to wish these two well today?

"Natey!" Heidi gushes, pulling over a chair from another table and plopping into it. She grabs hold of my face with both hands and pulls it toward her, planting a firm, moist kiss on my cheek. After releasing me, she states, "You've been awesome today. Thank you so much for everything!"

"Everything?" I look to Nick for some clue, but he's too busy gazing lovingly at his new wife.

"You know, being such a good sport and doing what Nicky needed before he ever had to ask."

I stifle a snort at the last minute. The effort results in a painful noise that resembles a hiccup. "Okay. It wasn't about being a good sport, but you're welcome, I guess."

Grasping my forearm, she leans even closer, which I didn't think was possible. I scoot back an inch, but it doesn't make much of a difference in my discomfort level. Oblivious to the "back-off" signals I'm giving her, she continues, "I know this hasn't been easy. It must be weird to see me with your brother—"

Oh gosh. Someone pull the fire alarm. Or anything.

Again, I shoot Nick a beseeching look, but he's trailing his right index finger down Heidi's neck, watching as it disappears down the gap her shoulder blades have created between her strapless dress and her back. Great. He's not even going to wait for the reception to end to start the honeymoon.

Finally, I find a way to address her assertion that seeing her with Nick is a problem for me. "I try not to think too much about it."

"Of course you don't," Heidi replies in that patronizing tone that makes me glad she broke up with me and chose, instead, to marry my brother. I can't imagine fifty years of hearing those four words in that tone of voice every time she didn't believe something I said or wanted to have the last word in an argument.

Well, she's not getting the last word today.

I gently remove her hand from my arm. "Really, I'm not just putting on a brave face, okay? I'm happy for you two. I've moved on."

"But Frankie's not here. I hope that doesn't mean something's wrong." She pooches out her bottom lip.

Consciously unclenching my jaw, I smile tightly at my new sister-in-law.

"Just a scheduling conflict. Right, Nathaniel?" Betty butts in.

I could kiss her. Platonically, of course. Not anything like what she did to me on her front step a couple of weeks ago. No. That should never be repeated. Because, well, it shouldn't.

It takes a few blinks and a concerted effort to pull myself back to the current conversation. "Right. Yeah. I wouldn't hear of her missing her dad's sixtieth birthday."

"Well, you know Nicky and I are here for you."

"Good to know." I try to keep the sarcasm from my tone, but it slips persistently through.

Heidi's too wrapped up in her wedding day euphoria to notice, thankfully. She reaches over and gives my hand one last squeeze but her grip lingers on my knuckles. My stomach drops when I see tears gather on her bottom lids. I almost forgot how she could cry at the drop of a hat. The two of us were quite the blubbering pair. Our sniffling got so out of hand when we saw *The Vow* that a lady sitting behind us in the movie theater leaned forward and offered each of us a tissue. Now I shake that memory loose like an Etch-a-Sketch doodle and focus on Heidi's sparkling eyes. She's always been a pretty crier, like she practices it in the mirror. I wouldn't put it past her.

"You're such a good guy, Nate," she fawns now, dabbing at the corners of her eyes with her perfectly manicured left index finger. "I spent a long time regretting that it didn't work out between us. But now I know why it didn't." She lets go of my hand and grabs Nick's unoccupied one over her shoulder. "I hope you someday have what we do. You deserve it."

"Mmm." I stand, my legs knowing before my head does that I need to get out of here, away from her. "Thanks. I'm working on it." I grab the garter from the table and shove it into my pants pocket.

Betty stands with me. "You promised me dancing," she declares. If she's as chagrined as I am that the DJ picked this precise moment to play the Macarena (when is that damn dance gonna die?), she doesn't let on.

Nick *finally* snaps out of his trance. He steps forward and offers me his right hand to shake. It's recently been halfway down the back of his wife's dress, but it would look rude and would most definitely be misconstrued by the people around us, who are surely watching, if I didn't shake it. So I do. Then, to seal the deal, I pull him in for one of those man-hugs—a slight lean forward so our chests are barely touching, followed by a swift thump on his back with my fist.

"Congratulations," I say next to his ear. "And good luck." I leave off the *"You're going to need it"* that's on the tip of my tongue. After all, maybe he won't. Maybe he's okay with Heidi getting her way about everything and forcing him to listen to endless analyses of her newest haircut or color. Then again, I thought I was, too. Until I didn't have to deal with it anymore. Then I realized what a major disaster I'd avoided.

After pushing away from my brother, I lean down and give Heidi a quick squeeze and a peck on the cheek.

Lightly, I say to them both as Betty tugs me away, "See ya!"

A slow Sting number follows the synchronized hell dance, but instead of walking back to our seats, we stay on the dance floor. I hold Betty—in a friendly, big-brother way—as we sway to the music. She smells like she did when she kissed me: clean, with more than a hint of hair product, but also soft and feminine, with undertones of citrus and something floral I can't place. I close my eyes. The weak me allows myself to remember how she tasted, how her lips felt against mine.

No. My eyes open, and I focus them across the dance floor at the DJ, who thinks he's cool, even though he spends his weekends playing the Macarena and the Chicken Dance for people who'd rather be in front of their TVs, not wearing pinchy shoes. During the week, he's probably an accountant or, worse, an engineer.

Betty's hand shifts in mine. It's soft and small and slightly sweaty, but so is mine (slightly sweaty, that is), so I don't necessarily take her damp palm to mean she's nervous or uncomfortable. It's just a byproduct of skin against skin. My skin against hers...

Away from her ear, I clear my throat, then look straight ahead again and say casually, "This wedding is one of the gaudiest things I've been a part of in a while. It's been a clinic in what *not* to do, wouldn't you say?"

She relaxes in my arms and laughs. "Right? Just so you know, Francesca will not be singing 'Endless Love' or anything by Adele when she's my maid of honor."

"I think that's probably for the best," I approve, recalling some of the times I've heard Frankie "sing" along to the radio. "And what's with the customized vows at every wedding nowadays? Someone smarter than I am thought of everything that needed to be covered in the traditional ones. Maybe we can leave out the 'obeying' part, but criminy! To go on and on and on."

"Yeah, I thought they'd never shut up in there today. I was waiting for them to reveal their birthing plan or their sex pledge. Glad it wasn't just me."

"It wasn't. That won't be happening when—*if*—I get married. Nobody needs to hear me gush about how wonderful I think my bride is. That's uncomfortable."

"You'd end up crying, anyway."

Grudgingly, I have to admit, "Without a doubt. Which might result in my being abandoned at the altar."

She flicks my pink bow tie. "And this is heinous. *When*—not if—I get married, there will be no matchy-matchy wedding party attire."

"On behalf of all men everywhere, thank you. It's not 'mauve,' like Heidi tried to tell me; it's straight-up pink, m'kay? And I'm not happy about it. I'll never make anyone I consider even close to being a friend wear something this color. Nick's lucky he's my only sibling. If I had a spare or two, I'd disown him for this."

"But hot pink looks good on you."

I look at her sideways, trying to judge if she's being sincere.

"Really, it does! It's still not nice to make a guy find that out about himself. But it could be worse. I went to a wedding once where the guys had to wear lavender top hats and tails. Lavender, Nathaniel. It was like the couple had hired Lewis Carroll on acid as their wedding planner. So count your blessings."

"How does that even happen, anyway? I mean, why don't guys get any say in what goes on or what their friends have to wear?"

"Do I really need to explain this to you?"

"Yes!"

She sighs as if it's a huge imposition. "Most women—not I, but most—have been clipping pictures of dresses and cakes and flowers from every wedding magazine on newsstands since they were eleven years old. It's their dream." She rests her head on my chest and flutters her eyelids at me.

In an effort to drown out the sound of my physical reaction to that gesture, I say, "It's *one day!*"

"I agree." She lifts her head and speaks normally. "So using that same logic, why do you care what *you're* wearing or how the floral arrangements or centerpieces look on that *one day?*"

I laugh. "I don't give a rat's ass about flowers or wedding favors, but giving either half of a couple complete and final control over all of the wedding-day decisions sets a horrible precedent for marital misery."

"Say that five times fast," she teases.

I ignore her. "Anyway, when I was eleven years old, I wanted every major event in my life to have a Transformers theme. Does that mean I get to say my vows in my best Optimus Prime voice?"

She throws her head back and shrieks at the ceiling, earning every attendee's attention. "Oh my gosh, I'm gonna pee!"

I clamp my hand over her mouth while trying to keep my own laughter in check.

When she calms down, I return my hand to her waist, and we snicker quietly together. Finally, she says, "That's different. You outgrew your Transformers preoccupation, I'm assuming?"

I grin. "Yeah, so what? My point is, I'm not going to let an eleven-year-old girl's concept of romance dictate what happens on my wedding day. No Optimus Prime, then no horse-drawn glass carriage, either."

A jazzier song comes on, so I spin her out and pull her back toward me in the only swing move I've ever mastered. She pushes away but remains facing me as she shimmies to the beat.

"Your cheesy move reminds me of something else that won't be happening at *my* wedding: the choreographed first dance."

I groan. "Oh, those are the worst!"

"And nobody better put condoms and toilet paper on the getaway car, like you instructed those young boys to do earlier. I'm riding away in a sleek town car, no shoe polish allowed."

"You're no fun."

"Yes, I am. I'm a lot of fun, where it counts."

I choose not to comment and instead focus on trying to remember how to dance to a fast song.

We don't say anything else for the duration of the peppy

number, but when it transitions into another slow dance, Betty says, "You're a decent dancer."

"Thanks, I guess." I turn to walk back to the table, but she snags my cummerbund.

"Wait. Nate."

I slingshot toward her, nearly slipping in my shiny, slick-soled shoes. Her unintentional rhyme and use of my real name get my attention more than her serious tone, but the latter two tell me she means business.

"What is it?"

"One more dance."

"People are going to start talking," I say, trying to cover up my unease with a joke.

"Who gives a shit? Come on. I need to talk to you about something. For real."

Rather than give her a hard time and make an even bigger scene, I acquiesce, pulling her against me. "Fine." Then I wait.

"I came to your house last Saturday, because..." She presses closer to me and lowers her head. After several seconds, she starts over and says in a rush, "I had a feeling you didn't know where Frankie was staying in Chicago, and I thought you *should* know, but once I was there, and it was clear you *didn't* know, I started to doubt my instinct to tell you."

Since I'm not sure it *would* have been right for her to tell me, I say nothing but simply stare over her head while biting the inside of my cheek.

Her hair grazes my chin when she abruptly lifts her head to look at me. "I'm sorry. I'm still not sure I did the right thing. I'm so confused."

That admission makes me feel like I did that time I drank a full jar of pickle juice on a dare: vindicated, yet nauseated.

"Say something," she begs in a whisper.

Feeling like I'm toeing a great, big, definitive, unambiguous line, a line everyone in a committed relationship is well aware of and can never claim ignorance about, I weigh each word before saying, "I understand how you might feel conflicted."

"You do?"

Her blue eyes sparkle hopefully, then dim when I answer, "You're friends with both Frankie and me, but you've been friends with her longer, so your loyalty is with her."

"Not if she's doing something wrong by you."

And there it is. The confirmation I've been dreading. Still wishing to hear anything to make it not true, to not make the past six months a complete waste, I ask, "Do you know she is? For a fact?"

My knees nearly give out when she shakes her head. "No. I don't have any proof. She hardly ever talks to me anymore, unless it has to do with Frank."

The hurt in her face awakens a fierce protectiveness in me. By instinct, my arms contract around her back, pulling her closer to my chest in a hug. "I'm sorry," I say against her hair.

She laughs bitterly. "My best friend might be cheating on you, and you're consoling *me*."

Still hanging onto every possible last shred of dignity I may have, I claim, "We don't know anything. According to her, nothing happened."

"Do you believe that?"

"I think I have to."

The song ends, and she separates from me. I'm dismayed to see tears on her face. Her mouth trembles as she opens it to talk, so she screws her lips to the side, pauses, then chokes, "Heidi's right. You're a really good guy," before rushing from the dance floor, leaving me there with my arms hanging limply at my sides.

People are definitely staring now.

18

DYNAMIC DUO

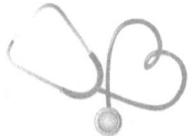

APPARENTLY, FRANK'S POPULARITY HASN'T MADE IT TO Duluth. There's still an hour left for today's event, but it feels like we've already been here for days. It's been one of the "painful" appearances the Phoenix bookstore owner derided all those weeks ago.

Prolonging the agony is the silence that's stretched—with few interruptions—for a month now between Betty and me, despite the fact that we spend nearly every weekend partici- pating in Frank-related pursuits. We've perfected non-verbal communication, as well as the use of the well-timed grunt or monosyllable. It's miserable. The longest "conversations" on these trips are between myself and the voice in my GPS (I call her Wanda) as she directs me to our event venues.

Following Betty's departure from the dance floor at Nick and Heidi's wedding reception, I returned to the table to resume hiding from my nosy, obnoxious, getting-drunker-by- the-minute relatives. Mom and Dad stopped by the table as I was finishing up my third whiskey and Coke, but their visit was a short one, probably due, in part, to my growled responses to their polite inquiries into my mental and physical wellbeing and their compliments on my fancy footwork with Betty. Taking the hint, for once, that I wasn't in the mood for a free therapy session, Mom simply informed me Nick and Heidi were changing into their "going away outfits" (#3,217 on Nate's List of Wedding No-Nos) and would be leaving any minute. Then she and Dad made their own escape, and I got to my wobbly feet to find my date.

I looked everywhere for her. An informal poll outside the ladies' room convinced me she wasn't holed up in a stall, but I couldn't find her anywhere else, either.

As the D.J. was announcing "Mr. and Mrs. Nicholas Bingham's" impending departure, I shot Betty a quick text: *Where r u?*

Almost immediately, I received the reply: *Home*

I wanted to know more, like "Why?" and "What's wrong?" but alcohol and a suddenly overwhelming and irrational sense of rejection were beating the shit out of my curiosity, so I simply shot back: *Fantastic. Thanks*

Not even my babysitter could handle a full evening with me.

Today, we're five hours from home, sitting behind a table in an independent bookstore, watching people walk past us. Most of them ignore us altogether, but a few of them have slowed down to glance at the books propped and stacked in front of us before speeding up again and studiously avoiding eye contact.

I'm sick of them pretending we're not here, but they're strangers; their indifference doesn't hurt. The detachment from the person sitting next to me is another story.

"Three hours is too long," I say, stating the obvious, rolling my signing Sharpie along my knuckles. My voice sounds rusty from disuse.

Betty, slumped over a stack of books—a stack too big for

the end of an event—sighs. "Yeah. This is awful. This store isn't even big enough to hold a crowd that would warrant more than a two-hour event."

"*If* anyone had shown up."

"I swear, I did all the usual advertising and promotion for this one, the same things I did for the signing in Eau Claire, and that was a huge success. I don't know what the hell happened."

I give her back a casual, consoling pat, then return my hand to the table. "It's not your fault. I bet this is pretty common."

She straightens, arching her back and pushing her arms over her head. "Still makes us look like major losers."

Studying her face, I take in the dark circles under her eyes. And is it just me, or is she wearing less makeup than usual? There's definitely something different about her skin. Duller, maybe. I fish a bottle of water from the cooler at my feet and slide it across the table. It stops directly in front of her, leaving a wet trail in its wake.

"You getting enough sleep?" I inquire, then nod toward the bottle. "Drinking plenty of water? Eating well?"

She shrugs. "Probably no, on all counts. Not enough time."

"It doesn't take a lot of time to drink water."

Twisting off the cap seems to require more strength than she has to give, and she winces. "Yeah, but water doesn't help me stay awake late at night while I'm updating Frank's website. Or sending out requests to book bloggers and searching for conferences for you to attend."

I'd prefer continuing my health homily, but the last thing she said has my undivided attention. "Conferences? Please, tell me you're kidding."

I have to wait for her to stop gulping water for her to answer, "Not kidding. Frankie wants you to hit at least two

216 | LET'S BE FRANK

before the end of the year. I already have you signed up for a smallish indie one in Atlanta at the end of August; now I'm trying to find another, bigger one that would give her books the most exposure."

I silently lament the vacation time I'll probably have to take to go to something I don't even want to attend. Not for the first time, I wonder what the hell we're doing and why we continue to keep doing it.

Before I can consult Betty to see if she has a better answer than the one I keep telling myself, she says while staring into the middle distance, "You're doing such a good job at all of this. You'll be a huge hit at conferences."

"You're giving me heart palpitations," I tell her.

She blinks and smiles over at me. "Oh, come on. It'll be fun. A chance to get away, meet some crazy writers. It'll be worth some laughs, if nothing else."

"I'm going to puke."

"Okay, I'll stop talking about it, then," she says, tenderly patting my cheek. "So sensitive." The plastic water bottle pops and crinkles in her grip as she returns her attention to it and sucks down the remainder of the liquid.

I avert my eyes, checking the time on my phone for the hundredth time in the past ten minutes.

Her voice cuts through my despair at the slow passage of time. "We've hit a bit of a sales slump, too. I need to figure that out."

I look up to see her nibbling on her thumb nail. Pulling her hand away from her mouth, I say, "From what I've read, that's typical going into summer. People spend more time outside, doing active things. Not everyone spends their weekends in bookstores. Remember when *we* didn't?"

"No," she says ruefully. "Anyway, Frankie's books are great beach reads. We need to capitalize on that. Maybe I can ask people to post pictures of themselves reading her books on vacation. Ebooks, paperbacks, whatever. Books in the wild." She muses about that for a while, staring into space once more.

"That's a good idea," I encourage. "But don't make yourself sick with all this work."

"Well, if Frankie's going to quit her job with Quimby-Rex so she can concentrate on writing full-time, like she wants to, I need to ramp up my game."

I drop the Sharpie and bend down to pick it up, nearly falling from my chair in the process. Righting myself, I sit upright and push Frank's glasses higher on my nose. I try to pretend her statement isn't a dreadful diagnosis I've just heard for the first time when I say, "Maybe it's not feasible for her to do that right now."

"She seems to think it is. Kyle crunched some numbers for her, and he says it's possible, if she withdraws some money from her 401K—"

"That's ridiculous, irresponsible advice!" I'm aware my reaction makes it obvious this *is* the first I've heard of all this, but at this point, I don't care.

In contrast to the strain between Betty and me lately, things have been better with Frankie. I woke up the day after Nick's wedding to a text from her that simply said, *I'm sorry. Call me.* We had a long talk about her weekend in Chicago, and she meekly reiterated there was nothing to be jealous about. She claimed he was at work most of the weekend, and she spent her time writing on the balcony at his place. When I eventually told her I believed her—it seemed petty to keep accusing her of lying when I didn't have proof she was—she said, relief heavy in her voice, "I'd never cheat on you, Nate. I love you! I wish I wasn't stuck here at my parents'; I'd come over there and prove it to you."

As much as I would have liked that under normal circumstances (whatever those are), I had to admit it was probably for the best she couldn't, since I was suffering through an astounding hangover attacking every pain receptor from my gut upwards. I told her I'd gladly accept a rain check.

I haven't been able to collect on it yet, because she's still spending most of her free time writing, but she at least seems regretful about it and apologizes often for not being more available. She's even backed up those apologies with some big promises. ("When I'm finished with this book, we'll go away for a weekend. Maybe in the fall? A spa weekend would be awesome, wouldn't it? I know how much you love soaking in bathtubs. You deserve it. You've been so awesome.")

I guess she's been too busy to let me in on this writing career plan of hers, though.

Betty has the grace not to make me explicitly admit my ignorance but simply continues as I catch up, "Yeah, well, she's determined. I agree with you about her retirement fund; that's why I want to do whatever I can to make sure she doesn't have to touch it."

"What is *she* willing to do to realize this goal?" I wonder out loud, making the executive decision to pull the plug on this event as I start to pack up nearly all of the books and merchandise we arrived with.

Betty follows my lead. "Type her fingers off, I guess."

"Helpful," I scoff.

"The bigger the back stock—"

"She has a big enough back stock. We can hardly market and sell the books she already has out there."

Glancing nervously around us, Betty says, "Hey, I just realized—maybe we should wait and talk about this later, when we're alone."

I roll my eyes. "Nobody here gives a shit or knows who the hell we are." But I drop the topic. It's only pissing me off anyway. Of course, just because we're not talking about it doesn't mean I'm not thinking about it while we finish our tear-down.

I'm so sick of being in the dark about everything, even though this has taken over my life. I'm so sick of Kyle MacDonald having more of a say about what Frankie does—what *I* do—than I do. I'm so sick of never seeing my girlfriend. I'm so sick of driving rental cars and turning in expense reports—*to my girlfriend*. I'm so sick of having one day every weekend—if I'm lucky—to do everything I need or want to do around my house, or nothing at all, if I'd prefer to simply rest.

While I violently stack boxes on the hand cart, preparing for our departure, Betty freezes me with a hand on my lower back. "Hey. I thought you knew."

I remain turned away from her. "Yeah. Well, I bet you're not *that* surprised I didn't."

"Let's put this stuff in the car and go for a walk before we hit the road," she suggests. "I can't handle the idea of sitting for another five hours right now."

Glancing at her over my shoulder, I can tell she's not exaggerating. She looks almost as undone as I feel. "Fine. I could use the exercise, too," I agree.

She smiles. "Great. I'll go find the manager and let her know we're leaving early."

* * *

The early summer weather's way too nice to have wasted the afternoon behind a table in a fusty bookstore. As soon as we've stowed the boxes of books and bookmarks and coffee mugs in the trunk of the rental car, we take off on foot in the direction of a park we drove past on our way to the bookstore.

We don't say much on our way there. I can't think of

anything to say that doesn't have to do with Frankie or Frank or selling books. Or heartfelt declarations. Or drunken kisses. Betty seems to be okay with not talking, so I eventually give up trying to conjure safe topics and decide silence is the best option.

When we get to the playground, I head for the seesaw and gesture to the lower end. "Climb on," I tell her.

That bewitching right eyebrow goes all downward-facing-dog and makes my stomach twitch pleasantly. "Are you serious?"

"Yeah! Come on. It'll be fun."

She looks skeptical, but she straddles the tiny plastic seat on the equipment and supports her weight on straight legs to bring my side closer to the ground. I climb on, suddenly feeling stupid but also feeling committed to this activity, since it was my idea. I let my body weight tip the balance more to my side, and I sink toward the dirt patch underneath me while Betty rises to the apparatus's maximum height.

"You better not pull any stunts, like dropping me from the top so I bust my ass. I won't be amused," she warns.

"I'd never do that! You could break your coccyx."

She smirks. "You said 'coccyx.'"

I push off the ground, sending her on a gentle descent, but her feet don't even touch down before my weight lifts her once more. "That's what it's called."

"It sounds dirty."

"Well, I know from experience it hurts like hell to bruise it or break it, so I'd never do that to someone." Again, I try to bring her down, this time with a stronger push from my legs, but she reascends before her feet contact the ground.

"You broke your ass once?"

"I've bruised my *tailbone* more than once, yes. Falls on ice, both times."

"Ouch. You need to be more careful, Nathaniel."

"I need to move to a place where there's no ice." After two more tries to make the seesaw work the way it's supposed to work, I sigh and admit defeat. "This isn't as fun when you're a grownup."

She laughs. "I guess when we're kids, our weights are more similar. It would probably take two of me on this side to make this work with you."

"Are you calling me chubby?" Again, I feel conspicuous in my tight-fitting jeans. I thought I detected the start of a muffin top when I got dressed this morning. Must make more time for exercise. I already get up at 7:00 every morning, no matter what day it is, but maybe on weekdays, I need to get up at 6:00, to work in a morning jog, or at least some crunches.

"Not at all!" She pauses to catch her breath after laughing at my indignant question. "But you're a guy. More muscle mass. Everyone knows muscle weighs more than fat."

"Damn right, it does." I wink as if I'm not taking any of this seriously. "All right, then. Off you go."

I straighten my legs to support both of us. She swings one leg over and hops off. I drop my side and step over the seat, brushing my hands together to rid them of the dirt from the metal handle.

"Wanna try the swings?" I ask, nodding in their direction.

Sadness and weariness take up residence on her face again when she says, "Nah. We should probably get on the road. Long trip home."

"Yeah. It'll be late by the time we roll back into town," I agree, closing the distance in the grass between us as we retrace our steps to the bookstore parking lot.

"Thanks for not dropping me." She threads her arm through mine and gives it an affectionate squeeze. As quickly, she lets go, putting a couple of feet between us.

I tuck my hands in my pockets and stare at my shoes. "No problem. We're in this together, right?"

She grunts, then says, "We don't have much of a choice, do we?"

I laugh. "I guess not, at this point."

Falling into step closer to me, she nudges me with her elbow. "Just kidding. Actually, you do have a choice. I'm sorry if anyone has ever made you feel like you don't." She abruptly stops talking. In the dusk, it's hard to read the expression on her face. Eventually, when I don't rush to fill the silence, she continues, "I'm starting to regret my part in all this."

"There's no use regretting it. I mean, good things have come out of it, right?"

At first, I think she's interpreted my question as rhetorical (which it may as well have been), because she says nothing to confirm or deny my theory. Then, as the rental car comes into view, I barely hear her whisper, "Right."

It's been so long since I've said anything that I've almost forgotten what she's responding to. When I do remember, her sad tone makes me wonder if she truly agrees or is just humoring me.

"Hey, I—"

"Listen—"

We laugh nervously at our simultaneous speaking as we stop in the middle of the parking lot, several yards away from the car, and face one another.

"You go," we say together, which makes us laugh harder and breaks the tension, somewhat.

Since I was about to propose something radical, something I think would make both of us happy while also making one of us quite sad, if that's possible, I decide I'd rather hear what she has to say first. "No, really," I insist. "You first."

She gives a short nod. "Okay. I'm sorry I ran out on you at Nick and Heidi's wedding."

Not wishing to revisit that night, I wave away her apology. "Don't worry about it."

"But I do. It was selfish. I hope you didn't look for me for very long before you texted me."

"I didn't. I assumed you were in the bathroom and wanted to be left alone, or something."

Her half-smile lets me know she's well aware I'm lying, but she lets it drop. "Right. Well, it was rude to desert you. Like dropping you from the top of the seesaw."

I smile. "Apology accepted."

"I know you want to make this thing with Frankie work."

I simply shrug, wishing I knew as much as she claims to know.

She slides her hands into her back pockets and looks down at her feet. "Other than that, I can't figure you out."

I take a deep breath and inject some uncharacteristic cheer into my voice, like I would for a nervous child about to undergo a procedure she's fairly certain is going to be unpleasant. "What's to figure out? I'm a guy trying to do the right thing. I said I'd do this; I'm doing it. Doesn't matter if I regret agreeing to it. The bottom line is, I did agree to it."

"But things are different now."

"Are they?"

When Betty's head snaps up, and she shoots me an incredulous look, I explain, "Everything's operating the same as it was when we started all this. Frankie's the same; the agreement's the same. The fact that I'm stuck doing something I don't want to do is nobody's fault but my own."

"Why do you always blame—"

"Really," I cut her off, voicing what I've said to myself a million times since the end of February. "It was my idea to be the face of her literary alter ego. I gotta live with the consequences of that suggestion and ultimately agreeing to go through with it."

Carefully, slowly, she asks, "Don't you ever feel like she's taking advantage of you, of your generous nature?"

I set my jaw. "I'm not a victim, if that's what you mean. Nobody's manipulating me."

She blinks at me for so long that I think she may be trying to send me a memo in Morse Code. I don't like the message, either.

I spin on my heel and stride toward the car. "Let's go. I'm tired and want to get home."

19

UNRAVELING

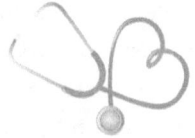

BETTY FALLS ASLEEP SOON AFTER WE HIT THE HIGHWAY, AND while I'm glad she's getting some much-needed rest, the silence gives me a lot of time to think. About four-and-a-half hours, to be exact. My thoughts keep returning to this:

I'm so full of shit, it's not even funny.

Even better, the only person I'm fooling is myself.

Frankie's going to cash in her 401K to fund her dream life; well, I'm ready to collect on *my* investment, too. I've spent months pouring myself into a relationship that's been far from ideal, all under the assumption that every good relationship is based on compromise and give and take. But good relationships have no room for resentment, and lately I'm starting to feel like I'm always giving, always the one compromising more, so the resentment is building.

I've been here before, facing this diagnosis, nearly four years ago. Back then, I chose the treatment plan with the most immediate results—people-pleasing, followed by major life-style changes. Oh, and large doses of denial.

This time, I've recognized the same things happening, and I thought I was choosing a different treatment plan. But it's the same plan, only disguised as something "new and improved." And now, unfortunately, my condition is too far gone to keep putting bandages on it and managing my symptoms.

My only option now, I'm afraid, is surgery. I need to cut out the disease before it starts to infect every aspect of my life.

The decision before me is similar to the one many women face when undergoing surgery for breast cancer. I believe one breast can be saved, but is it worth the risk? Perhaps the safest choice is to remove them both and move forward with healing and possible reconstruction later.

I decide to stop for gas, so I can stretch my legs and get some fresh(ish) air. I mean, I'm comparing my relationship with Frankie and being Frank to two cancerous boobs.

"You're a cancerous boob," I say out loud to myself, taking the next available exit from the highway.

Betty stirs. "Huh?" she mumbles.

"Nothing. Never mind. Gonna make a quick pit stop."

"Where are we?" she asks, sitting up and blinking.

"About halfway home. You can keep sleeping. I didn't mean to wake you."

At the service station, while waiting in line to pay for the coffee I hope will keep me alert for the rest of the trip, I text Frankie to check her status and plans for the evening. *Staying up late tonight?*

As I'm getting back in the car, she replies: *Can't text. Writing*

That settles it, then. Surgery it is.

* * *

It's late but still before midnight when Betty and I roll into Green Bay. Frankie never goes to bed before 2 a.m. when she's in the middle of a creative tear, so after I drop off yawning Betty at her place and ensure she makes it inside safely, I point the rental car in the direction of Frankie's apartment.

Outside Frankie's door, I take a deep breath and reassure myself this is the right thing to do. Our relationship is never going to work, and it's better to know that now, seven months in, than continue in denial and face it months—or years —from now.

My knocks go unanswered. Sometimes she writes with music blasting into her earbuds. She ignores the door and the phone, but she always replies to texts, so I pull out my phone and key: *I'm at ur door. Let me in?*

I'm beginning to think she may be indisposed—or ignoring me—when more than a minute goes by with no reply. As I consider my options (none of which are going home and trying again tomorrow), the door swings wide, and a flushed, robe-clad Frankie appears in front of me.

I smile nervously. "Hey!"

"What are you doing here?" she greets me coldly, stepping back.

"I know you're writing. Sorry for dropping in unannounced, but I... *we* need to talk."

I pocket my keys and advance into the apartment, standing behind a chair at her dining table, where her open laptop rests. I glance down at the laptop screen, a white background jammed full of single-spaced words, the file name at the top, "CEO-Oh-Oh," distracting me for a second.

I shake my head and look back at her, but she's no longer standing by the front door. She's rushing toward me, and not in a "catch-me-in-your-arms-and-make-passionate-love-to-me-on-the-floor, you beast!" way. She stomps, her teeth bared, her nostrils flared, the true human incarnation of the raging bull we all hear so much about but most of us never experience the horror of facing. I have an urge to say, *"Olé!"* Or whimper, *"Mommy!"*

When she arrives at the table, she slams the laptop shut. "Excuse me, but that's private."

"I didn't read anything but the title," I reassure her. "Clever, by the way."

She retreats a few steps, bites her lower lip and looks away from me, something suddenly interesting on the baseboard nearest us. "It's a working title," she snaps, making eye contact with me once more. "I'd like to get back to what I was doing, so..."

I have to hand it to her; she's making this a lot easier for me than I expected. That doesn't mean I'm not nervous. I am. My heart could have probably done without that cup of coffee. Uncertainty about her reaction to what I'm about to say makes my pulse pound in my ears.

After a deep breath, I begin, "Right. Okay, then. I'll make this quick. I came by here to say that I don't—"

The flushing toilet stops me mid-sentence.

Her eyes maintain a lock on my face, but she mutters an obscenity under her breath.

"Who's here?" I ask, my tone weirdly solicitous, even to my own ears.

Without hesitating, she answers, lifting her chin, "Kyle."

What does it say about me that the first thing that pops to mind when she drops that gem is, *"I hope he sprays the air freshener before he comes out"*?

Of course, my second thought has more to do with the guilty look on her face when she answered the door to me and the way she's dressed—or more accurately, *not*. Mixed with those images are her still-echoing denials regarding her weekend in Chicago: *"Nothing happened."*

Today, she claims, "He's helping me with some research for my book."

I bite hard on the inside of my cheek, bark bitterly, then say, "I'm sure he is."

The man himself chooses that moment to enter the living room. He has the good sense to have all of his clothes on. Well, most of them. He's barefoot, and too many buttons are undone on his untucked dress shirt. When he sees me, he smiles like we're in a sales meeting, and he's going to pull out his A-game to sell me a bunch of shit I don't want.

I stride to the door, painfully aware that Frankie's not saying or doing anything to explain herself. Even if it's more lies, I'd appreciate the effort.

But Kyle's the next one to speak. "Nate! Good to see you, man." He extends his hand, which I don't feel inspired to shake, so I don't.

Instead, I roll my eyes at him and snort. "Right. Well. I was just leaving. I'll let you guys get back to *whatever* you were doing."

Finally, Frankie snaps from her trance. But rather than give me the explanation I deserve, she states coldly, "Don't play the injured party here. I know about you and Betty. I've known it for a long time."

I turn to face her, but I refuse to say anything else with Kyle as a witness.

She takes my silence as a confession, apparently, because she sneers and continues, "I even know about the kiss. So spare me the righteous indignation."

I use supreme self-control to open the door calmly and close it quietly. No temper tantrums or flouncing out for me. Not going to give the two of them the satisfaction.

By the time I get to the parking lot, I can feel my hands

shaking and my eyeballs jiggling from the spike in my blood pressure, but I focus on breathing deeply through my nose, even when I spot the silver Jaguar that would have stuck out like a well-manicured thumb on a nail-bitten hand if I'd been thinking of anything but rehearsing my breakup spiel when I arrived here.

In my much-less-than-$70,000 rental car, I sit behind the wheel and stare at the sleek convertible through the windshield. Seething, I wonder how often it sits in this parking lot lately. Are Frankie's neighbors more used to seeing it than they are my car? Something tells me the answer is, "Yes."

And he's either extremely arrogant or stupid to leave it parked out here with the top down. Then again, it probably has a more sophisticated alarm and anti-theft system on it than most homes. Is he flaunting his wealth among the Toyotas and Fords and Hyundais? Jag-off.

He's probably the Bigfoot of the carbon footprint world.

And yes, I'm aware it's not normal for me to be dwelling on Kyle's personal impact on the environment right now, but it's keeping me conscious, so I'm sticking with it.

I rest my forehead against my steering wheel and breathe away the tightness in my chest that I wish I could say was the physical manifestation of heartbreak. Then, I'd feel more like a normal person. Then, I'd feel less guilty. Then, my outrage would be justified. Then, I could embrace the role of hapless pawn I now know I've been playing all along, despite my vehement claims to the contrary.

But I still can't go there. I can't admit the extent to which I've been played. Because then, everything has been for nothing.

Well, almost.

* * *

A PROPER VICTIM would go to a bar tonight and drink by himself. I don't want to drink, though. I don't want to sulk. I don't want to cry or rage or vent. I don't know what I want to do. But I definitely don't want to be alone.

Betty squints and blinks through the porch light at me. "Nate? What are you doing here?"

"I wish everyone would stop asking me that," I grumble, stepping past her without an invitation inside.

She rubs her eyes and closes the door. "I just fell asleep. Is everything okay?"

I have so much to say, but I start with, "Do you always answer the door in the middle of the night dressed like that?"

She looks down at her baby tee and boy shorts. "Huh? No. I don't think I've ever answered my door in the middle of the night, come to think of it."

"Well, it's not safe. You're lucky it was me."

Snorting, she shuffles past me and motions for me to follow her into the kitchen. "I looked through the peephole and saw it was you before I answered. Dad."

In the kitchen, she stretches to reach a shelf in one of her cupboards and pulls down two pint glasses.

"I don't want to drink," I immediately tell her what I've already told myself a hundred times in the past fifteen minutes.

Ignoring me, she opens the fridge, reaches inside, and comes back out with a gallon of milk. "How's this, Boy Scout? I'll even try to find some cookies that aren't too stale."

She scratches at her bare leg with her foot while pouring the milk.

"It's over," I say quietly, testing out the sound of the words before repeating them, louder.

"What happened this time?" she asks with a sigh as she disappears into an impressively organized walk-in pantry.

"This wasn't just a fight. Kyle was at Frankie's."

With a clatter, a package of Oreos skids through the pantry doorway and across the kitchen floor, Betty following closely behind it.

"Damn," she mutters, crouching down to pick up the creme-filled cookies, some of which have shattered on the hard tile floor.

I join her, kneeling and reaching for a few bits that have skittered under the fridge. She allows me to throw those away, but the ones she's picked up from the middle of the floor she sets next to one of the glasses. "I'll eat those; my floor's clean," she explains, before saying, "I'm so sorry."

"They're just cookies."

"No! About Kyle. And Frankie. I really thought it might not be true. I'd hoped, anyway."

"Yeah. Me, too. Apparently, he's her CEO-Oh-Oh."

She laughs. "What?"

I tell her about the title of the manuscript that was open when I got to Frankie's, before Kyle made himself known.

"Yeah, I'm the Hippocratic Oaf, and he's a CEO-Oh-Oh. She never even gave me a chance to..." I trail off, suddenly remembering I'm a) not alone and b) thinking out loud. "Anyway!" I smile sadly. "Whatever. I mean, I went over there to break up with her."

"You did?"

I nod. "Yeah. I should be thanking her for making it so much easier."

"Still, that sucks."

I shrug. "Whatever. I've had more intimate relationships with my cable company. *And* they screwed me more often, too." Immediately regretting that last sentence, I tack on, "Sorry."

I watch, mesmerized, as she holds a cookie in her milk for

several seconds, then gently lifts it and drops it whole onto her tongue. After chewing and swallowing, she grins at me, her teeth an odd grayish-brown. "Good one," she says, approving of my comparison.

I grin back before realizing I shouldn't be feeling so giddy. I just caught my girlfriend of seven months, a woman I fancied —in my wildest delusions, granted—as the mother of my future children, cheating on me. I shouldn't be yukking it up with that ex-girlfriend's best friend a whopping twenty minutes after the fact.

As if confessing to something much darker, I swallow my smile and say, "I don't feel sad. I mean, I'm pissed about, you know. I feel like an idiot that those two have been going at it behind my back, but I don't feel the way I should. I feel happy. No, that's not the right word. Maybe relieved?" Suddenly unable to focus, I watch Betty repeat her soggy cookie routine, then wash down her mouthful with the rest of her milk.

Brushing crumbs from her fingertips, she says, "You said you were going to end it. It makes sense you're relieved."

"Yeah, well. I'm not completely off the hook. I'm still Frank."

She shakes her head and chuckles like someone in the presence of a crazy person and nervous about it. "Seriously?"

Immediately, I reply, "Yeah. I was going to break up with her, but my offer to be Frank still stands. I don't go back on my promises."

"You wouldn't be," she says quietly, looking down at her restless hands.

I think about that for a second and let it sink in. The way in which my relationship with Frankie ended does make a difference, I suppose. I *don't* have an obligation to her anymore. In fact, I *can't* continue to be Frank. That would just be weird.

"Oh, my gosh. You're right," I mumble.

"Yeah, I know."

The anvil that's been sitting inside my chest cavity for months disappears. "I don't have to be Frank anymore. No more scarves, no more glasses, no more Facebook posts or tweets. I'm..."

"Free," she finishes for me.

Without thinking, I step around the counter, lift her off the floor, and spin in a circle. "I'm free!" I repeat after her.

"Put me down, you dumb-ass! You're gonna make me barf!"

I do as she says and quickly exit the kitchen.

"Hey! Where are you going?" she calls after me.

My answer is to return less than a minute later with some of the boxes from the trunk of the rental car. "Where do you want all this shit?" I ask, my voice shaking slightly.

She blinks at me. "I guess it doesn't matter. Anywhere?"

I place them next to the door I assume leads to the garage. "I'll stack them here. You can give them to Frankie. Or burn them. Or whatever." Before she can respond to that, I leave again, returning with two more boxes. After the final trip with the last two boxes, I come back to see her staring at the stack, her right elbow in her left hand, her right hand cupping her chin.

"Wow. It's really over, huh?" she murmurs.

For the first time since leaving Frankie's, I feel the type of pang typically associated with a traumatic breakup. Only it has nothing to do with the breakup. My smile fades with my evaporating euphoria as I watch her open the box on the top of the pile and pull out one of the paperbacks. She turns it over and looks at my picture on the back.

I want to go to her, but my feet feel glued to the floor, and I'm too far away to reach out and touch any part of her.

"Yeah, it is," I simply say.

"Like that."

"Like that."

She holds up the book, a copy of *Girl Noir*, cover out.

I tilt my head, my heart pounding. "Let me guess. That one's yours."

She nods. "Yep."

Judging by the set of her mouth and the tears gathering in her eyes, I know, "Not a flattering portrayal?"

Her head-shake jars a few tears loose. "No, but you already know that."

"Still haven't read it. Don't plan to."

Any surprise at this information is quickly covered by resolve as she extends her arm, offering the book to me. "You should," she tells me.

I begin to object, but she interrupts. "Please. For me."

I straighten my arm and reluctantly take the book. "Why?"

She shrugs. "You'll know why after you read it."

I turn it over in my hands and stare at the glossy, stylized cover. "Okay. Fine. For you."

Crossing the kitchen, she opens her arms and wraps them around my torso, burying her face against my chest. "Goodbye, Nathaniel. I'm so happy for you."

"Bye?"

She raises her face and nods. "Yeah. I think so."

I try to imagine keeping in touch with her, how that would work, considering everything, and I finally have to say, "Oh. Yeah. You're probably right."

"Usually am," she quips, sniffling and pushing away from me before I can fully return her hug. "Sometimes it sucks."

She walks me to the door. Since this is goodbye, I'm tempted to return the kiss she gave me two months ago on this very spot, the kiss she *must* have remembered and told Frankie about, but something stops me. Not something nebulous, something specific. Something called "self-preservation."

Because the fact she mentioned the kiss to Frankie but has never acknowledged it with me tells me she regrets it and wants to forget it. She probably only told Frankie out of some strange sense of duty to the type of honesty that exists in a friendship as old as theirs.

So I don't even turn around for one final hug or wave or smile or "bye" or anything. I get in the car and drive away without so much as a glance in the rearview mirror.

It's better that way, I tell myself.

20

THE END

So far, being single again isn't much different than when Frankie and I were together. As a matter of fact, I can't think of a single thing I miss about her.

There's plenty I *don't* miss, though. I don't miss the passive-aggressiveness, the pouty lip-pooching, or the petty arguments. I don't miss the random factoids about football players. I don't miss the sullen silences when I'm unable to hide my indifference about said factoids. I don't miss the sexual bribery that rarely amounted to anything and when it did, made me feel like a dirty scumbag. I don't miss the lies, the half-truths, or the secrets, either. No, life without Frankie is a-okay.

I certainly don't miss much about being Frank, either. Not the social media duties, not the glasses, not the scarves, and definitely not the skinny jeans. I don't miss the nerve-wracking public readings, either, but my weekends are depressingly empty.

Because there is something—or rather, *someone*—I miss like crazy. But that's just too bad. There's nothing for that but time and distance. And beer. Lots of beer.

Plus, I know from experience it'll get better. I just have to remember who the hell I am. And I have to stop thinking so much about starting over with someone I haven't even met yet. It's possible I might never meet someone else, so worrying about starting over with someone who may not even exist is pointless.

Somehow, that doesn't make me feel much better.

I can't truly start over, anyway, until I have absolute closure on the Frankie chapter of my life, which is what I hope to have in less than an hour, if all goes well when we exchange the things that have migrated to each other's places during the past seven months.

In order to avoid yet another awkward encounter with my replacement (is someone a "replacement" if they were installed before the incumbent's departure?), I've carefully arranged this meeting via one phone call and two confirmation text messages on a day in the middle of the week, when Kyle *should* be in Chicago, taking over the oh-so-adult world of video gaming. But I wouldn't put it past Frankie to ask him to make a special mid-week trip home for this, as if I'm the big, bad ex-boyfriend. When I arrive at her apartment, however, I'm relieved to see Kyle's ostentatious auto is conspicuously absent from the parking lot.

Really, I want to get this over with as quickly and amicably as possible. If we could do it without speaking to each other at all, that would be great. Somehow I don't think that's going to be possible, though.

After listlessly inviting me inside her place—hopefully for the last time ever—Frankie takes the box I'm carrying, glances into it, and sets it aside on her couch with a dull, "Thanks."

"I washed and sanitized your Packers travel mug," I inform her, not sure how else to start this conversation. "It was pretty nasty. You left it at my place a long time ago, and it was full of coffee... and cream."

She wrinkles her nose. "Gross. Why didn't you just throw it away?"

"I knew it was your favorite. So I gave it an extra soak in bleach water. It's fine now."

"Thanks," she repeats, shifting from foot to foot and looking me up and down with pursed lips and a slight roll of her eyes. "Nice scrubs."

I glance down at my chest and will myself not to blush at my rubber ducky ensemble. The kids love these scrubs, and I wear them for the kids, not for her. Still, my attire is yet another reason to be glad Kyle isn't here. When I don't give her the satisfaction of a defensive response, she edges past me and leads the way down the hallway to her bedroom.

"I have your stuff back here. You're early, as usual, so I wasn't quite finished tracking everything down."

"No biggie. I can help you find things."

"I'd rather you didn't poke around."

Standing in the doorway to her bedroom, I rub the back of my neck and watch her carelessly toss my belongings onto the center of her unmade bed. My lip hurts from biting on it to resist pointing out that I carefully folded each of her t-shirts and double-gloved to wash her favorite travel mug before placing everything neatly in a box, so the least she could do is handle my things with similar respect, especially while I'm standing here, watching.

Instead, I hint at the suggestion by saying, "I don't want to turn this into some big fight, because it's not worth it."

She whirls on me on her way into her bathroom and blinks at me.

My testicles ascend a little higher at that look, but I wait for her to tell me what I said that was so wrong.

"Not worth it?" She disappears into the bathroom and

returns with my toothbrush and baking soda toothpaste, which she tosses on the pile.

"You know what I mean."

"No, I don't. Enlighten me. I'm not worth it?"

I drop my hand to my side. "C'mon. Are you trying to make this more dramatic than it needs to be? I'd think you'd be relieved I'm not mad. I have a right to be, you know? Livid, actually. But I'm trying to keep everything in perspect—" I stop short and grin as it hits me. "Oh, I see. You want Kyle and me to fight over you, is that it?"

"Not even close, Duck Boy." But the vaguely guilty look on her face tells a different story. As does the blush creeping up her neck.

No longer amused, I state bluntly, "Well, forget it."

She taps her foot and crosses her arms over her chest. "Maybe *that's* why we failed as a couple. Because you've always given me the impression you didn't care all that much."

Heat climbs my neck and creeps into my ears, which I can feel reddening. "Um, no. We failed, in all aspects of our relationship, because you manipulated me and lied to me. And cheated on me. How long has it been going on, anyway?"

"You mean with Kyle?"

"Yes, with Kyle! Who else?" I swallow. "You know what? Don't even answer that second thing. Let's focus on Old McFratBoy."

"There wasn't anyone else anyway."

Instead of belaboring the issue and asking why she asked me to be more specific, I simply stare at her and wait for her to answer my original question.

Finally, she shrugs. "A while."

"A while. One month, two? Six?"

Again, all I get is a shrug.

I figure I can assume the worst, although I'm not sure I can allow myself to believe she's been with him the whole time, that *I* was "the other guy." There are too many horrifying implications involved with that scenario. I try to cling to the scant relief she's no longer insulting me by denying everything, but her taciturnity points less to honesty and more to conceal-ment to avoid exposing the extent of her dishonesty.

"Well. That explains a lot. A *lot*. About everything," I mutter, feeling sick.

"You're not blameless."

"Not this again. I didn't kiss her. *She* kissed *me*. After drinking a *lot* of wine at a dinner you and Lover Boy abandoned."

"Of course, you'd defend her and somehow make it my fault that she came onto you."

"It was your fault she had the opportunity. Maybe that was planned all along, huh? And you goaded me into an argument so you'd have an excuse to leave?"

"Whatever. I wasn't even referring to that kiss, originally. I meant, you played an active part in our relationship not working."

"What did I do wrong, other than continue to give you chance after chance after chance, hoping after the novelty of this venture wore off, you'd appreciate everything I'd done for you and reward me for sticking it out? And before you mention it, I don't count one manipulative blow-job that filled me with self-loathing and instant regret a proper reward."

"What, you wanted me to marry you, out of some sense of gratitude? That's... pathetic."

A montage of moments flashes through my memory. "You said you wanted to marry me! Many times! Without my prompting!"

"I said a lot of things to get you to do what I wanted you to do."

I close my eyes, hoping I won't feel as foolish if I can't see the self-satisfied look on her face. Nope. Still feel like an ass.

My eyes open to her smug consideration of me while she waits for a dramatic reaction I refuse to give her. Instead, I say calmly, "Anyway, I don't consider myself blameless. I did suggest being the face of your pen name, so the whole mess resulting from that is something I take equal responsibility for."

Snorting, she tosses my spare Kindle charger onto the bed from across the room, like she's playing a casual pickup game of basketball. "Okay. Whatever."

That flippant remark erases any remaining magnanimous feelings I may have been harboring. "No, not 'whatever.' If you want to be a bitch about it, I don't have to be so generous." When she sighs at that, I snap, "You were *wrong* to use my picture without my express permission, only based on a tipsy conversation in a bar. I think I was more-than-understanding and accommodating when I *caught* you in that ruse."

"I explained to you why I did what I did!"

"Yeah, you did. Now, I know it was probably all lies, but at the time, I believed you, which is why I agreed to go along with it. That doesn't excuse your continuing to use me to further your writing career."

"Oh, poor you! Well, Betty has some great marketing ideas, but they're not easy to implement. They're time consuming and require a lot of effort. Seven months of time and effort, in some cases," she tacks on with a pointed look at me.

Her insinuation confirms my earlier horrific suspicion that I was never her boyfriend and makes me feel faint. I back up to the wall and lean against it, hoping I won't need more support than that to keep me upright and conscious.

She smirks at me. "Yeah. You may flatter yourself that you came up with the idea to be Frank, but don't kid yourself."

Through gritted teeth, I demand, "Stop trying to turn this around on her."

"Then stop trying to blame *me* for everything. I know it's easy to make me the villain, because your ego's bruised, but—"

"It's easy to make you the villain because you *are* the villain!"

"That's completely unfair."

"Oh, we're talking about fairness now? Okay. Good. Let's do that. I have quite a long list of unfair things to discuss with you. Starting with skinny jeans."

"Betty's the one who designed Frank's image, not me. So you can take up your petty wardrobe whines with her."

"You're really going to stick with blaming Betty for everything, huh? Because as far as I can tell, she worked ten times harder than you did to try to make this whole ridiculous charade easier for me."

"Well, she would."

"What's that supposed to mean?" Rage replaces my light-headedness. I push away from the wall and jab my index finger in her direction. "Stop hinting around at things and come out and say what you want to say!"

She flutters her eyelashes. "I don't have time to spell it out for you. Ask her yourself." When all I do is stare her down, she looks away, sweeping her glance around the room, as if searching for more of my things. Ultra-casually, she mumbles, "If you defended me a tenth of the times you've defended her in this one conversation, maybe we'd still be together."

I laugh mirthlessly. "Really? If I had said out loud, 'I'm sure Frankie doesn't mean to be a manipulative, self-centered narcissist' a few of the thousand times I tried to convince myself of that, you wouldn't have been screwing Kyle while I worked my ass off to try to make a completely fictitious relationship work? Oh, wow. If only I'd known that."

So much for "amicable."

Her eyes flash my way again. "Betty's not the angel you think she is."

"I don't think she's an angel. But she's genuine. And she hasn't lied to me."

She hurls a sarcastic laugh at me that makes me flinch. "Gosh, you're dumber than I thought you were. And that's saying something."

When all I do is blink at her, she shakes her head, chuckles bitterly again, and snaps, "She'll deny it, but using you was her idea."

Bile gathers at the base of my throat.

"Well, not *you* specifically," Frankie qualifies. "But it was her idea for me to go out on dates to try to find a face for my pen name."

"What the hell are you talking about?" I croak. "Our first date—"

"Was more like a job interview. And you were perfect. I knew it right away. Not only did you have the right look, but you had that people-pleasing personality that would make you putty in our hands. I couldn't believe when I introduced you to Betty, and she suddenly turned against the idea. Then again, I don't know why I was surprised; she's always been a bit of a flake."

I remember back to that night, the inexplicable tension at the table when I returned from the bathroom. "You never loved me," I say out loud what I've known for a long time but haven't had the guts to admit.

She rolls her eyes. "Oh, don't get all mushy now. I became fond of you. You're a nice guy. And a hard worker. And I lucked out finding someone who didn't pressure me to have sex with him in exchange for all that work. Trust me, I didn't take any of that for granted."

Gritting my teeth, I close my eyes and focus on not puking. "Unbelievable," I mutter. I step forward and sweep my pile of clothes, toiletries, and other random belongings into a tighter pile that I can pick up. "I think this is everything. If you find anything else of mine, feel free to throw it away. I don't want it."

"If you insist."

"I do. And Betty has all the merch and inventory for the public appearances Frank will *never* be making again." I struggle with the armful of stuff as I make my way back to the door. "Good luck with everything," I toss over my shoulder.

At the front door, I scramble to shift items so I can turn the handle and make my grand exit. I lose my grip on half of the things in my arms, however, so t-shirts and underwear flutter into a pile at my feet. When I bend over to pick them up, I drop my toothbrush, which clatters across the tile entryway and under the small table where Frankie throws her keys and mail. On my way up from retrieving the toothbrush, I bump my head on the table, knocking it off-kilter and sending her bills flapping and keys clanging to the floor.

Cursing under my breath, I let everything in my arms go while I right the table, bills, and keys, and open the door. Keeping the door propped with my foot, I gather my personal belongings in a heap, not caring that several t-shirts are hanging as I carry everything down the stairs and to my car. I also have to backtrack halfway across the parking lot after I throw my stuff into my backseat and notice while getting into my car that I've dropped a pair of my underwear.

Not the most graceful, impactful exit I've ever made, but it was probably memorable. That has to count for something.

* * *

A Prius doesn't lend itself to angry, aggressive driving, but if it did, I'd be grinding gears and flooring the gas pedal and squealing my tires during my retreat from Frankie's. As it is, I'm doing all those things in my head and ignoring the fact that the car is carrying on, as usual, with its smooth whirring and humming and silent idling, oblivious to my destructive intent.

How dare she? How *dare* she? It's everyone's fault but hers, the person who manipulated and lied and cheated her way through the better part of a year of my life? What the hell?

Trust me, I blame myself plenty. I blame myself for being blind and stupid and passive and naïve and spineless and for not learning anything from my past relationships, apparently, no matter how much I've tried to tell myself I'm smarter for having lived through them. This proves I've learned *nothing*. In fact, I'm *dumber* than ever, because I've allowed past experiences to blind me to current truths. And I'm right back where I was a year ago.

Only, I'm even worse off than I was before I'd ever heard Frankie's name. Because at least back then, I was somewhat happy with my life. I'd just bought a house, I still had some faith in humanity, my brother was equally single and unattached (or so I thought. Ignorance *is* bliss), and the biggest worry I had was feeling uncomfortable about the fact that I didn't buy my boss's house and may have offended her.

Plus, I was seven months younger. Let's not forget that I recently "celebrated" a birthday. I'm fast-approaching my mid-thirties but back to being perpetually single Nurse Nate. Time is relentlessly advancing, and I'm no closer to having the life I want than I was when I first graduated from nursing school and felt like life was full of possibilities.

What a crock! Life isn't full of possibilities; it's full of false hope and disappointment. And my closet is full of ridiculous clothing I'll never wear again.

Fuck. I don't want to go home. I want to drink. But that's probably not the wisest decision—mentally or physically— right now. Anyway, who would I drink with? I've fallen hopelessly out of touch with all of my friends during the past few months, and my brother—I don't want to be in the presence of Nick and Heidi's newly-wedded bliss tonight. It might send me over the edge. The only other person whose name pops persistently to mind is off-limits. Gone. Another part of the past. And probably not the person I thought she was, anyway.

She knew the whole time. She knows what a fool I've been. She knows. She knew. She *knew*.

To my horror, I feel my eyeballs starting to sweat. Oh, hell no. I'm not going to cry. Uh-uh.

I blink and sniff and swallow repeatedly, willing myself to think of something happy. Or funny. Or maddening. But not sad or pitying. Anything but that.

As I'm waging this Herculean war against my emotions, my thoughts return to what I really need in my life: loyalty, appreciation, and unconditional love. I was a fool to think I'd get that from a woman, much less Frankie, that lying, manipulative, cruel bitch.

Well, no more bitches for this guy! The only bitch I'm interested in right now is a dog. And even then... I have a sinking feeling a female dog might be too complicated and high-maintenance for me to handle. Male creatures only, please.

I sniff and dab my nose on the back of my hand, the idea taking root now. I'll get a manly man's dog. Yeah! I'll call him something cool, something that screams, "I'm a bachelor, and I love it! Look at my awesome, bachelor-y dog." Schwarzenegger. Or Stalone. Or, I'll Google some other sweaty-looking dudes later. Or not. That doesn't sound like a very fun Saturday night, now that I think about it.

Whatever his name ends up being, I picture my future companion as a yellow Lab with a lolling tongue and delightfully vacant eyes, like that dumb dog in the movie, *Up*. (Oh, gosh. I can't think about that movie, or I'll really start crying.)

My furry pal and I are going to be great friends with our compatible IQs. He'll go for runs with me. I'll bathe him with a hose in the backyard in the summer and in the bathtub in the winter. He'll let me rest my feet on him in the evenings while I read on the couch or watch TV. We'll be swingin' single guys.

No girls allowed.

21

REBA

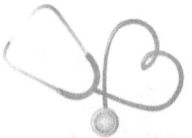

I'VE BEEN STALKING THE LOCAL ANIMAL SHELTERS' WEBSITES for a couple of weeks, waiting for the perfect dog to come up for adoption. I didn't want to show up at a shelter without a specific dog in mind, because I knew I'd get suckered into adopting the most pathetic mutt there, possibly even one of those hairless things that can't keep its tongue in its mouth, because it has no teeth. No, I had to have a plan. A firm plan. And now I do. Because today, I spotted Sherlock on one of the sites.

Sherlock's going to help me pretend to be a little less lonely. Maybe I can train him to bring me beers. Or carry my tool belt.

That thought elicits a goofy smile. Man, this is going to be great!

Someone drives into the lot and pulls behind the building, where I assume the employees and volunteers park. A glance at the clock on my phone tells me I have ten minutes to wait until they open the doors. My car's still the only one in the parking lot, which is good, because it means I won't have to fight anyone for Sherlock.

My heartbeat picks up pace, though, when a minivan glides beside me and pulls even with the parking space in front of mine. Without being too obvious, I size up my competition. Shit. A family with one of those stick-figure renderings on their back window. The only thing they're missing is a stick-dog.

Well, they're not getting *my* stick-dog. Sherlock is mine. I hope things don't have to get ugly in there. That kid staring at me with his nose pressed against the back window will be just as happy with some beagle-shepherd mix. Sherlock's the only dog for me.

I decide to ignore the gaping kid and train my eyes on the shelter's door, the tingling in my stomach reminiscent of the feeling I used to get in the blocks at track meets. Back then, pride and a district or state title were the only things at stake. In contrast, all of my future happiness rests on today's victory.

Okay, perhaps that's slightly hyperbolic, but not by much. My world is a lot smaller than it was a few weeks ago. It doesn't take much to make or break my day anymore.

When the door to the shelter twitches outward as the person on the inside twists the locks and flips the sign from "Closed" to "Open," I vault from my car like a world-class sprinter. Screw that little kid. I'm nice to kids all week long. It's my day off. No mercy.

Inside, I ignore the quizzical look from the middle-aged woman behind the counter when I tell her breathlessly, "I'm here to adopt Sherlock," and nod toward the door that separates us from the holding pens, judging from the barks on the other side.

"Okay..."

Urgency grips my insides when I hear the voices of the family coming closer to the door as they traverse the parking lot. I don't have time for this lady—Wilma, according to her name tag—to try to figure me out.

"I saw the posting online," I explain quickly. "And he's the exact dog I've been looking for."

"Oh, well, we have a lot of dogs—and cats—needing adoptive, loving families—"

"Sherlock will be fine," I interrupt, almost not caring how rude I'm being. "No need for me to browse."

Her tight smile softens to a more sincere one as the minivan family enters the shelter, and Johnny Gawker announces, "We wanna get a puppy!"

His mom gently admonishes him to wait his turn, but Wilma turns her attention away from me and says to the boy, "How nice! Do you have a specific dog in mind?" Am I imagining it, or did she put extra emphasis on the word "specific," like a jab at me?

"Nope!" the toothless kid answers.

"We'll know it when we see it, though. Right, kiddo?" the dad says.

I force myself to smile at them, hoping they're in the market for a lap dog.

"Well, why don't you all follow me, and you can take a look around, find the perfect new friend to take home?" Wilma offers, ushering us through a heavy steel door into a concrete-floored chamber full of chain-link cages. The smell of flea shampoo, dog food, and crap hits me like a wall, but I'm too busy scanning the room of now furiously barking animals to care or react to the smell.

I see my dog right away and stride to his cage. He sniffs my fingers through the metal fencing. "Wilma? Here he is." I relax when I notice the family has zoomed in on a pug with a propensity for licking. Another volunteer has entered the room and is helping them.

Wilma takes her sweet time joining me. "Yes. He's recently become eligible for adoption."

"I know. Like I said, I've been watching the postings for a while, waiting for the right dog." I scratch the top of his head with my forefinger. "Aren't you a handsome guy?" I say to him.

Wilma observes us silently. When I return my attention to her, her jaw juts forward. "Is there a particular reason you want *this* dog? You have a specific plan in mind for him?"

I don't understand her suspicious tone, but I answer her nonetheless. "No. I mean, yeah. I like this breed."

"Well, you can't breed him. He's been neutered."

"I know that."

She steps to the cage next to Sherlock's. "If I might suggest Reba here."

What does this woman not understand about what I'm telling her?

Since time doesn't seem to be of the essence anymore (the family hasn't even glanced at Sherlock), and I've been border-line rude so far, I decide to tone down the intensity and humor Wilma, if for no other reason than to stop her suspecting me of having dastardly designs on yellow Labs. I look at the dog to which she's referring, a squat orange and white thing that can't even be bothered to rise from her curled-up position near the back of her cage.

"She's cute. I think. It's hard to tell from here."

Wilma smiles tenderly toward the pooch. "Oh, she's a sweetie. A Corgi. An expensive breed, you know. She's full-blooded. No papers, of course, and she's been spayed, but I'm sure that's not an issue."

"I don't know much about Corgis," I admit, stepping back to Sherlock's cage. He grins up at me, his tongue flopping from the side of his mouth, his eyes twinkling.

"Hey, buddy," I murmur. "You're a fine fella."

"Corgis are the Queen of England's favorite breed," Wilma persists. "Do you have children?"

I shake my head, trying to focus on the fact and not the emotion behind the answer. "No. Sherlock here will be my only kid."

She returns to my side, finally seeming to get the message I'm not interested in Reba. "What about your backyard? Big? Fenced?"

I'm prepared for this, the "interview" portion of the process. I read online that they make sure each adoptee goes to a home environment that matches the breed's needs.

I nod eagerly. "Yep. Privacy fence. Nice and high. He's not gettin' out. And I love to run, so I'll take him for jogs and—"

"And you'll have lots of time to devote to a dog? Are you single? Work long hours?"

I wave away her questions. "I've installed a doggy door for the days I have to be gone a lot. And I'll come home on my lunch break."

"That's a big doggy door," she says, nodding toward Sherlock. "Intruders can get through a doggy door big enough for that guy. Reba, on the other hand..."

I sigh and turn away from my new best friend. "Look, I appreciate your help, Wilma, but I already know which dog I want to adopt."

She wrings her hands, looking down at them. "Yes. You've been very clear about that."

"Then what's the problem? I'm sure Reba will find a nice Corgi-loving family to take her home and treat her like she's a member of the Queen's household. But I'm no queen." I blush at how that sounds but resist the urge to joke, *"Despite what some people may think,"* and rush on, "Well, not to sound like a sexist jerk, because I'm not, but I sort of had a manlier dog in mind. That's why I've been waiting for *this* dog." I jab a thumb over my shoulder at Sherlock.

Glancing mournfully at Reba, she says, "And I respect that, but we haven't had any success adopting Reba to anyone. Not for long, anyway."

"She's been returned?" I ask, adding this to my reasons *not* to take Reba home with me (as if I needed more).

Wilma nods. "Yes. Well, in effect."

"What's wrong with her?" I can't see anything obvious, but maybe she bites. Antisocial? Her dogged position at the back of her cage supports that hypothesis.

"She's a runner," Wilma admits. "Animal control has picked her up three times and brought her here. And the last time we called the owners, they told us to keep her; they couldn't keep up with her."

"That's too bad," I say. "Now, about Sherlock. What's the adoption fee?"

"Wait. There's more."

I close my eyes and count to three, then open them and smile indulgently at Wilma. What's another couple of minutes, right? At least then I can pretend I kept an open mind, and she can say she tried her best.

Again, she steps to the front of Reba's cage and taps the laminated card attached to the door by the latch. "Today's Reba's last day."

I gulp, hoping she doesn't mean what I think she means. "Last day?"

"Yeah. We can't keep her any longer. If we don't find someone to adopt her—someone with a nice yard and a high fence and someone who can keep her on a tight leash—then... Well, we'll have to put her down."

Now I look more closely at Reba. She gazes balefully up at

me, her chin resting on her paws, as if she knows what we're talking about. My heart lurches.

Desperately, I gesture to the family walking out with the pug. "Wait! Tell *them* Reba's story. They'll take her, I bet."

"Looks like they've already set their hearts on a different dog," Wilma observes, waving at them and smiling. "Congratulations on your new family member!" she calls cheerfully to them before turning back to me with a somber frown.

I point to Sherlock. "I already have my heart set on a different dog, too. And you knew that up front. What's the deal with the hard sell?"

She shrugs. "I don't know. I can tell you're a nice, sensitive guy—"

I snort.

"And you may think Sherlock's the only dog for you, but he'll fit in with a hundred families. Reba's special. She needs someone special. And I could tell you were that someone as soon as you ran through the door."

Now I *know* the woman's crazy, but before I can say, "No," again, she implores, "Look at her! She's sorry for being so much trouble, but with the right owner, she'll be perfect." Moving closer to me and lowering her voice, although we're the only two people in the room, she says, "Between you and me, I think the little girls in the family who had her before kept leaving the back gate open and letting Reba out, then blaming the dog."

"That's sad, but—"

"It is! Reba was only doing what was natural—exploring."

I rub the back of my neck. "Listen, Wilma, I think it's sweet that you're lobbying so hard for Reba, but she's not what I had in mind. It sounds like you're pretty fond of her, though. Why don't *you* take her home?"

Her face hardens. "She's *not what you had in mind?* She's a living creature, not a china pattern." With a subtle head-bob, her tight curls quiver. "And for your information, I'd take her home in a heartbeat, but I already have three dogs and two cats. It would be irresponsible of me to take on any more pets. But you sound like you have plenty of love and room at your place. And you've thought through your adoption and will be a wonderful, responsible dog owner."

I puff out my chest and stand at my full height. "I have thought a lot about it. I purposely bought a dog-friendly house with a fenced yard so I could get a dog. But not *that* dog." I nod at Reba.

"Please, I couldn't bear it if they had to put her to sleep," Wilma begs.

"Are you like this with all the animals? How do you work here if you get so attached?"

"It's not all the animals; but this one is special. It's not her fault she's here. She's a sweet dog!"

"We've established that, but..." I shift from foot to foot. "You have the rest of the day to adopt her out. It's Saturday; I'm sure it'll be busy later, and you'll find someone."

Her eyes fill. "I don't think so. We've had her three Saturdays now. Everyone wants a Lab. Or a puppy."

Helplessly, I look back and forth from Wilma to Reba and back. Reba lifts her head and cocks it at me, as if to say, "Please?" Oh, gosh. She *is* really cute when she does that.

I consider taking home both Sherlock and Reba but instantly know it won't work. Taking care of one dog is going to be enough of a stretch, especially on weekends when I work double shifts at Urgent Care. And I want to do this dog ownership thing right, which is expensive. I can't afford two dogs.

Like a true glutton for punishment, I study Reba. Her strawberry-blonde fur is thick and shiny. The white ring around her shoulders and chest is bright and contrasts nicely with the rest of her fur. Her dark brown eyes shine, hinting at a playful personality. Suddenly, I get a horrifying flash of her lifeless body on a steel table somewhere cold and sad on the premises.

Toward my shoes, I mutter, "Eff me."

Wilma grasps my upper arm as if I've uttered a romantic marriage proposal. "You'll take her, won't you? She'll be grateful to you forever and love you for it, you'll see."

"That hasn't been my experience," I blurt but smile into Wilma's suddenly dry eyes. "Yes. I guess I'll take her."

Before my agreement is even fully out, Wilma unclips a leash from the chain link of Reba's cage and opens the door just wide enough to snake her arm through. Reba, as if in on the plan all along, jumps to her stumpy legs and waddles within arm's reach, obediently standing and waiting for the sound of the metal clasp closing on the ring on her collar.

"Let's get your paperwork filled out and get you on your way," Wilma suggests brightly, widening the opening to the pen and tugging gently on Reba's leash to get her moving. She hands the nylon strap to me. "There you go, Dad."

Automatically, I grasp it. Reba, pulling the leash taut and yanking me forward, cheerfully follows no-nonsense, business-like Wilma. On my way past Sherlock, I give him one final, longing look, all my manly dog fantasies evaporating like fog on a hot, sunny morning. He gives me a parting endorsement bark, as if to reassure me I made the right decision.

I'm starting to think word is getting around among females of all species that I'm the world's biggest pushover. Or maybe they can spot me coming from the length of Lambeau Field.

* * *

"First things first. Your name. It's gotta go. I'm a modern, enlightened guy, but if you have a habit of getting loose, I can't be heard calling for 'Reba.' People will think... Well, I don't know. That I like country music or something."

The Dog-Soon-to-be-Formerly-Known-as-Reba blinks at me, obviously bored with this conversation. I set a bowl of water in front of her on the floor, then lean against the kitchen counter. While I consider naming options, she laps lazily at her refreshment. I must say, I'm starting to think Wilma made up this dog's backstory. I can't imagine the Corgi doing anything close to running. She used up all of her pep at the shelter. Since we've been home, she's barely shown interest in anything more energetic than sniffing her new environment.

I cross my legs at my ankles and my arms over my chest. "So, let's go a little less country and a little more rock-n-roll, shall we? Or even hip-hop. Shorty. Shorty's a good name, and quite fitting. You wanna be my Shorty?"

She collapses to the kitchen floor, which in her case means she lowers herself about three inches, her chin resting on the edge of her water bowl, as if she's humoring me with this conversation.

"Is 'Shorty' insulting? I didn't realize dogs were concerned with political correctness. Okay, you want something that sounds like your current name but doesn't make me want to wear a paper bag over my head every time I have to say it? Amoeba? Nah. Zebra? Tebow? No? Well, we can come back to the name thing later. I'm sure I'll think of something in the shower. That's where I do all my best thinking. But we have plenty of time to learn those intimate things about each other."

Her eyes droop, and she heaves a great sigh before wiggling her head, obviously trying to make herself comfortable.

"Hey, I know!" I say, startling her awake. "Why don't I give you a tour of the place? You should make yourself at home, you know. Like, I have a doggy bed for you, and everything. You don't have to sleep on the kitchen floor."

She doesn't rise but gives me a huge yawn.

"Here. I know you're tired. I'll just show you the basics for now." I gesture to the flap at the bottom of the door that leads from the kitchen into the backyard. "That's for you. You can use it as many times a day as you like. Out there is the yard, where you'll do your business. Outside. Not inside. That's one of the few rules I'm going to have. You can't poop and pee in here."

Having said that, I don't know what I'll do if she *does* relieve herself in the house. I'm never taking her back to that shelter. And I'm not exactly the type of guy who kicks or beats his dog. I can tell by looking at Reba that she knows I'm a sucker with no actions to back up my tough talk, too. "I'll think of something, trust me," I answer her unspoken challenge. "No treats, or something. Just do me a favor and don't test me, all right? Pooping outside is awesome. You'll love it."

Clearing my throat, I push away from the counter and walk through the dining and living rooms and down the hall to my bedroom. When she doesn't immediately follow, I whistle and try, "Here, Jane," thinking a nice, generic name will suffice for now.

My call gets nothing.

I sigh. "Reba, come." Immediately, I hear the clack of nails on the hardwood floor, and she appears around the corner, her tiny legs working in a blur to get her to me not-so-quickly.

When she finally stops at my feet, I say, "Listen, I know you've had the name Reba for three years now. But whoever did that to you wasn't a nice person. So, we're going to change it. You'll have to get used to answering to something else. When you hear me whistle, come, no matter what I call you.

You'll get the hang of it." To soften the news, I give her a scratch behind her ears.

She grunts and slides to the ground, rolling onto her back.

I laugh. "Maybe later. I mean, we just met. You don't want to get a reputation, do you?"

She remains posed with her legs in the air—or as far in the air as they can get. I have to admit, I like this a lot better than the hard-to-get act she put on at the shelter. I can relate to this more. *Love me.*

Still, it's fun to make her work for it just a little. "Do you want to see your bed, or what?"

No reaction.

"It's in here," I walk into the bedroom, leaving her in the hallway. "See? I was expecting a bigger dog, so you'll have plenty of room on it." I pat the green-and-navy plaid dog bed next to mine.

Finally, she joins me and sniffs the stuffed mat, then turns up her nose at it.

While she blinks at me, I say, "I'd offer to let you sleep on my bed, but it's a bit of a jump for someone of your stature. You might be better off sticking with the cushion on the floor. It's an improvement over that concrete pen at the shelter, right?"

Apparently not. She turns and leaves the room.

I follow her down the hall, back to the living room, where she hops neatly onto the loveseat, turns a couple of times, and curls up in one of the corners.

I rub my neck. "Yeah, see... About that... I wasn't planning to let you up on the living room furniture. It's nothing personal, but I was thinking, with your fur and everything, it would be best if you stayed on the floor in here. You know, when people come over, they don't want to get hair all over their clothes after sitting on the couch. I can move your bed out here, if you'd prefer. We don't have to share a bedroom."

She closes her eyes.

"Or whatever. I mean, I want you to feel at home, so... We'll see how this goes. I guess I can always vacuum before having company." I watch her ignoring me for a few seconds. "Okay, then. Well, I can show you the other stuff later. Or we can go for a walk. Or play in the backyard."

Tentatively, so as not to disturb her, I sit on the cushion next to her and retrieve my e-reader from the coffee table. It's not exactly how I pictured my life with a dog, but it's not a *bad* picture, either. Like Wilma said, Reba's sweet, in a low-energy way. Sure, despite being labeled a "runner" by her former owners, I don't think she'll be game for the kind of runs I like to take, but as far as companionship is concerned, I think she and I will get along just fine.

Eventually, I tear my eyes away from her and turn on my e-reader, tapping to the first page of a brand new chick-centric book.

Page One, Chapter One.

Less than five minutes later, my arm flinches when something cold and wet nudges against it. I glance down and see No-Name has edged closer and closer to me in her sleep and is now bumping against me with her face. I lift my arm and rest it along the length of her body, giving her rump a tentative pat. She rests her head in my lap.

Warmth spreads through my chest while a smile takes over my face. I guess *this* is the closest thing to love I'll be experiencing for a while.

I think I might be okay with that.

NORMALIZING

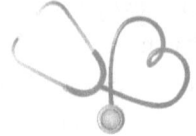

LONG SHIFTS AT WORK, LONG RUNS, LONG BATHS, LONG, lonely nights... I mean, long, uninterrupted reading sessions. That's my new life. It's... peaceful (a.k.a., "almost as boring as football"). But peaceful is good. Boring is good. Beats living a double life with a lying, cheating girlfriend. That's what I tell myself every evening when I eat alone, watch TV alone, read alone, and go to bed alone. Well, not completely alone.

I've fallen in love again. My new girlfriend is hot, too. Often. But she pants for a while and lies on the floor near an air conditioning vent, and that seems to take care of it. She also has four legs and a tail. I've always been a leg man and have been known to chase some tail now and then, so it works.

Yeah, yeah, my main squeeze is a dog. Literally, not figuratively, like so many of my former girlfriends, according to my older brother. She's a dog, and she's the best thing in my life. After all, the only time she hurts me is when she tries to jump on me when I come home from work, and her claws scrape down my legs. Oh, and there was that time she stepped on my balls in bed when she was trying to get comfortable. That hurt pretty bad. But I got over it a lot faster than anything a human female has ever done to me. I learned an important lesson: cover thine balls with thine hands whilst thine pooch is walking in endless circles on thine bed. Hasn't happened since. I wish I was as fast a learner with members of my own species.

Reba the Wonderdog. I've given up on renaming her. For one thing, she won't answer to anything else, no matter how hard I've tried, no matter how many treats I've used to bribe her. After I got over the frustration of not having any control over the situation, I realized something: I respect the hell out of her for persevering. She's Reba. She's not going to let anybody—not even the person who saved her from Doggie Death Row—change that.

As for her escape artist reputation, she *does* run out the front door every chance she gets, but she rarely ventures farther than the front lawn or driveway. Only once did she wander as far as the street, where she collapsed onto her side as soon as I caught up to her with her leash. I think she's simply putting me on notice that she *can* run if she wants to. I'm glad she doesn't seem to want to right now. Her company has been a vital component in my life.

I have a reason to get up in the morning (she paws at my hand to "remind" me to feed her at exactly 6:30 every single day). I have someone to come home to at night. She makes me laugh. She keeps me company in the kitchen when I make my dinners for one. She loves to snuggle. I mean, what more can a guy ask for?

Well, I can think of a few things, but...

No. She's enough. Really. *I'm* enough. Life is good. At home *and* at work.

They may not be my own flesh and blood, but the kids at the clinic are the next best thing, and I'm enjoying my job again. I have the energy to enjoy it, now that I'm not moonlighting as Frank. The kids notice the difference, too. One of the patients who comes in bi-monthly for allergy shots actually said to me the other day that he was glad I wasn't "sad" anymore. He never mentioned noticing I was sad, in the first place, that I can remember, but it must have been bothering him for him to remark about the positive change in me.

When he said it, I ruffled his hair, laughed, and said, "Me, too," like I'd been suffering a silly stretch of bad moods based on nothing deeper than getting up on the wrong side of the bed every morning for half a year. But it stuck with me the rest of the day—hell, it's still sticking with me—how unpleasant I must have been for one of the patients to notice it.

I spent the rest of that week trying to make it up to my co-workers, bringing in breakfast the next day, giving each of them a bag of their favorite candy the day after that, and taking everyone out for drinks that Friday. It was an expensive, tiring week, but it was the least I could do.

At the pub, Lynette—after a few too many appletinis—wrapped me in a hug and gushed, "I'm so glad you're back to normal!"

Around Lynette's headlock, I could see Dr. Reitman looking on with amusement. The doctor raised her glass in salute and gave me a subtle wink before turning away and joining some of the others at the dart boards.

I'm glad I'm back to "normal," too, whatever that is. I may be boring, but it's because that's who I am, who I want to be right now. There's a comfort in giving myself permission to be whatever I want to be. My evenings and weekends are my own again. Sometimes they're too much of my own, but never mind that. Most of the time, I'm okay with getting to know myself again. Homeostasis is a beautiful thing.

So is healing. I'm doing that. I beat myself up pretty good for a while after learning the extent of Frankie's betrayal, until I realized I wouldn't change anything, if I had the option. I don't want to be less trusting. I don't want to be smarter, if it means being cynical. Maybe that makes me dumb. So be it.

As for what Frankie told me about Betty, how unfair would it be to believe a pathological liar's account of someone who never gave me a reason to doubt her? At the same time, it's unlikely I'll ever talk to Betty again, so I may never know the full story. I'm confident, however, that the full story doesn't involve Betty scheming against me. Reading *Girl Noir* banished any remaining doubts I may have had on that subject.

Girl Noir. Yeah, I read it on one of those unbearably quiet Friday nights that lead to self-indulgent moping. Devoured it, more accurately. Started it at bedtime, planning to skim a couple of chapters, not sure I'd be able to handle reading something that would remind me of the person I missed so much, and finished it, dazed and bleary-eyed, only a couple of hours before I knew Reba would be giving me my Saturday morning wakeup nudge.

In the book, the reader meets an insecure woman named Lauren, a serious college student with some serious baggage. She's never known her biological father and while growing up, her mother brought home a series of "uncles," before finally settling down with a wealthy older man. In exchange for Lauren staying out of their hair, Mommy and Step-Daddy gladly act as bankers when Lauren goes to college, so they can travel the world and pretend they don't have domestic responsibilities.

In college, Lauren throws herself into academia, spending much more time at the library than at parties. (Attagirl!) One night, during a marathon study session, she meets a guy who seems equally disciplined and focused, and they fall in love. Or so she thinks. Until she tells him she's going to have his baby. Then he goes home between semesters and never comes back. (Asshole!) Heartbroken, Lauren decides she doesn't want to repeat the pattern begun by her mother and puts the baby up for adoption, never even holding the little guy before he's whisked away to meet his new parents, a young couple suffering from infertility.

Fast forward ten years. Lauren's now a successful public relations executive. She's a germaphobic neat-freak preoccupied with control, almost to the point of obsessive-compulsive disorder. She spends her weekends watching old movies and emulating the tough-talking leading ladies. Her hobbies include making lists, refinancing her mortgage, organizing her closets, and ensuring the vacuum tracks in her living room carpeting make pretty patterns. (In other words, she's hawt!) Her life is orderly and perfect, until a certain little boy named Ben tracks her down, with the help of his adoptive father, who happens to be a handsome, youngish widower whose wife died after a short, intense battle with ovarian cancer. (Nasty stuff.)

The reappearance of Ben in Lauren's life is not a welcome one. Not only is he the spitting image of his biological father, but he's a precocious, spoiled—albeit cute—little scamp determined to matchmake his bereaved dad with his birth mother, so they can be a complete, happy family. His methods are adorable and funny and ultimately successful, and they make for entertaining reading.

If I were an ordinary reader with no connection to the author or the inspiration for the book, I would have been charmed by little Ben and rooting for his dad and Lauren. I would have enjoyed the story, and the characters would have stuck with me. As so often happens after I read a great book, I probably would have had trouble finding something to follow it. But I was no ordinary reader of that particular tale, so the hangover it gave me was more significant, more haunting. I spent much of the book preoccupied, trying to figure out what was fact, fiction, or something in between.

I'm still not sure which plot details fall into each category. Some of them are fairly clear. The OCD-like traits, obviously embellished, ring true, as does the detail about the old movies. I realized with a start as I was reading that I wasn't at all sure about Betty's parentage, but considering she never mentions her mother and father (stepfather?) unless she's talking about using their luxury cabin for the weekend, I'm inclined to believe those details are at least somewhat true.

Then it gets a bit murky on me. Her intelligence supports the picture of her as the studious college co-ed, but I always assumed she was more the life of the party, with a trail of heartbroken guys in her wake. She's Frankie's friend, after all. Some of the stories I heard during the fateful snowmobiling weekend (before things went tits up) left no doubt in my mind that Frankie was a lot of "fun" in college, so it stands to reason her best friend was present during at least some of those exploits. But perhaps I'm assuming too much. Maybe Betty was in the library boning up on marketing strategies while Frankie was... boning the football team.

Everything else about the college portion of the book... who knows? I'm at a complete loss there. Obviously, Betty's never mentioned giving up a baby for adoption, but that's not exactly something you discuss during a skinny jeans shopping spree, is it? *"Wow. Those make you look like a complete douche. By the way, did I ever tell you about the asshole who knocked me up in college and abandoned me? Funny story..."*

No, I can see where that never came up in conversation.

As for the rest, I know it's fiction, other than the career choice. There's no hunky adoptive father lurking around. Nor is there a mischievous kid vying for her attention. So maybe there's no kid at all? Maybe the baby was invented for the sake of dramatic storytelling. I keep reminding myself almost none of the events in *Hippocratic Oaf* matched up with my life—the similarities ended with the character's personality and physical traits—so maybe *Girl Noir* follows the same pattern.

Why, then, would Betty practically beg me to read the book? I'm still not sure. "Lauren's" psychological attributes could hardly be the revelation Betty was going for, considering I already know them. It has to be something more, even more than, "I never knew my real father, my mother's always treated me like a burden, and my step-dad throws money at me as long as I make myself scarce."

Maybe it doesn't even matter. Maybe it was simply to let me know, "You're not alone; she does this to everyone."

One thing is certain: I'm becoming obsessed with it. During the day, when I'm busy with work, it's easier not to think about it. In the evenings, when I'm alone with my thoughts and my dog, it's a lot more difficult. More than once, I've gone as far as to have my keys in my hand, ready to drive to her place and ask her to tell me her version. Not just her version of *Girl Noir*, either. Her version of everything.

That's usually when I take a walk alone, a walk that nearly always ends at my brother's doorstep.

* * *

I HAVE to hand it to Nick; he seems to have it all figured out. For him, anyway. I wouldn't want to cut into people, holding their lives in my hands several times a day, much less be up before dawn most days to do so. Nor would I want to be married to Heidi (I think I've made that clear enough) or rattle around in a house big enough for six times the number of people who currently live in it. But it works for him. And he seems happy. So I'm glad for him. It's not his fault people always compare the two of us.

At his core, he's a good guy. He's been my friend my whole

life, which is more than I can say for anyone else. And he never turns me away when I show up at his house, no matter what else is going on, and no matter how many pictures of his bachelor party I've sprinkled on Facebook.

Tonight, he takes one look at me and leads me straight to the patio under his deck, next to the pool, where he opens the fridge in the outdoor kitchen and retrieves an armful of expensive imported beer. We recline on two side-by-side pool chairs, our legs stretched in front of us, and drink our first beers in silence.

As he pops off the caps on our second drinks, he asks in his typical, mind-reading way, "Whatever happened to that Betty chick?"

Hearing her name makes me wince, like he's broken his bottle on the stamped concrete and jabbed the jagged edges into my chest.

Seemingly oblivious to my reaction, he stares straight ahead at the sparkling pool. "She was hot. You two had something."

"No, we didn't," I automatically deny. "She was Frankie's best friend."

"So?"

I manage to laugh. "Oh. Right. I forgot who I was talking to. The guy who marries his brother's former fiancée doesn't worry about pesky details like that."

He laughs with me. "Is this how it's going to be for the rest of our lives? You're going to bitch and moan about how I married a woman you didn't even want to marry anymore... if ever?"

"No," I grumble, barely audibly.

"It's every man for himself in love and war, Natey-Boy. Love doesn't give a shit about social norms. Even if she's your brother's ex. Even if she's your girlfriend's best friend. *Ex*-girl-friend now, anyway."

Am I in love with Betty? It sure felt like it when I was reading *Girl Noir*. It was all I could do not to jump in my car, drive to her house, wake her up in the middle of the night, and take her in my arms. Even if most of the book is a fabrication, the kernels of truth that inspired it are heartbreaking. The fact that Betty calls it "her" story is incredibly sad.

"That's not even... Whatever," I mutter lamely, worried if I tell Nick about the book or how it made me feel while I read it, I'll start crying.

"Okay. You don't want to talk about Betty. Got it. So, Frankie? Is that why you're here?"

"Why does it have to be about a woman? Or anything at all? Maybe I just wanted to hang out with my brother."

His only reply to that is a snort and more drinking, so I sigh and admit, "Fine. I'm a little down."

"No," Nick drawls. "You?"

"Hey, I'm trying, okay? Some nights are harder than others, that's all." I swing my legs over the side of the chair and move to stand. "I'm sorry. It's probably annoying that I always come over here to sulk."

He extends his left arm, placing his hand on my knee. "No. Stay. I'm just busting your balls, bro, but I get it. She screwed you hard."

"Actually, no. Never." We both laugh at that, my chuckles more rueful than his and punctuated by a groan. "Oh, man." I return to my reclined position, falling back against the weatherproof cushion and staring at the darkening sky.

"What a mess," he commiserates.

"You don't even know the half of it."

For the next hour, I fill him in on the whole Frank Lipton affair while we throw back a twelve pack between us. At the end of my account, he admits, "I knew some of this, but wow. You wore skinny jeans?"

"Shut up. Yes. And what do you mean, you knew some of it?"

As if it should be obvious, he answers, "Mom showed me your picture on the internet. The glasses were a smart touch, by the way. *Nobody* would recognize you with *those* on," he snarks. "What is this, Metropolis?"

I laugh. "Right? Oh, well. It actually worked okay. Nobody around here ever asked me about it. Mom knew?"

"Of course, she did. She knows everything."

"Why didn't you guys say something?"

He shrugs. "You obviously wanted it to be a secret, with all your lies about working those Urgent Care shifts. By the way, hello! How did you think I wouldn't figure out you weren't on duty when you said you were?"

I feel like an idiot, but I defend myself, anyway. "I dunno. I figured you'd never check. Why would you?"

"I didn't go out of my way. I was called in for an emergency surgery one Saturday, and afterwards, while I was in the neighborhood, I swung by UC to say hi, but you weren't there. I joked in passing to the girl at the admissions desk that I must have misunderstood or assumed incorrectly, based on the fact that you were there *every* weekend, and she shot me a weird look and said, 'Huh? He's hardly ever here anymore. Trades shifts with people whenever he can.'"

Based on his spot-on impersonation, I grouch, "Gretchen. She hates me."

"Sounds like you were a major pain in the ass, always shirking your shifts."

My eyeballs are floating, but too relaxed to go inside to relieve myself, I continue to swig at the bottle in my hand.

"Yeah, I guess. I've made up for it since then, so she can suck my... butt." The last word comes out on a belch.

"Nice one."

Rewinding our conversation, I return to the last interesting thing he said. "Hang on. I can't believe Mom and Dad didn't confront me about posing as Frank."

"They figured you didn't want to talk about it, since you didn't tell us yourself."

"Since when has that ever stopped them? Remember all those interventions they used to stage with us? 'Nick, we've called this family meeting, because we're concerned you're spending too much time on your XBox and not enough time with real people.'"

He laughs. "I guess they figure we're too old for that shit anymore, unless it's something truly destructive, like drugs or alcohol, or gambling. I got a private lecture about that recently."

"Seriously?"

He shrugs. "Yeah. Whatever. They're always right. That's what's so annoying. What I don't get is why you kept the Frank Lipton stuff so hush-hush."

I think about it for a second. "I figured you guys wouldn't approve. Hell, *I* didn't approve."

"Why'd you do it, then?"

All of the reasons I had for going along with Frankie's scheme are suddenly absent from my memory. The only justification I have is what—or who—kept me doing it, even after I knew Frankie and I were going nowhere—*especially* after I knew that. I'll be damned if I'll admit that to Nick, though.

Finally, I settle on, "I don't know. At first, it seemed like it wouldn't be that big of a deal, and it made her happy, so..."

"Dude. You have some serious issues with boundaries."

I sigh. "Tell me about it. No. Don't. I already know. Mom

and Dad sat me down about it a long time ago. Which was ironic, come to think of it."

Again, we revert to silence, and I'm about to doze off when he says, "So, how's Reba?"

"Fine," I slur back.

"Okay. And work's good?"

"Yeah."

"You know, you're keeping me from having the sex my wife promised me earlier for watching figure skating with her."

Wide awake now, I groan. "Really? Is that necessary?"

"It's so necessary. It's the only way I'm watching that crap."

"Well, thanks for sharing."

"No problem."

"You accuse me of not letting go of the past, but you're determined to make it always feel weird that you married someone I used to *be* with."

"Yeah, well, I think it's important we never forget who won in the end. You screwed up, big time." According to his gloating tone, we might as well be talking about a bowling trophy.

"You're sick." My proclamation contains no venom, though. What's the point? I know he's kidding, trying to make it less awkward in his completely boneheaded, male chauvinistic way. If we never speak seriously about it, then it's not a big deal, according to his logic. I get it. But I'm not built that way. "It would be awesome if you would never talk to me about your sex life ever again."

"Jealous?"

"Nope."

"Right. Says the guy who has to pretend to be a completely different person to get laid. Then again, I guess that didn't work out so well, either, did it?"

"Are you trying to make me feel better, or worse?"

He playfully punches my shoulder. "Aw, bro, I'm sorry. But I'm kind of confused. You're not sorry to have broken up with Frankie; you don't have to pretend to be that nerdy author now. So why the long face? How can I help you if you don't tell me what's wrong?"

I shrug, my slight buzz making me sullen. I'm not about to spill my guts. Not to him, not to anyone. Not even to myself. Is it too much to ask to be allowed to just sit here with him so I can claim I don't always drink alone when Mom and Dad inevitably confront me about it?

We don't say anything for a while. Then Nick stands up, stretches, and asks, "More beer?"

I stare off into his dark backyard. "I should probably get going," I reply dutifully but without much conviction and without moving a muscle.

He pats my shoulder. "I'll be right back. Gotta drain my lizard first."

I hate to be such a pathetic imposition, but the thought of leaving fills me with nauseous dread. It's not just about being alone, either. More than anything, I'm delaying the moment when I get home and know with absolute certainty that Heidi and Nick are... pleasing each other. I won't be able to shut out the mental images, either. Sometimes it's a curse to have such a vivid imagination.

Like right now (while Nick's inside, probably commiserating with Heidi about how "he won't leave"), I'm not at all curious about what Frankie's up to, but I can't help but wonder what Betty's doing. Her lips hurtle toward me, behind my eyes, but I quickly blink them away. I push down the guilt and picture her doing something—anything—besides kissing me.

A few months ago, I'd think she was probably on a date, making some poor guy sweat with her witty one-liners. Now, I know it's more likely she's spending the evening alone, toiling away on Frankie's marketing efforts. Or in a hot bath with a good book and a large glass of red wine. Maybe thinking about me?

No! Not going there. Won't. Can't. Shouldn't.

Nick returns with an armful of beers.

I smile gratefully at him, take the bottle he's offering me, and use the underside of the lounger to pry off the cap. "Bottoms up," I demand grimly.

He complies, and we both gulp half our bottles before setting them down on the tiny table between us and belching in stereo. Neither of us asks to be excused.

"So, have you decided to tell me why you're so mopey? Mopier than usual, even? I mean, I haven't seen you act like this since..." He stops, seeming to think about it and reach back into his memory. "Well, the only other time that comes close is your senior year in high school, when..."

"Please!"

Through his laughter, he talks over me. "You wanted to ask Britta Kaepertowski to the prom, but your buddy Ted had the hots for her, and you had this insane idea that you weren't allowed to ask her, out of respect for Ted."

"It's the Bro Code! Are you honestly unaware of the concept?"

"No. I just think it's ridiculous. And pointless. And let me remind you—in case you've forgotten and haven't learned a damn thing in the past fifteen years—that in the case of Britta 'Big Boobs' Kaepertowski, you and Ted gallantly agreed that neither of you would ask her out, but the minute Michaela Whatshergut—"

"Pecklehoffer."

"Yeah, her! As soon as Michaela Peckerhopper..."

"Pecklehoffer, asshole."

"Whatever. As soon as she accepted your invitation, Teddy

marched himself up to Britta in the cafeteria, and what happened?"

"He asked Britta to the prom."

"And what did she say?"

"She turned him down."

"But not just that. She said…"

I sigh. "You know the story, so why are you making me say it? You're such a douche sometimes."

He snatches his beer bottle from the table and holds it to his lips but doesn't drink, yet. "Maybe you forgot. I could see why you'd want to block it out." Now, he sips, lowers the bottle and says in a high-pitched voice like no high school girl I've ever known, "'I'm waiting for Nate to ask me out.'"

"What's your damn point?"

"My point is, you went to prom with a girl who had to shave her face more often than you did at that age, because you were too nice. And if Ted had been able to go with Britta, it might have been worth it—you gotta admire the guy's balls —but he wound up not going at all. And to top it all, Britta went 'as friends' with Rex Reidy."

I finish my beer and move immediately to the next. Tossing the cap onto the table with a clink, I say, "See? It all worked out."

"How do you figure? He bragged for the rest of the school year about getting lucky with her at one of those after-prom parties at his best friend's house. Where he, incidentally, knocked her up, the moron."

I flinch at his harsh tone and bristle on behalf of all people who find themselves in that position, one person in particular for whom I feel protective and defensive. "It happens. And it was obviously meant to be, in their case. She and Rex have, like, five kids now. I recently saw their second-youngest, Theo, a couple of weeks ago at the clinic." I drop my voice confidentially. "Earwax build-up like you wouldn't believe. I thought we'd never get it all out. Never did, in fact. Had to send them home with some wax-softening drops and instructions on how to use a bulb syringe to flush out his ears."

"Are you finished destroying that patient's right to privacy?"

"I'm just saying, Britta and Rex have been together ever since. So it's not like it was a waste."

"You're unbelievable, you know that?"

"It wasn't meant to be with Britta. Or Heidi. Or Frankie. Or..."

Nick waits, then reaches for another beer. "Or? You're already planning the next Never-Gonna-Be-Mrs.-Nathan-Bingham?"

I shake my head. "No."

"Are you sure?"

Instead of continuing to lie to both of us, I mutter, "Stop being such a dick. Let's talk about something more interesting, like pre-season football."

He chuckles. "Suit yourself, bro."

23
THE PROPOSAL

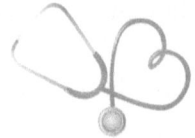

Much later, I was pathetically broody. I may have even choked up at one point while lamenting that I'd never find The One and have the family I've always wanted. I think my exact words were, "I'll probably wind up being that creepy guy who calls all his patients 'my kids.'"

That's when my brother claimed he was all out of beer and started pumping me full of espresso. It didn't take long before I was fit to walk the two blocks home. And just in time, too. Heidi had joined us by then, and she was scrolling through her phone, tossing out the names of some of her more desperate, single sorority sisters, trying to convince me to go out on a blind date or two.

The resultant nightmare from my last blind date is still too fresh for me to fall for that one.

This morning, I'm thirsty and feeling puffy, but I'm surprisingly not hungover, so I chug a glass of water while watching The Weather Channel, which promises a cool-down by the end of the week. Until then, we're stuck with record highs for this time of year. I lace up my running shoes, planning to sweat the toxins from my system on an easy run. Reba presses her cold, wet nose against my shin.

"Since when?" I say with a laugh, giving her a consolation scratch behind her ears. "I'd wind up carrying your big, furry butt all the way home. Not fun."

Her reply grunt probably has more to do with the ear-scratching, but I like to think she's also agreeing with me. That's another thing I love about her: she hardly ever argues with me.

"I'll be back soon," I promise on my way out the front door. "Make sure the couch doesn't go anywhere. I plan to use it a lot later."

Forty-five minutes later, while I'm deep in thought, recalling some of the things Nick said to me last night, my endorphin high wanes. I head for home, hoping I have enough gas left in the tank to get me there. It's apparent I don't when I'm still more than two miles from the house. I can smell the alcohol mingling with the sweat oozing from my pores, and it's nause-ating me, so I stagger to an empty bench at a bus stop and collapse onto it. Stretching my legs in front of me, I bend over, bringing my nose as close as I can to my knees, hoping I don't cramp, or barf, and cursing myself for letting my musings about last night's conversation with Nick put me in this predicament.

When I've caught my breath and straighten to an upright position, I notice a scruffy guy, who looks like he might smell even worse than I do, eyeing me and inching ever closer, so I rise to my feet and shuffle down the sidewalk. Even if I have to walk the rest of the way, it's better than sitting somewhere, miserable, wishing I were home.

What I see in my driveway as I limp the last block stops me as if I've stumbled into a patch of fast-drying concrete.

Exhaustion prevents me from turning and running the

other way. It doesn't stop me from looking around to see if any of my neighbors have some shrubs I can lie behind while I wait for my visitor to give up on me and leave.

Then I realize how irrational and immature my thinking is. Anyway, if I'm being honest, the sight of Betty's dark green Fiat thrills me as much as it terrifies me.

One foot in front of the other, slowly at first, then picking up momentum until I'm jogging at a clip I didn't think possible for the rest of this day (or week), I close the gap between my house and me, hoping I don't stink as much as I suspect I do.

She waits for me on the wooden bench on the covered stoop, holding two plastic, insulated coffee mugs. As I traverse the inclined driveway that normally feels like nothing but today might as well be Everest, she holds up one of the mugs in greeting.

"Hey. Salted caramel, right?"

I grin, even though the thought of drinking hot coffee right now is less than appealing.

"You remembered."

"It's the only thing you order that makes me reconsider my theory you're a robot."

"Thanks?"

She laughs as I reach for and take the mug. "You know what I mean. You never eat junk food."

Keeping at least an arm's length between us, I'm also careful not to let our fingers touch during the hand-off. "I have you fooled."

I key in the combination on the front door, then stand aside to let her walk in ahead of me. It makes me look like quite the gentleman, although I mostly do it so she's not downwind of me as we enter the house. Her summery, clean scent wafts toward me. I close my eyes and steady myself against the door frame.

She glances over her shoulder and notices me stagger. "Are you okay?" she asks, relieving me of the hot coffee.

I smile wanly. "Yeah. I overdid it on my run. Not in very good shape anymore. I wasn't expecting it to be so hot today, either." Little white lies are okay, right?

"Maybe I should come back some other time."

"No! I mean, that's okay. I'll be fine. Just need to drink some water and get a shower."

She looks relieved. "Are you sure? I didn't mean to barge in." Laughing, she amends, "Well, I guess I did mean to. I didn't call ahead, because I didn't want to give you a chance to say 'no' to a visit from me."

"I'd never do that," I promise, my heart pounding again, as if I'm still in full stride in the middle of my run.

Looking down at her feet, she says quietly, "Maybe you should wait until you hear why I'm here before you make such a bold statement."

Before I can ask her to elaborate, Reba waddles from the direction of my bedroom. She extends her front paws, lowering her head even closer than usual to the ground and arching her back in a huge stretch while yawning.

Betty laughs. "Oh, my gosh. Who's this?"

"My new roomie, Reba."

"She's adorable!"

I grin proudly. "Yeah, I know. And she knows it, too."

After setting her coffee on an end table, Betty hunkers down on all fours and crawls toward the dog, murmuring sweet nothings to her. Reba immediately flops onto her back and assumes the "love me" position. Betty's only too happy to oblige.

I could watch them all day, but now that I'm indoors, my

pong is even more pronounced. "I'm going to leave you two to get acquainted while I hose myself down, if that's all right."

Betty barely glances at me as I skirt the two of them, exchanging my mug for the dog-eared *Sports Illustrated* on the coffee table on my way through the living room, rolling the magazine into a tube to conceal the photo of the model in the wet, white swimsuit on the cover.

"Yeah. We'll be fine," she says distractedly, then, "Ah, there it is!" when she locates the "sweet spot" that makes Reba's leg flap rapidly. "You like that?"

During the fastest shower of my life, my mind works in double-time to try to predict why Betty is here. Based on her worry I may have refused to see her if she'd called ahead of time, I don't have high hopes. That still leaves endless possibilities.

Maybe... Frankie and Kyle are getting married? (If so, good for them; they're made for each other.)

Or do I owe her money? No, I paid for everything during our Frank weekends.

It's no use. I can't imagine what she could possibly have to say that would make me refuse to see her. Whatever it is is obviously not as bad as she thinks.

Meanwhile, this is a golden opportunity to ask about what Frankie told me when we broke up. I may go insane if I don't find out what—if anything—Betty knew all those months.

Asking her about *Girl Noir* is another story. Do I have the proverbial balls to broach that topic without my typical fumbling and blurting and making it sound like her answers will affect how I feel about her? Because her answers don't matter. Maybe it's best to leave it.

When I backtrack to the living room, self-consciously fingering my wet hair, hoping I don't look too much like a little boy all spruced up for school picture day, Betty and

Reba are no longer on the floor or even in the room. I follow my ears and my nose to the kitchen, where Betty stands at the stove, with Reba not too far away, eyeing the bacon I smell.

"What are you doing?" I ask with a chuckle.

Betty flinches and glances over her shoulder at me but quickly returns her attention to the sizzling, popping pan in front of her. "I hope you don't mind. Reba showed me where everything was. I figured you were hungry after that run. Thought I'd make you an omelet and some bacon. Protein, right?"

I smile at her back. "Yes. And no, I don't mind. But you don't have to do that."

"I want to."

Pulling out a chair at the kitchen table, I say, "Well, I'm not going to object. This is nice." After a few seconds, it feels too weird to sit and watch her, so I join her at the stove. Under the guise of observing her cooking technique, I stop just shy of pressing my chest against her back and rest a hand on her shoulder, again taking in the intoxicating smell of her, now improved—is that possible?—by the scent of bacon. It's like an ultimate fantasy, almost more than I can process. "Make enough for yourself, too."

"Not hungry," she declares dully.

Uh-oh.

I withdraw, then lean against the facing counter, bracing my hands behind me. She's given me a perfect opening to ask her why she's here and what she wants to talk about, but I can't seem to concentrate. All I can think about is, *Gosh, I've missed her!* I can't tell her that, though.

When all else fails, go into Nurse Mode. "You should eat something."

I can't see her face, but I can practically hear her eyes

rolling when she says, "I've been up since six. I ate a banana and some cereal."

Knowing better, I retort, "You had a Pop-Tart."

She laughs. "Okay. I had a Pop-Tart. It was all I had in the house. Grocery shopping hasn't been a high priority lately." She flips the omelet in front of her. "You, on the other hand, are all stocked up, making bachelors everywhere look bad."

"I have nothing better to do than hang out in the produce section," I say, then realize it makes me sound pitiful and add, "Plus, I like to cook. It keeps me busy." Marginally less pitiful, but at least it doesn't conjure the image of me spending my Friday nights all misty with the lettuce misters.

The bacon goes on a paper-towel-covered plate and receives a firm, de-greasing pat-down. Wordlessly, Betty hands back the damp paper towel, and I take it from her, crossing the kitchen and depositing it in the flip-top trash can while she plates my food and sets it on the table.

"There you go. Spinach and feta omelet with dead pig." She adds the coffee mug to the arrangement. "This should still be hot. Would you like some orange juice?"

I shake my head. "No. This is fine." I grab a fork from the cutlery drawer and sit, staring at the perfectly golden egg pocket in front of me. "Wow. This looks… great."

I wish my stomach would unknot enough for me to eat, but the anticipation of the conversation we're about to have— whatever it ends up being about—is killing me. Under her watch, I cut a bite with the side of my fork but promptly set the utensil next to my plate with a clatter, telling myself my hands are shaking due to low blood sugar but knowing I'm full of shit and literally quaking in fear.

"So, what's up?" I finally have no choice but to ask.

She nods at my plate. "There's nothing worse than cold eggs. Eat."

"I can't," I admit. "Not until I know why you're here."

Instead of taking the seat directly across the table from me, she chooses the one next to me, so I have to turn my head to watch her face, which looks decidedly apprehensive. That ramps up my anxiety level. What is she afraid of telling me? Is she afraid of *me*?

Before thinking better of it, I curl my hand around hers on top of the table. "Hey. Are you okay?"

She nods and gives me what's probably supposed to be a smile but looks more like a grimace. "Yeah! I mean..." She thinks about it for a second, then repeats, "Yeah," a lot more firmly. "Everything's fine."

Thinking maybe she needs me to say whatever it is for her, I smile encouragingly. "Wait. Let me guess... You need me to be your date to Kyle and Frankie's wedding?" I half-joke, gratified when she relaxes enough to laugh.

"You *do* owe me one, you know," she replies. "But no. Those two..." She wrinkles her nose but doesn't finish her thought.

I don't want to know any details. "Okay, so this isn't a walking wedding invitation. Darn. I was so looking forward to doing the Macarena again."

She laughs, and I congratulate myself on diffusing the tension. Her expression is so much less strained than it was a few seconds ago that I feel confident enough to take my first bite of the breakfast that smells so good.

As I'm chewing and shooting the chef a major thumbs-up and closed-mouth smile to let her know it tastes delicious, she blurts, "I need you to be Frank one more time."

Medical fact: solid food can go down the wrong "pipe." This particular mouthful certainly does. Then it comes back up. Which is a good thing, actually; aspiration can be dangerous and ultimately lead to complications like pneumonia. It's unfortunate my chewed-up food chooses to exit through my nose, but better out than in. Until I realize I don't have a napkin to catch it.

Betty jumps from her chair and circles behind me, pounding me on the back. I try to tell her that's unnecessary (and ineffective), and I'd rather she hand me the towel from next to the sink, but talking is impossible at this point, so I merely cup my hands under my nose and mouth and ride out the coughing, sneezing fit. Eventually, I recover enough to stand and get the towel for myself. At first, I keep my back to her while cleaning up, but since bits of egg are stuck in my nose, a dainty wipe-job ain't gonna cut it.

I choke out an "Excuse me" and retreat to the nearest bathroom.

"I'm so sorry!" she calls after me (and Reba, who's decided whatever I'm doing is even more interesting than bacon).

While my humiliation fades with each forceful blow of my nose into tissue after tissue, my rage builds. Having the parents I do, I know all too well that anger is a secondary emotion, needing something to feed it, but I don't want to explore the hurt and disappointment feeding this particular case of it. I prefer to be angry. "Angry" is a hell of a lot easier than those other things. I throw tissues at the wastebasket, hardly any of them hitting the target, slam the medicine cabinet and bang the heel of my hand against the sink.

Reba doesn't enjoy Angry Nate, so she quickly turns tail and trots to my bedroom, where I hear her tags jingle as they make contact with the wood floor on her way under the bed. Good. I don't want her to witness this.

My sinuses de-egged, I return to the kitchen to find Betty sitting at the table with a familiar pair of specs in her hands. I cross the room in three huge strides, snatch the glasses from her, and carry them to the trash can. Stomping on the pedal, I drop the hateful accessories with a flourish before letting the lid fall with a clang.

She looks unimpressed by my gesture, so I follow it up with, "Trust me; it's not where I'd prefer to put them, but count yourself lucky I'm too polite to follow through with that impulse."

Now she blushes. "I wouldn't ask you unless I had no choice."

"You have no *right*."

"It's not for forever," she says after a long silence, during which she looks as miserable as I feel.

"Yeah, it's for *never*," I verify. "I'm not doing it."

She sighs, puffing out her cheeks. "It's just one more appearance, at that indie conference in Atlanta I told you about. That's it. We've already committed to doing it, and—"

"*We* haven't committed to doing anything!"

She stands and walks toward me. I physically recoil, my arms rising to position my hands, palms out, close to my body. I step backwards when she continues her advance.

"Hear me out," she pleads.

"Don't ask me to do this," I beg in return, all former bluster gone. "Please, I can't."

She stops in front of me. "I know this is awful. I thought Frankie would be ready to reveal herself as Frank by now, but it hasn't worked out that way, and if we back out now... Well, among other things, it will be extremely unprofessional. The conference is next weekend, and Frank is one of the headliners. His name's on all the promotional literature, and everything."

I snort and groan. This keeps getting better. "Then, the answer's not just 'no.' It's 'hell no!'"

With that, I escape the kitchen, unable to be in her presence or the vicinity of the brown-nosing breakfast she cooked, not because she cares about me but because she wanted to butter me up before requesting I do the one thing I won't—can't—do for her. Need a kidney? I'm your guy. Blood transfusion? I'll insert the needle myself. Sperm donation? Sign me up! Lord knows I'm not using it. But this, no.

Of course, walking away doesn't accomplish anything, because all she has to do is follow me, which she does, into the living room. "It's only one more appearance."

"A big one," I point out.

Her dismissive, "Yeah, yeah, yeah," makes me widen my eyes, so she rushes on, "It'll be fun! Like old times!"

I feel myself waver on those last three words but force myself to focus and remain strong. *Concentrate on the anger.* "'Old times'? You mean the times when I was a pathetic fool? Those times? Oh, yeah. I long for those halcyon days!"

She stares me down for a second, and I see her chin wobble, but she grits her teeth, and it stills.

"You knew," I state simply. My heart races while I wait for her to deny it, while I silently beg her to tell me definitively that she had nothing to do with Frankie's plot. When she seems incapable of speaking, I ask, "Were you two laughing at me behind my back while I made an ass of myself?"

"No! It wasn't anything like that."

It's difficult to breathe, much less talk, but I manage, "What was it like, then?"

Her eyes flash. "Is that what she told you? That I was in on her stupid, selfish plan?"

I'm torn between not wanting her to know exactly what Frankie told me and giving her all the information she needs to satisfactorily deny her involvement, so I strike a compromise. "She said it was your idea."

All the color drains from her face, and for a second I'm afraid she's going to faint. I want to go to her, catch her, but my pride holds me to my current position, across the room from her.

She lowers herself slowly to the couch. Staring at her knees, she says, "I guess that's accurate."

Now *I'm* the one in danger of passing out.

Before I dissolve into a puddle in front of the dormant fireplace, she adds, "I said it in jest, though! Way before she ever met you. She was talking about using a male pen name, but she wasn't sure how she'd find the right guy to pose as her pseudonym, and I joked that it sounded about as impossible as finding the right guy to marry. She snapped her fingers at me and said I was a genius, but she didn't elaborate. Then, weeks later, she introduced me to you. By the end of that evening, it was clear to me what she was trying to do."

"So you *did* know. And you didn't tell me."

"I thought I could stop her." She looks up at me now, her eyes full.

"Don't you dare cry," I demand, feeling the mucus production going into overdrive in my own sinuses. My mouth twitches downward while I work to control my voice. "Don't. I don't want to feel sorry for you."

She blinks her tears away. "I don't want you to, either. I want... I need you to believe me."

I pinch my fingers into my eyes to block the sight of her—and to poke away the water threatening to spill from my own sockets—as she continues, "When you went to the bathroom at the bar, we argued about what I knew she was doing. And we argued about it every day for a long time after that. But the longer you guys were together, the more she seemed to really care about you, and she kept telling me she loved you. She gushed about what a great boyfriend you were and how she hoped to marry you. The hopeless romantic in me wanted to believe it was fate, that maybe something could blossom and become love, despite one person's original selfish intentions. And I thought as long as I kept an eye on things, it would be okay. I told myself the minute I thought she was using you, I'd tell you."

The hand that's been rubbing my eyes during her monologue drops to my side and swings uselessly as I remember her visit the day after Nick's bachelor party and our conversations at Nick's wedding and on our walk after the Duluth reading.

"You tried," I mumble.

She nods. "Yeah. But I wasn't sure enough to make an outright accusation." She stands and creeps closer to me but doesn't come within touching range. "I'm sorry! She kept me enough in the dark that I could never be certain. She knew I wouldn't tell you anything to hurt you if all I had were suspicions and no proof."

"And yet, despite all of that, you're here today, asking me to be Frank again. Why? How?" I wonder, close to whining the last word.

Massaging her temples, she turns away from me and says in a steady voice, "I told Frankie I'd try."

I'm glad she can't see my face, because I can *feel* what it looks like, and it's not attractive, but there's nothing I can do to change how slack and pale it must be. My voice is the uncontrollable oral equivalent. "Well, tell Frankie she has a lot of nerve."

Still showing me her back, Betty nods. "You're right. It was selfish and wrong to ask you to do this."

"But you did it anyway. You came here with my favorite coffee and... and... you loved on my dog. All to manipulate me. Just like *her*." My hands bunch into fists.

She spins and shakes her head resolutely, quickly swiping at the tears that track down her face with the sudden movement. "No. That was... I wasn't going to ask you. I'd decided not to.

But then it slipped out. I'm desperate. You're still the same old Nathaniel, and—"

"No, I'm not. Not even close."

She swallows thickly and curtly bobs her head. "Right. I understand, of course. I'm sorry I upset you."

I can't seem to make myself say it's okay, because it's not okay. Nothing is okay. But I'm not mad at her, either. I *can't* be mad at her when she's looking at me like that. Knowing it and telling her are two different things, though.

She heads for the door. Part of me wants to crawl across the floor and grab her leg to keep her here. Another part can't wait for her to leave. That second part is responsible for my cold tone of voice when I say, "You might also want to tell Frankie to stop sending you to do her dirty work. It's not fair to you."

Or to me, I add silently.

Betty's chastened head tilt kills the last of my anger—and almost kills me, too.

As she opens the door and gives me one more feeble finger wave, I gird myself to say the last words I'll probably ever say to her. For real, this time. "Hey, Betts."

She faces me, her brow crinkled expectantly. The words are right there, working up the nerve to jump from my tongue, but my overprotective heart pulls them back.

At the last second, I dully declare instead, "Thanks for the omelet."

24

RECONSIDERING

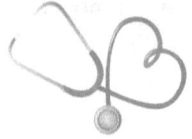

I'M STILL KICKING THE SHIT OUT OF MYSELF THREE DAYS later.

"Thanks for the omelet."

"Thanks for the omelet."

The words echo and taunt me nearly every spare second of the day.

Yeah, thanks for the omelet. The one that I couldn't eat but also couldn't bear to throw out and would have sat on my kitchen table indefinitely if Reba hadn't finally used the pulled-out chair to climb up and scarf it—and the bacon—in three neat swallows.

Scarf.

I stare at my closed closet door and contemplate whether I have the energy—or heart—to do what I've been putting off for two months: packing up all of Frank's clothes and giving them away to charity. I'm not sure I want to add insult to injury by donating these clothes to someone already going through a rough time, though.

I've also told myself they're not *hurting* anything in my

closet, and I have plenty of room for them. Plus, Halloween's only a couple of months away. I could go this year as "random douche," "pretentious a-hole," "complete tool," or "hopeless sucker."

Anyway, I'm too busy to pack them up and take them to the nearest collection station. (Yeah, *so* many chick flicks to re-watch and new releases to go see by myself, *so* little time.) And every time I psych myself up to do it, to rip those clothes from their hangers and stuff them into black garbage bags, banishing them from my life forever, I think of something else I *really* want to do. Like scoop Reba's poop in the backyard.

But now, three days after Betty's visit, I know I need to kill the possibility of ever donning another pair of skinny jeans. I need to forget—for good—the "manliest" way to wear a scarf (it doesn't exist, anyway). I need to give myself a failsafe, so I can legitimately say, "I can't be Frank; I don't even have the right clothes anymore."

"I need a walk," I say out loud, urging Reba into action at the w-word.

She nearly trips me in her haste to beat me down the hallway to the hook by the front door, where her leash hangs. Not for the first time, I marvel and laugh at how fast she can make those stubby legs move when she wants to.

"Chill, Rebes. I'm not leaving without you," I reassure her as I clip her leash to her collar. Before heading out, I pat my pockets to make sure I have my keys, wallet, and phone (because nothing completes the "lonely man with his dog" ensemble like a silent phone crammed full of saved texts from "Mom").

Ten minutes into our walk, I'm assuming another such text has arrived when my butt vibrates and chimes as I'm bent over, picking up Reba's latest offering, my hand shoved into an inside-out scented pet waste bag. Before I can complete the task at hand, the device gives me another jolt.

"For crying out loud," I mutter, carefully turning the bag right-side in and knotting it. When I'm absolutely sure I don't have any dog dirt on my hands or on the outside of the bag, where it can get on me, I hold the plastic baggie and leash in one hand and pull my phone from my pocket with the other.

Instead of seeing the expected texts from my mother, asking me what I'm doing and inviting me over for her latest fishing expedition into my psyche, I find two texts from Frankie. The first one says, *U owe me $2500.*

The second one adds, *Paypal is fine*

At first, I think it's a sick joke, but as the minutes pass with no further communication or explanation from her, I tap and send: *??*

She immediately fires back, *do u want an itemized invoice?*

Yes, since I have no idea what ur talking about. Not gonna hand over an entire paycheck to u. Sorry

The Wicked Witch of the West's song from *The Wizard of Oz* suddenly bursts from my phone. In spite of everything, I can't help but laugh. That's what I get for leaving my phone unattended with my brother while using the bathroom at his house the other day.

"Yello," I sigh more than say.

"Listen, you bastard, I'll be damned before I'll be out that money," Frankie launches, mid-rant.

"Uh, what?"

"You heard me. You're paying me for the conference registration, promotional merch, plane tickets, hotel rooms, rental car, plus all the tax and cancellation fees for that indie conference you backed out of."

"'Backed out of'? I broke up with you! Because you were sleeping with someone else!" My words seem to echo in the quiet neighborhood, so I blush and turn my back on the guy across the street, watering his lawn and (now) openly gaping at me.

"Same result. If you were still going to that conference as Frank, we wouldn't be having this conversation. You're not; therefore, I want my money back."

I lower my voice a few hundred decibels. "And I never want to talk to you again, but something tells me neither of us is going to be getting our wish any time soon."

She ignores my snark. "Whatever. The point is, it was too late to get refunds—"

"We broke up two months ago!"

"Yeah, well, Betty 'forgot' to cancel everything. How does someone so anal forget something like that, I wonder?"

I have to admit, that doesn't sound like Betty at all, but since Frankie's question seems more rhetorical than anything, I don't reply to it. Instead, I try to get back on track. "I don't owe you anything. You, my dear, are getting hit in the pocket-book for your transgressions. And I can't say I'm sorry." The leash jerks in my hand, so I aimlessly follow Reba as she leads me down our usual circuitous route of sidewalks.

"I can't afford to absorb that kind of loss," Frankie states unemotionally.

"I'm shocked that wasn't your primary consideration. You certainly didn't take into account my feelings. In any case, I'm sure your new boyfriend will buy your shampoo and groceries this month."

She growls something about leaving Kyle out of this, then huffs, "Fine! If you're going to be a jerk about it, then I'll just make Betty pay me. I'm sure her rich step-daddy will step up."

"Wait a second. Why does *Betty* have to eat the costs? They're *your* business expenses."

"Because it was her mistake, not canceling everything in

time to get refunds." In a tantalizing tone, she adds, "Of course, if you *were* to go ahead and attend the conference as Frank, I'd be getting something for my money, a return on my investment. I'm sure you and Betty would manage to sell some of that merch and all of those books. Plus, the exposure would be huge."

"Screw you. My answer is no, just like it was on Sunday, when Betty asked me."

Frankie's laugh surprises me. "Oh, my gosh! Did she really?"

"What do you mean? Yes. You told her to!"

"I never told her to ask you that! I don't think you're *that* much of a suck—" She stops short and gives a tiny gasp. The smirk strong in her voice, she says, "I see now. She didn't *forget* to cancel the arrangements; she purposely didn't, because she's been holding out hope all this time, trying to get up the nerve to ask you to go." Again, she laughs, but she pairs it with a sarcastic, "Oh, how sweet!"

I'm too flustered to remember Betty's exact words during our conversation three days ago, so I simply say, much less convincingly than before, "It doesn't matter. I'm not doing it. Suck it."

"It wasn't that great the first time."

"Hey!" Thinking I'm talking to her, Reba halts, sits abruptly, and looks over her shoulder at me. I twitch the leash to let her know she can keep walking, but she acts like it was her idea to stop and take a breather and doesn't budge.

Barely controlling her giggles, Frankie continues, "So she threw *me* under the bus, did she? Said *I* wanted you to do it? Well, that was a shitty plan, if she wanted you to agree."

Momentarily mute, I stare at the back of Reba's panting head while I consider everything Frankie has told me.

She takes my silence as my final offering in our negotiations. "Okay, then. God, I bet that that broke her heart, when you told her no and left her holding the bag. She thought you were different, but you're just like every other guy who's left her in the lurch—including that Chris asshole in college. She says *I'm* attracted to jerks. I tried to warn her you weren't the saint she's made you out to be, but she wouldn't lis—"

"I'll do it."

At first, she's quiet for so long that I think we've been cut off. Then she smugly states, "That's a good boy."

"I'm not doing it for you."

"Oh, I know. Trust me."

"Did you tell Betty you were going to call me?"

"No... Why?"

"Good. As far as she's concerned, this conversation never happened."

"Then how—?"

"I'll call her and tell her I changed my mind because I *want* to go to the conference," I explain rapidly. "When she informs you of this development, you do what you do best: lie and act surprised."

"So you look like the hero?"

"No, exactly the opposite. So she'll let me do it. If she knows I don't want to do it, and I'm only agreeing out of a sense of duty, she'll refuse."

Frankie pauses, then hums what sounds like an affirmation. "You have a point there," she mumbles. "Aren't you two quite the sickening, selfless pair?"

"Unlike *some* people, I wouldn't be able to sleep at night knowing I could have done something to help someone I call a friend, and didn't."

She sighs. "How noble. Whatever. If those are your terms, fine. I won't tell her anything about this conversation. One tiny suggestion, though?"

"What?"

"Do everyone, most of all yourselves, a favor, and screw each other already while you're in Atlanta."

I bite my lower lip, flare my nostrils, and hang up on her without another word.

STAR OF THE SHOW

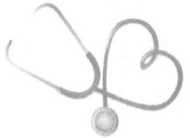

THEY SAY WISCONSONITES ARE OBSESSED WITH CHEESE. Well, we have nothing on Georgians' preoccupation with the peach. I get that it's the Peach State, but for crying out loud. They've turned a fruity mascot into something of a god. Since I don't see any peach trees growing in planters in the lobby of Atlanta's Peach Blossom Hotel and Resort on Peachtree Road (surprisingly), the sickly sweet scent of the fuzzy fruit must be coming from the ductwork. Am I the only one who thinks it smells like body odor? It *reeks* in here.

If my room smells like this lobby, I may have to stay somewhere else.

Betty and I split a Valium for the flight, in the hopes we'd be a mellower pair for our travels to Atlanta than we had been on the way to and from Phoenix. The drug helped with our fear of flying, but it didn't do much about our apparent nervousness around each other.

Now, as we stand at the reception desk at the hotel, checking into our rooms (plural, thank you), she says for at least the sixtieth time, "Thanks, again, *so much* for doing this. It means so much to me. To Frankie."

I roll my eyes at the last two words but soften the gesture with a smile and a casual, one-armed squeeze of her shoulders that I almost immediately regret when it feels anything but casual to me. Quickly dropping my arm, I pick at my jeans, then fiddle with the buttons on my plaid shirt.

"You're welcome, again. It's Frank's last hurrah, right? Let's make it count."

She grins. "Yeah." This time, she's the first to break eye contact, standing on her tiptoes and craning her neck. "Where the heck did the desk clerk go to get those key cards? China? I'd like to get checked in sometime today."

On cue, the clerk reappears, slides two plastic cards across the slick, shiny granite counter, and says in a syrupy drawl, "Y'all have a nice stay. I just need your signatures here, here, and here."

After we comply, she looks down at the paper, then back up at me, recognition dawning in her eyes. "I almost didn't recognize ya without your glasses, Mr. Lipton! Thought someone was signin' in for ya."

Another eligible citizen for Metropolis, or maybe Smallville.

My stomach drops to my feet. "Oh. Yeah." I reach up and touch my face as if verifying I'm not wearing the frames.

"Contacts," Betty quickly explains, pulling me away from the desk, toward the elevators. "Thanks!"

The way we collapse against each other, half-laughing, out-of-breath, as soon as we're alone in the elevator, you'd think we'd duped someone willing to kill us if they discovered our treachery, not some guileless front desk clerk.

"How could I forget the glasses?" I marvel, digging in my shirt pocket and coming up with the replacement pair I bought online and had overnighted to my house.

Betty presses the button for our floor. "I don't know, but

you're going to have to think a little faster on your feet this weekend."

"Yeah, I know. I froze. I'm rustier than I thought, I guess."

Oh, my gosh. This weekend is going to be an unmitigated disaster. I'm never going to be able to pull this off. Any of it. Being Frank, being around Betty, keeping it all together. It's going to be an epic fail. I can feel it. I can also feel that Valium wearing off, so I soon won't be able to contain the panic all of this is causing.

In a trance, I follow her from the elevator and down the hall, reading the room numbers, finally stopping in front of the ones that match the digits on our registration paperwork.

She's looking at me now, like she's expecting me to say something.

"Huh?" I eloquently seek clarification.

"Do you want to meet for dinner in a couple of hours?" she asks slowly, obviously repeating something she's already said.

"Oh. Yeah. Sure. Whatever."

She turns to insert her key card in the lock. "What's your deal, Nathaniel?"

I step to the door across the hall from hers and fiddle with my lock, too, so I can avoid her eyes. "Uh, I don't know. Jet lag?"

"We crossed one time zone," she points out, pushing open her room's door.

I shrug. "I'm distracted, I guess. Thinking about stuff."

When that admission receives no response, I quickly glance over my shoulder at her. Based on her expression, you'd think I'd just said I hated her guts.

"What's wrong? Are you okay?" I check.

She nods and swallows thickly, rubbing her pale forehead. "I don't know. Maybe it's the Valium. I've never taken one before. I think I'll just..." She backs into her room. "Take a nap."

"Hey." I step forward to follow her, but she already has the door half-closed.

Peering around the edge of it, she smiles shakily. "I'm fine. Just tired. I'll see you in a bit."

I give her an encouraging smile, trying to allay whatever worries are on her mind. I hope she's not afraid I'll make fools of both of us this weekend.

Clearing my throat, I assert more confidently than I feel, "After dinner, I'd like to look around the expo rooms, too, see where everything's going to be happening."

She nods. "Okay. Good idea. After that, though, we'd probably better hit the hay for the night. The less you wander around, the less chance you'll run into people who want to talk to Frank."

"Right. I didn't think about that."

"That's why I'm here. To keep you out of trouble." The wink that accompanies her quip makes my guts jump.

I return to my door, where I finally get the green light from the lock. "Then I'll see you in a bit. Get some rest."

"Yes, Nurse."

We enter our respective rooms, both smiling, but as soon as I close my door, my expression rearranges itself into a grimace.

What the hell am I doing?

* * *

BETTY MAY BE SPENDING the next couple of hours napping, but I'll be brushing up on being Frank. It's apparent from the short encounter at check-in that I desperately need to practice. Plus, traveling across time zones—even if it *is* only one—

is going to throw off my biorhythms plenty; I don't need a nap to confuse the situation further. Right now, if I'm going to get through the next two days without making a complete ass of myself (I'd be thrilled with half-assing the making of ass), I need to focus.

It's been a while since I forced myself to think like Frank, so I sit on the side of the bed, close my eyes, and breathe deeply through my nose. I ask myself, *What are the main attitudes Frank exudes?* and immediately, the words "guilelessness" and "arrogance" pop to mind. Yes, that's good. They seem at odds with one another, but they coexist harmoniously in the Frank persona. He considers himself the poster child for talented independent authors. He's not a hack who has an idea, barfs it onto a computer screen and publishes it on the Internet without proofreading, editing, and revising. He's a professional. He's proud of it—extremely proud of it.

On the other hand, any time it seems he's started to believe his own PR, he displays a humility and innocence that endears him to the reading public and the industry as a whole. I finally got the hang of this toward the end of my tenure as Frank, mostly by reading and studying the posts on *Quite Frankly*. Frankie had it mastered. She'd skewer someone in one sentence, then simper and defer to them in the next, ever the master manipulator.

Having recovered the Frank mindset, I work on his mannerisms. I open my eyes and move to the foot of the bed, so I can watch myself in the large mirror attached to the dresser. Recalling all of those book signings and readings, I practice my pontification pose: a slight lift of my chin while I rub it with my palm. This is usually what I do when talking about Frank's "craft." I feel it signifies that strange mix of pride and self-consciousness seeming to war within many creative people.

The pontification pose almost always precedes the "sooth-ing" behavior, since I inevitably ruffle some feathers during Frank's sermons. I smile sheepishly into the mirror while scratching the back of my head. Then I look down at my hands, breaking eye contact and conceding victory to whomever has challenged my previous offensive remarks.

There are plenty of other gestures in my repertoire—pushing my glasses higher on my nose (gearing up to say some-thing "smart"), chewing the inside of my cheek (listening to questions and considering my answers), letting my mouth drop open and pushing my tongue into the corner of my lips while chuckling (reacting to over-the-top flattery), among others—but the key is to alternate them and blend them together into a natural behavioral pattern that blends seamlessly with Frank's personality.

If it starts to look rehearsed, I'm toast, so I practice answering some of the more complex frequently asked ques-tions ("Where do you get ideas for your stories and charac-ters?" "Which character is most like you?" "Where do think the publishing industry is headed?") to utilize all the mannerisms.

What feels like minutes later, a knock at my door abruptly interrupts Frank practice, and I notice with a quick look at my phone that I've been at it for over an hour.

I approach the door with a smile, surprised Betty's finished napping so soon but glad, since it'll be helpful for her to critique my practice performances.

When I open the door, however, Betty isn't the person I see. Rather, three blonde women, dressed like they're prepared for a night of clubbing, stand before me, all smiling as if we're good friends. I've never seen them before in my life.

"Hi," I say uncertainly. "Can I help you?"

"OMG, it's really him!" the one in the middle says to her

companions, then directs at me, "Frank Lipton, right?" Before waiting for my answer, she digs through her purse and plows ahead. "We heard you were staying here and found out your room number, but we're not stalkers."

The one on the right adds, "We wanted to say hi and get an autograph and maybe see if you'd like to join us for a drink downstairs in the hotel bar."

"Just one little drink?" the one on the far left wheedles.

Oh, shit. I'm Frank. What would Frank do here? I want to slam the door in their faces and hide under the covers. But that won't do.

I lift my chin and summon the man I was only minutes ago talking to in the mirror. Flashing them a tight smile, I say, "Ladies, I'd love to, but I already have plans tonight, and I'm running late. I'm sure I'll see you tomorrow at the conference, where I'll have my autograph pen ready."

To my own ears, I sound self-assured, but I feel like I'm about to rattle apart on the inside.

The woman on the right bites her full lower lip. "We're not gonna be at the conference. It was sold out by the time we heard you were gonna be there. But we're your biggest fans—"

"Biggest!" the original spokeswoman reiterates. "Like, we have every one of your books." She holds up the e-reader she was apparently digging through her purse to find earlier. "All of 'em!"

The other two suddenly produce their own leather-covered e-readers and thrust them at me. Lefty says, "Please. Sign my Kindle cover."

"Really?" I squeak, then clear my throat. "I'm not sure about that... That's so... permanent."

Frank wouldn't give a shit, you nimrod. Stop being such a mamby pamby pussy. Take those devices and scrawl your John Hancock all over them, like a boss. Don't even leave room for future autographs.

"I want you to!"

"Me too!"

"Ditto!"

Suddenly, the door across the hall swings open, and a new, albeit familiar, voice breaks through the chorus. "Hey! What's going on?"

I look through the gaps between the bodies of the trio in front of me and try not to sound as relieved as I feel when I say, "Betty!"

The three visitors whirl to see who's interrupting their private meet-and-greet with me... Frank... whoever the hell I am.

While Betty skirts the small group and comes to stand next to me in my doorway, I explain, "These lovely readers want me to sign—"

"Who told you Frank's room number?" Betty cuts in brusquely to ask.

Righty looks down her nose at Betty, obviously unaware of who she's dealing with. "We don't have to divulge our sources." Her expression relaxes, and she grins proudly at me. "That sounded like Jess, didn't it?"

I stifle a laugh at her reference to the journalist protagonist in *Free Press* and allow, "Uh, yeah. It did," even though I've never read the whole book, only the synopsis.

Betty glares at me for my perceived encouragement, but now that she's here and I'm not as worried about what these chick lit junkies want from me, I can't help but see how ridiculous the situation is, and I'm starting to have fun with it.

Betty doesn't appear to be sharing my delight. "You don't have any business up here, and I'll be complaining to hotel and conference security for this," she informs the women.

I put a hand on her arm. "Well, they're here now, so..." I reach toward the women's electronic readers. "Hand 'em over. But, please, don't tell anyone my room number. I really need to get some stuff done, and I won't be able to do that if people are knocking on my door all night. Right?"

They nod in unison.

"Plus," I continue, feeling a lot more confident and finally finding my Frank feet, "it's much better if you three are the only ones to get these exclusive pre-conference autographs, don't you think?"

Lefty's nodding so hard, I'm worried her head's going to fall off and roll down the hall toward the elevators. The other two simply giggle and blush and hand me their e-readers in turn.

Emboldened by their success, the woman in the middle thrusts a phone at Betty. "Can you take a picture of Frank with the three of us? Pleeeeaase?"

Betty snorts. "Absolutely not!" She tries to hand the phone back to the woman, who steps away. For a minute, I think Betty's going to throw the device or drop it on the ground and stomp on it, but she helplessly holds it at arm's length, shaking it insistently in the owner's direction, to no avail.

What would Frank do? What would Frank do?

I shoot them regretful winces. "Gosh, guys, I don't know. It's been a long day, and—"

"Oh, please?? You look great. You're so cute! Even cuter in person than in your author photo. Just one picture?"

I consult Betty, who widens her eyes and tilts her head in a *"Don't even think about it"* silent message. Frank wouldn't let his manager/agent/whatever boss him around in front of a group of fans.

I pass the phone owner's newly signed, pink-covered Kindle back to her and stand between her and Lefty. "Aw, c'mon, Betty. Be a sport," I tease with a wink. "Just one little picture."

Betty scowls at me but aims the camera-phone at the four

of us and takes a hasty snapshot. "There. Now go." She commands, practically tossing the device across the hall.

Before I step away from them, Righty sneaks in a hasty peck on my cheek, knocking Frank's glasses askew. She smells like expensive whale piss, I mean... perfume. I hide my surprise at the kiss with a cocky laugh, like this happens to me all the time.

"Thank you for being such a gentleman!" the kisser gushes, moving reluctantly down the hall with her friends, who are tittering their way to the elevators.

Straightening the glasses on my nose, I give her a flirty finger wave before a firm tug on my arm pulls me backwards into my hotel room, and the door slams behind me.

"Oh, man, I almost blew that," I say with a laugh, wiping lipstick from my cheek while turning to confront a stone-faced Betty.

"Any of them would have been happy to return the favor."

"What?"

"Never mind," she mutters, flouncing on the bed. She lies on her stomach, staring out the sliding doors to the tiny balcony, which overlooks the indoor pool seven floors below.

A bit more gently and gracefully, I take up a similar pose next to her on the bed. "Are you mad because I suck at being Frank? I couldn't keep in mind that I was him and not me! I've been practicing in here, but it's not the same. I forgot how hard it is to stay in character. And they weren't like the women at the signings. Those ladies in the hallway were so so aggressive!"

"And hot."

I'm not going to insult her intelligence by denying that, but only an idiot would verbally agree with someone who points out something in such a derisive tone, so I say nothing. When I simply stare down at the pool, she continues, more softly,

"And you didn't blow it. Although you were probably more enthusiastic than Frank would have been. He's a loner, after all."

"True. But you couldn't tell I was afraid?"

"Afraid of springing a stiffy in front of three strangers?"

I nudge her with my shoulder and laugh. "No! I was too scared for that."

"Yeah, well, I'm not kidding about complaining to hotel management about this. That's a major safety issue. There are crazy people out there!"

"What's crazy is that crazy people would want to do crazy things to someone, just because they've read a few books with his picture on them."

"Yeah, some people need to get a life."

"Betts..."

She turns her head to look at me. The uncontrollable "stiffy" she accused me of nearly springing in the hallway threatens to make an appearance when I think too much about her lying next to me on the bed, and I lose my train of thought.

"What?" she prods while I try to think of the most un-sexy images possible. Frankie's refrigerator pops immediately to mind.

I lick my lips, roll away from Betty, and sit on the edge of the mattress. "Is it already time for dinner?" I pull my phone from my pocket and see it's only been about ninety minutes since we've arrived.

"It can be. I was dozing off when I heard all the noise you guys were making in the hall. Forget sleeping now. I guess I could eat. Oh, in other news, I called the conference organizers and told them you'd like a look around tonight. It occurred to me they may not let people wander around the convention areas, if they're still setting stuff up."

"Good thinking."

She taps her head. "It's not just a platform for gorgeous hair. And it's a good thing I asked. At first, I didn't think he was going to let us, but when I mentioned Frank's name, he got a lot friendlier."

"What time is our meeting with him?"

"Eight."

Again, I look at the time on my phone. "Okay. Let me freshen... do some things before we head downstairs."

While I'm crossing the threshold into the bathroom, she stops me with, "Hey."

I turn around. "Hm?"

"You handled yourself great out there." She bobs her head back toward the room's door. "If you keep that up, you'll be fine."

A grin bursts onto my face. I hope it doesn't look as goofy as it feels. "Thanks!"

"You're welcome. And what about me? Did I nail the role of the pushy, cranky manager?"

"Oh, that was an act?"

Reaching behind her, she grabs one of the pillows from my bed and hurls it at me while I laugh and sidestep the flying bedding. "You were perfect," I say more seriously.

She pushes herself into a sitting position, then stands and stretches. A sliver of belly peeks out at me, drawing my eyes inexorably to it. And that's when I see the unmistakable silver-and-pink, faded stretch marks. Too late, my eyes snap back to her face, which pales, then reddens.

So I do what any brave, mature man would do: I say something about needing to "tinkle," rush into the bathroom, and slam the door.

SCOPING OUT THE DIGS

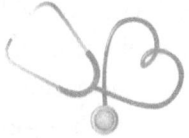

WE'RE SUCH AMATEURS AT THIS. AND WE'RE NEVER GOING to get better at it, since this is our last "gig." But like morons, we chose to eat at one of the restaurants on the resort's premises, so we hardly had a moment to ourselves at dinner. Betty eventually summoned a manager to try to keep people away so we could eat. By then, though, it was getting close to our meeting time with the conference organizers, so there was no time for talking, only eating. Fast eating. It probably saved us (okay, me) some awkward silences and conversational dead-ends, but it wasn't good for ingestion or digestion.

I stifle heartburn burps as we make our way from the restaurant to the convention rooms.

On our way past the front desk, Betty slows. "You go ahead. George should be wandering around in there, and he's expecting you. I need to put the fear of God into someone about security issues."

I swallow, glad I'm not the desk clerk or the hotel manager, as I watch Betty stride to the counter, her head high, shoulders back. Someone's about to get the ass-chewing of their life. I'd feel bad about that, but the idea of having gaggles of giggly women knocking on my door all weekend horrifies me enough to assuage my guilt. It's for the greater good. *My* greater good, granted. But still.

So I don't have to witness the bloodbath, I obey Betty and follow the arrows on the signs already set up for tomorrow's events. The first room into which I poke my head contains an endless sea of white cloth-covered tables with authors' names tacked to the front and stacks of books and swag covering the tables. Ooh, the meet-and-greet room. And there's my table smack dab in the middle of it all. Awesome. I'm getting claustrophobic just looking at it.

I clear my throat and cough, reminding myself I still have a full day before I have to worry about it, and it will be exactly like book signings. The table will protect me. The flow of traffic will prevent the crazies from loitering too long. It will be okay.

Before I can refute every single one of those naïve thoughts, I scuttle to the next room. It holds a long table on a dais and rows and rows of folding chairs facing the stage. The sign outside the door proclaims it to be tomorrow's Q&A room. The media will kick things off, but after the first hour and a short break, fans who have bought tickets will be allowed in to ask their questions.

The room is empty, so I walk closer to the dais and stare at the long table, trying to envision myself up there, next to a familiar and very intimidating name. My heartburn flares, licking at the back of my throat.

A full-blown panic threatens but retreats when Betty stands next to me and threads her arm through mine. "So, what do you think?" she asks.

"It'll do," I manage, keeping my reply brief to avoid my voice cracking. I stare at the letter "Y" in my seat-neighbor's first name, my unfocused eyes making it easier to travel to my happy place, far away from here.

Betty approaches the stage and points at the table tent with Frank's name on it. "You're right in the middle, the star attraction."

"Yeah. Goody."

"You're in good company, too." She rattles off the other names I've already noticed. "Lots of quality chick litters on the panel."

Snapping out of my trance and joining her at the front of the dais, I chuckle. "Chick litter? Sounds like waste from barnyard fowl."

"Chick littists?" she tries again.

"I prefer contemporary women's fiction author-publisher," I toss out snootily.

"Oh, lah-dee-dah."

I laugh but quickly pull myself together. "Really, Betty, you must take this more seriously. This is my craft, my *art,* we're talking about. It's not some frivolous drivel to make women— and men—feel all ooey-gooey about the power of love. There's *meaning* in my words. I'm making important statements about human nature and personal relationships and politics."

"Politics?"

"Yes. Definitely about gender equality, for starters."

She rolls her eyes. "Save it for the stage tomorrow, Descartes."

"Please, Betty, you can call me Frank."

When she hides a snicker behind her hand, I take it as encouragement to continue my Frank act and continue, "For real, though, I have to sit next to that hack, Yardley Cummins? He claims to drink his own blood, says it puts him in touch with his vampire characters. How'd he get in anyway? I didn't realize they allowed paranormal romance riffraff in."

"Everything okay?" a voice at my back asks, prompting a startle of epic proportions.

"Ohmyholyshityouscaredme!" I breathe more than say, whirling on the guy.

"I'm so sorry, Mr. Lipton," coos the man in the pinstripe suit with the gold name pin that dubs him "George." "I didn't mean to sneak up on you."

From the corner of my eye, I spy Betty struggling not to laugh behind her fist, but I try to ignore her and regain my composure. "Yeah, well, uh... whatever. We're fine. Getting a feel for the layout before tomorrow."

"George Nichols, author liaison." He extends his hand to me but says to Betty, "Miss Tate."

I want to punch him for talking to her chest.

Betty shakes George's hand. "Mr. Nichols. Thanks for letting Frank get a feel for the room tonight."

"Is everything to your satisfaction?" he asks both of us while still mostly looking at Betty's boobs. I clear my throat, so he tears his eyes away and blinks at me. "The seating arrangement may not be to your liking, is that what I heard?"

With the sort of agility not usually found in a man his size, George hops onto the stage, walks behind the long table, and stands behind the seat reserved for Frank. He lifts the name card and walks it down a few chairs. "We purposely put you in the middle, Mr. Lipton, to bring as much focus to you as possible, but..."

"Oh, that. I'm the headliner, or whatever. Right?" Blood whooshes in my ears as I remember Betty mentioning something about that in my kitchen after my near-death by omelet. Frank would relish the flattery, if not the attention, I remind myself, struggling to regain my character.

Say something Frank-like, you dumb-ass, I taunt internally.

"Maybe you'd rather be next to Ms. Delaney?" George

prods.

My eyes land on Margot Delaney's place card. I happen to know from scoping out her website on the way here that she's a hot redhead who not only writes chick lit but also erotica. She's here to promote her more mainstream books, but I'd still much rather sit next to her than Yardley Cummins.

I'm about to say just that when Betty shakes her head forcefully. "No, no! He's fine where he is."

He looks back and forth between her and me. "Or I could switch Ms. Delaney with Mr. Cummins," he posits unsurely. "It's just, she doesn't get along with Willa Nightsong, so then I'd have to move her, too, and—"

"It's perfect the way you originally had everything," Betty assures him, grabbing my arm and pinching me above my elbow.

"Ow!" I hiss, pulling away from her. Since she's resorting to physical abuse, I decide to defer to her expertise, and I grudgingly agree that George should return Frank's name card to its original spot.

"Remember, it's good to meet new people," Betty says. "I'm sure Yardley's interesting claims are mostly for show, you know, part of a persona. He's appealing to his readers' obvious interests."

"Well, it's dumb," I mutter like a sulking child. "If the guy shows up in a cape, I'm moving."

"That's fair," she replies, patting my arm in a placating fashion and tossing a long-suffering smile at George, who's either too used to this brand of behavior for it to be remarkable or too professional to show when he thinks someone's being a diva.

"I'm glad you approve, Betty," I say in the haughtiest tone I can muster. "Now, I'll be able to sleep tonight." Turning my attention back to George, I state dismissively, "Okay, then.

You've been very helpful. See you tomorrow at ten. I'll be bringing my own water."

"Uh, very well, Mr. Lipton."

Betty rolls her eyes toward George as if to commiserate about the eccentricities of creative types. He quickly looks away, and we make our exit.

Once clear of the room, she whispers through clenched teeth, "If you think I'm lugging around your stupid cooler for you all day tomorrow, you're crazy."

I giggle under my breath while we wait for the elevator. "I believe, as part of my entourage of one, that responsibility falls to you. Sorry."

"You're an idiot." Her statement has no bite to it as she steps into the newly arrived elevator car and faces front.

I follow her, jabbing at the button for our floor. "Well, after Sunday, you won't be subjected to my idiocy anymore, so..."

I tried to deliver it lightly, while staring at the floor numbers lighting up above the double doors, but the words have fallen like medicine balls between us in the peach-scented box. Neither of us says another word for the duration of the ride.

When we step onto our floor and make our way down the hall, she murmurs, "We keep saying goodbye; yet..."

Coming to a stop at my door, I stare down at the key card in my hand and chuckle. "Yeah. Well, maybe this time, it's for good. And maybe that's for the best." I'm saying what I think she wants to hear, trying to make this easier for her, even though it makes me want to puke. I glance up and smile ruefully.

Her face falls so far, I think it might drop right off the front of her head. She turns and jams her key card into the slot —hard enough that I worry she's going to snap it in two. Without another word, she storms into her room.

I stare after her, my mouth hanging open, much like the door in front of me. Tentatively, I cross the hall to follow her and close the door behind me, but I keep the bed between us as she stands by the balcony, her back to me. Unlike my pool view, her room looks down on a blacktop parking lot, complete with grotty dumpster.

"Hey," I begin. "I'm sorry if I said the wrong thing."

She tersely shakes her head but doesn't say anything. I'm afraid she's crying, but I'm too much of a wimp to move closer and confirm or disprove my suspicion.

Finally, her choked voice verifies my fear. "I get it," is all she manages before she can't continue.

Now I do draw nearer to her. Only a heartless bastard could maintain such a distance from someone so obviously distressed. "Betts, I—"

"No." She halts me with one word when I'm still a good ten feet away. Swiping under her eyes, she takes a deep breath, then sniffs. "It's fine. Well, it's not fine, but I'd rather you be honest than feed me a line."

"Feed you a line?"

She turns and hugs herself. "Yeah. You know, tell me we'll stay in touch, that we'll still be friends, when really, you want nothing to do with me."

"I'd never—"

"I know. You're not like that. You're a good, honest guy. And I understand if *this*"—she runs her hand up and down in front of her body, then circles her face with her index finger —"isn't something you want to take on."

What is she even saying? My throat aches and burns; my head pounds. "I love you, Betty." Unfortunately, because I've tacked her name on the end, it comes out more like a friendly reassurance than a heartfelt declaration, but it's a start.

She smirks and chuckles bitterly. "Right. Everyone does. I

work hard to make sure of it."

"I can relate to that."

"I know you can. That's why I wanted you to read that book." We both know which one she's talking about, so she doesn't have to specify further. "I hoped you'd understand me better, not think less of me."

Her presumption makes my temper flare as hot as my indigestion. "There's only one person I think less of after reading that book, and it's not you. It's *her*."

"She didn't tell any lies. It's all true. Well, up to a certain point in the timeline, obviously. And even then, she used details from a long-running fantasy I've had about being reunited with him."

"Your son?"

She nods, and two tears shake loose, plopping onto her shirt.

I step forward. She steps back.

Taking the hint, I halt but say, "She took things she knew, things you told her in confidence, and used them, capitalized on them, for her own ends. That's so wrong. She exposed your most private experiences to strangers."

Betty shrugs. "Whatever. At that point, it had been a long time. And the book has a happy ending."

"Well, I'm pissed off enough for both of us, then. She's a user. A manipulator! And she doesn't give a shit about anyone else or anyone else's feelings but her own. Can't you see that? Why do you continue to let her walk all over you?"

"Why did *you*?" she retorts.

Staring at her for a few seconds, I think about it. Then I sniff and clear my throat and give her a less-than-honest, "I don't know," because it's better for her to believe I'm stupid than for her to know the painful, embarrassing truth.

She lifts her chin. "Well, my story is as much her story as it is mine."

"Bullshit."

"I really believe that."

"So, *Frankie* was abandoned by Chris..."

"What? Wait. How do you know his real name?"

Rather than lose steam on my argument, I trust she'll figure out I learned his name from her so-called best friend and continue, "*Frankie* had a baby and gave him up for adoption; *Frankie* came out stronger—yet more vulnerable—for it? Is that it?"

"She was there for me through all of that, when nobody else was."

"Big fucking deal. Hundreds of other people would have been there for you, and they wouldn't have held it over your head for the rest of your life."

"But nobody else was. Who are these hundreds of people? Where were they? My own mother couldn't deal. She wrote me a check for an abortion because, 'Having a baby when you're as young as you are will ruin your life.' She was twenty when she had me, a year younger than I was at the time *I* got pregnant."

I bite my lower lip as her revelation actually causes me physical pain—in addition to the burning—in my chest.

"Don't look at me like that," she orders.

"I'm not."

"You are. I didn't tell you to read it so you'd pity me; I told you to read it so you'd understand me."

"And I do. Mostly. What I don't understand is how someone as strong and beautiful and smart and funny and... wonderful... as you are can let someone like Frankie convince you otherwise."

"She knows the real me."

Before she can react or move away, I close the gap between us and grasp her upper arms. My need to convey the following overrides my paranoia that my breath may singe off her eyebrows. "She invented the 'real' you. It's a figment of her imagination. And you've suspended your disbelief, like a good little reader, and have bought into it, most of the time."

She squeezes her eyes closed and shakes her head as if she can't bear to hear what I'm saying. That, or my breath really does smell bad. But I can't worry about that right now. I have a point to make.

"Hey," I say, barely above a whisper.

Eyes still closed, she replies at the same volume, "What?"

"Look at me."

She does, through wet eyelashes.

"You know better. I've seen the flashes of self-awareness—true intuition—you've had around her. I've seen you break from the trance and assert yourself. And I've witnessed her punish you for it every time."

"You make her sound so evil."

I widen my eyes but don't verbally commit to that exact assessment. Instead, I say carefully, "Anyone who treats people the way she does is not a nice person."

"She didn't use to be like that," she says defensively, as if to justify their friendship.

"I'm sure. But even if she was, it's not your fault." I take a deep breath. "Earlier, you asked where your other potential supporters were. And all I can say is this: people rarely apply for a job that's already filled."

She blinks up at me, and I can see the concept sinking in for her. Eventually, she whispers, "You're right," and her face crumples.

I pull her gently against me, and she hugs me with an intensity usually reserved for parents of scared children. I return the hug, but with more tenderness than force.

And for the first time in a long time, I feel like myself.

PANEL PANDEMONIUM

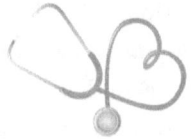

MY SWAGGER IS FALTERING UP HERE. I CAN FEEL IT FADING with every passing minute. The media questions were predictable and dull, good warm-up confidence-builders. The readers' questions, however, have been going on for nearly an hour now, and some of them are beyond intrusive and odd.

Who knew hardcore chick lit/romance readers cared so much about what style and color of underwear their favorite authors wear, how they're typically dressed while writing their books, and how they take their coffee? I've never given any of those things a single thought. Every time a reader asks something I deem either private or irrelevant, I have to bite back my urge to say, "None of your business."

It doesn't help that I seem to be the only author up here who seems to be bothered by the questions. Is that in character? Maybe. I wish I could convincingly act a little more like Yardley, though (and trust me, I realize how wrong that is), and smirk and leer my way through each question.

"What do you wear while you're writing?" His answer: "Depends on the kind of scene I'm working on, if you know what I mean," followed by wiggling, drawn-on eyebrows. My answer: "Shorts and a t-shirt?" Not surprisingly, my reply received a much less enthusiastic response.

Seriously, though, they want to picture me sitting naked in front of a laptop, stroking myself while typing out a sex scene? I can't encourage that thinking. It's bad enough they think I wrote the sex scenes, period. The closer we get to the end of this charade, the less tolerance I have for it.

Betty knows it, too. Seconds ago, my phone lit up with a new text on the table in front of me. I glanced at it and had to bite the inside of my cheek not to laugh out loud. *Your t-shirts are hot. Hang in there*

Her kind support and mild flirting, at first comforting, quickly reminded me of our conversation last night, though, and my mind started to wander, imagining what would have happened if I hadn't run from her room like a sexually repressed idiot.

Oh yeah, that happened. Actually, what happened was that I started to feel more and more sick due to my heartburn, and after we stood, locked in that embrace for what felt like an hour—yet at the same time, an instant—I had to step away. I didn't *have* to come right out and tell her I felt like the fire-burping gross-ass in a Pepto commercial, but I did, anyway, because, well, I'm me.

As soon as I got to my own room, though, and had chugged a bottle of antacid and a pitcher of water, my mind wandered, like it's doing now, to what would have happened if I hadn't ordered the mango salsa chicken breast with a side of garlic roasted potatoes for dinner. What if I'd kissed her? What if I'd let her yank off my "hot" t-shirt and run her cool hands against my warm chest? What if she'd given my lips the same treatment I've seen her give to countless glasses of dark red wine? What if...?

The room is disconcertingly silent.

Since every eye seems to be locked on me, I blurt, "What if?" then cough and correct, "I mean, what?" Blushing, I scan the room until my eyes land on a woman standing near the back, holding one of the handful of cordless mics that have been circulating the room. "I'm sorry, I didn't understand what you said."

She smiles nervously and repeats what she asked, a semi-intelligent and interesting question, although it's one I've answered a million times in multiple forums the past few months. Still, I reward her with a smile, grateful nobody here can read my mind (I hope), and she hasn't asked about my masturbation schedule but has instead inquired, "How do you continue to write and publish so many books while also marketing the ones you've already published and maintaining your social media presence?"

This is a topic on which Frank can pontificate all day, and I can, thankfully, speak about it without thinking too much. Still recovering from my R-rated fantasy, I stall by rubbing my chin as I collect my more relevant thoughts, then say, "Well, it all boils down to discipline. Ass in chair, peeps. Are there other things I'd rather be doing sometimes than writing about women who whine that there are no good single men left? Sure. Sometimes a colonoscopy would be preferable, no offense. But if you want to be successful, you have to be prolific. One-hit wonders don't cut it anymore. None of us up here is going to be the next Harper Lee, all right? If you don't have a back stock of titles, you're not going to make the type of money you need to make to survive."

"But how do you do that," she persists, "when you're pulled away from the writer's chair so often, for so many things, things like this conference, for example?"

"Late nights," Margot interjects from down the table. "Also, Frank has an advantage over some of us."

Annoyed that she butted into my answer *and* is presuming to know anything about Frank and his writing, I smile tightly. "Oh? And what's that?"

She grins. "Well, you obviously sell a lot of books because readers want to picture you naked while writing them. So you can pretty much slop anything out there at this point."

The rest of the panel laughs, but I grit my teeth at what's become apparent today, based on these readers' questions. Frankie was right all along; part of the draw to her books is her readers like the idea of a guy writing them. Clothed or not.

Still, Frank wouldn't let that stand, so I say, "I wouldn't go that far. Anyway, I'd appreciate it if you'd give my writing a little more credit than that."

She rolls her eyes upward into her stick-straight, thick bangs. "Cut the crap. 'I love cuddling and watching chick flicks.' Please! Why don't you tell us who your ghostwriter is and stop this silly, liberated-man act?"

My heart and stomach freeze in tandem, as if someone's injected my chest and abdomen with anesthetic. An audible gasp comes from the audience. The woman who had asked me about my writing schedule is still standing, but her eyes are wide, her hand covering her mouth.

I press the tip of my tongue to the center of my upper lip while the others watch eagerly, waiting for my reply. It's clear from my fellow panel members' expressions that this has been an oft-discussed topic behind my back, and they're all just as interested in my response as Margot is.

Suddenly it hits me that this is it. I can end it all now and extricate myself from this situation a whole day earlier than planned. But some shred of self-preservation keeps me from confessing to Margot's supposition. I glance at Betty, and the panicked look on her face reminds me of the huge financial risk she has riding on the success of this weekend. Plus, my head screams, *We've come so far; don't fuck it up now!*

Before I can respond, Margot says while playing with a strand of her hair, "Lots of authors use ghostwriters. There's nothing illegal about it. Sometimes you have the right image, and equipment…" She drops her hair and gestures toward me. "But not the talent to back it up."

Maybe it's the adrenaline. Maybe it's the desire to eliminate the worry wrinkling Betty's brow. But somehow, the Frank who's been absent for most of the morning asserts himself. I lift my chin and chuckle confidently. "I can assure you, I'm well-equipped in both departments to which you're referring." *Bonus points for using correct grammar, Bingham!*

Before I can congratulate myself too much, though, Yardley gives a snort and a sneer and drops, "Ah, well. It's not like the writing's that great, anyway, so if you *do* use a ghostwriter, you might want to get your money back, buddy."

I turn my scorching attention to him. "I think it's rich that you—Mr. Jump-on-the-Vampire-Bandwagon—would dare criticize someone else's writing. You're only here because the average reader is operating on an eighth-grade reading level, and as a whole, they've shamefully lowered their standards and can't get enough of your genre. You've been riding housewife hobbyists' coattails your entire career, writing glorified fanfic."

The crowd alternately boos and cheers me, revealing the lines between the camps of vamp-lovers and -haters, as well as reacting to my inadvertent insult to their intelligence… not to mention my slam of the entire stay-at-home mom community.

"Fuck you, Lipton!" Yardley screeches. "Why don't you go

back to your room and jizz out a love scene? You can blame your typos on your sticky keyboard."

My heart pounding and face flaming, I growl, "Typos? Your books singlehandedly give indies the bad reputation they have for lax editing."

For a second, I worry Yardley's going to live up to his weird reputation and bite me. He actually bares his teeth at me. Then something over my shoulder grabs his attention. I glance back and see Betty's joined us onstage.

"Let's go," she murmurs near my ear, tugging on my shoulder. "You don't have to listen to this guy's bullshit."

Instead of helping my cause, though, her appearance has given Yardley more ammunition. "Is this your real-life inspiration? How cliché... author in love with his manager. Although, in this case, I can't say I blame you. She's hot."

"Shut up," I demand through clenched teeth.

He continues, "We all use our sexcapades as inspiration. Don't be so embarrassed."

I stand and loom over him. "That explains why the love scenes in your books are so flat. When your only experience comes from dry-humping a blow-up doll with fangs, what can you expect?"

Apparently, insulting Yardley's favorite sex toy is the wrong move, because he pops from his chair and launches himself at me, taking me down to the pin-dot patterned, low-pile carpeting behind our chairs. The weirdo is stronger than he appears and quickly traps me against the wall, which he uses to hold my head still while he pummels it with both fists. After the first couple of blows, I manage to raise my arms and block the other punches with my forearms. Still, every once in a while, one of Yardley's wild swings lands against unprotected skin.

I can tell by the noise level that pandemonium has broken

out in the room, and the number of legs in my view tells me people have rushed the stage, but I have to focus mostly on protecting myself, figuring out a way to turn this fight around before I require a trip to the ER.

Where the hell is George, or anyone else sort of in charge? Hotel security? Dog the Bounty Hunter? Anyone!

As I'm about to use my legs as leverage for flipping over, Betty runs behind Yardley, and I know I can't kick my legs without kicking her, so I remain limp while she pulls on his long, black duster coat.

"Get off, you idiot!" she yells at him.

"I'm not done kicking your boyfriend's ass," he answers between swings.

"He's not my boyfriend!"

At that statement, Yardley stops his beating and half-turns to look at her. "Really?" He pushes his greasy black hair off his forehead and winks at her. "Because I'd be glad to stop this and take you out for a drink—in my room."

As she stares incredulously at the Gothic goober, I sit up, pull my lips into a straight, white line, rear back my head, and buck it forward as soon as Yardley faces me once more. The people gathered nearby give a collective gasp at the sickening thunk of our two skulls colliding. Yardley immediately falls to the side, where he slides down the nearby wall. One hand on my forehead, I use my other hand to push myself free of the passed out writer.

A hush falls on the room as we all catch our breath.

"Bad-ass!" one of the audience members finally hisses to the person next to her.

Margot laughs deeply in her throat, something I'm sure she's spent hours practicing. "Oh, my God! What a couple of morons!"

"Are you okay?" Betty asks, kneeling next to me.

"No," I admit, collapsing, exhausted, onto my back, my arms flopping to my sides. I want to check on the unconscious guy, but I have no energy right now.

"I'll go get help," she offers.

Somehow, I find the strength to grab her hand. "No. Stay here with me."

"Why didn't you just punch him?" she wonders. "Why the head-butt?"

I wince and hiss as she pokes at the goose egg forming in the center of my forehead. "Arms dead," I answer her succinctly, jerking away from her fingers. "Ow! Stop that!"

"It looks really bad."

"Well, it feels worse, so stop touching it."

"You're bleeding."

"Yeah, I know." I can feel the blood dripping down the side of my face and pooling into my ear, but I don't care. I'm worried more about going to prison for murder.

Fortunately, I don't have much time to dwell on that possibility before I see Yardley stirring and being helped into a sitting position by George, who must have arrived on the scene sometime during Betty's ministrations.

"Wait!" I say, my training kicking in. Despite the pain it causes, I sit up and crawl toward Yardley and George. "Don't move him."

"Stay back!" George commands. "You've done enough."

"I'm not going to hurt him," I promise, sitting next to Yardley and straightening my skewed glasses. "Help him lie down, please. And Betty, grab one of the bottles of water from my cooler." She does and hands it to me. I press it to the bump that makes Yardley my twin. To George, I say, "Can you—or someone—find me a penlight or flashlight? And it might be smart to call an ambulance, to be on the safe side."

Before George is even gone from the room, I turn my

attention back to Yardley and ask him some of the usual questions to ascertain his awareness level. "Do you know what the date is?" "Who's the President?" "Do you know where you are?" "Who am I?"

To the last question, he answers, "A complete asshole."

I can't help but laugh at that, mostly from relief. "I think you're going to be okay, but I'd be more comfortable if you got a second opinion from someone who may not also be suffering from a concussion."

George returns with a full-sized flashlight, something a police officer may carry and could double as a weapon.

"This is the smallest one you could find?" I ask, exasperated. When George stutters defensively, I wiggle my fingers impatiently in his direction. "Never mind. Just give it."

He slaps the flashlight into my hand. I turn it on and wrap my hand around the beam of light, trying to focus it. I sweep it in front of Yardley's left eye, then his right.

"It's hard to tell with this monster, but your pupils seem to be responding equally and appropriately to light." I turn to George and ask, "Did you call that ambulance?"

"It's on its way," he confirms. "You look like you could use some medical attention yourself."

Feeling dizzy, I find a chair and plop into it. "I definitely could," I agree. "I'm gonna sit right here and wait for the paramedics. Nobody let either of us fall asleep."

Betty sits next to me and blots the blood from my face and inside my ear with a wet paper towel. I widen my eyes and blink them rapidly, rolling them in my sockets like someone trying to blink moisture into a pair of contact lenses.

She turns my face toward her with a hooked finger against my jaw. Grinning, she says, "Oh, my gosh. Look at you, you idiot!"

I try to focus my droopy eyes on her and reply, but the

exhaustion and pain are too much. The last thing I'm aware of is her yelling, "Nate!" before the blackness engulfs me.

* * *

YEAH, I know. It's not very manly to pass out like that, but is anyone surprised I did? It also wasn't masculine to wake up to a burlier-than-me female paramedic waving smelling salts under my nose. But that happened, too.

Considering it came on the heels of nearly being beaten to a pulp by a vampire wannabe wearing penciled-on eyebrows and shoe lifts, I'd say losing consciousness after a stout blow to the head is the least of my shame.

Several hours later, after a more thorough once-over at one of Atlanta's fine medical establishments, Betty and I return to the hotel, both of us pretending we don't notice everyone staring at us as we cross the lobby and duck into an elevator. With the exception of a few rare moments here and there, including last night in Betty's hotel room, I've been pretending about one thing or another my whole life, so ignoring a few stares is nothing.

Head trauma makes me philosophical.

In my room, I stride straight for the bathroom, where a hot shower beckons. Considering I spent the majority of the day among the sick and wounded, it feels like I've been at work all day.

As I wordlessly shut the door between us, Betty picks up the old-school phone on the bedside table and calls to me through the wall, "What do you want from room service?"

We determined in the rental car on the way back from the hospital that we weren't going to brave the Author's Ball later, even though it's included in the conference's registration fee.

Before answering, I turn on the taps, then strip. I'm not at all hungry, but since it's late afternoon, and we missed lunch, I know I need to eat something. Something marginally healthy. With some protein. I'm contemplating all of this when the door swings open, cutting a swath through the steam.

"Whoa!" I object reflexively, lifting my leg and showing her my butt and right flank, crossing my arms in front of me.

She immediately backs through the door and pulls it closed on her way. "Sorry! You didn't answer! I was worried you'd passed out on the toilet or something!"

"I was thinking!"

"Well, can you think out loud, so I know you're still conscious? It's my responsibility to keep an eye on you." She sounds more irritated than concerned.

"I'll have a chef salad!" I snap in return. "The biggest one they have." I may not be hungry, but I'm vindictive. I can't wait to submit the expense report to Frankie for *this* trip. An ER visit, room service... How else can I rack up some charges?

Thirty minutes and three "Are-you-still-okay-in-there?" knocks later, I emerge, lightheaded.

Betty, watching TV from the bed, closes her eyes to block out my towel-clad form.

"You've already seen it all, so what's the point?" I grump.

"You still have the right to *some* privacy," she explains but opens her eyes.

Despite my big-talking, I keep the towel on until both my underwear and pajama bottoms are fully covering my best friend and his boysenberries. To let her know there are no hard feelings, though, I blindly toss the towel in her direction when I'm finished with it, as I pull my UW-Milwaukee t-shirt from the hotel dresser.

She catches and clutches the damp towel to her chest but doesn't even try to hide her staring at me.

"What?" I ask self-consciously, hurrying to put on the shirt.

I remember her laughing at the bachelor party pictures of Nick, declaring him, "so hairy!" and wonder if she's thinking the same thing about me. My blushing makes my head pound harder. "Where's the bottle of acetaminophen we got from the hospital pharmacy?" I ask to cover my embarrassment.

Turning off the TV and hopping from the bed, she says, "I'll get it. Just get comfortable."

"I'm fine," I insist but make a beeline for the bed anyway, where I pull back the covers to unearth the pillows. While I'm arranging them against the headboard so I can sit propped up, she returns to the bed and takes over the job for me, practically pushing me aside.

"I can fluff my own pillows," I assure her, taking the rattling bottle of non-prescription pain medication from her.

"No, I'm going to take care of you."

"But I don't need—"

"I know it feels weird, but you're going to be the patient for once."

"I'm a horrible patient," I warn.

"I can tell that already. Your glass of water is right there, on the table next to you." She jerks the pillow away from me while I'm distracted and gives it a good, stiff beating before placing it exactly where I had it before. "There. Now take your medication—you're allowed to have four at a time—and get comfortable. Room service should be here any minute."

"I know the correct dosage," I mutter, shaking the tablets into my hand and tossing them into my mouth. I wash them down with most of the water in the glass, so Betty intercepts it before I can set it down again on the table.

"I'll take that. Looks like you need a refill."

Her fingers brush against mine as she pulls the glass away from me. I want to grab her hand or wrist to keep her from leaving, but my reflexes are too slow, so I settle for saying to her back while she pours more water from the pitcher on the dresser, "I'm not going to be able to relax if you're fluttering around me like... like... a mom!"

As soon as the words tumble from me, I want more than anything to take them back. Since I can't, I verbally backpedal with, "*My* mom, I mean. I don't need to be mothered," I finish weakly, closing my eyes and standing next to the bed with my hands in fists at my sides.

After a few tense, silent seconds, I feel her cool hands wrap around the fist closest to her. Calmly, quietly, and gently, she says, "I'll stop 'fluttering around' as soon as you do as you're told and get in bed, Goose Egg."

I nod my cooperation and start to do exactly that when we hear a knock on the door, followed by, "Room service!"

She bustles away from me, and I settle myself without an audience. When she returns with a tray full of food, she inquires, "Don't you want to get under the covers?"

"No, I'm about to eat."

Her shrug says, *"Suit yourself,"* and she hands across a large glass bowl with a napkin-and-cutlery bundle balanced on top of its plastic wrap. "Your salad."

"Thank you."

I'm still not hungry, but at least eating will keep us too busy to talk. I hope.

I slit the paper ring holding my utensils and tuck my napkin into the collar of my t-shirt. Betty purses her lips at me but doesn't make a comment, so I pretend I don't notice. I don't want to give her an opening to offer to feed me herself, which is where I'm afraid this is headed.

I pick at my food, shuffling the lettuce leaves and taking tiny bites of turkey and egg when I notice Betty watching me as if waiting for me to put the fork to my lips, but eventually the act is too exhausting. "I'm tired," I declare, ripping the napkin from my shirt and moving the bowl from my lap to the bedside table.

Without missing a beat, Betty pulls her phone from her pocket. It clicks as she taps on its screen. "Setting an alarm for an hour from now, when I'll need to wake you up to check your pupils."

My groan is to no avail, I know, but I let it rip anyway so she'll be aware of my displeasure.

"Head injuries are nothing to screw around with, Nathaniel."

"You don't say. I never learned that in *nursing school*."

"Don't get snippy with me, Mister. I'm helping you follow the doctor's orders. I shudder to think what would happen if I weren't here."

"I'd get lots of uninterrupted sleep."

"And possibly fall into a coma and go missing until house-keeping got suspicious and made a grisly discovery."

I laugh, but it hurts my head, so I stop abruptly. "Ow."

"Exactly. Now." She tugs at the bedspread trapped under me. "Just... Get... Under... These... Covers."

"I'm not sleeping under this nasty thing."

"I know. Ew. But I can't get it off the bed with you on it."

"I don't need covers. I'm still hot from my shower."

"But you'll cool off and catch a chill while you're sleeping."

"What? 'Catching a chill' is not even remotely medically accurate."

"Your body temperature drops when you're asleep."

"I'll be fine." Still upright, I close my eyes. "Now, shhh... Watch TV or something."

"I don't want to disturb you. I'll read a book. Are you going to sleep sitting up?"

Tucking my hands under my armpits and crossing my feet at my ankles, I grunt an affirmative reply.

"That doesn't look comfortable," she declares, her warning tone predicting something direr than a chilly or unrestful sleep.

"It's only for an hour, tops, so who cares? I just need to rest my eyes. And my ears."

"Right. Message: received. Zipping my lips."

I crack my left eyelid to shoot her a one-eyed glare, but I can't hold a sufficiently stern expression to make the proper impact.

She laughs as I try to pull my lips downward into a frown and fail. "Sorry!" she says through her giggles. "I'm nervous. It's like I'm holding your life in my hands, or something. I don't know how nurses and doctors do this every day."

Closing my eyes and adjusting my neck against the pillow again, I casually drop my hand, palm-up on the mattress between us. She correctly reads the cue and clamps it with her own.

"Don't think so much about it," I advise, giving her fingers a squeeze. "Everything's going to be fine. Now shut up."

She so faithfully follows my half-joking command this time that I worry I've hurt her feelings and can't resist peeking one more time at her in my peripheral vision. Fortunately, my check through slitted lids reveals she's the mirror image of me, resting her eyes with an enigmatic smile playing on her full lips like a teasing kiss.

I pinch my peepers closed more tightly to shut out the vision, but it's burned on my brain, eliciting a dangerous tingle I know is only the beginning of yet another embarrassing moment I'm powerless to prevent.

As subtly as possible, I let go of her hand and turn onto my side, facing away from her, pulling my pillow downward with me as I scoot into a fetal position.

"Told ya you wouldn't be comfortable sitting up," she murmurs.

At this point, I'm perfectly content to let her think she was right and have the last word.

KISS IT BETTER

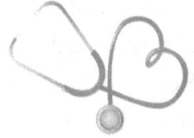

AT FIRST, I WAS HYPER-AWARE OF BETTY IN THE SAME BED with me, but exhaustion took over, and I fell into a deep, dreamless sleep. As promised, she woke me up about an hour later, looking nervous, like she wasn't sure what she was going to find when she looked into my eyes.

To put her more at ease, I joked, "It's a lot nicer waking up to you, not that scary EMT."

She held back to prevent laughing in my face, so I continued, determined to get a proper response from her, "Someone needs to tell her 'No-Shave November' is still two months away, although I do applaud her dedication to making sure head trauma victims *really* know the date and aren't working off visual clues to guess."

At that, Betty tossed back her head and shrieked at the ceiling, and my chest swelled. When she dropped her chin again to look at me, I winked, then laughed at her chiding head-shake.

"You're mean," she said, covering her mouth to hide her continued amusement.

"Oh, whatever. You were thinking it."

"I was not! I didn't even notice! I was too worried about you."

"Okay, fine. I'm sorry. But I was up-close-and-personal with her hair follicles, so it was hard for me not to notice. Maybe as a show of appreciation, I should sign her up for that Dollar Shave Club service my dad uses."

Her warning look as she took her e-reader to one of the chairs in the tiny seating area between the bed and the wall seemed more sincere after that dig, so I quit while I was ahead and slid under the covers, where I almost immediately fell back to sleep, grinning at the memory of her laughter.

Now, after about the third check (I think), I get up, and after Betty finishes staring into my eyes at intense, close range, I use the toilet, wash my hands, take some more painkillers, splash water on my face, inspect the bump on my noggin, make myself a fresh ice pack, and return to the bed.

"Mind if I watch TV?" I ask, holding up the remote.

She shakes her head and smiles. "Go for it."

As I channel-surf, she inquires, "How are you feeling?"

"Fine." Giving up on finding something to watch when so many shows are in commercial breaks, I pull up the on-screen guide and peruse the list. Considering it's a summer Saturday night, I don't have high hopes for finding anything interesting.

"'Fine,' like, 'all better'?" Betty digs deeper.

"Not exactly. My head hurts like a sonofabitch, but that's to be expected, I guess. Ooh! *The Notebook* is on." I push the button to take me to that channel and toss the remote onto the mattress next to me.

"So, I take it we're not going to join the party downstairs, huh?"

"I thought we'd already established that." I adjust the pillow between my back and the headboard. Her question reminds me of dinner, and I realize I'm hungry, finally, but the salad bowl is missing from the bedside table.

Without a word, she crosses to the mini-fridge and produces my wrapped-up dinner. "Looking for this?"

"Yeah. Thanks."

While I tuck into the wilted greens, cold meat chunks, and eggs, she perches on the foot of the bed, her right foot tucked against her left thigh, her left foot swinging off the side of the bed. "I can order something fresher for you. Or we can go downstairs and see what's on the buffet at the author mingly-thing."

"Nah." I chew and stare at the TV, then swallow and point to the screen with my fork. "Have you ever kissed someone in the rain like that?"

She looks over her shoulder. "I've never kissed anyone like that. Ever. Anywhere. In any weather."

"Me neither," I agree, transfixed by what Rachel McAdams and Ryan Gosling are doing to each other's faces.

I blink and return my attention to my salad, not quite able to achieve eye contact with Betty when she twists at the waist to face me after watching that scene. I'm also suddenly thankful for the very cold, very large bowl on my lap. Frantically, I try to remember what we've been talking about. The formal dress Author's Ball. Or whatever. Right. "You can go, if you want," I offer.

"I don't want to go alone. I'm not an author, anyway."

"Ha! Join the club." I push a particularly nasty piece of lettuce to the side to get to some crispier stuff underneath.

"You know what I mean, though. I'd feel out of place without you. But I dunno, I'm starting to feel bad that we're not doing what we're here to do, which is market and promote and network."

I smile ruefully. "I think Frank has done enough 'networking' for one day."

She sighs. "You're right."

"You don't sound happy about that."

Picking at the bedspread, she mumbles, "I'm mostly bummed I won't get to wear the dress I bought especially for tonight. It's smokin'."

Seeing that dress is almost enough for me to forget every other factor in the decision and agree to go. But I hold firm. "I don't think I'd be able to stay in character with this headache. I say we let the excitement die down and keep a low profile tonight. Tomorrow, we attend the meet-n-greet, as planned. Except you might want to double-check where Frank's table is in relation to Yardley's. Could get ugly if we're too close." Since she still looks so dejected, tracing her finger along the outline of a flower on the ugly comforter, I nudge her with my foot. "Anyway, *The Notebook* is on! I can't believe more authors aren't skipping the party to stay in their rooms and watch this."

I'm relieved when she laughs and seems willing to drop the debate. Finished with all the edible parts of my meal, I set the bowl aside once again and gently press the ice pack to my forehead, hissing as my bruised skin adapts to the cold.

"It looks a lot better than it did earlier," she lies straight to my face.

I shoot her an appreciative smile but counter, "Where's the fire extinguisher? Because your pants are going up in smoke."

Before she can commit further to the fib, her phone rings. She winces at the display, rushing to the balcony. As soon as she closes the door behind her, I mute the TV and strain to listen. I can immediately tell by her side of the conversation that the caller is Frankie.

"No. What do you mean? Oh. That. Really? On an RSS feed? Slow news day. Well, it wasn't like *that*; I'd hardly call it a 'brawl'. I don't know! It just happened. He's going to be okay, by the way, in case you're wondering. Nice. No, I don't think the other guy is going to sue; he was the one who threw the first punch. No, no charges pressed; the police didn't even come. And if anything, Nate would be pressing charges against *that* freak. Well, that's all just speculation"

Then there's such a long silence that I think maybe the call has ended, and I've missed the heartfelt goodbyes. I grip the remote more tightly, ready to restore the volume and pretend I've been watching TV the whole time, not eavesdropping. Seconds later, though, while my finger's still hovering over the mute button, Betty snaps, "I don't remember, okay? Maybe I did! I was worried about him. Well, I'm sorry, but at that point, I didn't give a shit if I called him his real name. He lost consciousness right in front of me!"

I blush at that detail. Great. The last person I want to have that information is now in smug possession of it.

"No, you can't talk to him. He's resting. I know what the itinerary says, but neither of us is in a partying mood, so we're skipping it. No! No! I said, 'no,' Frankie... Frankie? Hello? Frankie? Sonofa...!"

The balcony door crashes open at the same time my phone sings, "Doot-dee-doo-doo-doo-doooooooot, Doot-dee-doo-doo—"

"Hello?" I answer as confidently as possible, cringing when the ice shifts and clacks in the bag in my other hand.

"You couldn't even do this one thing right?"

"Good evening, Frankie. I'm fine, and you?"

"Cut the crap. You two have managed to make a major mess of things out there."

"Seems so, doesn't it?"

"Well, fix it."

"We will. We still have the meet-n-greet tomorrow. Everything will be fine."

"You're supposed to be one of the headliners, but you've made a complete ass of yourself and my books."

"Your books are probably selling better than ever. Go download a sales report and calm down."

"You need to make an appearance at that thing tonight."

"Not happening."

Her frustrated growl would be funny if it weren't so loud in my ear. I close one eye and pull the phone away from my head while she vents her anger. That's when Betty grabs the device from me, turns it off, and tosses it in the dresser, where it lands softly on top of my clothes.

"What are you—"

"That's enough," she states, slamming the drawer shut, her chest heaving, her pulse thumping in her neck.

"You shouldn't have done that. She's going to think *I* hung up on her."

"Who cares? She's being a bitch. She doesn't even care that you got hurt."

"Well, that's not surprising. And it's not like it hurts my feelings."

"It hurts *mine*." She plops into the armchair she's spent much of the evening occupying and rubs her fists into her eye sockets.

"Don't do that to your eyes." I switch off the TV, placing the remote on the bedside table.

Her hands drop, and she looks miserably at me. "I said your name—your real name—in front of everyone this morning."

I let that information register and try to recall it for myself, but it's no use. The day's earlier events are mostly a blur of Yardley's fists, physical pain, and humiliation.

Trusting she's remembering correctly, I say, "So what? I've called myself my real name at appearances before. We have a cover story for that: Frank Lipton is a pen name."

"Yeah, well, since we've never made that public knowledge, people are coming up with their own explanations. The most popular theory happens to be the truth."

I transfer the ice bag to my other hand, tucking my frozen hand under my thigh. "So? That doesn't mean it's true."

Her eyebrows nearly touch. "I think that's the definition of the truth: it's true."

"Yeah, *we* know their conjectures and the truth are one and the same, but *they* don't know that. All we have to do is give them the pen name explanation at tomorrow's meet-n-greet, and everyone will shut up."

"Or we can skip the meet-n-greet and let them think whatever the hell they want to think."

"We have books to sell and sign and merchandise to unload." *To the tune of about $2500*, I add silently.

"Fuck it."

"Betty..."

"No, I'm serious. Fuck it, and fuck her."

"Never managed it myself," I quip, then cough when she glares at me. "Never mind. The important thing is that we came all this way to do something we promised we'd do, and we're going to do it. Then—in my case, at least—I never have to do another thing for her. I send her a cease and desist regarding the use of my image, and it's over."

"I'm sick of this, and I don't want to do it anymore," she mutters to her lap.

I swing my legs over the side of the bed, toss the ice pack aside, and drop to my knees in front of her, grasping the arms of the chair with my frigid fingers. "I've been sick of this since the first day. So, I get it. But it's almost over. And if nothing else, someday we can say we did it. And laugh about it. I'm sure we will. I mean, I got beat up by a vampire romance writer. That's funny!"

A tiny laugh escapes her, but she quickly sobers. "It's not funny. You could have been seriously hurt."

"But I wasn't."

"It's not fair that Frankie keeps profiting from our hard work and trouble."

I nudge her under the chin with my cold forefinger. "Hey. We'll make her pay some other way. My ER bill will work quite nicely, for starters."

Those reassurances don't erase the frown lines on her forehead. In fact, the creases deepen. "Who cares about money? She doesn't anymore. She was ready to take a complete loss on this weekend when I told her you refused to do it. Now that she has Kyle, even your ER bill will be pocket change to her. She has him wrapped around her little finger. If he wasn't such a douche, it would be sickening to watch the way she manipulates him."

"Like she manipulated me," I choke, rising to my feet.

She winces. "Like she manipulates everyone."

I know she's trying to make me feel better about being duped by Frankie, time and time again, but it only makes me feel worse. At least Kyle has the excuse that he's getting laid on a regular basis. My only defense for believing Frankie's lies is that I was desperate and pathetic and hopelessly gullible. I turn so she can't see my shameful blush.

"Anyway," Betty continues to my back, "when you broke up with her and said you were finished being Frank, I warned her about this weekend and told her we needed to cancel everything, but she said to hold onto all the reservations. At first, she mentioned a 'coming out' plan and the possibility of attending the conference herself. Then the date drew nearer, and she changed her mind. That's when she told me to ask you. I was actually proud of you for saying no."

I gulp at the realization that I went and screwed that up, ultimately, but I remain silent and let her continue.

"When I gave Frankie your answer, she shrugged it off and told me to give her a few days to see how she felt about revealing Frank's true identity. She said if worse came to worst, we could claim that Frank came down with some horrible, contagious virus, or say he'd had a death in the family."

I snort, marveling at how effortlessly Frankie devises lie after lie.

Betty groans. "Yeah, I know. I hate lying. But whatever. At that point, it would have been unprofessional to back out for any other reason, and my name was connected to all of the arrangements, so I left it at that and hoped she'd do the right thing and attend the conference herself. Then Wednesday, you called me and said you'd changed your mind, and all of our problems were solved."

"Except your losing all respect for me," I mumble.

"What? No!" I hear rustling behind me, and her voice is nearer when she says, "I was relieved you were saving our skin." I flinch at her unexpected touch on my shoulder blade, but I don't have the guts to turn and look her in the eyes. Her voice softens. "I was touched that after everything..." She stops, takes a deep breath, and sighs. "Anyway, at that point, I didn't care why you changed your mind. I was just relieved you did. And grateful. I knew you didn't want to do it; yet, there you were, willing to do it, anyway. But you've done enough now."

"Not technically, I haven't. If we don't show up at the meet-n-greet tomorrow morning, you'll be facing the same problem you had before I said I'd do this: your reputation, Frank's reputation, the conference's reputation—they'll all suffer. And you'll be eating ramen like a college kid for the next month."

Oh, damn. Did I say that out loud?

She steps around me, forcing me to look at her.

To her confused expression, I say, "All that sodium and MSG is horrible for you," even though it clarifies nothing.

She screws her mouth to the side. "What are you talking about? Why would I be eating ramen noodles?"

Damn, I stare at the ceiling and confess, "I didn't change my mind about this weekend based on anything you said at my place last Sunday."

"Okay. That still doesn't answer my question, though."

It takes supreme courage, but I lower my chin and focus on her eyes when I reveal, "Frankie called me. She wanted me to pay her the $2500 she claimed she'd be losing if we didn't attend this thing. And she said if I refused, she'd go after you for it."

"What? She cut me a check ages ago and hasn't mentioned another word about the money!"

All I can offer her is a lame shrug. I don't understand any of this, either. The only thing I understand is that I've probably been hornswoggled, again.

Betty jabs her fist into her hip, as if *I'm* the one who has some 'splaining to do, but says, "When she proposed asking you to come to this conference, it was strictly so we wouldn't look like jerks for backing out at the last minute."

"She told me *you* were liable for the expenses, since you forgot to cancel the arrangements."

She tucks her chin closer to her chest. "Excuse me? I don't forget to do *anything*."

Knowing what I'm about to say, I preemptively blush and scratch my ear. "By the end of the call, she had come to the same conclusion, saying you must have been lying about forgetting."

She throws her hands up. "A) I never told her I forgot anything, because I *didn't* forget; and B) Why the hell would I ever do something like that? To purposely make a mess for myself and eventually make myself look like the worst PR rep of all time?" Now she quiets and turns sideways, mumbling into her fist, "She asked me to ask you. Period. And if I'd known it had anything to do with money... forget it. I would have never approached you." Her hand falls from her mouth, but her voice remains subdued. "I realized at your place, when you reacted the way you did, that my reputation wasn't worth it, either. I felt horrible for putting you in the position of having to say no."

I stare at her, struggling to make the connections that are right there but evading my temporarily (I hope) lower-functioning brain. Fighting through another furious blush, I mutter, "I see. So, I haven't learned a damn thing when it comes to Frankie, have I?" I pivot, placing us essentially back-to-back. Then I move to the foot of the bed, where I sit dejectedly, my hands resting limply in my lap.

I mean, could I *be* any stupider? Is "stupider" even a word? I'm so stupid I don't even know. Why on Earth would I *ever* believe a single thing that comes out of Frankie's mouth, after everything she's put me through? Why? Am I destined to keep making the same mistake over and over with her, just in ways that are different enough to make me believe I'm actually learning from those mistakes?

Oblivious to my internal berating and obviously coming to grips, herself, with the lies Frankie told me about her, Betty cries, her voice coming closer to my shoulder, "I'm so confused!"

I close my eyes when she rests her hand on the back of my

neck. As unemotionally as possible, I explain, "She said you purposely kept the arrangements—then hid behind forgetting —in the hopes that I'd feel obligated to do this. She said you had... *have*... feelings for me. Now, I know she was merely telling me what I needed to hear, what I *wanted* to hear, in order to agree to do what she wanted me to do all along. I'm such an idiot."

"You're not an idiot."

It's subtle at first, so soft I think I may be imagining the pressure against the top of my head. But then I feel her warm breath filtering through my hair to my scalp, and I know the kiss is real. Like a kiss you'd give to an upset child, granted, but still a kiss. She turns her face sideways, resting her cheek against my skull.

"You're not an idiot," she repeats in a hypnotic murmur.

Instinctively, I reach over my shoulder and cup her neck against my palm, an acknowledgment of her reassurance, a thank you for her kind words.

Cooler air hits my back, and my hand falls away from her neck as she withdraws. I open my eyes, but I continue to stare at the outdated brass drawer pulls on the dresser, not sure what to say or do next. As I'm about to tell her I'd understand if she wanted to pack up and leave tonight, that I'll handle the meet-n-greet alone tomorrow and finish what we came here to do, I feel the mattress dip behind me, and her body heat returns.

She curls against my back. Her lips brush against my cheek.

Not sure how to interpret what she's doing (is this a pity kiss, another "It's-okay-you-were-bamboozled-again" consolation kiss, a "Don't-be-sad" kiss?), I tense and hold my breath.

She presses her lips more firmly on my face. Her soft mouth contrasts with my rough stubble, whispering as it travels from my jaw to my neck. Since I'm still holding my breath, a lack of oxygen eventually makes my head pound enough that my brain sends the message to my respiratory system to start breathing again. I try not to take huge gulps of air, try not to do anything that would spoil the moment.

Meanwhile, I struggle to determine if she's been drinking. She doesn't seem drunk, and I haven't seen her drinking, but I've been asleep for much of the evening. I turn my head slightly and surreptitiously sniff, trying to detect alcohol on her breath. I smell nothing but that intoxicating, clean scent that I would know anywhere, even if she were standing among a hundred other sweet-smelling women, and I were blindfolded. That visual's actually kind of doing it for me. *Oh, yeah...*

But wait! If this is another drink- or pity-fueled grope, I don't want anything to do with it. That's what I tell myself, anyway. Then it strikes me that I haven't seen Betty drink in months, not even at my brother's wedding. The last time I witnessed her imbibe alcohol of any kind was—I frantically search my memory—during that horrendous double-date at the French restaurant.

And anyway... let's be frank—who cares? I don't, at this point. I know what's motivating *me*, and it's not drugs or alcohol or pity or even lust (purely). I love her. I've loved her for a long time. I'm sick of denying it.

I turn my head even more toward her lips, conveying my active participation in what she's started. She leans over my shoulder, takes my face between her hands, and presses her mouth to mine. I twist at the waist to make the position less awkward, and I brace my weight on my hand, which I place on the mattress behind me. She swings her leg around me and straddles my right thigh. For a second, I think I may pass out.

This kiss is lighter and less frantic than the drunken one she gave me on her doorstep all those months ago, but it somehow conveys more passion, more feeling. It definitely feels more sincere, less silly. There's nothing silly about this kiss, or my reaction to it.

I push my mouth harder against hers and tease my tongue against her teeth, then farther inside the silky folds of her lips. When she mimics my behavior, I move my free hand to the base of her skull, tangling my fingers in her soft, wavy hair as I hold her head firmly in place so I can continue devouring her mouth.

After several minutes, I pull my face away from hers but don't move any other part of my body (voluntarily, that is). Her hands fall to my shoulders.

"Wait," I pant.

What? No! something other than my brain wails.

Parts of her body may be screaming the same thing at me, based on the rapid rise and fall of her chest, so I explain to all the screaming body parts in the room, "Hang on a minute. I mean... What's happening?"

"Has it been *that* long, Nathaniel?"

The arched eyebrow I love so much is almost my undoing. But I have to be strong. I have to be sure of one more thing. I let go of her head and laugh nervously. "Nearly. But that's not what I meant. I know about *that* part, but you don't have to do this."

"I'm well aware of that."

"No, I mean... You're not obligated to deliver on her lies." The possibility of her feeling that way, of her going that far to do Frankie's bidding, nauseates me.

She returns her hands to my face, so I can't look away, even if I wanted to. I don't want to. I could stare into her eyes all night. I could stare into her eyes for the rest of my life. As a matter of fact, her eyes could inspire a guy to go into optometry, easily one of the most boring specialties.

As I'm contemplating a career change, she says softly,

tracing her thumbs along my cheekbones, "As usual, she knew exactly how much truth to include in her story to make it ring true. But this has nothing to do with her. And it definitely has nothing to do with obligation."

"I don't want you to think—"

"I'm not thinking, for once. Please, reward me."

She learns forward abruptly, shifting me off-balance so I fall onto my back on the bed—directly onto the ice pack I tossed aside earlier. I hiss and arch my spine. She reaches under me and shoves the ice-filled bag away, sending it sailing off the side of the bed like an air hockey puck. I recline once more against the still-cool spot on the sheet, pulling her down with me. Our chests collide, expelling the air in our lungs with brief grunts.

I replenish my oxygen supply before diving once again into a pool of hormones and pheromones, which are now effectively drowning any of that remaining pesky fear. Fear is for wimps. And smart people. I refuse to be the former anymore, and I've never been the latter.

That means the only remaining obstacle is clothing. Rolling her onto her back, I dispense with hers like she's a coding ER patient. Okay, not the most romantic comparison, but it's the first thing that pops to mind as I quickly unbutton her shirt. My hands play the part of the crash cart paddles on her torso, but there's no "clearing." On the contrary, our mouths crush together for another thorough tonsil check. She blindly pushes down on my pants, only pausing when my elastic waistband hangs up on the most currently intractable of my body parts.

Lips still locked, we take over some of our own disrobing, me de-pantsing, her shrugging off her shirt and shucking her bra. My underwear's still hanging from one ankle when I consider my job done well enough for now and focus on the zipper and button of her shorts. She lifts her hips just enough to make easy work of removing her outer- and underwear in one smooth motion. Skin slaps skin when my t-shirt finally gets the hint and leaves the party, my briefs following closely behind with a final shake of my leg.

Betty rests her right knee against my ribs and breathes into my mouth, "Now. Please."

Condom! screams the nurse who's apparently *never* off-duty in my brain.

I sigh but mutter the word in a tortured rasp against Betty's lips. The only movement from either of us for several seconds comes from our heaving chests while we contemplate our frustrating dilemma.

Finally, she pulls her head back and says, "Tell me it doesn't matter," her eyes searching mine and packing volumes into her plea.

"It does, though," I manage to answer. "It matters a lot. You matter." I tilt my head and kiss her trembling lips.

Her closing eyes push tears down both sides of her face.

"Don't cry," I whisper. "Why are you crying?"

"I'm so happy," she whispers back, her eyes opening and proving with their sparkle that she's telling the truth. "Are you happy?"

"Yes. Very."

She cups my butt in both hands. "Then just love me."

"Oh, God, I do." I've barely spoken the last word, giving neither of us time for reconsideration, before I plunge myself deep inside of her, and it's as if a row of laboratory pipettes has sucked every remaining coherent, responsible thought from my mind.

The next few minutes (okay, probably more like seconds, unfortunately) are frantic, frenetic, and frenzied, but brain function eventually returns on a basic level, and I realize something wonderful, yet terrible, is about to happen.

"Oh, gosh," I whisper, the tell-tale tingling in my extremities a surefire warning of the end. I freeze and think about football.

"What's wrong?"

To my utter horror, I slur, "Football."

"Football?"

Burying my face in her neck, I take a deep breath and laugh at myself, even though I want to cry. "Never mind." I risk my immediate release by resuming some movement, rising on one elbow, trailing kisses down her shoulder, anything to get past this moment. But that damn nurse—I'm starting to hate him—compels me to stop and blurt after another few seconds, "I'm about to... you know... already." I barely prevent the highly unsexy declaration from escaping in a highly unsexy whine. My only consolation is that I didn't use medical jargon to let her know. ("Ejaculate" is such an ugly word.)

She halts all hip movement, kisses my temple, and says, "I'll be right there with you."

I can feel my pounding heartbeat everywhere, including in the bump on my forehead. "Really? Already?"

She wraps her hand around the back of my neck. "Already? I've been waiting for this for months," she murmurs next to my ear. As if to prove it, after the next couple of thrusts, she contracts around me, and her head falls back, exposing her neck to my lips. Her vocal chords vibrate under my mouth as she moans while we buck against each other, and I attempt to channel all the feelings I have for her through such an admittedly coarse, primal activity.

"Ohhhh!" I groan, as the last of my control finally falls away. For an immeasurable amount of time, I exist on a plane not governed by anything but pure biology in its most glorious form. Every nerve ending is humming; every hair follicle is standing at attention; every blood vessel is pumping and whooshing. I hope it's the same for her. I think it is, based on her reaction.

"Kiss me," she practically begs, bringing me back to a time and place connected to the physical world. I do as she says, and my heavy limbs reawaken. I run my hands up and down her body, smiling at her squirms and sighs of delight.

Out of breath, I'm forced to break off the kiss, so I don't do something humiliating, like stroke out.

She tightens her embrace around my back. "Don't leave."

"I'm not," I reassure her, shifting subtly on top of her. "I'm just breathing."

With a grin, she declares, "Overrated."

"Actually, not. And it would be a shame to die right now."

"I'd be okay with it."

"Don't even think about it." I touch my forehead to hers, then jerk back when another piece of my reality transmits a painful reminder. I roll away from the sensation, landing on my back with an "Oomph."

She follows, hooking a leg over my side. Her ankle brushes against a still-very-sensitive part of me, which makes me flinch and her chuckle.

Still lightheaded, I place my hands behind my head, my elbows pointing to opposite corners of the room, like someone cooling down after a long run in high altitude. She runs her finger along the pale underside of my exposed upper arm, and I contract my bicep so it stands out in contrast.

"Are you flexing?" she asks with a bemused smile.

Sheepishly, I admit, "Yeah."

"Why?"

After I think about it for a second, I angle my head to look into her face and answer, "I don't know."

"You don't have to pose for me or try to be anything you're not."

"Including muscular, right?"

She laughs and slaps playfully at my chest. "You're fine. Mighty fine." A different muscle flexes as she cranes her neck and presses her lips against mine.

Too soon, the kiss is over. "Oh, and *that* part of Dr. Nathanson was no fiction," she states, looking down my body at the appendage more persistently nudging her foot with every complimentary word from her swollen lips.

I blush. "You're just being nice."

"There's nothing 'nice' about it. It's very naughty, indeed."

"You keep talking to me like that, I'll show you a whole lot more 'naughty.'"

"Excellent. First, though, let me check your pupils."

This is definitely the most erotic pillow talk I've ever experienced.

GHOSTING

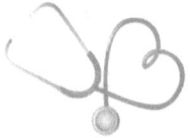

AFTER THE MOST AMAZING NIGHT OF MY LIFE (NO, REALLY, I mean it), sharing a pizza with Betty at midnight, sharing a lot of other things with Betty following that, receiving a private fashion show of the "smokin'" dress she bought for the Authors' Ball we never attended, nearly destroying that dress, and falling into a dead, exhausted, satisfying sleep at around 2:30 a.m., I wake up refreshed and energized at my usual time, according to my body clock. That means I have two hours to prepare for the meet-n-greet that starts at 9:30.

I prod gingerly at the bump on my head and take stock of my pain level. The contusion itself is still tender, but my headache is all but gone. Score one billion for endorphins!

I chuckle at myself, shifting so I can get a better view of my overnight guest, who's still out of it. Way out of it. I watch her closely for any signs of stirring that I can use to justify touching her. Breathing doesn't count (although I'm glad to see she's doing it), so I eventually stop torturing myself and slide from the bed with one last look at her over my shoulder. She's a sight to behold, but I figure I'd better get my head in the game. The head on my shoulders, that is. There'll be plenty of time for shameless ogling when we get back to Green Bay. That thought pastes a goofy grin on my face.

When I emerge from the shower, Betty's still sacked out, so I dress as quietly as possible in my stupid skinny jeans and stupid Beatles t-shirt (no offense, fans) and stupid waistcoat and stupid scarf, which I wind around my neck perfectly the first time, much to my mixed pride and chagrin. Even after applying about 100 cc of product to my hair and dabbing some concealer I've found in Betty's purse onto my forehead, I'm bemused by how little Betty has moved. I don't have time, however, to stand here and admire her cuteness or reminisce about all the things we did to tire her so thoroughly. I need to get downstairs to eat some breakfast before taking my post at my table.

We're still two hours away from the 11:00 check-out, so it makes sense to let her sleep. She obviously needs it. I scrawl a quick note on the comment card on the desk (*"Down at meet-n-greet"*) and leave it on my pillow, where she'll find it immediately upon waking.

I'd say more, but I only have two stubby blank lines to work with. No matter how much I might like to, I can hardly write, *"Down at the meet-n-greet. By the way, my love, last night was amazing, and I can't wait to spend the rest of my life with you. If that's what you want. But we can talk about that some other time. And now... for a love poem, Ode to Betty..."*

I figure it's best to stick with the facts, since I'll be seeing her in a matter of minutes.

After a few more seconds of self-indulgent-yet-not-too-creepy gazing at her, I do one final sweep of the room, gather my bags, and leave. I won't have the opportunity to return before check-out, and although we didn't discuss logistics last night (for some reason, it never crossed my mind), I have faith she'll figure it out. I also trust she's responsible enough to wake well before check-out, with plenty of time to dress and clear her belongings from both of our rooms.

Just in case, I make a mental note to call or text her in an hour, to make sure she's up and about.

Fast forward *three* hours.

Yeah, I know. But it's *insane* down here. I barely had time to stow my luggage under the table and inhale a bran muffin and a cup of coffee before the incompetent conference organizers let readers into the meet-n-greet room, several minutes early (I'm *so* not coming back next year... ha!). I was instantly surrounded and overwhelmed by readers and authors alike. The area in front of my table has been like the blocked artery of a bacon addict.

The readers want pictures and autographs—and in some cases—full-blown conversations, including reassurances I'm working hard on "my" next book. The authors want the scoop on my injuries and why Betty yelled "Nate!" I had to bite back the response that they'd have to be more specific about that last question, since she yelled it a lot last night, but I gave straightforward answers to the same questions, over and over again. Well, straightforward lies, of course. I stuck with the pen-name cover and supplied vague answers to inquiries about where I was last night during the Authors' Ball (if they only knew), all the while trying hard not to think too much about how Betty and I truly spent our night.

It wasn't until my stomach growled that I even thought to check the time. It feels like mere minutes have passed since I've taken up my spot behind the table. When I pull out my phone to check the time on it, I nearly hit the floor. It's 12:30, ninety minutes past check-out.

"Shit!" I hiss, immediately tapping out a text to Betty that simply says, *WAKE UP!!!!*

When my message receives no response, I call her. When

my call gets no answer, I take a few deep breaths and tell myself she's in the shower. Sure, she's overslept and missed checkout, but it isn't the end of the world. Explaining to Frankie how *I* missed check-out when I was manning the meet-n-greet table will be interesting, but actually, that thought fills me with vindictive glee. I push it aside, though, and resolve to try contacting Betty again in fifteen minutes.

Forty minutes later, I'm frantic. And stuck at this stupid table.

Ten minutes later, I decide, "Screw it!" and abandon my post.

On our floor, housekeeping is hard at work along the hall-way, including in both of our former rooms. Like a proud idiot, I pretend I've forgotten something in my room; I just don't mention it's a person. There's no sign of Betty in either room, so I backtrack down the hall.

As I board the elevator to ride back to the lobby, I realize I need to start asking around about her. What if something horrible has happened? I can't let pride and embarrassment delay an investigation, if foul play is involved. I also despise myself for hoping for even a second that foul play, not a simple run-of-the-mill case of morning-after regrets, is to blame for her unexplained disappearance.

On the main floor, I stride to the reception desk and ask the clerk—the same woman who helped us check in—if she's seen "Ms. Tate."

She looks me up and down, pauses, then says, "She checked out hours ago, Mr. Lipton. I called a cab for her."

"What? Did she say anything else?" I demand, my voice rising and echoing in the peach-scented atrium.

That's when she hands me a piece of hotel stationery. "She left this for you."

I snatch the paper, hoping for an explanation, but the only

thing it contains is a to-do list for conference tear-down, including the address of the nearest FedEx, where I should take any leftover books and merchandise to ship back to Green Bay. Betty even thoughtfully wrote down her address in neat block lettering, in case I don't know where she lives.

"What... How did she look when she left?" I hate asking, but I'm desperate for information.

The clerk wrinkles her nose. "Not good. I could tell she'd been crying. I hope everything's okay."

I want to grab her by her ugly uniform lapels and shake her, but I know it would be a classic case of strangling the messenger, so I merely mumble a thanks at her, ignoring her blatant fishing for more information, and return to my table with my to-do list, which I promptly crumple and throw in one of the empty boxes I'll supposedly be refilling in a couple of hours and preparing for shipping.

From several rows away, Yardley sneers at me and mouths, *"Nice scarf, asshole."*

I flip him the bird.

He laughs. I don't. I'm too busy to deal with him. Too busy freaking out. Too busy wracking my brain, trying to figure out what the hell happened. Too busy thinking frantically about how to get out of here as soon as possible.

Within minutes, I have a plan concerning that last thing, at least. Everyone who walks past my table receives a free, hastily autographed book, a mug, t-shirt, bookmark, and poster. It doesn't take long for word to spread that Frank Lipton is giving away swag. My table becomes more popular than ever. I bundle my wares as if I'm in a race, or on speed. Sweat collects at the base of my scarf-covered neck and under my arms. When I run out of merchandise, lucky visitors to my table get a book and a picture with a harried, distracted fraud. In no time, I have nothing left to give away.

I dive under the table, grab my bags, and nearly run for the doors leading to the parking garage, where the rental car sits. While speeding to the airport, I talk non-stop to my phone, trying to arrange for the fastest flight out of this godforsaken town. Unfortunately, the only other plane to Green Bay departed hours ago, probably carrying a white-knuckled Betty, so I'm stuck with my original flight, which means a three-hour wait.

I fill the majority of that time going over every single word, look, action, and interaction with Betty from last night, searching for clues to what went amiss. The rest of the time I spend texting Betty, who's finally answering me.

What the hell is going on?

Did you get my list at reception?

Yes. Call me

No

Can I call you?

No

Why not???

Are you already done? Did you ship that stuff overnight or two-day?

There was nothing to ship

??

I gave everything away and drove to the airport as soon as I realized you were gone. WTF?

I'll take care of everything else, don't worry

Don't worry?? I'm coming to see you as soon as I get back

Please don't

I don't understand! What did I do?

Forget it. Let it go

That's it. I've typed about a hundred different responses to her final text, but I've never sent any of them. The only thing I need to tell her is something I can't—won't—say in a stupid text message.

Now I'm on the plane, regretting that I was too apathetic to take a Valium before takeoff. My jiggling leg and I have already received several dirty looks from the lady next to me. The usual me would apologize and explain to her my situation (at least the fear-of-flying part, not "the-woman-I-love-ran-away-from-me-as-fast-as-she-could-after-our-first-sexual-encounter-do-you-think-that's-a-bad-sign?" part), but the me today wants to tell her to save her dirty looks for someone who cares, or wants to live. All I can think about is getting off this plane and driving as quickly as possible to Betty's.

Except I can't do that. Because I have to get Reba from Mom and Dad's, where she's been staying all weekend. Oh, shit. I have to face Mom and Dad like this? I close my eyes and take deep breaths through my nose.

The woman next to me sighs. I move to the aisle seat that should be holding Betty, leaving an empty seat between the stranger and me and decreasing the chances of an FAA-reportable incident.

One more hour.

DESPERATE MEASURES

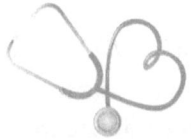

I'VE GIVEN UP ON THE TEXTS AND VOICEMAIL MESSAGES, BUT I've shown up at Betty's house every single day for nearly a week, hoping each day will be the day she's home. So far, none of those days have been the day.

Tonight, desperate and feeling no shame, I do something I told myself I'd never do again. But I have no choice.

"Well, well, well. Calling to face the music?" she says after we've dispensed with the pleasantries (and by "dispensed," I mean, "skipped").

I will not let her get to me, I vow to myself.

"I don't know what you mean by that, so no. I'm calling to see if you know where Betty is."

"Like I'd tell you?"

My heart races. Still, I keep my voice remarkably steady when I answer, "I hope so. That's why I'm calling."

"Well, you're an idiot. But I guess we already knew that, considering you gave away hundreds of dollars' worth of merch and books that I had been planning to make a hefty profit on. I *will* be sending you an invoice for that."

"Whatever. I won't charge you for that ER visit, and we'll call it good."

"Oh-ho! Someone learned how to play hardball."

I sigh. "Frankie, I'm not in the mood for this. I just want to know where Betty is. Or at least know she's okay."

"You know, when I told you to screw her in Atlanta, I didn't mean to screw it *up*."

What does she know? What did Betty say? What did I do?

Before I can figure out a way to ask any of those questions without sounding like a complete loser, she reveals, "Ah, well. It's been fun messing with you, but I have to run. Kyle and I are leaving for Paris in, oh, about now, actually. And I don't know where Betty is. She's pissed off at me, I think. Hasn't said two words to me since coming back from Atlanta. I'm too busy to drag it out of her. But you say she's not home, huh?"

"No."

"I'd check the cabin, then. That's usually where she goes during her anti-social kicks."

"Oh. Right." *Why didn't I think of that?* "Thanks for the info."

"Don't mention it. And you still owe me for that stuff you gave away. If you think I was ever going to pay that ER bill, you're nuts. It's not my fault you got into a pissing match with a vamp-queen. Pay your own damn medical bills."

With that, she hangs up, and I back out of Betty's driveway to drive two hours to the cabin.

* * *

WELL, at least it's a beautiful night. The mosquitoes think so, too. They're keeping me company on the front porch of the cabin. I haven't been here since the snowmobiling weekend/disaster six months ago, and I have to say, tonight's visit isn't doing anything to redeem the place in my eyes.

Frankie was right (oh, how it galls me to say that); Betty's here. Inside. Sans mosquitoes. Resolutely refusing to see or even speak to me. As a matter of fact, she's so emphatic that I expect a sheriff's deputy to pull into the gravel driveway any minute now to escort me from the premises.

Then again, maybe she thinks I'm not here anymore. I've been quiet and still for about ten minutes now, and I haven't seen as much as a twitching curtain in most of that time. Now, I emit a low whistle, trying to decide what my next move will be. I've tried begging ("Please, let me in. Or at least tell me why you won't"), joking ("If this is about your dress, I didn't mean to rip it. I can learn to sew"), crying (just a little), and threatening ("I'm going to kick down this door and make you give me a straight answer").

That last one was definitely not the right way to go, but I was frustrated! And it wasn't a horrible, scary threat. She knew I wouldn't do it. *Couldn't* do it. That door looks like something recycled from a medieval castle, not one of those wimpy jobs you can pick up on clearance at the local home improvement store.

Anyway, now I'm out of ideas. I just want to talk to her face-to-face. I want her to look me in the eye and tell me what happened, what I did that was so wrong. I want her to tell me I imagined that night and all of the feelings associated with it. I want her to tell me there's nothing I can do to change this, that I need to move on.

But she won't tell me anything. She's giving me nothing to go on. Only, silence.

Well, that's not entirely true. She did say one thing: "Go away, Nathaniel!"

That statement wasn't very elucidating, though.

I slap another mosquito and wipe the streak of blood from my arm. "Sonofa...!" I hiss, then mutter, "Effin' West Nile virus, malaria, shit..." I pop to my feet and speak at the front door again, my nose pressed against the wood. "Betts... Are you there?"

Nothing.

"I'm going to assume you are. I'm going to say one more thing; then I'm going to go away. For real. Because you don't want me here. And you won't tell me why. I can't take this anymore."

I guess Plan E is crying, again. I clear my throat. "So here goes. For the first time in my life, I'm going to lay it all out there, and I'm not going to give a shit how it makes me look or sound."

Yeah. Tough talker. It's a bit harder than that, isn't it? Now you have to follow through and do it.

I take a deep breath and poke at a knot in the wooden door with my left index finger while swatting distractedly at a mosquito on my neck with my right hand. "Okay. So, last weekend... I know it may not be right, and I wouldn't even admit it to myself for a long time, because it means I wasn't any better than *her,* but... what happened last weekend is something I've wanted to happen for a long time. For most of that time, I denied it was even true. Then I told myself if it *was* true, it was wrong, so I couldn't allow it to be true. What was wrong, though, was staying with Frankie when all I really wanted was to be with you.

"Last weekend, you asked me why I stayed with her so long. The sad answer is, because it was easier. And because she felt like my last decent chance at, whatever."

I stop, realizing I'm generalizing in an effort to save face. Punching at my thigh, I grit my teeth and say, "No. Not 'whatever.' I used her as much as she used me. She seemed like my last chance at settling down, at having the family I want. That's part of why it took me so long to give up.

"The other, stronger reason I stayed with her was that I knew if she and I were over, then *you* and I were over, and I couldn't face that. That's why, even while planning to break up with her, I told myself I could still be Frank. But you were right when you said it wouldn't work. I wanted to be free of him *and* Frankie. But I didn't want to be free of you. It sucked that it was a package deal."

I sigh at the hopelessness of it all. "I should have known you didn't need me to rescue you from an oversight as stupid as forgetting to cancel Frank's conference registration. I should have known I was just falling into another one of Frankie's traps. Maybe I did know, deep down. It seems so obvious now that I *had* to have known. Maybe I just didn't care. Or maybe I allowed myself to be tricked so I had an excuse to be with you again. Or maybe I wanted to pretend I was rescuing you, playing the part of the big hero, whether you knew it or not."

I chuckle bitterly at myself, feeling the heat from my blush radiating from the top of my head. "Gosh. It was such an effing Mr. Darcy stunt, now that I think of it. Arrogant, but well-meaning. Ultimately selfish, though. Because doing it made me feel good. And it was an outlet for how I felt about you. *Feel* about you. It was nice to finally find an acceptable way to show you how I feel. I was so sick of denying it, hiding it, being *in the closet* about it. Because I can no more tell myself to stop feeling the way I do for you than I can tell my heart to stop beating, to tell my cells to stop regenerating, to tell my brain to stop organizing my scrubs by color."

Clawing my fingers down my face, I moan at myself. "I'm rambling. Sorry. It's just... I'm determined not to say something dumb, like 'Thanks for the omelet,' then spend the rest of my life hating myself for not telling you exactly what I wanted to say. I'm going to leave here, knowing I said what needed to be said, so I can live with myself." I reflect for a few seconds, mustering all of my remaining nerve.

Go big or go home. Or in this case, *Go big* AND *go home.*

"I love you. And I know at one time, even if it was only for that one night, you felt the same way about me. I *know* it. I felt it. And I'll never forget it. You made me believe that maybe it was okay to be me. Even better, that it was okay for me to be me and to love *you.* Like, none of the factors that kept me from acknowledging my feelings for you up 'til then made a damn bit of difference. All that mattered was you. And me. And our happiness. Because we *were* happy. So happy."

I brush away the tears I'm glad she can't see. "I'm starting to accept I'll never know why you've changed your mind, but understand this: I haven't changed mine. I still love you. And I can't imagine that changing. Ever. But I love you enough to let it go, if that's what you want. I just wish you didn't want that."

I push away from the door, then stop on the top step and announce at the top of my voice, "I'm leaving now!" willing her to run onto the porch, to throw herself into my arms. It would happen in a chick flick. Or a Nicholas Sparks book.

When it doesn't happen in real life (that bastard, setting us up for letdown with every new release!), I swallow my disappointment and call, "Make sure you have that door locked! Crazy rednecks up here. And gosh! Have your step-father spray for frickin' mosquitoes. Damn health hazard."

It's a beautiful night for a long, tear-soaked drive, if I do say so myself.

NEW NORMAL

I'M GOING TO BE OKAY. I *AM* OKAY. THINGS ARE FINE. I'M fine.

This is what I've told myself every day for a month, even as I've spent my days around other people's kids and my nights listening to Jon McLaughlin's greatest breakup hits, my nose in a girlie book while the rest of my family whispers about me behind my back and speculates about the personality quirks keeping me from finding my other half. But no matter what *they* think, *I* think I'm okay. I really do.

However, that doesn't mean I'm ready for today's events.

Once again, I'm in front of a mirror, practicing for my next performance. I'm wearing my normal clothes—simple (non-skinny) khakis, a long-sleeved, sage-green t-shirt, and a pair of Vans—so there'll be no mood inspiration there. I have to do this as me.

I stand in the bathroom and test out my smile. It still works, amazingly. I guess that's because there's still much to be happy about in my life: French-press coffee, chick flicks, chick lit (that I don't have to pretend to have written), hot baths, long runs, peace and quiet, cuddles with Reba...

Who cares if it's a tad bit boring? And lonely. Maybe it won't be for forever. Then again, maybe it will be. And if it is, forever is plenty of time to get used to just about anything.

And when I want a taste of chaos and companionship, I can always count on my family. Like this afternoon, the reason for my latest acting gig.

It's a beautiful fall day, and I've been invited to Nick and Heidi's for a "special announcement." I've been telling myself all morning they're calling both of our families to their house on a precious football-watching day to tell us Nick's been promoted to Chief Surgeon-Big-Wig-Head-Dick at the hospital, or something. Yeah, that's it. I'm getting damn good at this "denial" thing.

Turning my attention to my reflection, studiously ignoring the tiny dot of toilet paper on the shaving cut next to my Adam's apple, I say now, "Hey! That's great!" My smile fades to a more thoughtful expression. "Hmmm, okay. A little crazed. And your eyes are dead. Is there a way to force them to smile, other than by being sincere, of course? Because that's too much to ask. I get it."

Again, I arrange my facial muscles into a smile, this one less manic, and try again. "Hey! What great news! I'm so happy for you."

I nod. "Better."

Clacking behind me distracts me from my task. I half-turn to see Reba sag to a sitting position in the bathroom doorway.

"Hey!" I test out on her. "That's awesome, man!"

She promptly rises, performs an about-face, and leaves.

"Too much?" I call after her. "Sorry! I know, you're not a man! Just practicing!"

I grip the edge of the bathroom sink, drop my head, and sigh. This is ridiculous. No matter what the announcement is, of a personal or professional nature, I shouldn't have to practice a positive response. Only a true jerk begrudges his brother —a brother who's been good to him, for the most part—all the success in the world. A) It's mean, and B) Nick's prosperity isn't the thief of my happiness.

I haven't even had to consult my parents for those pearls of wisdom. I haven't consulted anyone for anything lately, as a matter of fact. I'm standing on my own two feet, not seeking validation from anyone else, and most days, when I remind myself I'm independent but not alone, it feels pretty freakin' fabulous. Okay, that's hyperbole. But it does feel good.

It's almost time for me to go, so I push away from the sink, flick off the bathroom light on my way out, straighten the bedspread that Reba's rumpled since I made my bed this morning, and stride down the hallway, whistling for the dog.

She's still a bit skittish around kids, which I found out the hard way when I took her to the farmers' market last weekend (See? I still have a girl to do things with, albeit one who knocks over apple carts when over-excited children get too close), so knowing Nick's place will be crawling with Heidi's nieces and nephews, I plan to leave her at home.

Filling her water bowl and food dish before leaving, I tell her, "Trust me; I'd rather stay here with you," pretending she looks sad to see me go. Really, I think she wants me to step aside so she can get to her bowls.

She nudges my ankle with her nose. Yep. If only I could read the nonverbal—and verbal—cues of women as well. Before I get too melancholy about that, I take a deep breath, straighten my back, and remove the toilet paper from my neck.

"I'm going in, Rebes," I say, rolling the paper between my thumb and forefinger, tossing it in the trash, and moving to give her access to her food, which she attacks as if I haven't fed her in days. "Send help if I'm not back by seven. That means I'm being sucked into the Sunday night football game."

She grimaces at me, but I know it's because she's trying to work loose a piece of food stuck in her back teeth, not because she's sympathizing with me, as I'd like to believe.

"Eat slower!"

Ignoring my advice, she buries her face in her lunch. I grab my car keys from the kitchen counter. "Whatever," I mutter. "I won't be here to give you the doggy-Heimlich, you know. And if you puke on the couch again, I'm going to be super-pissed."

Her only response is enthusiastic crunching and a subtle cough.

Since the conversation is only getting more and more pathetic (on my part), I exit without another word, silently vowing for the umpteenth time to put both of us on a strict diet this week.

Not gonna happen.

* * *

DESPITE MY USUAL PATHOLOGICAL PUNCTUALITY, I'm the last one to arrive, so when I step onto the deck, my parents, my former future in-laws, and all three of Heidi's siblings, plus their spouses and children, are crowded around Nick and Heidi. Everyone's smiling and laughing, and my mom's crying.

My smile becomes more forced while I anticipate receiving the "news." Mom takes an interest in our careers, but I don't think a promotion announcement would ever bring her to tears.

Cautiously, I enter the melée, put up a hand in a tentative wave, and say, "Hey, everyone. Sorry I'm late, although I didn't think I was."

Nick pushes through the crowd to get to me. "You're not. Everyone else got here early, and we couldn't wait to tell them our news."

"Big job news?" Maybe if I pretend for a few more seconds, it won't sting as much when I finally hear it.

He grins. "No, we're going to have a baby!"

I let loose with an "Aaagh!" of fake-delight, the most unconvincing performance in the history of bad acting, and pull him to me in a hug. "That's great, bro!"

Bro? That's his word. I never call him that. Oh, shit. I'm blowing this harder than an emphysemic octogenarian in front of a birthday cake. I look at the group gathered around us and can tell I'm not fooling anyone. My mom's no longer crying tears of joy; instead, she looks worried. Or is that pity I see in her drying eyes?

I smile at her. It must come off more genuine than my previous act, because her face relaxes, and she smiles back.

I let go of Nick and reach for Heidi. "Give me a hug, Mama," I say quietly.

For some reason, that ridiculous request sounds completely natural.

After my hugs have been delivered, everyone seems to breathe a collective sigh of relief. Hands in my pockets, I look around at the dispersing conjecturers and try to exude confidence, but I must have used up my finite stores of thespianism during those months of being Frank. I can tell by the way most people are avoiding eye contact with me that I look as awkward as I feel.

Heidi's dad bravely nods at me, so I nod back and smile.

Her mom breaks away and says, "Hey, Nate. How's it going?"

I reply with a simple, "Fine, Mary Jo. How are you doing?"

which launches her into a ten-minute gush about how excited she is that her baby girl is going to have a baby.

My dad, thinking he's rescuing me, approaches us, places a hand on my shoulder, and booms, "What's new?"

While I search for an answer, he searches my face. Finally, I say, "Not much," which seems to disappoint but not surprise him.

He rushes to fill the resultant void. "How's Reba doing? It's too bad she's not a fan of these big gatherings."

Mary Jo's face brightens. "Tell me about this new girl of yours!"

I blush and fidget. "Uh. No. I mean, Reba's... She's a corgi." When it's obvious Mary Jo still thinks we're talking about a person (a social-phobic person from the little-known island of corg?), I clarify further. "A dog. My dog."

Her eyes widen, and her face flushes. She fingers the pearls around her neck. "Oh, I'm sorry. I thought... That is, I assumed... Because I heard you were, um, unattached again."

"I am."

To prevent another worry-filled silence, I inform Dad, "Hey, I enrolled in UW-Milwaukee's nurse practitioner certification program."

Dad's eyes light up at that information. I'm sure he's mostly just relieved to have something to talk about, but I'd also like to think he's proud I'm furthering my career. "That's great!" He sounds a lot more sincere than I did saying it to myself not too long ago in the mirror.

When he calls my mom over, she smiles expectantly and joins our circle. "What's going on over here? More good news?"

Dad squeezes my shoulder. "Nate's going forward with his practitioner certification."

Mom leans forward and kisses my cheek. "Good for you, sweetie."

Mary Jo interjects, "You're so good with the kids."

I'd almost forgotten she was still standing there with us. Shooting her a grateful smile, I reply, "Thanks. They're a lot of fun."

"It's a waste you don't have any of your own," she says more to the watered-down drink in her hand than to me.

I feel Mom tense next to me. "Still plenty of time for that, right?" She places a supportive hand on my forearm.

"Sure," I humor them all, like a good sport. "Anyway, it's good to see you again, Mary Jo," I say, edging away. "I'm going to see what the kids are up to."

Without waiting for them to reply, I trot down the deck stairs and approach the unorganized Wiffle ball game in the large area of thick grass to the side of the now-covered pool. I wonder if Nick realizes how badly his nieces and nephews are trampling his sod. Oh, well. He'd better get used to not having nice things, now that he has a booger-muncher on the way.

"Hey, Captain Poop Head!" Kingsley greets me. "Wanna play?"

"Heck-to-the-yeah, I do!" I reply, holding up my hands so he'll throw me the holey ball. "I'll pitch for you guys."

Remus cheers and runs for home plate, where he snatches the hollow plastic bat from his younger brother. Percy promptly screeches indignantly. *Should have named that one Hedwig,* I can't help thinking with a private chuckle.

I'm still—technically—the adult here, so I call to Remus, "all right, hang on! Give that back to your brother. We'll let him go first."

After several minutes of barely contained chaos and at least two knocked noggins, I notice Nick hanging out on the periphery of the game, probably lamenting the condition of his lawn. Looking more closely at him, though, I see he appears to be studying *me* with that disapproving look on his face.

What did I do now?

Pretending not to notice or care that he's staring at me, I pitch to Amber, then Ruby. As Kingsley's catching a fly ball, Greta, hugely pregnant with yet another witch or wizard, waddles to the deck rail and calls down for the kids to wash their hands for dinner.

Nick helps me round up the half-dozen Wiffle balls.

"You okay, man?" he asks me as we drop the balls into a pile in the middle of the yard.

"I'm fine," I say dismissively before swiftly changing the subject. "I was wondering, though, what theme are your kids' names gonna follow?"

"Huh?"

"Well, it's a Plotzler family tradition. Heidi's parents chose the Lederhosen theme with Hans, Greta, Sonya, and Heidi. Greta's stickin' it to the Muggles with her *Potter* theme. What's the new baby's name? Hagrid? Sonya's kids, Jude, Justin, and Jeremiah, are rockin' the J's. And Hans, with Amber, Ruby, and Violet, has made his colorful contribution to the population."

Under the deck, Nick finds the mesh bag that holds the balls. Holding it open for me, he says, "I'm not sure we're going to have enough kids to have a *theme* for names."

We're alone in the backyard, so I feel safe joking, "Aw, come on, now! That'll never do. The rule is, you have to have at least three, so you better be priming that pump."

"Dude."

I'm on a roll, though, and don't heed the warning in his tone. "Heidi's family has made it their personal mission to make sure we continue as a race, in case of a zombie apocalypse. So chop, chop! What's it gonna be? You can go with flowers. I personally think Hibiscus is a beautiful name for a boy *or* a girl. Then there's Rose, Iris. Oh, the possibilities are endless if your swimmers are XX. Or you can go with famous athletes. That way, you have lots of options for both boys *and* girls. Satchel is a great name. Paige: equally great. Or what about names that really aren't names? That's very Hollywood, which Heidi would totally dig—"

"What the fuck is wrong with you?"

His question is quiet, but his word choice brings me up short. "What?"

"'That's great, bro!'" he mocks me. "'I'm gonna go play with the kids and be completely anti-social, bro.' 'I'm gonna make fun of your wife's family, bro.' 'I'm gonna make assumptions about your family planning and be a sarcastic douchebag, because I'm a miserable asshole, bro.'"

"Hey! What the hell?" I toss the last ball into the bag and step back, my hands on my hips.

He throws the sack on the ground, as if it's a gauntlet. "Why don't you come out and say what's bothering you, huh? Let's get it out in the open, once and for all."

"I have no idea what you're talking about."

"Bullshit. I guess I'll say it for you, then, if you're not man enough."

"Please, enlighten me." I cross my arms over my chest.

"Why don't you admit it's hard for you to see the only woman you ever came even remotely close to marrying, married to me, and now having my baby? Huh?"

"What? That's not—"

"Come on. I know, okay? I know. I have the house and the wife and the baby on the way, and I know those are all things you want, too. Well, I'm sorry. We've tried to make this as easy for you as we could, but—"

"As easy for me as you could?" I snort. "Like, by inviting everyone else over here a half-hour earlier so you could make your happy announcement and get your cheers out of the way without worrying about my feelings? Like that?"

"We're sensitive to the fact that all this may be awkward for you."

"But it's not! How many times do I have to tell you people that? It's not awkward for me! You guys *make* it awkward for me by constantly pointing out that it *should* be. If everyone would shut the hell up about it, I might have the chance to forget that I ever saw your wife naked. Or that I know her favorite erogenous zones. Or that she has a tattoo on her left ass cheek that she didn't have to change when you got married, because you and I have the same damn initials!" I'm marginally aware I'm shouting, but it feels good, and I'm to the point that I don't care who hears me. "See? I know a bunch of private details, too! But I don't feel the need to constantly bring them up just to prove to everyone I know them and I'm okay with them. That's moronic!"

"Keep your voice down, all right?"

"No! I hope everyone hears me! Because every nonverbal cue I've been tossing out there since you announced you were marrying her has gone unnoticed. Or ignored. Or whatever. And I'm sick of it!" I tick them off on my fingers, "I don't want your life. Or your wife. Or your ugly-ass monster house with your pretentious landscaping and your idiotic seasonal décor. Or the hideous, gas-guzzling SUV you'll surely buy now that you're adding *one* extra person to your household. I like my Prius, damn it! And I *have* a house. And a dog. And I get to wear pajamas to work!"

Even though nobody's in sight, I'm sure they're all inside the back doors, listening. Except the kids. I hope to God the kids are deep enough in the house that they haven't heard this.

I don't want to be "Weird Uncle Nate." I mean, "Weird Captain Poop Head."

"Okay! Dude. I was just trying to figure out—"

"Well, stop it! Stop trying to figure me out, then assuming you know what I want. I'll tell you what I want. I want the pitying looks to stop. I want the special arrival times for Nate to be a thing of the past. I want people to know that I don't like tattoos, and I definitely never wanted my initials on some-one's ass!" Now, I shove my hands in my pockets and say more quietly, "And the parts of my life that aren't so great right now have nothing to do with *you*."

"Hey." Nick puts his hand on my shoulder. I shrug it off.

Oh, no. Don't touch me, man. I'm totally gonna lose it.

Since I can't say that without losing it, he persists, "Hey, what's going on with you?"

I stare at my feet. "It's complicated."

"But it's about a woman, right?"

I hate that the cliché is so true, but I nod. I mean, I'm not depressed because I couldn't find the right shade of floor stain at Home Depot last weekend. (Sure, that was frustrating, but I got over it.) No, the truth is so much sadder than that. I can tell everyone I'm okay with myself until I'm blue in the face, but the fact remains that I can't seem to find someone to share my life who is just as okay with me. And that sucks.

When he opens his mouth to say something that will surely be trite and make me feel even worse, I cut him off. "Listen. I don't want to talk about it." I pick up the discarded bag of balls and the bat and turn toward the house. "This is your day. That's why I was hanging out with the kids. I knew they'd keep me too busy to think about... stuff. Because when I think too much about everything..."

"I'm sorry, man. I just thought you were being a dick."

"I sort of was when I was talking about all the kids' names.

I'm sorry. It's always cracked me up, though. I thought you'd think it was funny, too, and I needed to laugh."

I set the sports equipment next to the deck stairs but continue along the side of the house to get to the street. Nobody wants to be around me after hearing me say all those things. Now *that's* awkward.

Nick catches up and falls into stride next to me. He doesn't try to convince me to stay. Instead, in a low voice, he confides, "Yo. It *is* funny. I mean, Heidi's already suggested the name Massimo for a boy."

"No way."

"Oh, it's not happening. Ever. I told her we Binghams are more traditional types. It's bad enough our parents gave us the same initials."

I can't help but smile on the sidewalk as I kick at the perfectly edged grass border. "I don't know. It's come in handy recently, wouldn't you say?"

The grin he shoots me across the roof of my car has a lecherous tint to it. "True. 'HIP & NAB Forever,' bro." Sobering after a few seconds of inappropriate chuckling, he asks, "Are you going to be okay?"

I wave away his concern. "Yeah. Of course, I—"

"I know you will, in general. But today. You don't have to go, you know."

Laughing ruefully at my shoes, I say, "Uh, yeah. I think I do. And it's fine. I have some stuff I can be doing around the house," I fib. More likely, I have a Maeve Binchy book on my e-reader just dying to be read.

He nods and pats my car before backing away. "Right. Okay, then. I'll, uh, call you later and tell you who won the game."

"Oh, will you? Please? That would be so great. I'll be waiting with my hand on the phone."

He mutters something about me being a jack-off before turning and crossing his front lawn, picking up an errant leaf on the way and tossing it in one of the trash cans lined up along the side of his house. It's such a grown-up, dad thing to do, and the emotion it evokes takes me by surprise.

That's my big brother, I think proudly with a shake of my head as I get behind the wheel of my car. He's in for the shock of his life, I think, but once he gets over not being the center of Heidi's world, he's going to be a good dad. I'm sure of it.

It feels good to be sure of something.

CHANGE IN PLANS

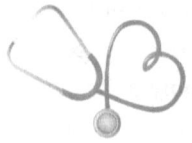

I DON'T GO ANYWHERE OR EVEN START THE CAR FOR SEVERAL minutes. *What am I going to do now?* And I'm not just talking about right now, today, on this Sunday afternoon, when most of my friends—the ones I've reconnected with since reclaiming my life—are watching football or raking leaves or hanging out in parks with their spouses and toddlers. I mean it in a much broader sense.

What am I going to do now?

I decide I'm going to spend the rest of my Sunday afternoon buying a shit-ton of the cutest clothes and toys I can find for my new niece or nephew, who I plan to spoil absolutely stinking rotten.

I press my foot on the brake, turn the key in the ignition, and cut the steering wheel to the left to pull away from the curb while glancing in my side mirrors to check for traffic. My foot, easing off the brake pedal, jams down again at the image in the rearview mirror. To make sure it's not some crazy mirage, I verify the sight over my shoulder, through the back window.

The green Fiat is indeed there. And Betty's stepping out from behind the open driver's side door.

I slam my car into park and turn it off with a shaky hand, my mouth suddenly drier than Mom's meatloaf. (How many times do I have to tell her, "Fewer breadcrumbs, more Worcestershire sauce"?) I hope I don't look too eager when I jump from my own car, wiping my sweaty palms on my pants.

Seeing Betty makes me feel like someone's stabbed me in the gut. It's all I can do not to pitch forward and grab my midriff like a shameless over-actor in one of the Sy-Fy Originals I've taken to torturing myself with on Friday nights when I can't face another happily-ever-after in the newest chick lit bestseller.

"Hey," she begins shyly before I can come up with a mental list of possible reasons for her sudden appearance.

"Hi. Uh, what're you doing here?" To my dismay, my voice sounds pinched and helium-filled.

Movement behind her car's windshield in the passenger seat catches my eye, distracting me from my bone-headed greeting, and I do a double-take. "Reba?"

Betty follows my glance and smiles indulgently. "This bitch was digging to China around the Japanese maple in your front yard. Figured you'd appreciate me putting the kibosh on that Asian fusion experience, and since you weren't home, I brought her with me to find you. This was the first place I thought to look."

"That predictable, huh?"

She nods. "Yeah. It's nice."

"Well, thanks for bringing her to me." I scoot between our bumpers and open the passenger side door, snapping my fingers at Reba to prompt her out. "Let's go, Houdini," I mutter at her, swallowing back the disappointment at such a mundane purpose for Betty's seeking me out. Opening the Prius's back door like a doggie valet, I usher the canine into the backseat. "In you go." I slam the door behind her and watch as she circles several times before plopping and resting her chin on her dirty front paws.

When I turn, Betty's standing before me, her hands behind her back. I lean against the door, watching as she studies her shoes, the silver stilettos she wore to Nick and Heidi's wedding, now matched with jeggings and a baggy, off-the-shoulder sweater, and sinking into Nick's lush front lawn. She looks different. Smaller, somehow. Or maybe that's just due to her meek posture. Since her face is pointed toward the ground, I stare at the slightly lighter strips of hair along either side of her part, wondering when I became the type of guy who noticed when someone was due to have her roots re-touched.

"You didn't ask me why I was at your house," she points out.

I feel like an idiot for the oversight but manage to quip, "What? Not on stray dog patrol?"

Her smile is grateful and brightens her otherwise pale face. "No. Just happened to work out that way. I stopped by to talk to you."

I squint into the afternoon sun, telling my eager, racing heart to settle the hell down and not jump to any conclusions. After all, maybe she's here to smack me for whatever it is I did that she wouldn't tell me about all those weeks ago. Maybe she's here on more business for Frankie. Maybe—

"Actually, I came to apologize."

Even worse.

"Ah. Apology accepted," I grant shortly, pushing away from the car and walking around the back bumper.

"Nate. Wait."

I stop, but I stare straight ahead, biting hard on the inside of my cheek.

"Can we go somewhere and talk?" she asks.

Still showing her my profile, I think about it, quickly playing in my head how this is going to go down (talking across a table at a coffee shop, outdoors on the patio, on uncomfortable wrought-iron furniture; her saying she's sorry and giving some lame excuses about not wanting to get involved with anyone, namely me; my telling her I completely understand and that I've moved on and am fine; both of us hugging and promising to remain friends, a promise neither of us plans to keep, for different reasons). After a few tense seconds, I answer, "Actually, I have plans this afternoon. I was just leaving here to get on with them."

"Oh." She blushes. "Of course. I didn't mean to presume or..."

"It's not a big deal. I usually don't have much going on." Now I turn my head and smile bravely at her over the roof of my vehicle. "Just sort of worked out that way."

She nods and frowns at my echo of her earlier words. "Right. It was rude for me to come by unannounced. It's a bad habit, I guess."

I don't confirm or deny her assessment. Instead, I step forward and pull on the door handle. At the last second, before opening the door all the way and ducking behind the wheel, I pause, search her eyes, and ask, "Everything okay? I mean, you're doing well? Eating your vegetables? Drinking lots of water? Getting plenty of sleep?"

Her arms fall limply to her sides, and her shoulders slump. "Stop being nice to me."

"What?"

Picking her way across the grass, toward her vehicle, she says, "Just stop."

I watch her wobbly progress, my mouth hanging open. "I only—"

"I don't deserve that, okay?" She jerks her door open and flops into the seat, collapsing against the steering wheel and flinching when her actions produce a plaintive bleep of the horn.

I gently latch my own door with a quiet click and slowly walk to her vehicle, where I drape myself over the top of the open door and look down on her. "I'm not being nice to be mean. If that makes any sense," I defend myself. "I asked because I genuinely care."

"I know!" she muffles against her arms. "You're killing me."

I sigh and come around the door, crouching next to her. "Hey." Moving my hand almost close enough to touch the side of her thigh, I stop before making contact and pull my hand back, gripping the rocker panel just before falling on my ass in the street. "I'm sorry."

She snorts. "Oh, God. If you start apologizing, I'm going to punch you."

My physical balance restored, I run my hand through my hair. "I don't understand you, Betts."

With a turn of her head, she trains her shining eyes on me. "You do, though. That's the problem. You're the only one who does."

Loathe to break the news that, in effect, nobody understands her, if that's the case, I simply bounce on my feet and take in how surreal this moment is.

She seems content with the silence, to a point. Then she drops, "I treated you like shit. I did exactly to you what Chris did to me: ran away with no explanation. But I couldn't have explained myself to you if I tried. I only knew I was scared."

"Of what?"

"Of changing everything."

"Why didn't you just tell me that?" I wonder, still not getting it.

"Because you would have tried to fix it."

"Yeah?"

"And I wasn't sure I wanted you to. And I was embarrassed about what that said about me, that I'd prefer a shitty status quo, just because it was familiar and seemed safe, rather than actually admitting I wanted something different."

"Change is scary. Even good change sometimes."

"Exactly!"

"See? I understand."

She pivots on her butt, facing me, bracketing my knees with her own. I swallow and concentrate on her face. When I realize I'm not breathing, I take in tiny sips of air until my lungs reach full capacity. Then I exhale in equally small measures before resuming normal respiration.

She touches the spot on my forehead that's long-since healed and is back to its usual, smooth self. "I kept telling myself that I needed to choose between Frankie and you. I already knew what to expect from Frankie; and although I thought I knew what to expect from you, I didn't really. Not as well as I knew what to expect from her, anyway."

"Abuse and heartbreak?"

"Yeah. But... I was used to it. Desensitized. What you were offering—or seemed to be offering—was foreign. And unpredictable. And what if you changed your mind when you got to know me better? You know, like when all my quirks started to be annoying, not cute. When you had enough and left, I'd have no one."

I look down, dismayed at her poor opinion of me but also knowing nothing I say can convince her that wouldn't happen. Because there are no guarantees in life. And I can't even promise myself it won't happen. I *am* difficult to please. Then again, I've never loved anyone like her, and I can't even think of anything she does—other than dropping in unannounced all the time—that would potentially become one of those grating deal-breakers I'm so good at finding. Anyway, even her most unpleasant unexpected visits wind up being the highlight of my day. I realize that might be a bigger commentary on my average day than the quality of her visits, but the result is the same.

It's all a moot point, anyway, I realize, so I swallow and say, "Well, I guess you made the right choice then."

"Oh?" she whispers.

Still staring at the pavement, I nod. "Yep. I mean, Frankie will never leave you."

"But—"

"I can only claim I love you. And that's nothing compared to the control that motivates her. So you're right; you'll never be alone as long as you have Frankie in your life."

My legs and knees are screaming at me, and I can't bear this position any longer, anyway, so I creak to a stand and look down on the top of her head. I give her a jerky pat, akin to something I'd give Reba before leaving for work in the morning, and say, "But I do appreciate your telling me. Better late than never, right? Tell Frankie I said hi." I turn to go, then stop and amend, "On second thought, don't."

"I won't."

While walking away, I toss over my shoulder, "Good. That would just be awkward."

"I won't, because I can't."

My hand freezes on my door handle.

The Fiat's door is blocking my view of her face, but she raises her voice and says more firmly, more confidently, "Well, I guess I'm *able*, but I won't. Because I don't talk to her anymore. Ever."

"Oh."

She stands and closes her car door again. "Yeah. Haven't talked to her since Atlanta."

I stare at a sparkle in the Prius's paint job, processing this information, suddenly experiencing an overwhelming sense memory at that last word, as if I've plunged my nose into a basket of peaches. "So..."

"Turns out being alone sucks, but it's working for me."

Turning sideways, I sag against the car and ask quietly, "Really?"

Her simple, contradictory head shake spurs me into action, and in three strides, I'm not only in front of her again, but she's in my arms, her feet off the ground. I cup the back of her head with my palm, pressing her cheek to mine and whispering, "Don't ever do this to me again."

"I won't," she whimpers hoarsely next to my ear. "I promise."

When she pulls her head back, I kiss the tears that have trailed into the corners of her mouth.

"Ew!"

Our heads snap in the direction of the chorus on Nick's front lawn. At some point, Heidi's nieces and nephews have crept around the side of the house.

I blush but don't put Betty down. "It's not nice to spy," I lightly admonish them.

Kingsley speaks for the group. "We're not spying! We wanted to see your dog."

I glance at the windows of Nick's house, but our only audience appears to consist of people under the age of twelve. "Where are your parents?" I ask, just to be sure.

"Watching football," Hermione answers, leading her siblings and cousins closer to my car.

Reba, cowering in the backseat, emits a whine as the curious group presses their faces against the back windows.

"Guys, she's afraid of kids," I explain with a regretful grimace, begrudgingly letting go of Betty and setting her on feet so I can mediate.

Betty chuckles while rubbing the tear tracks from her face. "Oh, the irony of *your* dog not liking kids."

I herd the children away from the car windows. "Yeah, I know. Some other time, guys. I promise. Now, you'd better go back inside."

Dejected, they slink away, kicking at the grass and muttering their collective disappointment.

I turn to Betty with a sheepish grin. "Oops."

She presses against me, fingering the front of my t-shirt. Through her eyelashes, she says, "All kidding aside, though... Reba's gonna have to adjust to being around little people."

"Yeah, probably. But not today."

Betty raises her head. Her wide, serious eyes hold fast to mine and make my heart pound. "Not today, no. She has about..." She bites her lower lip, then releases it. "Nine months —give or take—to get over it."

"Nine months?" I question faintly then feel the blood return to my extremities. "Oh! You mean, because of Nick and Heidi. Right. Well, less than that, I guess. Probably more like six months."

She pulls her head back, looking surprised. "Wait. What? Nick and Heidi are expecting?"

I laugh. "Yeah! Isn't that what you were saying?"

She smiles and shakes her head. Suppressing a grin while she watches me work through the seemingly impossible logic puzzle she's given me, she nods encouragingly. "I'm confident when I say nine months. Well, more accurately, about thirty-six weeks, if you're going to be a stickler, which you will be. I expect nothing less."

"Thirty-six weeks," I echo, reaching behind me for the car

when I feel my knees give out and blinking through my narrowed, tear-filled vision while I do the math.

"So, I guess I fibbed a bit when I said I've been alone for the past month," she admits with a wince. "But I didn't want to make you feel like you *had* to forgive me."

Pulling her against me in a crushing hug, I finally dare to ask somewhat more directly, if incompletely, "You're going to have...? We're going to be...?"

"Yeah," she answers. "Yardley used a condom that weekend, so it has to be yours."

"That's so not funny," I chastise, laughing into her hair.

"Liar. It's hilarious, and you know it."

I push her gently away from me and flutter my fingers against her midriff. "Thank you," I whisper, pressing my forehead against hers.

"No, Nathaniel. Thank *you*. For this and so much more." She clears her throat and steps back. I reach for her again, but she continues retreating. "No, I'll call you later. I'd better let you get on with your plans."

"My plans?"

"You were on your way somewhere when I showed up, remember?" the right corner of her mouth creeps upward at my short-term memory failure.

I laugh and lunge for her when I remember my self-preserving cover story. "Major change in plans." I tug on her hand, pulling her toward Nick's house. "Suddenly, I'm in a much more family-oriented mood." On the front porch, though, I remember everything I said in the backyard and blush. "On second thought, it wouldn't be right to leave Reba in the car. I said some pretty offensive things before you got here, so maybe we should hang out at my place and keep a low profile."

She shoots me a naughty grin. "Ooh, I seem to remember enjoying myself the last time we 'kept a low profile.'"

My heart flutters and races. I walk faster to the street and hurry to open my car. "I'll meet you there."

Betty laughs, trotting to her own vehicle, her sassy heels tapping on the pavement. "Maybe we'll feel like stopping back by here later."

Frankly, I doubt it.

EPILOGUE: GEORGIA

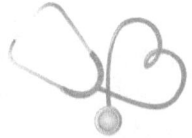

TEN MONTHS LATER...

"Oh, gosh, check out the purple sling Nick's wearing," Betty mutters to me from the corner of her mouth while we watch my brother and his family walk through Mom and Dad's front door.

I smirk. "Forget that. Did you see the Packers jogging suit Massimo's wearing? If the kid didn't already look like Mike McCarthy, he sure does now."

"Holy shit! You're so right! Gosh, it's uncanny! And creepy. I guess it's better than looking like Vince Lombardi, though."

"Debatable."

"What the heck does a four-month-old need with a jogging suit? Plus, it's July! Poor kid must be roasting."

"Heidi always thinks he's too cold, especially in the air conditioning," I explain. "I'm sure there are layers under that hoodie."

"Your parents have already set up a savings account for his psychiatric fund, right?"

"I hope someone has."

"What are you two in here whispering about?" Mom's voice comes from behind us. "Nick, Heidi, and Massimo are here."

Betty and I both look guiltily over our shoulders from our gossip spot at the kitchen sink, where we're supposedly rinsing the pacifier our newborn daughter has a habit of spitting out approximately every three seconds if someone's not holding it in her mouth.

"Is that really a two-person job?" Mom inquires.

"Well, it wouldn't be much fun to laugh at Nick in here by myself," I state.

She waves her hands at us. "You two!"

I pop the binkie into Georgia's mouth and keep my index finger on it. "Stay," I command the piece of plastic and rubber. Slowly, I move my finger away. On cue, the infant spits it out.

"Have you ever considered that she just doesn't want it?" Mom asks, standing next to me and smiling down at her grand-daughter.

"Wait for it," I say, holding the pacifier aloft.

"One, two, three." Betty points at the baby nestled in the crook of my arm. Georgia squirms, squeaks, squeals, then gears up for a good scream, which I head off by plugging up her cry-hole.

Mom shrugs. "Oh. Well, maybe she's hungry. Or wet. Or..."

"Wants me to hold this for her," I provide the correct answer, determined by intensive, hands-on, often middle-of-the-night research.

Betty tilts her head and gazes at her daughter affection-ately. "She's a tad high-maintenance, isn't she?"

I grin at my wife. "I don't care."

She grins back. "I don't, either. Plus, she's nothing compared to *some* people."

"And she's much cuter," I add.

"You're going to spoil her," Mom warns us.

"That's kind of the point," I reply. "So if you want to hold her, holding her pacifier is part of the deal."

"Deal," she readily agrees, waggling her fingers at me. "I bet you haven't used two hands to eat all weekend."

After transferring Georgia to Mom's arms, I shrug, keeping my eyes on my daughter's face. "I haven't noticed," I say truthfully.

Betty confirms my mom's suspicions as we parade into the dining room, where Dad, Nick, and Heidi are already settling into their usual seats around the table.

"Look who I have," Mom brags.

"Nate's letting someone else hold her?" Heidi fakes a heart attack, complete with clutched chest and protruding tongue.

"What is this?" I object to their teasing, nodding toward Nick. "You're wearing your kid like a fashion accessory, and nobody's giving you grief."

"You think I volunteered for this?" he grumbles across the table at me. To his wife, he gripes, "Seriously. How am I supposed to eat with this thing attached to my chest?"

"That 'thing' is your son, and you'll figure it out, like I have nearly every meal of my life for the past four months."

"I meant the sling, not the baby."

"The answer's the same. Deal with it."

Dad chuckles. "What happened to letting kids cry it out?" he wonders.

Heidi and I talk over each other, trying to explain why that's an outdated practice. Her reasons are more emotional, while mine are rooted in medical research, but the result is a cacophony of rhetoric.

Betty places a hand on my knee. "Yo. Save it, T. Berry Brazelton," she says mildly, passing me the serving dish of mashed potatoes. "You don't have to explain yourself to anyone. Plus, they're only kidding. It's cute how you want to hold her all the time."

I take the bowl from her and swallow the next thing I was going to say but start, "I just—"

"Yeah, I know. You were about to break out the hernia facts, and that's not good dinner conversation."

"It's valid, though."

She bats her eyelashes at me.

I sigh but smile. I can't resist that look. She could probably talk me into a sex change operation with that look. Well, maybe not. Oh, who am I kidding? Yes. I'd do anything for her.

The feeling is mutual, anyway. I mean, the woman stood her ground and barely flinched when I cried all the way through our [highly traditional] wedding vows a mere month after our reunion in front of Nick and Heidi's house. When it was her turn to repeat her vows after the minister, she said, "I, Betty, take you, Nathaniel, to be my lawfully wedded husband." There was a collective rustling of bulletins throughout the congregation as everyone rushed to double-check that the bride had, indeed, called the groom by the wrong Christian name. She didn't say it for anyone but me, though. And she achieved her goal, which was to get me to stop crying by making me laugh. She always knows exactly what to do or say.

Just like she knew I had way too much medical knowledge rattling around in my brain to get through our daughter's birth without multiple panic attacks and insisted I have Dr. Reitman write me a legitimate script for Valium.

"Forget the soothing music, focus item, and tennis ball, Nathaniel. You're going to need drugs," she announced bluntly, tucking the bottle of pills into her overnight bag with all of her other hospital supplies. And she was right. I took the pills and made it through. (Oh, Betty did a great job, too.)

Nothing prepared me, though, for the first time I held Georgia. I expected to blubber like one of those televangelists claiming to be filled with the Holy Spirit, but I was surprisingly dry-eyed, taking in her birth-swollen features and lubricated eyes. Frankly, I think I was too stunned by what I was feeling to even cry. Crying wasn't a strong enough reaction. So I stared. And felt. And thought, *It's all been worth it. Every single minute of fear, heartbreak, and doubt before this second, worth it.*

And I haven't wanted to stop holding her since then. Unfortunately, a week after her birth, I had to go back to work. But when I'm home and awake (and sometimes when I'm not awake, although I try to resist the urge to nap with her, having heard way too many horror stories about smothered infants), she's in my arms. That's how it goes. Even Reba's used to it by now.

Actually, Reba's been surprisingly chill. I think she's convinced Georgia's a puppy, and she, Reba, has to protect her. Whatever the reason, we haven't had any issues with her freaking out around the baby. She's still not thrilled about older kids, but over the past year, we've exposed her to more children in controlled settings, and we hope being around *our* child every day since her birth will make Georgia the exception to the rule.

I also think Reba recognizes there's no contest between her and the baby. Probably because I told her so in no uncertain terms when Reba got her first sniff of Georgia. "You even look at her funny, and I'll kill you, Rebes. Not even kidding. I love ya, but I won't hesitate." As if to demonstrate her agreement with my tough-talking demands, she gave Georgia a gentle lick on the tip of her nose, turned tail, and walked away, as if she had much more interesting business to attend to in another room.

Betty turned down the corners of her mouth at me and

bobbed her head. "Well. There you have it. All that worry for nothing."

I snorted. "I wasn't worried."

She pushed my shoulder, then we stared down at our baby.

"She's real," Betty said, rubbing her belly, as if to prove it to herself. "I mean, two days ago, she was here." Her hands stilled but remained on her midriff. "And now, she's there." She pointed to the infant carrier on the couch. "And I got to take her home with me."

I'd been waiting for her to acknowledge this wasn't her first experience with childbirth, but until then she seemed determined not to mention it, and it wasn't my place to push it. I hoped she knew I was there if she needed or wanted to talk, but I wasn't going to force her to relive something painful.

I didn't know how to verbally respond to her statement, so I simply put my arm around her shoulders and squeezed her to me.

She rested her head against my pec but kept her focus on our daughter. "And I gave another couple this feeling, all those years ago. So that's pretty cool."

"Pretty cool, indeed," I finally managed to say, when I was able to speak.

She quickly changed the subject, saying something about "unpacking our new toy" as she undid all the straps holding Georgia in her seat.

Tonight, she deftly changes the subject again. "Tell everyone your good news."

"Oh. That." I pass the last side dish across the table to Nick and place my napkin in my lap. "It's not a big deal."

"Yes, it is!" Betty insists.

"Well, I mean, it is. To me. To us. But not earth-shattering, or anything."

"Spit it out already," Nick demands. "You're worse than a

woman sometimes with your qualifiers and provisos. These babies will have graduated high school, and we'll still be sitting here, waiting for you to tell us you're having hemorrhoid surgery, or whatever."

"Nick!" Mom admonishes.

I laugh. "No. It's okay. He's right. Well, the final ruling came in on the cease and desist against Frankie for using my image on her books. I won, of course. And she has to pay me a percentage of every sale she made as 'Frank Lipton' between last September and now."

"Honey, that's great!" Mom cries, waking up Georgia, who spits out her unsecured pacifier and lets rip an angry howl.

Without any argument, Mom hands the crying baby and the pacifier back to me. I pat Georgia's butt and replace her binkie, which she sucks more lustily than before.

Betty picks up the pace on her eating. "I'll be done in a sec."

"No rush," I reassure her. "She can wait a few minutes to eat. You take your time."

Staying with the original conversation, Dad growls, "It's about time. And it's sad that Frankie needed a judge to tell her all that."

Nick swallows his mouthful of food and says, "So, between that and the rental income on Betty's house and your pay raise in January, after you've finished your practitioner certification, you'll be rolling in it, bro."

I laugh. "Hardly. Those royalties will be going straight into Georgia's college fund, anyway. I'm mostly happy it's over, and Frankie has a court order to stop hiding behind my face. And the raise in January is a bonus to what I really want at work, which is more autonomy. But you're right; it's nice not to have to worry so much about money, since there's one more mouth to feed at home now."

Heidi smiles enigmatically across the table and sets her fork down next to her plate. "Speaking of more mouths to feed..." She grabs Nick's hand on top of the table. He plasters a forced smile on his face. "We're expecting another baby!" she finishes with a tiny squeal.

Betty kicks me under the table. I shift in my seat and hide my "ow" in, "Wow! That's great!" Really, I'm silently cursing that I lost the bet Betty and I had going about how soon Nick and Heidi would be having their second child. I said Nick would make Heidi wait until Massimo was at least a year old. I should have known better than to bet against Heidi. Damn it.

"Thanks, Natey!" Heidi says, patting her flat belly. "It's still early, but we figured it was safe to tell family. We're due next March."

While Mom, Dad, and Betty offer their congratulations, Nick mouths across the table at me, *"Help me! Vag rage!"* causing me to nearly baptize my daughter with the drink of water I've taken.

My reaction wipes the grimace from my brother's face, but he hides his laughter behind his fist.

"What's so funny, you two?" Mom demands.

Nick and I answer together, "Nothing!" then dissolve into giggles like two teenage girls.

"Some things never change," Dad remarks with a shake of his head as he returns his attention to the food on his plate.

Some things don't. Then again, many things have. And for that, I'm grateful.

ACKNOWLEDGMENTS

So many people to thank, so little space! But here we go! When a book takes as long as this one did to write and goes through so many permutations, there are a LOT of support people to thank.

As far as large groups are concerned, I need to thank the folks in ChickLitChat HQ for their much-needed input on choosing a title and the Chick Lit Goddesses and WIP Support Group for being there when I needed to cry, rage, despair, and threaten to give up writing forever. It helps to know people who don't roll their eyes at my melodramatics, because they don't have to live in the same house—or town— as me. You guys have done a wonderful job of saying, "There, there," and holding my virtual hand through a lot of dark moments. I'm always glad to return the favor.

More specifically, Kathleen, Tracie, Laura, and Martha... thank you for pep talk after pep talk, valuable insight and input, and all-around girl-power camaraderie. You've seen me at my worst and still choose to be friends with me. I don't know what that says about you (ha ha), but it tells me that I'm one lucky woman to have such lovely friends.

Which brings me to blurb-writing. In the past, I've employed the expert services of Ms. Francine LaSala (hire her; you won't regret it), and I so longed for Francine's expertise this time around, but I was resolved to do it myself. Like a big girl. I won't bore you with all the depressing reasons. Well. The experience stank as much as I remembered. But with the help of fellow writers Martha Reynolds (author of the amazing *Chocolate...* trilogy and *Bits of Broken Glass*) and Tracie Banister (author of *Blame It On the Fame* and *In Need of Therapy*), I managed to do it without inflicting any self-harm. Martha instilled the confidence I needed and helped with word choice, while Tracie urged me to "chick lit" it up and provide readers with more info about the plot (I'm stingy and paranoid about spoilers). What resulted was something I was proud to attach to my book. Thanks, ladies! You're the best! (Francine, expect a message from me for future books, though.)

I always have a great group of beta readers, and this time was no exception. However, the beta readers for *Let's Be Frank* were exceptionally awesome. I asked them to read a 114,000-word book during the holidays and get back to me as soon as possible, and every single one of them did it. Not only that, but they returned with amazing comments, suggestions, and catches of some pretty epic mistakes that would have caused major embarrassment had they not been caught. Amy, Martha, Sharon, Hans, Bethany, Vickie, Laura... thank you! You made Nurse Nate a much better man and *Let's Be Frank* a much better book.

They weren't the first beta readers, though. I'd like to say a special thank you to Cindy and Heather for reading the very first-ever draft of this book, back when it wasn't really this book but merely the concept that eventually became this book. Thank you for being brave enough to say, "This isn't your best work," and for forcing me to rethink the entire project. Several times. If it hadn't been for you, I would have published a book that was "okay" but didn't live up to the potential of the idea. That would have been really sad, I think. I would have always wondered how good it *could* have been, if only I'd worked a little (okay a LOT) harder at it. You're Nurse Nate's heroes. Oh, and mine, too.

Thanks also to my husband, who gave up his solitary early mornings so I could work on this book before getting the kids up for school each day. I really enjoyed our quiet together-but-not-really-talking-to-each-other time as you watched ESPN before going to work and I sat with my earbuds in my ears and my nose against my laptop monitor and furiously typed draft after draft after draft of this infernal book. Thanks for listening to Nurse Nate stories. Thanks for giving me advice and insight into the male psyche, which I then invariably disregarded as not attractive enough for a chick lit audience. (Sorry, but we like our guys slightly... well... realistically unrealistic.) Thanks for *not* punching me all those times I whined and complained about never being finished with this book. I can only imagine how you felt the second time I said, "I have to start all over again, from scratch." But you held up so well. You're my rock. A lesser man would have taken the kids and run.

As for the rest of you who have stuck by me, you patient readers and friends and family members, thank you! I'd like to especially thank the insatiable fans of *The Secret Keeper* series for giving me the time away from *TSK* to write something different. I know you're anxious for the next *TSK* installment, but I also hope you read *Let's Be Frank* and decided it was worth waiting a little longer for the continuation of the series you love. Your unselfishness has been inspiring. And I promise to get to work in earnest on *TSK VI* as soon as possible. I already have a good start and many, many exciting ideas. Just a little more patience, please!

And while I'm at it, a preemptive thanks for the reviews and kind words you'll have for *Let's Be Frank,* not because it's the best book ever written (as if!), but because you're always so generous with your praise, and I know that will never change. Thank you!